To all the shadow daddy lovers,
And to Jen, for her need for a trigger warning for the use of the
T word. It's actually in here twice now.

She's a dark, little artist with ink in her veins
    She's been through the hardest, but prospered
from pain
    She appears to be heartless, surrounded by flames
    But through all the darkness, a lover is chained

BRYCE SAVAGE

Forgotten Kingdoms Collection Introduction

Forgotten Kingdoms Collection

Eight women.

One sacrifice to save their kingdoms.

A chance to reclaim the love they lost.

Collection notes:

Forgotten Kingdoms is a collection of full-length stand-alone fantasy romance novels with fated mates and a guaranteed happily ever after. With vampires, fae, shifters, and everything in between, each book features a unique heroine and her epic love story that can be read in any order.

Authors and books in this set include:

Of Blood & Nightmares by Chandelle LaVaun

Of Dragons & Desire by G.K. DeRosa

Of Death & Darkness by Megan Montero

Of Shadows & Fae by Jen L. Grey

Of Elves & Embers by Robin D. Mahle & Elle Madison

Of Mischief & Mages by LJ Andrews

Of Serpents & Ruins by Jessica M. Butler

Of Claws & Chaos by M. Sinclair

FORGOTTEN KINGDOMS

OF
ELVES
&
EMBERS

USA TODAY BESTSELLING AUTHORS

ELLE MADISON
ROBIN D. MAHLE

KINGDOM OF FUOCO

COURT OF MOON AND STARS

KINGDOM OF EYRE

KINGDOM OF TERRE

THE NEVER COURT

DRACONIA

KINGDOM OF AQUOS

AEI

KINGDOM OF NIGHTFALL

KINGDOM OF EVENTIDE

VARGR

SACRE

ISLE OF WILDCREST

COURT OF BLOOD

KINGDOM OF KROPELKI

KINGDOM OF OGNISKO

COURT OF NIGHTMAI

SEPEAZIA

ISRAMAYA

T E R

MAGIARIA

MYRKFELL

COURT OF
FIRE AND SUN

RIA

SANCTUARY
OF
SEERS

VONDELL

THE WILDLANDS

MOUNTAIN

ISRAMORTA

SWAMP CLAN

SLATE CLAN

TEMPEST CLAN

CINDER CLAN

SUMMER COURT

WINTER COURT

TALAMH

REA

Court of
Moon and Stars
Thalassa Village
Akri
Village
Koilas
Village
Ourania Bay
Portal
Telikos
Village
Tower
of
Chasoura
Vasi
Village
Fengari
Zoferi
Mines
Borderlands
The
Never Court
Nefritis
Palace

AELVARIA

KINGDOM OF THE ELVES

MOUNTAINS

MONIRIS
VILLAGE

KÓKKINOS

MI...
...AGE

CHRYSÓS
VILLAGE

ILLIOS PALACE

NI...
...AGE

FAVÓRI
VILLAGE

POTÁMI
VILLAGE

M
O
U
N
T
A
I
N
S

ANAPTO
VILLAGE

AGIOS
VILLAGE

IEROS LAKE

MITERA TREE

COURT OF
FIRE AND SUN

Author's Note/Content Warning

This book contains some spice

Usually ElBin books are known for being more fade-to-black or fade-to-gray, but this story is for a more adult audience and contains open door, though not explicit, sex scenes.

We try to focus more on the intimacy and emotional connection versus the mechanics, but they are here and you are more than welcome to skim/skip them. We just didn't want anyone walking in blind or to base your reviews on the fact that the heat picks up for this story.

If you would like a comprehensive list of the scenes that are spicy, or to view our trigger warnings for our other books, please visit our website: https://mahleandmadison.com/faq/

Prologue

DEATH. FOR THE SAKE OF LOVE.

I repeated the words over and over in my head, reminding myself of why I was here. Why I was willfully allowing my body to be ripped apart, to endure pain unlike anything I had ever felt before.

For love.

My skin burned as the Sacred Tree's roots wrapped around my limbs, slowly embedding themselves into my flesh. A breath hissed past my lips. There was an explosion of light, then nothing but stars.

All my life, I had been haunted by the dying embers of stars sparking across the night sky. Ruled by them. Captivated by them.

It was fitting that they were here now to usher me into death, too.

Blood pooled from the cuts in my hands, streaming down into the glowing water at my feet. My bones ached, and my skin burned, the pain threatening to bring me to my knees. So I focused on the stars at the edges of my vision, reminding myself that I had chosen to be here.

I had chosen to die...for *him*.

And given the chance to do it all again, I would still choose this.

A quick glance at the women around me revealed expressions that were just as determined as mine. They were the Goddess's chosen warriors from all over Terrea, full of resolve to endure and to die for the sake of something more than themselves.

If I were a better person, someone less selfish, I would be content that my sacrifice was saving my people as well. But I wasn't that noble. Maybe I had been once, but now... Now all that consumed me was the visceral need to keep *him* alive.

I swallowed hard, bracing myself against another wave of pain and squeezing the hands of the mage and fae on either side of me. Then I met Abba's lavender gaze, filled with untold amounts of grief. She had been with me my entire life, and now she would be here at the very end.

At least I wouldn't die alone.

A scream shook the air, and the Sacred Tree trembled as her roots began to glow and stretch around the vampire strapped to her trunk. His red eyes lit up with fury, and another anguished wail wrenched from his throat.

My mind flooded with memories of blood-stained battlefields, of shadow monsters that rose from the ashes and tore through my armies. Of death and pain and loss.

All of it was his fault.

He was the reason Abba had called me from the battle back home. He was the reason I was leaving everything behind.

My body shook as I sent the last few waves of my power toward him, wanting to burn him alive for the death and chaos he had wrought throughout Terrea. Another wave of agony washed over me, followed by another and another.

My chest caved in. My vision darkened until I could no longer see the glowing waters we were standing in or hear the screams of the vampire king.

The Sacred Tree blocked it all out as its roots climbed up to cover my throat, pulling the last drop of magic from my blood.

Finally, I gave myself over to the darkness, letting it swallow me whole while I pretended it led, not to death, but to quiet reprieves and whispered promises against my skin. Promises and lies, the hallmarks of everything I was leaving behind. Of everything we had been.

Mortem pro amore. I chanted the words in my head, over and over, heralding me into the endless abyss.

Death for the sake of love.

At least this was a vow I could keep.

Chapter One

I DIDN'T BELONG HERE.

Of course, that feeling was nothing new. Even as a child, when I still had parents who were alive and adored me, there had been a persistent sense of being *other*. While the other children played and made friends, I stayed indoors alone to draw things that only existed in my mind, never quite able to escape the restless, empty feeling that plagued my soul.

Then my parents died, and that feeling only intensified.

Tonight was different, though. My skin itched with an almost eerie feeling, contributing to what was more of a pervasive insistence that I was out of place than the normal vague intuition. Then again, this wasn't exactly my scene.

Smoke clung to every surface of the crowded casino in the middle of the Vegas strip. It was bad enough on a normal day, but intolerable on Halloween. Bodies crushed against each other, the masks and costumes making everyone even bolder than usual.

I could barely breathe in here. All I wanted to do was go back up to the relative quiet of the rooftop where I could see the stars. One look at my best friend's wide grin and bright brown eyes as she took in the fairy-themed bar, though, reminded me of why I had left my solitude to begin with.

Isa excitedly pointed at the careful details of the gazebo. It was covered in flowers and vines while artificial stars lit up the ceiling and smoke machines made it look like the partygoers were dancing on clouds.

It was pretty cool, I supposed. For a crowded club full of drunk assholes.

The hair stood on the nape of my neck, and I spun to find someone's eyes on me. That wasn't unusual, in and of itself. My fiery ombre hair tended to catch attention, even when I wasn't wearing a black dress and combat boots, dressed like a shadow in a sea of sparkles.

But this man smiled at me like we were already friends. I narrowed my eyes, trying to figure out if he was drunk or hitting on me or just a rare genuine person, trying to decipher the odd melancholy that surged in my chest when I took in the details of his costume.

Before I could make sense of it, my best friend stepped between us.

"*Mira, Mami.* I'm going to give you a pass for taking your ears off again since I know you didn't want to come." She pointedly glanced at the headband with glittering cat ears that was wrapped around the strap of my purse instead of on my head. "But at least come get a drink with me."

Isa's brown eyes widened like some sort of anime character, her full lips pursed in a delicate pout that had me rolling my eyes.

I knew she wasn't pleading for her sake, but for mine. She had wanted me to take a break so badly, from life and work and the restless energy that made me want to sell my shop, pick up in a new town, and start all over until I finally found somewhere that felt like home.

When I got the literal golden ticket announcing an all-expenses-paid trip to Vegas this weekend for two, I had already been strangely tempted to accept. That was weird, in itself, because I didn't like casinos or crowds or Halloween. Hell, the entire thing felt like a scam, but I had called to verify the details through the airline and the hotel, and everything was confirmed.

Still, I normally would have declined, but instead I had an inexplicable urge to accept. Then my only other friend, Ivy, received the same ticket. She shouldn't have wanted to go, either, but Isa had insisted it was a sign, from the universe or whatever powers that governed our lives. And of course, she insisted on joining us.

That's how I found myself here on one of the busiest weekends for my burgeoning tattoo shop, instead of losing myself in an endless line of clients gushing over the new psychedelic inks for the fantastical creatures that I was quickly becoming known for.

But Isa was a better friend than I deserved. Open and kind where I was distant and closed off. For her sake, I put the ears back on my head and made an effort to smile.

"All right, let's go."

She let out a squeal of excitement, linking her arm in mine as she dragged us to the fairytale-like bar.

The counter was carved to look like a fallen tree, while branches wrapped around to form shelves behind the bartenders. Twinkle-lights lit up the bottles of liquor while blue and pink flowers covered dark green vines that stretched around and between the shelves, giving it the feel of a real enchanted forest.

Isa took in every detail while I studied the menu, finally ordering something called Faerie Fire for her and a whiskey on the rocks for myself.

The frazzled bartender nodded, disappearing to take several more orders before he got to making the drinks. I diverted my attention to the sea of dancers.

"You should go."

"I said I wouldn't leave your side, and I won't. I'm still holding out that you'll want to dance after two or three more of those whiskeys," she said with a wink.

It wasn't completely outside of the realm of possibility. I did like to dance, and I had a dagger in my combat boot for anyone who got too handsy with either of us.

The sound of two drinks sliding across wood pulled my attention back to the bar. Two glasses sat in front of us, holding identical red concoctions that were very much not whiskey. I looked up to tell the bartender he had gotten it wrong, but he was already well away from us with his back turned.

Another masked, drunken moron bumped into me.

"Meow, kitty cat." He slung an arm around me.

My hand twitched toward my dagger, but Isa was already there, using all hundred pounds of her weight to shove him off me.

"*Chinga te, Pendejo*. Not tonight," she cursed him in Spanish, and I might have laughed if I hadn't been so irritated.

He put his hands up and backed away. I ripped the ears off my head, and Isa tucked them back around my purse strap with an apologetic look. She shoved my drink a little closer to me.

I eyed it dubiously, noting the bartender was still an ocean away and not so much as glancing in our direction.

To be buzzed on whatever disgustingness was in this cup, or to be sober? They set the strobe lights to pulsating, and my decision was made.

I took a sip, nearly gagging at the sickly-sweet taste of it. It was like raspberries had a vodka-and-rum-soaked baby with some lemons in a gallon of sugar. Isa, however, looked delighted while she drank hers, nearly downing it in one go.

Gross.

Then again, it was the only alcohol I had at my disposal to dull the throbbing bass and strobing lights wreaking hell on my cranium. The urge to take another sip overwhelmed me. So I did.

It was...better. *Maybe?*

The man who had been looking at me earlier leaned over to whisper something to Isa. She giggled before turning to me.

"The dance floor misses me," she said with a half apology.

Then she flounced off into the crowd. *What the hell?*

That drink must have hit her fast. I surveyed her steady

movements for signs that I should go after her. She appeared to be okay, just buzzed, so I kept my seat, making sure her bouncy black ponytail and sparkly cat ears were in sight.

"You don't like to dance?" the man who had spoken to Isa, the one who had been watching me, asked in a lightly accented voice.

British? Australian? It was too loud for me to try to narrow it down when I could barely hear him.

His deep brown skin had undertones of blue that only highlighted the pale glowing blue runes painted on his arms and face. Silver hoops lined the tips of his pointed ears that looked far more real than they should have.

When they began swimming in my vision, I realized I had been staring for far too long. I blinked and shook my head.

"It's more that I don't like people," I said a bit bluntly.

My words felt further away than they should have. I took another sip of my drink, almost taking comfort in the fruity flavor I couldn't quite place.

He chuckled. "Fair enough. I'm Kallius, by the way."

He scooted closer, so I leaned away.

"Ember." I didn't want to encourage him, but whatever courtesy lessons my parents had instilled in me in the brief decade they'd been with me had stuck. There was no need to be rude to him. Yet.

In truth, he had a kind, open face and a genuine smile. He looked at me like he already considered me a friend, with none of the lewdness I had come to expect from men. Something in me wanted to trust him, which sent up immediate alarm bells, making me go the other way.

Appearances could be deceiving. Anyone who has lived on the streets learns that fast.

"How's the drink?" He tilted his head and shifted away, taking my cue to give me some space.

"Disgusting." I scowled.

He pursed his lips and arched a dark eyebrow.

"Is that why it's halfway gone?" Kallius teased.

A laugh bubbled out of me, unexpected and loud.

I tilted my head, studying the lines of his face as he grinned. In another life, I wondered if I would have found him attractive.

But I didn't have it in me to be deeply attracted to anyone, as I had discovered the hard way in one too many failed relationships. I always hit a wall, and I was tired of feeling like a failure, an outsider, like there was something wrong with me. Tired of feeling the constant disappointment emanating from the other person when I had no desire to rip their clothes off with reckless abandon.

After several lackluster relationships, paired with underwhelming experiences in the bedroom, I had stopped trying. I only clumsily shook my head at his teasing, pulling my phone out of my small leather purse to text Ivy.

Where was she, anyway?

I tried to ask her, forcibly tapping letters on the glass screen, to tell her that Isa had left me here. Which was... strange. Wasn't it?

My head was light, each of my thoughts dancing just out of reach. Everything felt off right now.

I scanned the crowd. Finding the familiar ponytail took me

longer than it had before. Isa was laughing and dancing in a sea of other women dressed in animal costumes.

Looking back down, I stared at the blurring words on my screen, but I managed something almost coherent. Hopefully.

"We should go somewhere quieter, so we can talk." The man's voice was loud, almost like it was resounding in my head. I started, nearly dropping my phone.

I went rigid, clutching my grossly addicting drink in my fist with one hand while I tucked my phone away with the other. "No, we shouldn't."

I had to work harder than I should have to enunciate the words. This drink really was strong. The thought should have made me stop, slow down. A buzz was one thing, but I never let myself get drunk in front of strangers.

Instead, I took another long sip.

"She doesn't even know you, Kallius. How did you think she was going to take that?" a lighter voice hissed.

All at once, the man disappeared, replaced by a woman who looked startlingly like him. Had I seen her before tonight?

"Sorry, my brother's an idiot. I'm Celani, by the way," she said, leaning against the bar.

I mumbled something that sounded vaguely like Ember while she ordered a drink for herself from the bartender.

The light reflected off her silver cloak, highlighting similar rune tattoos her brother had painted on. Her whole Vikings-meets-Lord-of-the-Rings costume was epic, and the silver-white hair peeking out from her hood gave her even more of an ethereal appearance.

The dye job was excellent. So good that it almost looked

natural. It had me thinking about every single time someone asked me about mine, the way my roots faded from a deep red down to a faint orange and golden blonde tips. Like I had a head of fire.

No matter how many times I tried to dye over it, the color peeked through within days. No one believed me when I told them it was that way naturally, and I didn't push, not wanting yet another thing to make me feel *other*.

"My brother's an idiot," the woman continued when I didn't respond. "He isn't trying anything untoward."

Untoward? The old-fashioned word went with her medieval costume and her polished accent, something that sounded close to British but maybe not quite. My shoulders relaxed without my permission, but I raised an eyebrow. Or tried to. My face felt funny. Numb.

"Of courshhh not." My efforts to enunciate were less successful this time. "Men always say that with...noble intenshions."

The corner of her mouth tilted up in a knowing grin.

"Just ignore him. You don't want to dwell on that anyway. You want to go look at the paintings in the corner." Her voice reverberated in my head, stronger than her brother's had.

Did I? My attention turned to the massive, floor-to-ceiling canvases in the corner. One was of a sunny spring day with an open forest filled with wildflowers. It was bright, and lovely, and everything I was decidedly not.

The other, though, held snow-capped mountains under a night sky. Silvery blue flowers peppered the snow while serene waterfalls cascaded from the cliffs into a glimmering pond.

Then there were the stars, painted so realistically that they seemed to be twinkling.

That was probably just my blurry vision, though. *Surely.*

Still, Celani was right. I did want to get a closer look.

I *needed* to.

I stumbled over there, drawn to the artwork with a magnetism I didn't understand, while Celani waited patiently next to me. I stared for minutes — or hours, maybe — transfixed, until Ivy's familiar voice sounded behind me.

"Not drinking whiskey, huh?"

Celani muttered a soft *dammit* as I spun around to find my friend. Or at least, a blurry shape that looked like her, wearing a pig onesie.

When my eyes focused again, I thought about how unfair it was that she looked pretty, even dressed in that.

Her strawberry-blonde hair glittered like a freaking halo around her head, and her pale green eyes reminded me of the spring painting behind us.

I turned to introduce her to Celani, but the Elven-dressed woman was gone.

Shaking my head, I remembered my text to Ivy and how long she had taken to show up.

"You. Bishhhhh," I gritted out, but my voice was far away to my own ears.

"Well, you did tell me to join you at farty bar. So, you know, shit happens." She gave me an unapologetic shrug.

I cringed, wrinkling my nose in disgust.

"Ew. No way. I said...Fairy Bar." *Probably.* I wasn't even sure I said it now.

Then I caught a whiff of her, a floral shampoo mixed with the heady scent of sweaty armpits, and I wondered all over again why she was wearing the onesie.

"A costume." She answered what I had apparently spoken out loud. "Unlike you."

"Don't celebrate," I reminded her. She knew I hated this time of year. A lifetime on the streets had taught me that people were even more unpredictable when they had masks to hide behind.

Something twisted inside of me at the thought.

I suddenly found myself in need of another drink. I shoved my glass into her hand and took off toward the bar, trying not to think about the way the crowd of people made me feel even more alone. The way all of the bad memories were creeping in. The way the painting had stirred in me an odd mix of nostalgia and longing and pain.

I stumbled against the wall, and a face appeared in my vision. It was a woman dressed as a guard, but she was the most beautiful person I had ever seen. Amethyst waves framed a face that was practically glowing in its perfection.

Her plump lips pursed into a concerned frown, and a gentle hand came to brush the hair off my forehead that was suddenly too hot.

"It will be better soon, Child," she said in a voice like wind chimes. With a last maternal look, she placed the cat ears that were hooked around the strap of my bag back on my head.

I opened my mouth to tell her I hadn't been a child in a long time, but she was already gone.

My head spun, and I wondered if I'd imagined the entire thing.

Somehow, I made it back to the bar. At least, I thought so. The woman was there, giving me a perplexed look while ethereal silver markings winked in and out of existence in my field of vision.

"I need another...drrrrink."

"I don't think you do. Stars, I didn't realize how human you would be."

I must have been even drunker than I realized, because that made no sense.

"You don't want another drink, Ember. You want to come with me."

I nodded, my eyes fixed on hers. Of course I did. Why wouldn't I? She was a beautiful moon fairy elf queen. I must have spoken the thought aloud, because she looked at me askance.

"Yes, you've had plenty," she muttered, amusement coloring her tone.

She led me back past the gyrating crowd toward the painting, supporting my weight. Ivy was gone. Where was she? And Isa was...still dancing? The thought sobered me slightly. I should find them.

"I need to find...friends."

"No, you don't. You need to come with me." Her voice dipped lower into a whisper, something earnest like a promise. "The shadow king is waiting for you."

Goosebumps lined my skin, and my eyes snapped to hers. Those words stirred something inside me.

A warning.

Dread.

Pain.

Some small part of my mind rebelled, but it wasn't strong enough to combat the soul-deep yearning I had to follow Celani. So I followed.

Right through the painting.

Chapter Two

A WAVE OF HEAT WASHED OVER ME, SEARING THE top of my head down to my toes. My balance was precarious at best, and I struggled not to fall ass over tits through the painting-doorway thingy.

Celani grabbed my wrists. To help steady me? To drag me the rest of the way through the door? I couldn't be sure. But her grip was cool against the inferno that blazed along my skin, so I didn't fight her.

I blew out a sigh as the heat wave dissipated, but when she pulled her hands away, there was a silver band on each of my wrists. Those weren't there before. Right?

I shook my head, my thoughts spinning as I stepped forward into a sea of stars.

I blinked slowly, frowning as I registered the snow beneath my boots. It was freezing here, a light dusting of frost covering glowing blue and silver trees and flowers that peeked through the snow on the ground.

I spun back to the painting — or what I had thought was a painting. From this side, it was like a window into Fairy Bar. Drunken partiers danced and threw their heads back in laughter, but no sound permeated the odd bubble. Instead, the air was filled with a constant whirring noise, a sound that was pure energy that had my skin prickling and the hairs rising on the back of my neck.

Tentatively, I lifted a hand, trying to figure out what kind of odd technology was at play here. Celani's hand clamped around my wrist before I could touch the strange sound barrier.

"Come on now," she said, steering me in the other direction.

Shaking my head, I tried to clear my fuzzy thoughts as I focused on the images unfolding around me.

Whoever had designed this room had gone all out. The sky was brighter here than the real one in the smog of Vegas. Brilliant stars lit up the night while purple and green and blue light danced between them like an aurora. Stranger yet were the two crescent moons. One silver, one gold, both exquisitely...painted? Sculpted?

I tried to figure it out as my blurry thoughts sluggishly crawled from one to the next. They weren't the cutouts you would expect from a special effects department. There was shading and dimension on them, the same faraway impression I got when I looked at the real moon and stars.

Or maybe my depth perception was just off from all the alcohol.

Something was off, because I didn't even notice that we

were moving until I nearly tripped over a tree root. My attention snapped back to the present. Celani's arm was still on mine as she guided me deeper into a forest that sparkled like a Cullen in daylight.

No.

I needed to go back to the club. To find Isa and Ivy. To get the actual hell away from this stranger leading me to some random corner of the casino that I was beginning to suspect was something else entirely.

I twisted around, inhaling a lungful of cold air. Frigid, really, compared to the mild Vegas night I had left behind. Goosebumps rose along my skin, intensifying when I saw the painting once more. Door. Whatever the hell it was, standing silent and alone on a snowy cliffside that even my addled brain knew couldn't exist in a casino.

Two sets of footprints led along the uneven ground, the downward incline we had been on since Celani pulled me through.

I opened my other senses, noting the woodsy scent of the trees too subtle and rich to be fake. The wind that blew through the luminescent blue leaves. The snow falling from a single puffy cloud moving sluggishly across the sky.

There was even a fat, fluffy creature bounding away, too smoothly to be a prop.

Dread pooled in my stomach, realization clicking into place like the piece of a puzzle I hadn't known I was trying to put together. My pulse raced, sweat prickling at my back, despite the freezing cold air.

I wasn't in the casino, but nothing else made sense. Unless I was hallucinating.

"You drugged me." My voice was far calmer than I felt. "That's why I'm hallucinating."

I had never been tempted to try drugs of any kind for this very reason. Not being able to trust my own mind was nothing short of terrifying, and now here I was, imagining an entire... world?

Celani sighed again.

"You're not hallucinating," she said. "It was elvish wine. Not harmful, and good when you need to compel a human to cooperate."

My brow furrowed as I tried to make sense of her words. They weren't fuzzy. Nothing was, for that matter. The trees were crisp in my vision, the stars twinkling a normal amount. Nothing to hint at a hallucination, even without her very droll insistence.

"I needed you to come with me willingly through the moongate, so I got you drunk on magic wine," she said when I didn't respond, speaking slowly and loudly, like I was an idiot.

Maybe I was. I certainly felt like I was missing something obvious.

What I did know was that I needed to get away from the woman who had drugged me and then dragged me to wherever the hell we were now.

I darted forward, taking my chances on my wobbly legs. I made it a solid two feet before pitching forward to eat a mouthful of snow. My knee snagged on a gnarled root, and pain lanced across the skin.

Celani pulled me off the ground, propping me up against her side. For a brief moment, I wondered about screaming, but there was a sound barrier of some sort to the club, and I wasn't sure I wanted anyone here to hear me. Maybe there was someone worse than Celani nearby.

"Are you done now?" she asked in a sardonic tone, arching a sculpted eyebrow like she was wrangling her drunk friend from the bar rather than trying to kidnap me.

The thought sent my mind racing back to the bar. To Isa who had been drinking the exact same abomination as me, and Ivy who drank from my glass. Fury burned through my veins, so powerful I felt it would catch fire. I wished it would.

"And my friends?" I spat the words at her. "Did you give them *magic wine,* too?"

"We had nothing to do with your pig-friend by the painting," she said, her eyes darting suspiciously back toward the door to the bar. "But Kallius is walking the kitten back to her room now."

I attempted to clench my weak fists, the wine robbing me of all of my meager strength.

"Well, that's a great comfort," I shot back. "The man who drugged me is carefully seeing my best friend back to her bedroom."

Celani flinched, her violet eyes narrowing at my words.

"What is your name?" she asked abruptly.

"I already told you that," I hissed, a fuzzy memory from earlier coming to mind. "But if you don't even know my name, why did you go through so much trouble to kidnap me?"

She opened her mouth, then closed it without answering, looking to the sky in exasperation.

"I can see this is going well." The deep voice startled me, and I spun around to find Kallius, having apparently crept up on us from the doorway.

"Indeed," Celani drawled. "*Ember* here was just worrying that you might have spent a little too much time with her kitten friend." She emphasized my name a little too much, some unspoken conversation passing between the siblings.

If she remembered my name, why had she asked me for it again? Kallius frowned before his expression turned thoughtful.

"Can't say I wasn't tempted." His lips tilted in a cocky grin. "Or that she wasn't extremely persuasive."

I lunged forward, ready to punch his smug mouth. Of course, I stumbled and Celani caught me. Again.

"Don't worry. I turned her down," Kallius assured me. "To my everlasting disappointment."

I wasn't sure whether or not to believe him, though something in my gut made me want to trust him. But that could have just been wishful thinking that Isa really was safe.

I needed her to be safe. My legs trembled as I considered making another run for it.

The thought must have played out across my features, because in the next breath, Kallius stepped forward, slinging me over his shoulder as he carried me farther from the impossible door.

Panic coursed through my veins as I tried and failed to fight my way free of his hold. But I was still so weak. I swallowed down the lump in my throat as I watched that door grow smaller in the distance, taking with it every hope I had of making it back to my friends.

That wasn't even the worst part. The worst part was that the farther he took me, the clearer my mind became.

And yet, the world around me didn't change.

The glowing trees just became clearer. The snow fell harder and the wind howled, like they were trying to prove to me they weren't some delusion.

My stomach lurched, and it wasn't just because Kallius had begun trekking down an even steeper path, throwing off my sense of gravity. It was because of the sinking realization that I wasn't in Kansas anymore...or Vegas, as the case may be.

Finally, I cleared my throat, watching the door disappear behind the hill as I worked up the nerve to ask the question I should have asked earlier.

"Where are we?" The words sliced through the silence like a dagger, and Kallius stiffened beneath me.

"Aelvaria," he answered. "The kingdom of the elves."

I scoffed, waiting for him to give some indication that he wasn't being serious. My mind whirled, my heartbeat pounding so loudly in my chest, I thought it might rip free from my skin.

"Not possible," I breathed out, arguing more with myself than them.

It couldn't be... Elves weren't real. That was ridiculous.

Then again, so was going through a painting in the middle of a casino and ending up on a snow-capped mountain in a land with two moons. I wasn't sure what made sense anymore.

Not this night or this world, and certainly not the strange feeling of déjà vu I got when Celani cleared her throat, gesturing vaguely to the land below.

"Welcome to the Court of Moon and Stars."

I WASN'T sure how long we walked, or rather, they walked while I was carried like a sack of unwilling potatoes. All I knew was that it was getting harder and harder to keep track of the footprints in the snow as fresh powder fell to cover it.

My skin was ice cold. The small amount of warmth from Kallius's shoulder and arms were the only things that kept me from completely freezing to death.

Both of my captors had refused to answer any more questions about where we were or what they wanted with me, and honestly, I was getting too tired and cold to wonder about much of it anyway.

Part of me hoped this was all in my head, a bad trip I could ride out and laugh about with Isa later. Sure.

When a dark form flew overhead, blocking out the stars, I froze. A frozen gust of air followed in its wake, then another form passed by, and another. Eight total that stirred up the snow, further covering the footprints I was trying so hard to keep track of and drenching me in more icy droplets.

Kallius tensed beneath me, and Celani stopped in her tracks. There was a quick crunching of snow as she spun around to march back up the path next to her brother.

"Did you tell them to meet us here?" Kallius whispered to his sister.

"Of course not," she hissed. "Go. Into the trees. Keep her hidden."

I felt Kallius nod, then he was darting through the woods.

He set me down next to the giant silver trunk of a knotted old tree. My muscles burned as he leaned me back against the smooth bark. His expression brooked no argument when he met my gaze, pressing a finger to his lips in a silent gesture to be quiet.

I wasn't sure why I listened when whoever was here might help me get back to the door. Still, I kept my mouth screwed shut, straining my ears as I listened to the forest.

Deep growls echoed through the trees, sending shivers racing down my spine. Then came voices. Men, or elves, or whatever the hell they considered themselves.

Kallius's shoulders relaxed at the sound of one of the voices, and then his sister was calling his name, telling him to bring me, too.

I gave him a look that told him exactly where he could shove the idea of slinging me over his shoulder again.

A crooked smile teased the corner of his mouth, and he nodded at the warning, sliding my arm over his neck as he helped me walk back to the path instead.

Eight soldiers stood around Celani, each of them with various shades of blue, silver, and purple hair pulled back into warrior braids or knots. All of them had the same pointed ears and rune tattoos painted along their skin, and they each had spears strapped to their backs.

"As I said, General," the tallest man at the front of the group addressed Celani. He was the opposite of her in every way. Tall and broad with fair skin, dark purple hair, and silver eyes.

Despite the way he towered over her, easily four times her size, he spoke to her with respect and maybe even a little fear.

"We came as soon as we spotted them."

"Spotted what?" Kallius cut in, his grip around my waist tightening.

"Wraiths." Celani's tone was grim as she turned to meet her brother's gaze. "Captain Xanth said there are at least three on the mountain."

The giant man nodded, his silver eyes narrowing on me. His lips pulled back as he bared his teeth.

"And they're headed this way," he added.

Fear crept along my spine at the images my mind conjured up of blackened spirit creatures in tattered, hooded cloaks. Kallius let out a steady stream of impressive curses that made me think my reaction was on point, while his sister's expression turned thoughtful.

"We'll need to dispatch them before we head to Fengari Palace," she mused, her violet gaze hardening as she looked between the captain and me.

"Kallius, Xanth, I need you with me. Everyone else, you'll stay here with..." She hesitated before saying my name. "Ember. You will guard the prisoner, and protect her with your lives, by order of the shadow king."

There was a long, pregnant pause where no one said

anything. Celani narrowed her eyes, her chin lifting in a challenge as she looked between each of them.

"Do you understand your orders?" She bit out each word, and the soldiers stood at attention, putting their fists on their chests before saying "Yes, General."

"Good. Everyone stays here until we return." She looked at me next, something unreadable in her delicate features. "You, too."

I rolled my eyes, gesturing to my legs that were still numb from the cold and the cut on my knee from my fall.

"Sure thing, General." I offered her a mock salute.

I could have sworn amusement danced in her eyes, but it was gone as quickly as it had come. Kallius rested me against another tree before following his sister into the darkness of the forest, along with the one they called Xanth.

Which is how I found myself alone with a group of elven soldiers. What would one call such a gathering? A gaggle? A flock? A council? A fluffle? An unkindness?

Here was to hoping that last one was inaccurate, but experience had taught me not to bet on the kindness of men. Somehow, I doubted elves would be any different.

Chapter Three

THE OTHER SOLDIERS GAVE ME MARGINALLY MORE space than Celani and Kallius had, though they were sending me a slew of confused, intrigued, and downright disgusted glances.

Even so, I took the opportunity to stretch out a bit. My skin was raw and frozen, but some of the strength in my legs and ankles was coming back. I rocked back and forth on my heels, elongating my calves.

The dagger in my boot dug into my ankle, a familiar comfort that helped me breathe a little easier.

I needed to get out of here before Celani and Kallius came back, but that was proving difficult with the watchful eyes of the soldiers scanning the small copse around us, and the low, distinct growls coming from the clearing on the other side of them.

I hadn't seen what cast the shadows above us when they first arrived, but judging by the vicious snarls and the heavy breaths echoing through the air, I had a feeling they were more than simple paragliders.

I dug around in my small leather purse, searching for a tube of lip balm with trembling fingers as if that would help me focus on anything but what those creatures might look like, or how badly they might want to eat me.

The lock screen on my phone lit up, a capital *R* flickering in the right-hand corner as it uselessly searched for a cell tower.

I swallowed hard. It was one more nail in my elvish coffin. I quickly powered it down, so the battery didn't drain, before grabbing the lip balm.

A slender woman with navy hair and pale-blue eyes watched me carefully, her hands moving to her spear as she nudged the man next to her.

She nodded toward me as I soothed my chapped lips, like the tube was some deadly weapon she needed to rid me of. I carefully popped it back into my bag, leaving the metal clasp unlatched.

"Leave her, Leda. You heard the general," one of the other soldiers spoke up, distracting the two whose attention had been fixed on me.

I flexed my ankles, watching each of the soldiers to see if they noticed the movement. When they didn't, I risked rubbing my legs, my fingers inching toward the dagger in my boot.

The one called Leda nodded, but one of the male elves scoffed.

"We all heard her threaten the lives of her own soldiers over..." His gaze slid to me. "*Her.*"

"Merikh," the same one who had chastised Leda intoned.

"A human, you mean?" a younger-looking soldier asked, staring dubiously at my rounded ears.

"Don't be an idiot, Cedar. You know who she is, and what she's done," Merikh spat.

That gave me pause. I wasn't aware of any especially heinous misdeeds in my past, certainly nothing a gaggle of elves would have reason to be concerned with.

Who do they think I am?

I didn't plan to stay to find out. My fingers rubbed against the hilt of my dagger, and I held my breath, waiting until they looked away before sliding it out and tucking it into my purse.

"Regardless, the general gave orders."

Merikh shook his head. "And we're all expected to hop, even though that *general* only got her title from being the king's cousin."

This was looking dicier by the moment. I had allowed a false sense of calm to wash over me when my limbs weren't working and Kallius and Celani were being almost solicitous in their kidnapping, but I wasn't stupid enough to stay here while the soldiers debated the merits of following Celani's order to keep me alive.

The youngest soldier laughed, the sound drawing the attention of the rest of the soldiers. Good. I could work with that.

"Then why don't you challenge her for the position?" Cedar's tone was taunting as he tilted his spear toward Merikh.

Leda joined in, raising a challenging eyebrow. "Come on,

Merikh, all you have to do is best her in combat and the king will give you her title."

I silently and fervently hoped their ribbing continued long enough to keep their attention away from me. Slowly, I inched around the side of the tree, counting the seconds between breaths, waiting for any sign that these so-called elves had noticed.

Merikh scoffed, and I froze, relief washing over me when he only spoke up to bluster at the challenge his friend had set for him.

"I could challenge her if I wanted to," he said, a false note in his tone.

The others laughed, having heard the lie as easily as I did, and I took advantage of the sound to move another step away.

My pulse quickened, my heartbeat thundering in my ears as I held my breath and took another step. Two more. I was almost to the next tree, my legs surprisingly steady as I crept away.

"Hey," a deep voice called, and the quick crunching of icy snow sounded behind me.

Panic clawed its way up my throat, and before I could think about it too much, I turned and bolted. I made it all of two feet before careening directly into the hard planes of Merikh's chest.

A small, choked sound hissed past my lips, ringing out in the silence between breaths.

It was weak. Pathetic. Merikh noted it, too, the corners of his mouth inching upward as his pale eyes hardened.

"Going somewhere, princess?"

I scanned the trees, my heart thundering in my ears as the other soldiers stepped forward. They held their spears in their hands, clutching them like I was some sort of wild creature that might attack.

They weren't wrong. I felt exactly like that. Like a rabid, feral thing. Like a caged animal.

I couldn't think through the panic, could barely breathe. Before I knew what I was doing, my fingers were wrapping around the hilt of the dagger in my purse, and I swung wildly at the soldier in front of me.

He growled as my blade scraped across the skin of his forearm but didn't draw blood.

Which was strange, since it was freshly sharpened.

In a lightning-fast move, Merikh reached out, grabbing hold of my wrist as he pinned me against a tree. Pain lanced through my hand. He squeezed, the pressure so intense I wondered if the bones in my wrist would break under the strain.

He didn't let up until my fingers were numb, the dagger falling from my useless hand as I cried out in pain.

The sound had the one named Aelle stepping forward, her gaze steely as she pointed her spear at her fellow soldier.

"That's enough, Merikh," she said as his free hand trailed from one leg to the other, his fingers dipping into my boots.

"Not yet, it's not, Aelle," he said, baring his teeth. Then his hand was tracing up my calves, my thighs, searching under the tight black dress.

Nausea rolled through me at his touch. I looked at Aelle, my eyes pleading as Merikh continued his search. She took another step forward as his hands cupped my breasts, squeezing harder than necessary until he found what he was looking for.

A small, dark laugh escaped him as he reached down into the center of my bra to grab the switchblade I had hidden there.

"Bastard," I hissed at him.

Merikh scowled and stepped forward, erasing the few inches of space between us. His lips parted, his hot breath cascading over my cheek.

"I can't wait to watch him break you," he said.

My stomach roiled again, at the rancid odor, at the threat his words implied, at the pervasive feeling of helplessness that always seemed to plague my life in one form or another.

"Merikh?" Relief coursed through me at the sound of Celani's voice, which was ridiculous since she was the one who put me in this situation to begin with.

The soldier spun around to face her, though his hand stayed clamped over my wrist.

"The prisoner," he spat, "tried to escape. She also tried to stab me."

He tossed the general my dagger and switchblade before wrenching my small leather purse from my shoulder. The thin strap snapped in half as he threw that to Celani as well.

That's when Kallius stepped forward. His tall frame towered over Merikh's as he forced him to back away.

As soon as the bastard's hand left my wrist, I hissed in pain, massaging the sensation back into my fingers with my uninjured hand.

"Aelle," Celani called over her shoulder. "Escort the others back to Fengari. The king will want a full report."

"Yes, General," she said, before issuing orders and marching the other soldiers toward the clearing on the other side of the trees.

"Kallius," she said a moment later. "Take Xanth and scout ahead to the moongate. We need to make sure the path is clear. No more disruptions."

The last two men disappeared down the path without a word.

There was a long beat of silence as Celani studied me, her violet eyes looking from the daggers in her hands to the bruise on my wrist. Her brows knit in confusion that she shook off.

Then she moved closer, reaching out to touch the goose-bumps on my frozen skin, and the faint blue tint to my fingertips.

She ripped off her cloak to wrap around my shoulders, and the warmth was immediate. Delicious heat soaked into my numb skin, and a shiver raked its way through my bones.

"I didn't think you'd be cold," she said after a moment, like it was some revelation.

I glared at her.

"Well, that was dumb," I managed through rattling teeth. "Who woul-wouldn't be cold in this weather?"

Celani only shook her head in response. When I risked a glance backward, her hand wrapped around my arm, the pressure of her fingers gentle but firm.

"Don't."

The urge to run was markedly less strong now. I wouldn't

get far without my weapons. Not that I'd gotten very far with them. It didn't help that my head was spinning, and I was pretty sure blood was dripping from a cut on my leg.

How far would I get like this? How far was the door?

My stomach hollowed, but I set my jaw, following the general down the mountain.

We walked in silence until exhaustion nipped at my aching bones and I wasn't sure I could take another step. And yet, the general kept the grueling pace, her hand fixed around my arm as we marched on and on and on.

I heard it before I saw it. The same distinct whirring in the air from before, followed by the sound of voices.

Celani led me to the left down a narrow walkway that opened into another clearing. This one was smaller than the last and filled with ancient, ruined stones that had likely once been buildings. And there, in the center, was a circle of wan light.

Another door, or portal, or whatever the hell it was.

I stopped abruptly, staring at the gleaming, smooth gray circle of stones. The middle shimmered, just like the other one had, but instead of the casino bar, this one displayed a castle straight out of a fairytale.

"You can't take me through unless I'm willing, right?" The words tumbled from my shivering lips. "That's why you used the wine before."

Celani's gaze met mine, her chin dipping in something like approval.

"Willing is relative, the isos—" She paused before translating. "Magic, isn't picky."

Merikh's words resounded in my ear, about *him* breaking me. It didn't take a genius to guess that I had no desire to meet the king who had ordered my capture.

"Well, unless you plan on cramming more of that fairy wine down my throat, I'm not going."

Celani sighed, her grip still firm around my arm.

"First of all, it's Elven wine. Not faerie." She shuddered as if the difference repulsed her. "And secondly, I will be taking you to the king. So, the way I see it, you have three options before you."

She paused as a shadow passed overhead, sending tendrils of fear down my spine. The elf named Xanth landed in the clearing between us and the portal.

His massive form was dwarfed by the creature he'd flown here. A black jaguar with celestial markings and giant black feathered wings like a raven's. A small lantern hung from its neck with dancing blue flames that lit up the ground around it.

Kallius touched down behind him on a similar creature. The animals must have been the source of the sounds I heard earlier from just outside the clearing.

Celani didn't so much as flinch as icy gusts of wind blew toward us and the jaguars stretched and yawned, showing off gleaming white teeth that were longer than my hands.

The beasts were larger than any horse I had ever seen, and undoubtedly deadlier.

"So," the general continued, "I can throw your ass over my shoulder and carry you the rest of the way down this mountain. I can also throw your ass over the saddle and let one of the baztets fly you down the mountain."

Every part of me recoiled at that, and I took a giant step backward.

"The hell you're putting me on one of those things," I barked back quickly.

Celani's eyes narrowed, her expression shifting into something unreadable as she studied me for several long moments.

"Or," she continued as if I hadn't just spoken, "you can walk with me through the moongate quietly. Willingly." She stressed the word. "But one way or another, I am taking you to King Hadeon."

So much for a way out.

Chapter Four

In the end, I walked through the stupid damned portal on my own two feet, as it was the least humiliating of my three crappy options.

We stepped out to the view of a giant palace made of shimmering blue moonstone nestled into the base of the mountains.

The towers stretched up into the starlit sky just above a waterfall that cascaded from the mountaintop. It glittered like strands of silver before crashing down into a vast lake right next to the grounds.

I had spent my childhood mired in fantasy, drawings, and books and everything that took me to a place where I felt like I might belong. It was almost funny that I wound up here, somewhere I might have called beautiful if I hadn't been dragged here against my will.

Celani didn't allow us to linger, quickly moving us from the pristine courtyards into what I assumed was

Fengari Palace. Portraits and paintings lined the smooth stone walls, some of them moving to watch us as we walked through the halls. They didn't appear to be sentient as much as animated, painted leaves rustling as we passed.

Before I could study them further, Celani ushered us through an austere room with looming ceilings and candles that seemed to float in the air before stopping at a large set of black, iron-clad double doors.

Kallius took what looked to be a steadying breath as his sister signaled to the guards to open them.

The metal brackets groaned under the weight of the doors, an ominous sound that had trepidation racing through my veins. The quiet hum of conversation cut off as we stepped inside, a crowd of elves parting for us as Celani moved through the center of the room.

I kept my head down, staring at the swirling lines of silver-and-white marble on the floor. My skin crawled as I felt a hundred eyes watching me, gawking like I was the evening's entertainment.

Not the sexy kind, despite my little black dress, but the kind that just showed up in a clown costume.

Kallius cleared his throat just as Celani came to a stop in front of me. When she stepped to the side, I finally risked glancing up.

Starlight streamed in through the open ceiling, highlighting the blue and silver marble walls and pillars, and the white stone statues of mythical creatures that lined the corners of the room.

Small constellations were woven into everything, like a delicate silver thread that pulled everything together.

While I took it all in, the rest of the room seemed to be holding its breath, the crowd of people — soldiers, courtiers, whatever the hell they were — behind us not even daring to move, like they were waiting for something to happen.

I braced myself, turning to ask Celani or Kallius what was going on, when a wall of darkness bounded toward me. An enormous creature leapt from the shadows, and my blood turned to ice in my veins.

I just had time to recognize that all of its heads — all three of its massive heads — were canine in form, sleek and pointed, as dark as the night sky. Its eyes glowed like six separate moons, all of them focused on me.

I froze, sure that I had survived growing up on the streets and being taken by whatever the hell these things were only to be devoured by a freaking celestial cerberus, far away from whatever semblance of home I had built for myself. Worse, I was unarmed and defenseless like I swore I would never be.

I dove to the side, for all the good it would do me, and Celani's cloak slipped from my shoulders. I felt the thing's breath hot on my back, heard it let out an unearthly noise, some kind of ethereally harmonized bark that probably signified it wanted to eat someone.

Celani and Kallius didn't intervene, nor did the handful of soldiers that I had met before. Was this why they brought me here? Not to face their king, but to be offered up like some human sacrifice to his pet cerberus?

In my panic, I had wedged myself into the corner of the

room. There was no way out. No one to come and save me. Nowhere to run.

My fingers trembled as I used the cool marble to center myself, slowly turning around to face my impending demise head-on.

Then, a voice cut through the air, low and cool and commanding, like darkness itself. I got the strangest feeling that the owner of this voice might be worse than death, might spell my end out as certainly as the massive creature would have.

"Nyx." The word whispered across my skin like shadows.

The dog — if you could call it that — retreated with a disappointed whine, its nails tapping against the marble floors, echoing through the room.

Behind it, wrapped in shadows, was a gleaming onyx throne. My heartbeat pounded in my chest, some long forgotten part of my brain willing me to look away.

Of course, I didn't listen. Obedience had never been my strong suit, and I wouldn't back down from a challenge, even in my own mind. So I lifted my eyes to a being even more ethereally beautiful than the strange cerberus — and more terrifying.

His skin was pale, almost to the point of luminescence, a striking contrast to the dark-blue hair that fell past his shoulders. Like everyone else here, his ears were pointed, studded with a row of gleaming silver hoops at the top and gauges at the bottom.

A crown rested above his chiseled features, the smooth silver twisted like vines or roots around his head before dipping down onto his brow. He scarcely needed it to convey the sense of command that bled from every ounce of his being.

Even his clothes spoke to his power. He was the only one in the room who hadn't bothered with some form of armor. Instead, he was sprawled arrogantly on his shadowy throne in only a sleeveless vest and trousers.

But it was his eyes that got me. Silver starbursts on a midnight canvas, reminiscent of the night sky, just as fathomless but twice as cold.

They were the kind of eyes you could drown in, so lost in exploring their depths you didn't know you were sinking until the sea overtook you entirely.

He looked down at me — and on me — a raised eyebrow giving away exactly how unimpressed he was by what he saw. I forced myself to lift my chin defiantly.

"Princess Phaedra." Something dangerous lurked under his cool indifference.

A gasp swept through the room, an echo of the one on my lips. The name pricked at something in my mind, something I instinctively wanted to shy away from.

Was Princess Phaedra who they thought I was? Why they had taken me?

"No," I said, shaking my head as the word came out as barely a whisper.

He glanced behind me, and I followed his gaze to where Celani was giving him a meaningful shake of her head. He was examining me once more by the time I turned back to face him.

"No," he said quietly, more in agreement than argument, though the word was soaked with bitterness.

"So...now that you know you have the wrong person, you can send me the hell home." My words came out less certain than I wanted them to, but no less barbed.

The uncommonly gorgeous king and this palace and that name were stirring up reactions in me that made no sense — hatred and panic and desperation.

There were a few muttering voices clearly offended by something I said, but the king ignored me entirely. He kept his attention on Celani and her brother.

"I heard there were obstacles on the way?" It was a demand as much as a question.

Was he referring to her little side quest to visit the wraiths, or the fact that I'd tried to stab one of his soldiers? Either way, it was infuriating that he had dragged me here and was now refusing to even acknowledge me, but I didn't press the issue.

Not when I suspected going unnoticed would be preferable to having his attention on me. I was outnumbered and outpowered here, and I hadn't survived as long as I had without knowing when not to draw unnecessary attention to myself.

"More or less, King Hadeon," Celani answered, her gaze sliding to the right. Toward Merikh.

If I had thought the king's eyes were dark before, it was nothing compared to the pure death that clouded them now. "I see."

I braced myself, my mouth going dry as my stomach churned. Would he kill me for this? Was there some sort of specialized punishment for kidnapped humans who raised their weapons to his soldiers?

"Nyx," the king said shortly.

The cerberus stepped forward, all three heads homing in on Merikh as it bared its teeth, a low growl rippling from its massive jaws.

The elf paled, turning to run, but Aelle and Cedar crossed their artfully wrought spears to bar his escape. The cerberus stalked toward him, and he turned to face it, fear widening his pale silver eyes.

I watched as the beast lunged forward, the middle head lifting his body like it was nothing, before the heads on the sides clamped down as well, all three tearing him apart.

There was a loud cry, then the spray of inky blood as the cerberus devoured him limb by limb.

My stomach twisted, and my breaths came faster — not for the man's sake so much as my own. Would that have been my fate, if not for the king's intervention? Being torn apart by three savage heads, the crunch of my bones echoing off the midnight blue floors?

Would it still be my fate, now that he knew I wasn't the person they were looking for?

I looked away from the bloody teeth and the few meager remnants of a man I couldn't dredge up much sympathy for, and my gaze landed on the king. He was studying me with a curious expression before he turned his attention to the rest of the room.

"Let that be a lesson to anyone who dares touch what belongs to me."

My lips parted at his implication, something visceral inside me balking at his threat. "I do not belong to you."

I wasn't sure where the words came from, but the hush that fell over the room was enough to tell me they were a mistake. So much for not drawing attention to myself.

Maybe I would end the evening as his pet's meal after all, but I couldn't find it in myself to cower. I glared at him like he didn't hold all of the power in the room. Like he didn't have control over whether or not I lived or died by celestial cerberus.

"Not Phaedra indeed," the king said, letting out an irritable huff of air.

"No," I agreed, though I sensed his sarcasm. "My name is Ember."

He scoffed. "The bare remnants of a dead star. How fitting."

"I'm not who you're looking for, so just let me go home," I said, crossing my arms over my chest.

I didn't let pleading enter my tone, since I doubted he would respond to it anyway.

A muscle twitched in his jaw on my last word.

Hadeon gave a lazy wave of his hand, and the bracelets around my wrists vanished. All at once, I was overcome with wave after wave of heat, just like I'd felt at the casino portal, only more intense. My skin flushed and burned as a rush of energy poured into me, an implosion of light that turned back outward in a single golden burst.

My hair turned to literal flames that licked across my shoulders and down my back. There was a painful stretching in my ears, my cheekbones, my jaw, and an unbearable heat searing along my body in patterns I knew all too well.

My tattoos, the artwork I had designed myself then painstakingly inked across my skin, were now glowing golden against the bronze backdrop.

I gasped, the air too dry, too hot to fill my lungs. I was going to burn up. I was sure of it. Turn into a pile of no more than the namesake the king had just mocked.

Just when I was sure I could take no more, when pure white light surrounded and filled me, blinding me from the rest of the room, searing into my soul like some sort of parasitic flame, something cool whispered along the nape of my neck.

A gentle touch that doused the consuming fire lining my skin. It would have been soothing if not for the implication of its placement.

My hands went to my neck, feeling nothing but a slight drop in temperature around the skin there, but I knew in my soul I had just been collared.

"What did you do to me?" I demanded.

Everything I had done was to ensure I was never at the mercy of another person and now... My heartbeat thundered furiously in my ears, but the bastard on the throne remained impassive.

"I can't very well have you incinerating my people," Hadeon said with a shrug. Then the corner of his mouth tilted up. "And this way, everyone will remember who you belong to."

"I already told you, I don't —" My words cut off when the collar around my neck tightened in warning.

"When I said everyone, I meant you as well." His voice was a low growl. "Nod if you understand."

"Rather. Die." I choked out.

He sighed, like I was the problem, but then loosened the collar before it could actually strangle me. "I see you are as savage as ever, my little Feralinia."

Feralinia? Another name that wasn't mine. And how the hell would he know how savage I had ever been? While I was still catching my breath, he turned to address the rest of the room.

"Leave us." His voice was low, quiet, but no less commanding for it. The courtiers and soldiers practically fled from the great hall, leaving me with only the king and the other vicious beast in the room.

He studied me for several heartbeats, his head tilting slightly. "You truly have no memories of who you are."

"I have all of my memories," I rasped. It was true. From a happy childhood to being orphaned in a single blow, to a slew of foster homes and nights on the street when those homes were even more unsafe, I had a glaringly vivid recollection of my life.

And I would damned sure remember meeting someone like him.

He made a noncommittal noise in the back of his throat. "If that were true, you would remember that you do, in fact, belong to me. We made a bargain in your...first life."

My first life? So they didn't just believe I was some long-lost princess, but that I was...reborn? I was torn somewhere between fury and maniacal laughter.

"I don't believe in reincarnation," I said in a tone that was calmer than I felt.

Hadeon gave another infuriating shrug, his strange eyes pinning me to the spot. "The goddess cares not for your feelings or beliefs. Nor do I," he said flatly. "But I always collect on my bargains."

"You're going to hold me to a bargain someone else made?" My temper flared to life. "It's hardly my fault if she was desperate or stupid enough, but I would never make a deal with you."

A bitter smile curved his full lips. "I would argue that you were both desperate and stupid, but I can see there's no talking to you tonight."

With a flick of his wrist, shadows streamed from his finger, stretching past me to open the iron doors.

"Celani, escort her to her rooms," he said evenly, keeping his eyes on me. "We'll continue this in the morning, Feralinia, when I trust you'll be more reasonable."

With that, he sat back on his throne, waving a dismissive hand in my general direction.

I was too furious to be afraid.

Chapter Five

Hadeon's mocking chuckle followed me for longer than it should have. His deep baritone crept under my skin, unnerving me and sending shivers racing down my spine.

Celani seemed unbothered by it, clearly used to taking orders from the king of shadows and asshattery.

She led me down a wide hall, wordlessly gesturing toward two soldiers standing guard. I wondered if silent commands were a Moon Court thing, or if everyone in Celani's family expected people to obey their unspoken orders.

Either way, the soldiers immediately fell into place behind us, perfectly spaced, their spears drawn like I was some monster from whom they needed protecting.

The scowls that seemed permanently etched into their faces made them almost more menacing than the sharp tips of their weapons.

None of them spoke, leaving me with no distraction for my racing thoughts.

I scanned the sweeping hallway, the gilded doorways, and the massive marble staircase as we climbed each step, searching for any sign of an easy escape. I knew it wouldn't be possible yet with the general at my side and the soldiers at my back. But there might be a chance later.

Unless, of course, the word *room* was a euphemism, and they were leading me to a dungeon where I would waste away for the rest of my life. Was that even the worst-case scenario?

The king had said I belonged to him. In what capacity?

I tried to banish the familiar panic at facing the unknown. After my parents died, I bounced around from one foster home to another, and it had never gotten any easier, the initial surge of uncertainty before I knew what I was walking into.

Each time, the same relentless wave of questions: Are they kind? What will be expected of me? How long will I stay?

On and on, it went. I spent my adult life clawing my way to some semblance of consistency even when every part of me begged to stay on the move. I had put down roots, opened a tattoo shop, bought a freaking plant, all to end up back where I started. Out of place somewhere that would never be mine, with no idea what to expect from the people who had power over me.

Resentment and anxiety battled in my churning stomach. Still, I walked with my head high and my shoulders back.

I may not have been a princess, but I had survived too much to be cowed now.

We finally came to a stop in front of a large door made from deep amethyst wood. Constellations were carved into the rounded frame, and the silver handle curved into a crescent moon.

Celani silently stretched out her hand, twisting the crescent downward to reveal a room that was decidedly not a dungeon.

From the high ceilings illuminated by floating candles to the gilded canopy bed and even the silver threading on the navy wallpaper, it was every bit as opulent as the rest of the moon palace.

I narrowed my eyes, knowing I was getting this luxurious accommodation at the low, low price of my freedom.

Celani scrutinized my reaction, and I wondered what she was looking for. Awe? Gratitude? Shock?

"Why this room?" I asked, not allowing any of those emotions to infiltrate my tone.

"Instead of a dungeon, you mean?" she guessed accurately.

I nodded.

She pursed her lips. "You are a royal prisoner, whether you remember that or not."

I shook my head, irritation rising in my chest.

"And what will be expected of me in return for this generosity?" I asked, shutting out memories of demands that had driven me to live under an icy bridge rather than stay and cave to them.

Celani surveyed me for a long moment, a muscle clenching in her delicate jaw as her violet eyes narrowed. "The king may have need of your services, but it will not be the kind you're insinuating. He's not a monster."

I thought back to his dispassionate expression as he watched a man get eaten not ten feet from where he sat.

"Maybe not to you," I responded. "But being his cousin and his general is hardly the same as being his prisoner."

She met my eyes for a long moment. "You have no reason to believe me, but I swear on my life and my honor and my isos that no one here will touch you against your will again."

She was right. I didn't have to believe her, but she hadn't lied to me yet. Drugged me and kidnapped me, sure, but no lies.

So I nodded my acceptance of her oath, taking careful note of the caveat. Celani continued in a brisk tone, as though the interaction never occurred.

"There's wine on the table, if you need a drink after the events of this evening. Don't worry, it won't compel you here when you have your own isos to counteract it," she said, gesturing toward the small table near the fire. "The lavatory is through that door. And if you need anything else, ring for your maid."

She pointed to a long strip of blue fabric embroidered with the night sky, that I presumed pulled a bell of some sort.

"I'll come to retrieve you in the morning," she finished up.

"For what?" I didn't bother to hide the wariness in my tone.

A small sigh escaped her. "Just breakfast, princess. And before you try to escape, you should know that the room is warded, and there will always be a guard at your threshold." With that, she left, closing the door solidly behind her.

The moment I was alone, I wanted to give way to the

wobbling in my knees and sink to the ground and close my eyes until this entire nightmare went away.

But I knew this was no figment of my imagination, no fantasy. In some ways, this felt sharper and more real than the world I had left behind, and if this was real, then I couldn't afford to crumble just yet.

So I steeled myself to investigate the room, searching for weapons, escape routes, lurking elves or creatures who wanted to make me their dinner. In the end, all I found was that Celani hadn't lied about the room being warded.

At least, I assumed that was the appropriate terminology for the way that every square inch of space along the edge of the sparkling Grecian balcony was enclosed by a clear...air shield of some sort.

Even if I would have risked climbing over the edge and miraculously didn't plummet to my death on the icy mountainside below, the barrier was impenetrable.

There were no weapons, aside from a sharp-ish quill in the desk. That was sure to do me a lot of good against magic and flying jaguars and carnivorous three-headed dogs.

Finally, I forced myself to examine the one thing I had been avoiding. The moonstone-framed mirror hanging in the biggest bathroom I had ever seen.

My gaze shied away from the unfamiliar pointed tips of my ears, the gold hoops and chains still looped through them like they were when I was human. Instead, I focused on the dark shadows swirling around my neck. I brought my fingers up to the collar King Hadeon had put on me, a chill running from the swirling shadows all the way down my spine. It felt like silk underneath my fingertips, but there was no give at all.

Would something in this stop me from going home, even if I could find a way out?

I shivered before scanning the rest of my appearance. A small bruise was forming on my cheekbone from where I'd faceplanted on the ground outside of the portal.

The sparkling cat ears Isa had insisted I wear were off center and tied up in my matted hair.

And this is what I had looked like standing in front of a king and his court, arguing about my identity.

A bitter laugh threatened to rip out of me, but I choked it down, walking away from the mirror. I was tired of looking at myself. Tired of looking like this.

Since I sure as hell wasn't going anywhere tonight, I could at least ensure that whenever Celani came to fetch me tomorrow I wasn't quite so disheveled.

I didn't want to be impressed with this place, but I couldn't help but run my hands along the dark gray stone with silvery blue veins. It shimmered in the moonlight streaming from the half-open ceiling and balcony surrounding two of the walls.

A silver tree with glowing teal leaves grew in the corner, its branches stretching across the room, up the walls and down the pillars, each one covered in small white flowers that smelled like jasmine.

A steaming waterfall fell from the open ceiling into what I might have called a bathtub, if it weren't easily ten times the size of my tub back home.

And tucked away in a corner was a wide, shallow basin that sat on elegantly wrought legs next to what looked to be a very fancy seat. On closer inspection, it was a toilet, also attached to a source of constantly flowing water. That would have been a relief if I had any intention of staying here.

Hell, who was I kidding? It was a relief now.

After taking advantage of said facilities, I peeled off my filthy clothes, letting them land in a heap on the floor before kicking off my combat boots and stepping into the steaming bathtub.

The water was like hot silk lapping at my aching skin, and for a moment I closed my eyes, allowing myself to just breathe.

When I finally opened them, my thoughts chased each other once again. They raced through my mind in frantic circles that all led back to Hadeon. To his fair skin and midnight blue hair, the tendrils of shadows that floated in the air around him.

It was impossible not to notice the similarities between the shadow king and the Greek god of the underworld. Aside from the name, there was the cerberus and the whole "dragging unwilling women to his palace to be his prisoner."

Though the joke was on him, because I sure as hell wasn't Persephone.

No, just an elven princess reborn, an intrusive, slightly hysterical voice corrected me.

I ignored that voice, dipping my head under the water as I began the arduous process of untangling the cat ears from my matted hair.

The king's condescending tone came to mind, telling me I

had made a bargain with him. Wasn't Hades known for that, too? I didn't remember much about the mythology aside from a few scattered references in books and movies.

Even his name, though. *Hadeon*. Was it a family name? A tradition?

If so, somewhere, at some point, a human had left this place and lived to tell about it. Just in time for it to become part of our mythology...a mere few thousand years ago.

So that was promising. Obviously.

The longer I stayed in the water the more the ache in my muscles eased, but I didn't want to linger. Something about the bathroom called to me in a way I wasn't entirely comfortable with, pulling at a thought in the back of my mind like it was a loose thread that would unravel if only I allowed it.

It was more than just déjà vu, stronger and ...sadder, a feeling I didn't want to touch right now.

Instead, I scrubbed my body and hair, carefully avoiding the bruise on my cheek and cut on my knee before exiting the bath again.

I dried off with one of the soft, woven towels, staring at the soiled, crumpled heap of my dress on the floor. I didn't want to wear someone else's clothes, let alone a dead princess's, but I wasn't about to sleep naked in an unfamiliar place.

Grabbing one of the pale silk nightgowns, I yanked it over my head. It should have been cold in here, with the open balcony and thin clothes, but my skin seemed several degrees warmer than I was used to it being. Just before I climbed into the bed, my eyes snagged on the desk again.

It wasn't much, but the metal tip of that quill was a better weapon than nothing. So, I snatched it from the drawer, tucking it under the pillow as I climbed into the giant bed.

It wasn't as comforting as the feel of my dagger, but since no one had seen fit to give me my purse back, it would have to do.

At least, until I could secure something better.

The candlelight intuitively dimmed as soon as I lay down, and the shadows at the edges of the room grew larger. I stared at them, my eyelids growing heavy as I watched the way they moved and crept through the room.

I fell asleep with the distinct feeling that they were staring right back.

MY DREAMS WERE VIVID, more like visions or nightmares that accosted me, chasing me as I slept.

Over and over again, I felt the click of the shadow collar snapping into place, only it was more oppressive in my dream, devastating when it severed me from my isos – the only defense I had.

I heard the shadow king's laugh dance along my skin, even colder than his shadows, beheld the hatred burning from his starburst eyes and felt the same resonating within myself, even as the time and scenery changed around us.

There were rooms I had never seen, tables filled with foods I had never eaten, and the only constant was the king's smug face and the fury I felt every time I looked at it.

The images spun until I saw razor-sharp teeth snapping inches from my face, heard the eerie keening of the cerberus creature, haunting and stretching on into eternity. Monstrous shadow creatures marched in the distance, and a man's deep, heated tone rang out over it all.

"This is Hadeon's doing. There will be no stopping him now."

Another wave of rage burned through me.

Then I was in the bathtub I used last night, only I wasn't alone. Instead of lying back against the cool stone, I was supported by a warm, hard body.

A pale, masculine hand pressed against a stone to remove a glass bottle. The hand briefly disappeared from my view before I felt the luscious sensation of shampoo being lathered into my hair. He dragged his fingers along my scalp with an aching slowness, sending zaps of lightning straight down to my toes.

The deft hands followed the strands of my hair all the way down until they were playing along the swell of my chest.

Not *my* chest, I realized. My array of tattoos was entirely absent from the smooth, tan skin, and this body was responding in a way mine never had, arching against the touch and relishing the slide of the man's hands with the slickness of the soapy water.

Distantly, something stirred inside me, longing or jealousy or both.

Then the vision dissolved, and the shadow creatures returned. Terror crashed over me in the dream and out of it. My entire being writhed with a visceral fear, the acute horror of losing something so much more precious to me than my own life.

I followed the thread of thought, trying to find what it was that was so precious to me until I ran into a wall of black shadows. They were colder than the creatures, stronger somehow, enveloping me until finally, I slept without dreaming.

Chapter Six

THE MORNING BROUGHT WITH IT EXACTLY ZERO clarity.

Well, that wasn't as true as I wanted it to be. When I made my way to the bathroom, I couldn't resist trying to find the compartment from my dream. Sure enough, it opened to reveal an artful collection of glass bottles, so I now knew with a degree of certainty the dreams were more than just dreams.

A glance in the mirror proved that, much to my dismay, I still had pointed ears and glowing tattoos and a freaking collar around my neck.

I wrenched my gaze away, going to find clothes to wear before Celani came to fetch me. Though it was dark on the balcony outside, I wasn't sure that was a good indicator of time. When did the sun rise here?

I froze when I realized my dress was missing from where I had left it crumpled on the floor, and my boots were lined up neatly against the wall.

Someone had been in my room while I slept. I grabbed the quill from under my pillow, trying to chase away the shivers that crept along my spine.

A knock on the door nearly had me leaping out of my skin, and my grip around the quill tightened.

An elf with long aqua hair braided back from her silver-freckled face stepped in before I gave her permission, and my anger surged all over again.

It was a maid, insisting on helping me dress. I couldn't help but shoot her a scathing look, though I knew this wasn't her fault. I didn't like people in my space, and I sure as hell didn't need help dressing.

"I'll manage," I told her.

She looked just as happy with that, casting a thinly veiled look of judgment at my — well, my everything. I couldn't tell if she objected more to my bronze skin or my tattoos or the flaming tendrils of my hair, but all of it was at odds with the moonlit color of her skin and hair and clothes.

It didn't matter.

"And I'd like to formally request that you not enter my room without my permission again."

I didn't know if she was the one who took my dress while I slept, but she had just let herself in before I was ready, and that wasn't going to work for me.

Her pale blue eyes narrowed, but she dipped her head in silent assent before turning and shutting the door behind her.

I sighed, grateful to be alone again, before moving to the closet.

I took my time shuffling through rows upon rows of white and golden dresses. Had Phaedra been a priestess of sorts, as well as a princess? Or just some kind of eternal virgin?

I scoffed, remembering last night's dream. Whoever had been in that tub was having more fun than I had ever had with...well, anyone. If those were Phaedra's memories, then my virgin theory was definitely wrong.

If those were Phaedra's memories, though, did that mean that they were also mine? That this whole ridiculous reincarnated princess story was true?

Dismissing the endless list of questions I had no answers for, I chose one of the pristine Grecian gowns and wrestled myself into it with more difficulty than I had anticipated. Layers of thin white material crisscrossed over my torso to cover my chest before wrapping around my shoulders.

Long, translucent sleeves trailed down my arms, cinching at my wrists with delicate golden chains.

There were even soft, delicate golden slippers to match. I took one disdainful look at them before chucking them back in the closet, opting for my combat boots instead.

Another knock sounded at the door, this one louder and more confident than the maid's, so I wasn't surprised to find Celani on the other side.

She eyed me, starting with the fiery hair that had dried in thick waves that fell past my shoulders and ending with my black boots, biting back what I could have sworn was a smirk.

"The king will see you now."

My heart pounded at the thought of another encounter

with the shadow king, a combination of terror and something more difficult to place. I quashed both feelings, striving for an outward display of nonchalance.

"How very magnanimous of him," I muttered. I didn't argue, however, not when my mind was swimming with questions and I suspected the enigmatic douchebag was the only one who would give me anything resembling answers.

Instead of taking me to the throne room, she brought me to an open room with a round table on the balcony. Mountains were visible in the background, punctuated by sleek, glowing waterfalls and silvery blue flowers.

The sun was just barely peeking over the horizon, painting the scene in an unearthly haze. Celani left me at the doors, telling me the king would join me shortly.

I had spent the walk there preparing myself to face him again, but it did little good. I felt him the moment he entered the room, an overwhelming presence that took up all of the available space.

He walked with the grace of a predator, on footsteps that were somehow both silent and dominating. The same silvery blue crown rested on his head, a symbol of authority he scarcely needed when it bled from every part of him.

His giant cerberus was at his side, the blue and golden star-studded pattern of her fur evocative of the view of the sky from my room. Like she was born under these stars or had been painted to reflect them.

The rational part of me knew I should be terrified of the three-headed Anubis-looking moon-dog, having watched it eat someone just yesterday, but some buried instinct told me to keep a wary watch on Hadeon instead.

Or maybe it was just hard to look away from his preternaturally perfect features. Had Phaedra been terrified of him?

She had hated him. That much I felt in the dream.

He watched me with a gaze that was nearly as cautious as my own, the way a lion might watch its prey to be sure it didn't try to escape. His starburst eyes swept over me before widening for a fraction of a moment.

"That dress doesn't suit you."

Just like that, anger eclipsed the smallest bit of my fear. Like I had been given any more choice in what to wear than I was in coming here to begin with.

"That's disappointing, when I dressed with you in mind. Of course, if you don't like it, you could always give me my own dress back and *send me home*." My tone grew flat on the last three words. "You can't possibly think I'm going to stay here as your willing prisoner."

He tilted his head like he found me particularly amusing. "Obviously not, or I wouldn't have bothered with the collar."

A wave of rage washed over me, so potent I felt like it was poisoning the air around us like oil spilling into a clear lake. But Hadeon was as impervious as ever, striding past me and taking a seat. He gestured for me to do the same, and I badly wanted to refuse.

The girl who had never known where her next meal would come from balked at that, though, so I reluctantly sank into the chair across from him, staying as far from the king and Nyx as I could.

Curiously, I peered into my cup.

"It's only coffee."

"Pity," I said. I didn't want to be vulnerable from elven wine, but I wasn't sure I wanted to face the day sober either.

Nonetheless, despite the lack of many modern conveniences, at least this place had coffee. I might have died without it.

I carefully picked up the ceramic mug, bringing it to my lips to test the temperature, then the taste. It was dark and rich with a hint of caramel sweetness, like freshly brewed espresso. I practically moaned as I took a long sip, savoring the flavor as much as I did the immediate effects of the caffeine.

I could feel Hadeon's gaze locked on me as I filled my plate with food, but I ignored him, focusing instead on the small waffles with berry compote and what looked like powdered sugar.

There were also long strips of some sort of grilled fruit that tasted like savory bacon, and white, fluffy eggs with a pale pink sauce that reminded me of cheese. But the most enticing thing at the table was what I could only describe as a pomegranate, with white skin and purple kernels that burst in my mouth with the flavor of dry red wine.

If I closed my eyes, I could imagine being back home at my favorite breakfast place, eating all of my favorite foods.

"Hungry?" Hadeon asked, his voice an unpleasant interruption.

I scowled at him, refusing to feel embarrassed, even as he made consuming his own meal look like a warrior's dance.

"Yeah, see, this asshole kidnapped me and didn't give me any food last night, so I'm afraid I skipped dinner."

The corner of his mouth quirked, but his tone was dry when he responded. "I assumed you could subsist off your righteous indignation."

I sighed, shoving another bite of the delicious waffle into my mouth as I stared at him. I took my time chewing and swallowing before sniping back at him.

"And I assumed you could subsist off the glee you get from casually murdering people, yet here we sit."

His navy eyebrow arched, either in fury or...amusement. "It's actually considered an execution when I do it."

I narrowed my eyes, and he made a tutting sound.

"Were you sad to see Merikh go? That is the punishment in the Court of Fire and Sun for daring to touch a royal." He deftly speared a piece of fruit with his fork, and my eyes tracked the movement, running over the tendons in his pale, powerful hands.

I watched the pale blue melon journey from his plate to his waiting lips, my heartbeat picking up in my chest as I noted the way his fingers tilted, trying and failing not to compare them to the ones that had been on my — *her* taut breasts in the dream.

When I lifted my gaze, it was to find him studying me. For a scant fraction of a second, I imagined something other than hatred stirring in his features. Then it was gone as quickly as it came.

Surely it couldn't have been him in the dream. Half the

elves I had met so far had the same pale, luminescent skin. I had felt Phaedra's loathing of the king and had witnessed his return of that emotion. Whatever happened in that tub didn't feel like sultry hate sex.

So a guard, then, or a courtier?

I was the first to lose our unspoken staring contest, turning my attention back to my plate.

"Why are you so convinced that I'm her?" I murmured, moving the remaining food around with my fork.

Somewhere in the back of my mind, I processed the court he had mentioned. With my skin and my hair, it wasn't a stretch to assume that the Court of Fire and Sun was my court, as the Court of Moon and Stars was his.

When he scoffed, I glanced back up.

"Even if you weren't identical – well, almost." He swept an assessing look over me, pausing for emphasis at the tattoos blazing across my chest and shoulders that must have been the exception to our similarities. "The priestess herself informed me."

Something niggled at the back of my mind, but I pushed it away.

"Well, your all-knowing priestess was wrong." The words fell flat, even to my own ears.

He shook his head in a chiding, irritating way. "Abba speaks for the goddess herself. So she may be arrogant and infuriating, with a rather wicked sense of humor, but it's unlikely she was wrong."

I opened my mouth to argue, but he raised a hand and I clamped my lips shut in spite of myself.

"Do you think it's a coincidence that you were there, at that establishment where the portal opened?"

"I...was invited." I heard it as soon as I said it, how little sense it made...how little sense it had always made that I was given an all-expenses-paid trip for a contest I didn't even enter.

"Naturally," he said sarcastically, sitting casually back in his chair. "And you seem like the easygoing type, so you probably enjoy spontaneous trips like that all the time. Certainly you didn't feel *compelled* to go."

The blood drained from my face. All of it was a ploy to get me here. But why?

Like he heard my question, Hadeon waved a hand and an honest-to-god scroll appeared on the table in front of me, unfurling with another motion from him.

"All of this was prophesied," he said tonelessly, gesturing for me to read the scroll.

On the night The Veil shall Open
Nightmares claim thy sacred tokens.
But magic stolen comes with a cost,
For by His hands blood will be lost.
Bound in war, triumph is hopeless,
Thy future lies In death and darkness.
Yet on the Eve thy battle ends,
Eight fierce souls will make amends.
Hand in hand they shall unite,
A pact in blood, heiress to fight.
When gifted power pays sacrifice,

Mother Terrea shall repay the price.
Blessed be her soul reborn,
Seek from where the Earth was torn.
In fifty years eight heiresses will return...

THE BOTTOM of the page was torn.

"Where's the rest?"

"Where, indeed?" Hadeon responded, his fingers drumming irritably on the arm of his chair. "Every time I have sought that answer, I have been thwarted by the goddess in some manner, so I'm sure she'll reveal it when she damned well feels like it."

"No love lost there, I see," I muttered.

He released a bitter exhalation. "You would defend her after she sent Abba to convince you to *die*."

I scrutinized his features, trying to read the subtext of a situation I didn't begin to understand.

"Were you that upset just because she confiscated your property?" I pressed, gesturing to my collar – the same one I had seen in the dream I now realized belonged to Phaedra.

Whatever trace of emotion had entered into his features effectively vanished.

"Everything the goddess does and is upsets me," he said flatly.

I studied him for another moment, gleaning about as much from his flawless features as I would have from the marble statues in his throne room.

With a small sigh, I returned to the scroll, my mind snagging on *eight fierce souls.*

"Eight?" I echoed aloud.

Ivy had received a ticket, also. What were the odds...but Celani had hedged when I asked her what happened to my friends.

We had nothing to do with your pig-friend by the painting...

I had been so focused on the other part of her denial that I hadn't considered it further. Nothing to do with Ivy, but something had happened to her. And maybe six other women that night.

"Where is Ivy?" I asked, not bothering to expound. He knew where to find me, and that meant he likely knew my friends and far more about my life than I was comfortable with.

"Your little fae friend?"

Fae. That was...I wanted to say impossible, but was it more impossible than this?

"Apparently not all of your senses were deadened by your human form. It seems several of you were drawn to each other on Earth."

I ignored the way he said human like it was an insult, my mind racing with the implications for my friend.

"Is she safe?" I pushed.

He gave another of his infuriating shrugs. "The Fae are hardly my concern. What is my concern is that you learn to channel your isos — or magic, as the humans so crassly call it — before you incinerate yourself and, more importantly, everyone else in Fengari."

His words had the intended effect, sending ice creeping down my spine, but I told myself I wouldn't be here long enough for that to be an issue. The portal was still out there, and there had to be a way back. Then maybe I could figure out how to get Ivy.

Hell, if there was another world connected to ours, there had to be someone somewhere who knew about it. Probably someone dismissed as insane.

"Well, if the person who kidnapped me thinks it's necessary, then I'll be sure and get right on that," I muttered.

"Is your own life not motivation enough?"

"To trust you? Not really." I was mostly lying. A survivalist at heart, there wasn't much I wouldn't do to stay alive, but he had already said his shadow collar would prevent me from burning myself up.

Would it disappear once I crossed back into Earth?

"I'm not sure what part of your collar made you believe you had a choice, but I have no intention of letting your short-sighted human stubbornness endanger my people." He got to his feet in a single fluid motion, ignoring the indignant scoff I let out. "You will train."

With a last look of distaste, he left before I could respond, gesturing for Nyx to follow. The massive dog looked back at me like she was disappointed, maybe because I didn't serve as her breakfast. Then she loped after him.

I barely picked at the remaining food on my plate, my appetite suddenly gone as I seethed and shook with wrath. But I also thought on everything else he said, about me, about the goddess and the priestess, the eight...about everything.

And I wondered if he was right when he said the goddess had a wicked sense of humor. Otherwise, why the hell had she gone to the trouble of getting me to that casino only to leave me at the mercy of my enemy?

Chapter Seven

CELANI ESCORTED ME BACK TO MY ROOM AFTER breakfast, where I was left to my own devices for the rest of the day. It was too much time to think. To feel. To try to remember a life that wasn't mine.

The room didn't get any less gorgeous with time. That was worse somehow, the way even the palace seemed to want to mess with my mind, tugging at memories like a word on the tip of my tongue. I paced the floor and tried jabbing at the wards with my quill to no avail.

It was frustrating, but the only way to pass the time until I could find a way back to the portal, which was still my goal.

I couldn't fight the elves, but I was quiet and light on my feet. As long as the collar didn't prevent me from leaving, could I make my way there without anyone noticing? Celani had said there was a guard at my door, but was that something I could talk my way around?

There was a small, unreasonable part of me that rebelled at the idea of going home. That wondered what I had to go back to besides the roots I had forced myself to put down and the career I gave most of my time to. Ivy and Isa both had lives outside of me.

Was that Phaedra? Did whatever was left of her soul want to stay in Aelvaria?

My fingers came up to the black collar around my neck that told the entire kingdom who my *owner* was, and I pushed the irrational thoughts away. Maybe I never quite felt like I belonged on Earth, but at least there, I was free.

For hours I paced the marble floors while coming up with a half-assed plan. I would have sold my left kidney to have my phone and earbuds back to drown out the world while I thought, to lose myself in the playlist I had painstakingly put together when I needed an escape.

Eventually, I made my way back to the bathtub, mostly to kill time.

The sound of the waterfall and the view of the starlit sky distracted me enough that I didn't hear the maids when they snuck into the bedroom again.

When I came out, in place of the dress I had laid out on the giant bed was a sheer silky nightgown and robe, similar to the ones I had seen in the vast closet the day before, only these were black.

A niggling suspicion formed in my brain, and I crossed the distance to the closet, wrenching open the door.

It was empty. His mocking words echoed in my head. *That dress doesn't suit you.*

A tendril of anger burrowed in my chest. Was he planning on replacing them all with black things, or would I be expected to wear a negligee around the palace? It hardly mattered. It would be a freezing trek back, but no one in Vegas would look twice at someone walking around in lingerie.

I could escape this.

At least they hadn't taken my boots.

I shoved my sockless feet into the combat boots, lacing them tightly around my ankles. Then, I pulled my stabby quill from under my pillow before going to try the handle to my door.

It turned easily and soundlessly. The hallway was dark, and empty, as far as I could see. There were no guards outside, which surprised me, given that the people here hated me and the king had a vested interest in my continued existence.

Maybe Celani had been bluffing to keep me in my rooms? Either way, I wasn't going to look this particular gift horse in the mouth.

I had learned the value of going unnoticed by my second foster home, so it was now second nature to creep on silent footfalls down the hallway. From here, I could reach the balcony with the trellis just around the corner. I only hoped it wasn't warded like the other rooms had been.

If it wasn't, then the climb would be easy enough and it was just a short sprint to the first moongate. From there, it was only an hour or so north to where the portal had been.

Adrenaline raced through my veins, a small spark of hope igniting for the first time since I came here.

I should have realized it was too easy.

It only took me two more steps before I understood the lack of guards. Or at least, the lack of Elven guards. An eerie keening sounded behind me, already hauntingly familiar to my ears.

Shivers raked down my spine, like my soul itself reacted to the sound. My mouth went dry, my heart beating so loudly in my ears that it nearly covered the sound of an enormous tail thumping against the solid castle wall.

Run, run, run, I chanted to myself, but there was no time. I hadn't even turned around before a massive glimmering form bounded from the darkness. I backed slowly away, blindly feeling along the wall and hoping I was closer to my door — or any door — than I thought.

But all I felt was solid stone.

Nyx slowly morphed from moonlight into a more solid being. She prowled closer, and I was sure she was going to make up for her disappointment earlier by devouring me on the spot.

Then the shadows behind her shifted and the darkness lifted, revealing a king who looked entirely unamused. Nyx whined before sitting back on her haunches, shuffling her giant paws in frustration.

Hadeon's starlit gaze roved slowly over my body, like he was cataloging every dip and curve and marking.

No, it was more than that.

There was a familiarity in the look, a sweeping assessment that was as territorial as it was primal, as though he was doing it more out of instinct than desire.

Or like he was searching me for weapons, which I realized a moment too late, just as the quill was plucked from my hand by a wisp of shadow. It sailed through the air and he examined it, raising an eyebrow. There was even more darkness in his expression than there had been earlier, something dangerous brimming beneath the surface.

I decided to tread more carefully than I had been.

"What did you expect?" I remarked quietly, not sure why I felt the urge to make excuses when he was keeping me prisoner.

"For you to display a modicum of common sense and refrain from traipsing half-dressed around a palace where people want to kill you, armed with a quill when your enemies have isos, but then, Phaedra lacked basic self-preservation skills as well." His voice grew colder with each word, the last few falling like icicles, shattering in the space between us.

For all that he said I was Phaedra, this wasn't the first time I noticed that he spoke of us like we were two different people whom he loathed equally.

"I guess it's not in my nature to stay put like a good little girl until you see fit to let me out of my cage," I seethed.

Hadeon offered a wicked grin in return, one that didn't reach his hard, icy gaze.

"I suppose *stay* is too difficult a command for you to master. Perhaps we'll try *beg* first and go from there."

Indignation flared to life in my chest, my hands clenching into fists as I glared at him.

"The day I beg for anything from you will be the day I

die." I hoped I wasn't bluffing. I had endured plenty of pain before, but I had never been outright tortured.

"Historically speaking, you'd be wrong." The corner of Hadeon's lips tilted up in a vicious smirk, and another wave of fury crashed over me.

It was bad enough he had all the power, physically, but he also had all of the knowledge. He held literally all of the cards, while I had none.

Had he tortured Phaedra, then? Did she break under it? Or had it been something different, a favor she asked of him? Whatever led to their bargain, perhaps?

I told myself I didn't care when I was leaving anyway. None of this mattered if I could make it back home.

As though he saw the thoughts play across my face, the king tipped his head.

"What were you planning, then? Going to murder me in my sleep?" He glanced down the hallway, and I swallowed a curse.

Of course his rooms were right next to mine, the ones shrouded in shadows. That's why the hallway was unnaturally dark and why his damned three-headed dog was sleeping in them.

I was further from freedom than I ever imagined.

"If only," I muttered.

"So you were going to the portal, then," he guessed accurately, damn him.

I didn't respond, but my face must have given me away again.

"And what were you planning to do if you found it? You can't very well pass as human anymore."

I gritted my teeth. Truthfully, I had hoped I would turn back once I crossed the portal, so I thought on my feet. "I can wear a sweater, get some cosmetic surgery. Dye my hair. I'll figure something out."

"Very well. Come along, little Feralinia." He held out an arm.

There was that word again, but I wouldn't give him the satisfaction of asking what it meant. I took a step back.

"Don't you want to see your precious portal?"

I weighed my options, considering the likelihood that he would actually take me there and the reality that I couldn't escape even if he didn't. So I took a step closer.

Shadows wrapped around us both, a cool contrast to the way my skin was always too hot here. Especially now, when I was this close to him. Close enough that I could smell the scent of nighttime and the mountains that clung to his faintly glowing skin, the bergamot wafting from his shiny midnight locks.

I subtly inhaled through my mouth, trying to shield against the sensory memories I could never seem to escape here. Seconds passed, minutes, while I squeezed my eyes shut, blocking out the feel of his shadows against my skin.

Then it was over. His shadows fell from my skin as he stepped away from me. We now stood in a familiar field. The view of the mountains was identical to the first time I beheld them, the trees around us in the exact pattern I recalled.

And there, just where I remembered it, was the portal, the moongate, whatever it was. Only instead of a view of Fairy Bar shimmering within, the inside was empty, still air depicting nothing more than the icy mountain behind it. Dismay seized my lungs, and I crossed the distance, unconcerned with the freezing temperatures or the snow melting against my thin robe.

"Turn it back on," I said, my voice more panicked than I wanted it to be, already close to the begging I had just sworn never to do.

"As flattering as your estimation of my power is, the goddess herself cannot activate that portal outside of its time." Hadeon's indifference rang out behind me.

"And when is its time?" I pushed, spinning to face him. "Every week? Every month?"

He let out a low, mocking laugh, enough to set the hairs on my arms standing on end.

"A year?" I whispered.

Could I make it through an entire year this way?

His expression was unreadable, but his voice dipped lower as he answered.

"Closer to fifty."

The blood drained from my face. No. That wasn't possible. Even the fates that ruled my life, even the stupid goddess's stupid priestess, couldn't be that cruel.

"I'll be half dead by then," I whispered to myself, but that didn't stop him from responding.

"You won't be," Hadeon said flatly. "Elves live long lives. Everyone else you know, on the other hand..." He trailed off with a shrug, like it couldn't matter less to him that everyone I knew would be dead or close to it by the time I returned.

I shook my head, horror clawing its way up my chest. No. That... That wasn't fair. Wasn't possible. It was an effort not to imagine Isa in her seventies, wrinkled with age, an entire life lived while I, what, stayed like this?

"I have to get back."

"Get back to what?" he demanded. "All the friends and family waiting for you?"

I set my jaw, my pulse raging in my temples. "No, I'll just stay here in your castle and wear my *collar* rather than return to the life I built myself."

Something passed over his features. "The sad excuse of a life you built yourself is gone. The earth itself has forgotten you, as has everyone you've ever known."

That...

No.

Just no.

"My shop —"

"Anything you had is now owned by another, who believes it has been theirs all along."

"Isa —"

"Doesn't remember you."

"How can you possibly know that?" I murmured, hating how feeble my voice sounded.

"Because, Feralinia, this is how it has always been when a human crosses into Terrea. It's part of the isos."

He sounded so sure, and for a rare change, his tone was absent of any mockery. But that couldn't be true.

"You're lying," I hissed.

"Of us, I have never been the liar." It was the conviction with which he said those words that convinced me more than anything else.

I stepped back, looking up at the star-strewn sky, the endless sparkling abyss and the two moons that I would apparently spend the next half a century looking at. Defeat settled into my shoulders, into my bones.

"This is why you brought me here," I observed aloud. "Not out of mercy or even to placate me, but so you could ensure I didn't have a single shred of hope left to cling to." My tone was undiluted bitterness and disbelief.

He didn't bother to deny it. "The sooner you realize the human realm has moved on without you, the sooner you can do the same."

I let out a huff of air, and with it went the last of the fight I had in me. What was there left to fight for?

"Very well. Feel free to return me to my lavish cell." My voice was flat, completely devoid of life.

He paused, examining my features like this was some sort of trick on my part, like I was the one who had upended his entire life on a whim.

"This is what you wanted, right?" I threw my arms out and gestured vaguely to myself. "My obedience?"

Something that might have been remorse and might have been acrimony flashed through his eyes. "Don't kid yourself, Feralinia. If I had gotten what *I* wanted, you would never have come back at all."

He shadow-whisked me back without another word,

leaving me at my door before my feet were even firmly on the ground. I didn't argue before going into my room and shutting the door behind me.

There was no point when I was going to be stuck here, a ghost whether I was in his world or mine.

Chapter Eight

My dreams that night were fitful and disorienting. My mind was intent on reliving moments I would rather forget, along with ones from a life I shouldn't remember.

I was on a battlefield, staring down at the broken and twisted bodies of dead soldiers covered in black veins and green smoke.

Then Isa's arms were around my neck, hugging me after her *abuela* died. The copper taste of blood filled my mouth, trickling in from a split lip the day I arrived at Ivy's gym for self-defense training.

I woke up feeling even less rested, and even more unmoored.

When a maid came to help me dress in the morning, I sent her away. She didn't leave immediately, but pretending to call upon the powers I in no way had access to had her scurrying away in no time.

Small favors I could still lie, one tiny remnant of my old life here to help me through my new one.

Or maybe Phaedra had always been able to lie. That was certainly how the king told it. How the hell would I know what was hers and what was mine anymore? *If anything had ever really been mine...*

Celani came to fetch me for breakfast, but I stayed in my massive bed, pulling the plush navy comforter higher over my shoulders.

"You don't want to pretend you'll set me on fire?" she asked, quirking an eyebrow.

I was too tired to rise to her bait, so I just met her eyes evenly.

"Would it work?" I questioned.

"No." Her tone was matter-of-fact.

"There's your answer, then." I made no move to get up, and she tilted her head.

"If you would agree to train, you wouldn't have to pretend to know how to use your isos." She kept her face expressionless to drive the point home.

No, I'd just have to give the bastard king exactly what he wanted, give up whatever tiny piece of self I had left.

"Pass," I said without lifting my head from the pillow.

She eyed me, but short of throwing my nightgown-clad form over her shoulder and physically hauling me to breakfast, we both knew I wouldn't budge.

"All right," she said after a beat, turning to leave.

If I had been capable of surprise, I might have felt it when she didn't, in fact, choose to drag me to breakfast, but I was too numb to care.

She must have ordered food sent up, because shortly after she left, breakfast came via a different maid than before. I feigned sleep until she left the tray on the table.

I tried the same when the door snicked open a third time, with sadly less effective results.

"If you're going to keep pretending, do me the courtesy of putting some effort into it." Hadeon's deep voice slid over me like the curls of his shadows, power concealed in each syllable.

Something inside me thrummed in answer. My own power, rising to meet his? Whatever it was, I ignored it like I wished I could the oppressive presence of the king in my room — cell, whatever.

I narrowed my eyes at him. "You could do me the courtesy of dying in your sleep, but you haven't yet."

A muscle ticked in his jaw, and he studied me the way a panther studies a mouse, like he was trying to decide how much to play with his food before eating it. "I see you're back to your usual savagery today."

"Only toward you," I informed him.

"Your maid this morning would argue otherwise," he countered darkly.

That was more necessity than savagery, but I didn't care enough to debate that nuance with him.

"You can channel all that anger into your training," he informed me in a tone heavy with condescension. "At least then it will be useful."

My lips parted in disbelief. "*Useful*? You think I should be useful in the way that I grieve when I've just lost everything?"

He stepped closer to me, his shadows clouding around him like an ominous aura, a portent of his ire.

"You and your short, mortal life cannot possibly comprehend what it is to lose *everything*."

"But you can?" It was as much a question as a declaration because I saw the evidence churning in his eyes, though it was hard to imagine the untouchable king doing something as pedestrian as grieving. "And you, what, picked up with your life being *useful* the next day?"

The air between us was charged.

"I had a kingdom to lead and things to attend to, just as you have training to attend to now. I lacked the luxury of wallowing." He glanced over me. "I have known you to be many things, but *weak* was never one of them."

"No," I snapped sharply. "You have known *her*. You have never known *me* to be anything at all."

"Are you so ready to die for that distinction?" he growled.

As if he gave a single damn about my life outside of whatever the hell it was he needed from me.

"After you've given me so much to live for, you mean?" Each word fell like knives sinking into a target. "Isn't that what you wanted to show me last night?"

He stiffened, looking at me with something akin to a warning. Then he shook his head, letting out a slow, controlled breath while his shadows receded into him.

"If I had known you were going to lie down and die the moment someone gave you the truth, I wouldn't have bothered." He leaned toward me as he spoke, his tone low and deadly. "Whether you have the basic common sense to see the use for it or not, your training begins in the morning."

With a small twitch of his fingers, the collar around my neck tightened in warning as he added, "And if I am forced to drag you out of here, it will be far less pleasant."

THE MAIDS RETURNED after he left, bringing in black and navy gowns for my closet, along with more useless matching slippers, none of which I had any intention of wearing.

On some level, I wondered if Hadeon was right, if giving up like this was beneath me. Hadn't I always been a survivor, even when there didn't seem to be anything left to survive for?

This felt different. A strangeness and emptiness and loneliness that stemmed from deep within my soul. It was like a phantom limb, pain radiating from a part of me that didn't exist anymore.

I would have thought it was all in my head, that it was only my own grief ravaging my mind, if it weren't for the dreams. Memories. Whatever they were.

That night, they came for me again.

First, I heard the man's voice. It was less heated, but no less booming. A gentler, feminine voice accompanied it, murmuring things that were just out of earshot or singing a song I couldn't quite place. The backdrop of it all was laughter, free and unfettered. The memories were vague, but they were encased by a warm, golden glow that I instinctively knew meant family.

Then came the darker dreams. Visions of a blood-strewn battlefield. Charred limbs. A voice begging me to stop. Those were crimson-tinged.

After that came a feeling of desperation. Of longing, underpinned with a deep purple hue.

"Then we have a bargain." Over and over again I heard that phrase, sealing my fate while dark amusement glittered in Hadeon's fathomless eyes.

Shadows crept in to obscure the dream, heated moments interspersed with war, and shadow creatures, and terror, and a crushing certainty that everyone I loved was going to die just before it all went black.

Then it started from the beginning. Once again, the visions took the same path, like Phaedra was trying to tell me something. Or maybe she was mourning, the same as I was, her mind retracing the set of decisions and circumstances and mistakes that led to her eventual downfall.

I didn't know what time it was when I finally tired of dipping in and out of the dream reality. Back home, it would have been deep into the night or late morning, but I had learned here that a sea of stars meant nothing. There were only a few hours of sunlight in the middle of the day to break up the endless darkness.

I shuffled over to my balcony, throwing open the glass doors to let in the cool air. It washed over my skin, instilling in me a small bit of the peace my restless slumber stole from me every night I could remember.

In the distance, framed perfectly by my doorway, was a constellation of seven stars that shone bigger and brighter than the rest, giving off a golden glow. I stared at it, transfixed until a sharp knock that was becoming irritatingly familiar sounded at the door.

Celani had arrived to escort me to her precious king.

Chapter Nine

ABSOLUTELY THE HELL NOT.

I nearly dropped the steaming mug of coffee Celani had brought as a peace offering as I stared up at the massive creatures in front of me.

I hadn't imagined them that first night. There really were giant flying celestial cats here.

Swallowing down the lump in my throat, I stared wide-eyed at a row of black and blue tigers and jaguars, waiting for one of them to open their mouths and devour me whole.

Three of the jaguars shifted, shaking out their long black wings as an elf stepped forward to light the small lantern around its neck. A feather flew toward me, glistening under the moonlight like black silk with silver threads.

Like their riders, the creatures had distinctive silver and blue glowing runes that wound through their fur, each one different and even more remarkable than the last.

Still, while my fingers might have itched to draw them, my feet itched to run away. I could admire something like this from afar. Or, like...in a zoo, but absolutely not up close like this.

They braced themselves, all three staring at the same empty spot next to the stables. Half a heartbeat later, Nyx bounded from those shadows, launching toward them playfully.

Large, pointed teeth and claws glimmered like well-sharpened blades while the beasts tumbled around the field, like giant puppies — which I suppose one of them kind of was. Their growls sent a shiver racing up my spine.

I took one step back before shadows slid around my waist, holding me in place.

"Feralinia," Hadeon's voice was a low warning rumble, and I glared at him.

"I thought the point of training me was to keep me alive," I hissed over my mug. "Putting me on one of those...things—"

"Baztets," Celani offered from my right, her tone carefully neutral.

"Baztets," I continued, "will completely defeat the purpose."

Hadeon sighed, arching a dark eyebrow as he stared down at me like I was a petulant child.

"Don't be so dramatic. Besides, it's the only way to get to the training grounds from here."

"Can't you just..." I gestured to the shadows that seemed to follow him everywhere. "Shadow us there?"

"That would take more trips than I am willing to make," Hadeon answered flatly. "From what I understand, it's much like riding a horse in your world."

I took a sip of my coffee, savoring the bitter taste on my tongue.

"Welp." I shrugged a shoulder, the movement tugging at the golden chains on my black gown. "I have no experience there either, so that's not really going to help us."

"She can always ride on my baztet." Kallius's voice was full of mischief and promise as he and his flying tiger landed behind us.

He winked at me, and Hadeon's shadows tightened possessively around my waist.

"That won't be necessary," the king practically growled before gesturing toward his general.

Celani did an admirable job of keeping her features completely impassive, putting two fingers to her lips to let out a piercing whistle. The creatures stilled, then stalked toward us.

Hadeon climbed onto the largest cat, a panther with several hoops in her ears that matched the pale-blue markings on her skin. Without warning, he used his shadows to lift me off the ground. I dropped my coffee mug while I soared through the air, gently landing right in front of him in the leather saddle.

The black panels of my dress separated to expose my thighs, the golden tattoos there contrasting brightly against Hadeon's dark trousers.

I quickly pulled the loose fabric of my cloak around my body, covering my lap before I could give everyone around us a free show.

I could have sworn I heard the distant sound of Kallius chuckling, but I could hardly focus on anything else as Hadeon wrapped a makeshift seat belt over my hips, securing me between his legs.

Every coherent thought left my mind in a whoosh.

The heady scent of bergamot and fresh snow and citrus filled my senses. He was warm, far warmer than his shadow touch usually let on. Heat emanated from his lap and the hard planes of his stomach and the muscled arms that wrapped around me to grip the reins.

"Hold on tight, Feralinia," he whispered just before spurring the baztet with his heels.

There wasn't time to respond, not that I was sure what I would say anyway, before the cat took off in a gallop. Its wings flapped soundlessly as it caught the wind and took us up in the air.

I tried not to think about how high up we were, or how fast we were flying, or the sharp edges of the mountains that waited for us below.

And I especially tried not to think about the strong thighs around my hips, and the corded muscles that were visible in Hadeon's forearms — or how easily I could picture them wrapped around me in the bathtub.

Surely it was all in my head.

Probably.

For all Hadeon's baiting about the severity of my training, so far, it was more an exercise in boredom than anything.

As soon as we landed, he removed my collar, announcing he was close enough to control my isos if things got out of control. Though he claimed I should have been able to access a fraction of it with the collar on.

But the joke was on him when I couldn't touch it in either scenario.

He covered us in shadow, blocking us from the rest of the world as he instructed me on meditation with an increasingly impatient tone.

I mostly ignored him while I let my mind wander.

"If you can't connect to your isos, you can't hope to master it at will," he said for at least the tenth time.

I didn't hope to master it at all, so that was not a concern for me. What good was having magic or isos when Hadeon controlled every damned thing I did anyway? It would just be another tool in his arsenal, not mine.

Hadeon's eyes narrowed on my expression like he could feel the mutiny in it, and I shrugged.

"Guess the isos doesn't want to be manhandled like a waitress at a titty bar."

Kallius snorted from somewhere behind me, but Hadeon's lips parted in what might have been horror.

"Is that something you have experience with?" he asked.

I looked down at my medium-sized chest. My breasts were perky enough, but not exactly show-worthy. Instead of denying it, I shrugged again.

"I've always done what I had to do. It's a quality you respect, right?" I harkened back to his asshattery from the day before.

The king's shadows crept farther out around him. He opened his mouth, no doubt to say something offensive, when Celani cut in.

"I brought lunch, if his majesty would like a break." There was something just slightly sarcastic in the way she addressed him, like the formality was an inside joke.

He shot her a sideways glance but nodded, letting his shadows breathe enough to lead us to a small makeshift table near the cliffside. Several logs were cut into small benches, and another was sliced in half to act as a table in the center.

She and Kallius set out a picnic of sorts, and I went to help. My time with my parents may have been briefer than it should have been, but ten years was plenty of time to learn better than to stand around while someone else worked.

Even the lofty Hadeon set out plates with his shadows. It was an oddly domestic sight, one that tugged at a long-forgotten part of my consciousness. I supposed if Phaedra had been prisoner in the Moon Court for some time, it was something she would have witnessed before.

The constant vague déjà vu was a feeling I grew more tired of by the minute.

"How long was she a prisoner here before?" I asked no one in particular.

It seemed like a relatively innocuous question, but by the odd three-way glance they exchanged, I gathered it wasn't one they wanted to answer.

"She was here for close to two years," Hadeon finally answered in a tone that invited no further discourse.

I pushed anyway.

"And then she left from here to die?" Had the priestess broken her collar? Could she do the same for me?

"No." Hadeon's voice was flat. "She left from the Never Court to die."

All at once, he lifted his shadows from where they surrounded us, and I let out a gasp. There in the distance was a kingdom on fire. At least, that was what it looked like. Endless mountains and valleys of blazing golds and furious reds.

I looked down at my skin, then back at the golden kingdom. "My court?" I whispered.

"The Court of Fire and Sun is where you were born," he confirmed.

I ignored his territorial distinction, still examining the gleaming mountains. The kingdom was gorgeous, but I didn't feel the pull to it that I had expected.

Still, I had to wonder if Phaedra's family was there. Were her parents alive? On the throne? Did they miss her? Did they think their daughter would come back to them still?

If so, they would grieve all over again when they realized it was only me.

I felt rather than saw Hadeon's stare on me, almost like he was waiting for me to ask the questions. I wouldn't, though. Not only had his answers so far proven unsatisfactory, but in the end, it hardly mattered.

They weren't my family. My family was dead.

Forcibly averting my gaze, I looked to the west next, where rocky mountains peeked out from under misty clouds with a faint greenish hue. The ground, however, was completely obscured, a void of nothingness that sent shivers racing down my spine.

I was used to the dark. Hell, in the many nights I had to spend sleeping on benches or under overpasses, I craved the cover of nighttime, where I was less likely to be spotted as something potentially vulnerable. Less likely to be noticed at all.

But the darkness from this place was different, more than the absence of light, it was a thick, poisonous miasma on the land. There was a wrongness to it.

"That's the Never Court." Celani's voice was almost...haunted.

Hadeon nodded, and Kallius chimed in.

"It used to be called the Court of Mist and Memory. Before..." Kallius trailed off, something in his tone telling me he was unwilling to go back down that road.

There was something...sad, about knowing it was the last place Phaedra had been before she walked to her death. I looked away, already tired of the way each new facet of Phaedra's life that I uncovered seemed to be worse than the last.

Hadeon put his shadow shield back in place, and we returned to meditating. Or rather, we returned to Hadeon trying to get me to meditate while my thoughts drifted between the three kingdoms.

My home, my prison, and my demise.

Chapter Ten

ANOTHER COUPLE OF DAYS PASSED, WHEREIN IT became glaringly apparent to everyone that I had no natural aptitude for meditation or isos, nor any real desire.

Nevertheless, I woke early and dressed like the obedient little captive that I was, if only because I had no other choice. This morning, though, it wasn't Celani's knock at the door that told me it was time to leave. Instead, Hadeon came barging in.

Well, he glided in through his shadows, but the effect was the same.

"No, please, don't knock," I said acerbically.

His lips tightened in an imperious look, his usual disdain for me seeping from the expression. "On my own door in my own palace to see my own pet? I won't."

I gritted my teeth. "I'd remind you that I might have been changing, but I suspect you've been watching me like a creeper."

His lip curled in disgust that was only moderately offensive. "If I want to watch someone undress, I can assure you I have no need to do it in secret from my shadows *like a creeper.*" The last word came out awkwardly.

I might have fought the urge to laugh except for the unwelcome image of Hadeon summoning me and ordering me to undress. Or the image of him summoning someone else with that order, which made fury rise inexplicably in my chest.

Because I was indignant on the hypothetical elf's behalf, obviously.

Dark amusement glittered in his eyes as he examined my reaction, the color that was no doubt creeping into my cheeks.

"Would you like that, Feralinia?" he mocked.

"For you to order your court to undress?" I said with all the flippancy I didn't feel. "I won't pretend it wouldn't be amusing, but I imagine it would get drafty for them."

I strode toward the door like I was the one in charge of this interaction, forcing him to trail behind me. It was surprising that he let me take the lead until I rounded the corner, when he called after me.

"Not that way."

Ah. So he had only delighted in the opportunity to make me look foolish, as usual. I spun around to see him looking just satisfied enough to confirm my thoughts.

"We aren't going to train?" I asked.

"Not yet. You don't appear to be properly motivated."

I gave him a mock pout, gesturing to my collar. "Whereas a long life as your pet would be enough to motivate anyone else?"

As I said it, I wondered if it was true. If Hadeon was king and had absolute power here, *would* people line up to belong to him?

He gave me an arrogant smirk that confirmed my suspicion, and I scowled, following him down an unfamiliar winding hallway. As huge as the palace appeared from the outside, it seemed even more so from within.

Having spent most of my life in tiny suburban houses or trailers before my even smaller apartment in the city, a palace was the kind of luxury that was still hard to wrap my head around. There were wings and endless corridors connecting rooms whose purpose I couldn't begin to guess at.

He led me through a set of double doors into what appeared to be a study. Bookshelves rose to the high ceiling, punctuated by gold and bronze astrolabes and telescopes. The domed ceiling was almost entirely open, and the wan sunlight filtered through to cast the room in long, lazy shadows.

"Why are we here?" I asked.

"Because there is an abundance of natural shadows here," he said, like it explained anything at all.

He waved his hand, and the shadows merged together to form a flat circle in the center of the room. It was thin, stretching up in front of our faces instead of out over the rug, just like...

"Is that a portal?" I asked. Hope surged in me, only to be dashed by him shaking his head.

"No. I suppose you could think of it as a window, though no living matter can pass through."

My forehead creased. "Then what is it for?"

"For viewing," he said shortly. For once, it didn't seem to be irritation clipping his words as much as...concentration? He stared into the darkness like he could see something I couldn't.

Then the shadows dissipated, and in their place was a picture.

An intricate chandelier made of vines and flowers hung over a large bed.

I gasped. A familiar form slept in the center of the plush mattress, peaceful and unaware.

Ivy.

"Is this really her?" I asked, just as she shifted to turn onto her other side, showing her face and her very pointed ears.

He nodded once. She really was fae, then.

I held out a hand toward her. "Can she hear me?"

"No." Threads of shadows crept into the edges until they obscured the picture entirely.

Then the portal, window, whatever it had been, was gone, leaving us alone in the room.

"Does she remember me?" I asked, hardly daring to hope.

"Yes. She has asked about you already," Hadeon said. "Someone from Talamh reached out about you. Apparently, she is as unyielding and insistent as you are."

Relief trickled through me. Someone remembered me. Someone in this world knew me as more than some lost princess. Isa, my clients, my single employee, even Stan, the trainer at the gym...they had all forgotten me.

But I still had Ivy in some small, abstract way.

I raised my eyebrows, wondering how he knew that for sure.

"Did you see her that way before?" I gestured to where the shadows had been.

"No, that's a difficult way to find someone, but I had already contacted their High Council about allowing her to communicate."

Allowing.

So was she as much a prisoner as I was? She looked well cared for, at least. Was that all we could hope for in this world? To be ripped out of our lives so that we could be pampered pets?

"Do you know why she was taken?" I asked. Was she also the unwilling captive of a bastard king?

"I don't. Abba — the priestess — only told me where to find you." He was being oddly forthcoming, no doubt with some sort of end in mind.

"The one who told Phaedra to sacrifice herself?" I clarified, seizing the rare opportunity to get answers from him.

He nodded, and I studied his features, trying to put together another piece of this that didn't make sense.

"If it's difficult to find someone that way, why did you bother to show me?"

He pinned me with his starlit gaze, the same contradictory combination of hot and cold as a burning star in the endlessly icy galaxy.

"As I said, you are unmotivated. There is a threat coming, one that your isos could help combat."

"From where?" I asked. I suspected I knew the answer.

His confirmation felt like the drop of a guillotine, striking a chord of fear from deep within when he said gravely, "The Never Court."

The place Phaedra had been before she died. Did everything come back to that?

"What does that have to do with Ivy?" I asked. "Or is that just the carrot and this is the stick?"

He blinked, and I surmised that wasn't a saying here, but he breezed past without addressing it.

"They won't stop here. The blight there is spreading. The wraiths will eventually consume the rest of Aelvaria, then they will go wherever else they can find isos to feed off of. Which includes Talamh, the fae lands where your friend is."

Another manipulation on his part, one I hated to admit was working.

"How do I know you aren't lying?" I demanded.

I expected another line about how Phaedra or I was a giant liar and a generally terrible person, but instead he only shrugged a single muscular shoulder.

"You don't. But is that a chance you're willing to take with the life of your only remaining friend?"

Once again, he had neatly boxed me into a corner. Helplessness and wrath warred in my gut. I had spent years working to be my own person and have my own life, to never again be dependent on someone or at their mercy, and he had stripped all of that from me, my pride and my agency, for what? Just because he could? To rope me into his war?

"No wonder she hated you." I hurled the words at him.

His eyes narrowed. "I assure you, the feeling was mutual."

He straightened to his full, impressive height, all business once more. "Will you let the fae girl suffer for your animosity, then?"

He asked the question like he already knew the answer. Worse yet was that he was right.

"No," I muttered. "I'll train to fight in your war. But first, I need something in return. I want my weapons back. And my purse."

Hadeon's lips twitched slightly, but he nodded. For a brief moment, I thought about asking for my freedom, but something in my gut told me that wasn't on the table.

Besides, I didn't have the slightest idea what I would do with it at this point, here in this realm where I had no friends or allies or understanding of how anything worked.

"Who knows, maybe we'll both get lucky and the Never Court will claim my life again," I added a moment later.

For all that I claimed to have no concern whether I lived or died, icicles still scraped along my spine when I realized that was a very real possibility. He went deadly still, his face like a thundercloud.

"Don't worry, Feralinia. I have no intention of letting you go that easily."

That answered my question about how optional my freedom was.

My lips parted, but no sound came out as he shadow-whisked me back to my rooms, leaving before I could decide whether his words were even more terrifying than whatever awaited me in the Never Court.

I DIDN'T DWELL on Hadeon's strange reassurance-threat for long once I saw what was waiting for me on my bed: the small leather purse I had worn to the casino, the one they had taken from me when they searched me for weapons.

It was an unexpected piece of home, one that brought tears stabbing at the backs of my eyes. Isa had bought me the trendy black leather purse for our trip, mostly to keep me from hauling my giant bag around the casino.

I picked it up cautiously, like it might disappear if I moved too fast. Slowly, I moved the clasp, scanning the few precious contents of the bag. A single tube of lip balm that was, thankfully, full. My lips hurt just looking at it, like its nearness reminded them of how dry they had been in its absence.

I pulled it out, squeezing it past my phone and my earbuds, and dislodging something crinkly in the process. It was the ticket. The gold foil piece of paper that ruined my entire life.

I would have gladly set it on fire, except for the memory that sprang to mind of Isa waving it in my face, jumping up and down with excitement while she insisted on our girls weekend.

My mind was moving faster than it had in days, waking the monstrous grief that seemed to live permanently inside me. Restless energy coursed under my skin, clawing to get out. It was too quiet in here, the still night sky and the steady flow of my waterfall bath too peaceful for the emotions rising up inside me.

I wanted to shove it back down again, but I was afraid to go back to the numb, uncaring way I had felt earlier. So I pulled my phone out of my purse, along with my earbuds.

I pressed the power button, and the phone took several long seconds to come to life. There was still no signal, but the battery was at seventy-five percent and my portable charger was still in the bottom of my bag.

Part of me wanted to squirrel it away, but it would only drain over time anyway, and I needed it now.

Once it was unlocked, and my earbuds were in, I hit play. It picked up in the middle of the last song I had listened to. The one Isa and I kept on repeat while we did our makeup for that damned bar.

I started it over, pushing down the pang in my gut as I flipped through my last few text messages, smiling as I read the words "farty bar" in my thread with Ivy.

Then I opened up my photos, scanning through several pictures of finished tattoos, my favorite pieces. There was one or two of me and the girls, but mostly, it was work.

A lump rose in my throat. Why didn't I take more pictures? Why wasn't I more present in my life before it was torn away? It had always felt like I was living someone else's life, in a way, which was ironic now that it was true.

Shaking my head and squeezing my eyes shut, I focused on Bryce Savage's gravelly voice. The bass from "Easy to Love" slowed my racing pulse and steadied my panicked breaths.

It was helping, but it wasn't enough.

I crossed the distance to the small writing desk where I'd first found the quill. There was another one in the drawer, along with a small black ink pot.

Surely, it couldn't be any harder to use than a tattoo machine.

I brought the stuff out to the balcony, setting up at the small table overlooking the snow-capped mountains and the star-studded sky.

It took me a few drops and spills to get the hang of it, but soon I was lost to the steady, mostly familiar motion of my hand across the page. I sketched furiously as memories ran through my mind.

Isa cleaning the shop with me before opening day, a bottle of champagne on the counter. The gym where I learned to defend myself with Ivy at my side. My first paying customer, gushing over the brilliant hues of the ink I had learned to mix myself.

My parents.

All of it was gone.

Of course, *her* memories encroached, too — the ones I had from the dreams — but I pushed them away. This wasn't her time. Everything here was hers, and I deserved to mourn my own family.

My own life.

With each measured stroke, I captured Ivy's furrowed brow and the tilt of her eyes, Isa's full lips pulled back into a wide smile, and the single potted plant in my apartment window. The gentle lines of my mother's hands and my father's proud eyes, things that were memorialized in all the pictures I would never see again.

I didn't want to forget them, the way everyone on earth had apparently forgotten me.

The small pot of ink was nearly gone now. My hands were on fire, but I didn't stop, trying to give the people and things I loved a small piece of space in this strange land where I would spend the rest of my life, or at least the next fifty years.

Some, I drew as I remembered them, and some were in the same geometric style I favored for my own tattoos. Only when my ink pot ran dry and my fingers were shaking, my mind just a fraction quieter than it had been, did I stop.

When I finally took a step back to stare at my work, my breath caught in my throat. I looked up into the night sky, seeing the seven golden stars shining brightly over the length of the mountain range.

Then I looked back at my drawings, pages upon pages of images so similar to the ones in my shop, the ones on my body, the ones I dreamt up every night when I closed my eyes. A single pattern I never would have seen, one I built my entire brand as an artist around.

Lifting my hand, I traced a line on my collarbone over the branch I had painstakingly inked into my skin — the first tattoo I ever gave myself.

It was backward, but it had the same framework as the constellation, its leaves reaching out from the knotted bark right where the three largest stars would be.

A reflection of the same constellation that was framed

perfectly by the balcony of the room where Phaedra was kept prisoner.

I shook my head in disbelief, frustrated that even my art didn't feel like mine anymore, and in sorrow for a girl who felt so far removed from me most of the time.

What had this place done to her, to haunt her soul so thoroughly that now it was haunting mine?

Even in death, she had never really been free of this place.

Maybe I never would be, either.

Chapter Eleven

THE FOLLOWING MORNING, CELANI SHOWED UP TO escort me to training again, and I followed her to the stables. Usually, I hurried to climb onto Hadeon's baztet before his shadows hoisted me unceremoniously into the seat.

Today, I stood waiting until he showed up, curious to see if he would uphold his end of our bargain.

He raised an eyebrow when he took in my expectant stance.

"Doubting me so soon, Feralinia?"

"Always," I replied simply.

He may have had some basic vested interest in keeping me alive, but I wasn't stupid enough to trust him over it.

Instead of looking offended, he only sighed and reached into his cloak. He withdrew a pair of daggers, holding them out to me, hilt first.

I studied them in confusion, and a small amount of awe I tried very hard not to display. They were exquisite, all sleek, deadly arcs and intricate engravings in fluid patterns reminiscent of Hadeon's crown.

The blades were made of the same silver-blue metal, and they held a faint glow under the starlight. But the hilts were what caught my attention most. They were gleaming black metal with an onyx jewel in the bottom.

They looked more like jewelry than something I would use for self-defense.

"These aren't my weapons."

He blinked. "Obviously. Your crude human daggers hardly scratched the skin of a lesser elf. I could have them brought for you instead, but I was under the impression you wanted a way to actually defend yourself."

Already, my mind rebelled at having those daggers instead of the ones he presented me with. My hand stretched out toward the deftly wrought metal, even as suspicion niggled at my brain over what his motives might be.

He wanted me alive, but wasn't he at all concerned that if he gave me a weapon to use against a non-lesser elf, I would turn it on him? Or did something in my collar prevent that?

"Brave of you not to worry I'll use them on you," I remarked, eyes narrowed as I closed my hands around the hilts. They fit perfectly in my grasp, like they were made for me.

The corner of his lips tilted up in the most arrogant smirk I had ever seen as he took a few steps backwards. "By all means."

Condescending bastard. In a movement fueled by irritation, I flipped the daggers one by one and hurled them through the air at him. His shadows reacted even before his expression did. Tendrils of darkness closed around the blades, snatching them right out of the air.

Kallius and Celani both watched casually, clearly not worried about any threat to their king. Hadeon actually let out a chuckle, the sound rumbling through me.

"I'd hate to see what you would do if we weren't allies," he commented, handing them back over to me.

"The fact that you used my only friend to manipulate me into training after you kidnapped and collared me does not make us allies," I growled.

I could appreciate that he kept his word about the weapons, but that didn't change anything else between us. Not when I hadn't been given a say in anything since that night in Vegas.

Hadeon looked bored rather than properly chastised.

"You'll find your limited view of the world serves you badly when you're surrounded by those who would just as soon see you dead." Reaching back into his cloak, this time he pulled out a set of bracers that were clearly made to match the daggers.

The way he said it wasn't hypothetical, but like he was speaking from experience. His, or someone else's...

"Was that what Phaedra became, then?" I asked, eyeing him warily as he gestured for me to hold out my arm. "Your ally?"

"No," he said shortly, his features darkening. "Phaedra only ever did things her own way, to serve her own ends."

It didn't sound like a compliment, but I detected a small level of respect in the way it was delivered, buried deep beneath the resentment. Whatever part of me had learned to read him could sense that his patience was coming to an end, so I held out my arm.

He fastened one around my forearm, then motioned for me to switch. The black metal was smooth against my skin, comfortable despite their size, and I wondered if they were designed with some sort of isos to make them that way.

Once they were in place, he showed me how to sheathe the small daggers into them. They fit seamlessly into the bracers, almost impossible to see once they were in place.

All the while, he avoided direct contact with my skin like it was poison to him. Maybe it was. Maybe that was something I could consider in my arsenal.

"So you can always access them," he said, taking a step away.

I bit my tongue before I could thank him. He didn't deserve gratitude for choosing when to cage me and when to arm me, when to bestow beautiful things upon me and when to order me around.

But I couldn't deny feeling better, and maybe just a touch more like myself.

HADEON MAY HAVE THOUGHT that motivating me to train would be beneficial, but so far, it was making no discernible difference in my ability to wield my isos.

Kallius called a gust of wind like it was as easy as breathing, as he had demonstrated every day.

Celani explained each thing her brother was doing, her tone far more patient than I felt when she spoke.

"The isos is there. We saw it that first day. You just need to dig until you find it."

"Sure. I'll just dig way deep down to the bottom of my — I mean Phaedra's soul," I muttered.

It wasn't the first time she had told me to try that. Hadeon had also helpfully locked me in a cocoon of darkness to incentivize me to break free. I hadn't, but I did stab it with one of my shiny new daggers. He claimed it didn't hurt, but the ill-tempered look on his face suggested otherwise.

"It shouldn't be this hard," Kallius mused.

I blinked several times while I tried to figure out if the usually congenial elf was insulting me.

"He means literally," Celani explained. "Kal was in charge of training the little ones before he made captain. It's not that you're inept. If anything, the problem should be that you have too much isos, not too little. It should be hard for you to control, not impossible to reach."

Hadeon took over. "She's blocking it somehow."

I might have argued, but for once, his tone lacked accusation.

They spoke about it like accessing isos was as easy as breathing, but I couldn't touch mine. There wasn't a single hint of the fire that had consumed me that first day.

Did that mean I wouldn't be able to? Was I not meant to have Phaedra's isos?

Since we were clearly not going to continue training, Kallius motioned for us to join him at the picnic area while he set out platters of meats, cheeses, fruits and bread.

It wasn't until we had laden our plates with food that I asked the question I'd been stewing on for a while.

"Does everyone in Aelvaria train to be soldiers or only the nobility?"

Celani shook her head. She finished chewing her bite of the sweet white melon before responding. "We don't have nobility or rankings outside of the military. We work based on merit."

I tilted my head, trying to understand. They were Hadeon's cousins. But contrary to what Merikh had insinuated that first night, they earned their places here.

"And that is why my little sister outranks me," Kallius said with a sigh as he slathered some of the soft cheese over a slice of bread. "Because her isos kicks my isos's ass."

"Regularly," she added with a grin.

"You're younger than he is?" I couldn't help the surprise that leaked into my tone, or my growing curiosity about what Celani's isos could do.

I had observed the general lack of sexism in the Moon Court, what with the soldiers being so evenly split, but I had just assumed the rank came from order of birth.

"Yes," Celani answered. "Kallius only acts like he's a teenager. He's a solid century old."

Kallius shrugged, loading his open sandwich with several slices of meat before topping it off with spicy peppers and a little bit of melon. He made sure everything was evenly distributed before taking a massive bite.

"Is that old for an elf?" I asked, taking in the muscled body that looked to be in its early twenties.

"If it is, then his majesty is ancient," Kallius responded with a laugh.

I very deliberately did not look at Hadeon's body, which I also knew to be...adequately formed. Fortunately, Celani brought it back around.

"No," she said. "We're not even really considered adults until forty."

I mulled that over for a moment, wondering if I would ever get used to the way no one here seemed to age.

"So your hierarchy is based entirely on power."

Hadeon studied me while I came to the obvious conclusion, and I ostensibly ignored him, something I was making an artform of.

If I could only manage it on the inside.

"And that includes the king?" I finished somewhat reluctantly.

Hadeon smirked arrogantly, his hands frozen in front of his lips, a piece of melon balanced between his fingers. "Indeed, it does."

Because of course he wasn't just the king, he was the strongest person in the entire damned kingdom. Which made me wonder where I — no, Phaedra would have ranked in all of that.

"Is it the same in Phaedra's court?" I asked.

Hadeon scoffed, finally eating his fruit. "No. The Sun

Court persists in the old ways of watered-down nobility and weaklings."

I narrowed my eyes at him, spotting at least one lie.

"Really?" I tilted my head in mock curiosity. "Is that why you need me to access my isos so badly?"

Kallius let out a snort, and even Celani smirked.

Hadeon stayed silent, his midnight eyes locked on to mine in some sort of challenge I wasn't sure I was ready for.

"Yes," Celani answered when it was clear her king wouldn't. "The royal family in every court is Goddess-blessed, meaning they're not only the most powerful family in their respective kingdoms, but also given an extra gift from the realm, like the king's shadows."

My lips parted. I had guessed that my magic was unique, but that kind of power... Was it strong enough to combat Hadeon? Weapons were apparently useless against him, but would this be a way to finally break free of him one day?

The hope was dashed nearly as quickly as it came. If that were true, he would hardly be encouraging me to use it. In any event, it wouldn't matter if I couldn't access any of it.

"Well then," I said, setting my plate down before heading back to the field. "Let's get back to training."

Chapter Twelve

By the end of the week, I was more than a little motivated to set Hadeon on fire, but for all of his claims that I could be the match, I refused to burn.

The desire only amplified when he left me at the doors to my rooms, sore and tired, with the beginnings of a migraine, ordering me to be ready within the hour.

"For what?" I gritted out the question, massaging my temples.

Usually, I had dinner alone in my room, the only real reprieve I got in the day. It was the one part of my day that I actually looked forward to after hours of trying and failing to do magical meditation — food and solitude.

It didn't help that I was extra exhausted today. After a night of gray-hued dreams that chased me with promises of endless, piercing agony, I had woken up less rested than I would have liked.

Three cups of coffee were barely enough to get me functional enough to talk to anyone during training, and now he wanted to take my one moment to myself away.

"Once a week, we dine with the court," Hadeon offered by way of explanation, as if this were something I should already know.

I blinked several times, waiting for him to take it back.

"The royal we, you mean?" I asked, gesturing toward his entire person.

A muscle ticked in his jaw. "No. You will be joining me from here on out."

I thought about the group of elves that filled his throne room. The way they'd just watched as Nyx cornered me, some of them appearing almost sad when she didn't make me her meal.

A night with all of them and their very clear prejudice or bloodlust — depending on the elf — sounded like an actual nightmare.

I crossed my arms over my chest, noticing the way Hadeon tracked the movement.

"Joining you," I echoed his words. "Because torturing me during the day isn't enough to get you off anymore?"

He blinked once. "Because it is important for you to be seen."

An unreasonable wave of fury rose inside of me, and I wondered if it was my imagination that my tattoos glowed a little brighter in response.

"You honestly expect me to sit at your side like a dog on a leash for your entire court to gawk at?"

Dark shadows snaked toward me, and I swallowed the

lump in my throat. They wrapped around the collar, gently tugging me forward until I was mere inches from his chest.

He invaded my senses. I couldn't breathe in air that didn't belong to Hadeon, didn't smell or taste like him. So I swallowed, holding my breath as he spoke.

"I *expect*," he emphasized the word, his warm breath washing over my face, "for you to be ready within the hour, Feralinia."

His shadows loosened their hold, and he swept an assessing glance over my disheveled state.

"I also expect you to allow the maid to help you to dress since I have no hope that you're capable of going it alone, considering the state in which you arrived."

I glared at him for several long heartbeats, finally risking a breath. This wasn't the hill I wanted to die on. After the baztets, how bad could dinner really be?

"Shall I assume if I refuse, you'll threaten to drag me from my room again, kicking and screaming?"

A cruel smile twisted his full lips, and he tilted his head in a predatory motion. "You catch on quickly. Perhaps you can be trained after all."

"You're an ass," I said flatly.

My chest was tight, irritation and something else clawing its way through my veins. I stepped backward and pushed open my door, before slamming it shut behind me.

There was no satisfying thud, however, since his shadows slid into place to catch the door, just before his infuriating voice rang out once again.

"Oh, and Feralinia? I also expect you to show a modicum

of decorum this evening. If you insist on eating like a barbarian at my table, I will force you to finish your meal with Nyx on the floor."

Anger clouded my vision, and I spun around just in time to watch his shadows close the door with a gentle click. I could swear I felt his dark amusement as he disappeared down the hallway.

I SPENT what time I could in the bath, mostly using the steaming waterfall like a shower while I tried and failed to stop thinking about all of the responses I should have given Hadeon. All of the things I could say or do to be just as infuriating to him as he was to me.

Then I thought about actually being forced to eat on the floor with Nyx, and my plans dissolved like the steam from the water.

A maid was already waiting for me by the time I emerged, impatience carved into her aquiline features. It was the woman with the cropped purple hair again, and she eyed me warily as she held out my gown for the evening — like she was bracing herself for the fight that was sure to come.

Sighing, I stepped out of my towel, holding up my arms for her to dress me like Hadeon's doll.

A flicker of surprise lit her aqua eyes, but she quickly blinked it away, stepping closer with the yards of navy fabric.

It took her several long minutes to secure the delicate

golden chains around my arms and thighs, connecting each strip of the smooth satin.

The dresses here were always a blend of elegant and revealing, but this one took the cake. Tonight's gown was more befitting of a Greek goddess, rather than a human girl with an obsession with needles and ink.

The panels of the dress hugged my curves and dimples, revealing the crescent moon tattoo on my chest and the array of images on my arms and thighs.

The golden chains accented the glowing ink even more, as if this dress was designed specifically with me in mind.

It is important for you to be seen...

Hell, maybe it was. Maybe Hadeon had methodically planned out all of this, down to the way the gown revealed every tattoo.

I stood in front of the mirror for several long moments, blinking at my reflection while my maid gathered cosmetics on the small dresser. She stretched her hand out hesitantly, reaching toward me with the brushes like she was unsure whether I would try to bite her or not. Or, more likely, set her on fire.

A memory pulled at the corners of my mind — not mine, but Phaedra's.

A team of maids readying me for a night like this. Dancing in a ballroom under floating candles on a floor made of clouds. Dark eyes staring down into mine before I switched partners. I hated this man, the one with the pale silver gaze and the white hair.

His hands were rough, digging into my skin too eagerly.

Fire erupted from my fingers in a brief flash of light, and he relented, his scowl deepening. There was a purr of approval somewhere in the distance.

The night ended in a sea of black silk, gentle caresses, and delicious, heady desire.

I shook my head, forcing myself back to the present.

This was the first time Phaedra's memories had assaulted me during the day, and I wasn't sure what to make of it. Was she getting stronger?

This memory must have dragged me away from reality longer than I realized because the maid was already gone, having somehow dried my long hair and combed it into gentle, flowing waves. Strands of gold with small, gilded leaves sat atop my head to add to the Grecian look and keep my hair back from my face.

She had painted my eyes in a shimmering gold, enhanced my lashes with a dark, winged liner, and dusted my cheeks and lips in a burnt red color that matched the flames in my hair perfectly.

There was a pair of gilded slippers resting on the bed, along with a long, delicate chain and matching earrings.

After sliding into the shoes, I picked up the necklace, brushing a finger over the two crescent moons and the star-burst at the end of it. I slid it over my head, and it tried to pull me into yet another memory.

Shaking the vision away, I finished donning the jewelry and made my way to the door without a backwards glance.

Maybe it was the familiarity of this dress, this necklace, and the forced attendance of a court dinner that beckoned

Phaedra more than usual tonight. Maybe it would have been better to let her in, let her handle whatever politics I would be subject to this evening.

She had been a prisoner here, but she was also a princess. She undoubtedly had more experience with all of this than I did. It became a moot point, however, when I opened the door to find Hadeon waiting for me.

It seemed the brutal king had used every minute of his time perfecting his already ethereal features.

Gleaming silver armor adorned his shoulders, linked with a narrow leather strap across his clavicle that housed several daggers on his hip. His navy hair glinted like starlight underneath his thorny crown, cascading over his armor and dipping down to reach the broad muscles of his chest.

I swallowed, staring at the hard ridges of his abdomen and where they led down into his fitted trousers. His pectoral muscles twitched beneath writhing black shadows that stretched up to hide beneath the armor, growing darker and more corporal the higher they went.

I had the sudden desire to trace the shadow tattoos with my fingertips, to feel the way they moved and memorize their whorls and curves.

My line of work demanded I focus on the naked torsos and arms of both men and women. Nudity was nothing new to me.

So why the hell couldn't I stop looking now?

He stared down at me, something like amusement dancing in his eyes. I stiffened, schooling my expression into something more like disinterest instead of some thirsty teenager staring at a real-life Shadow Daddy.

"You know," I sighed, looking down at my gown and the ridiculous amount of skin that I was showing. "When I said I wanted you to order your court to attend to you naked, I was actually joking."

"This is the ceremonial garb of the Moon Court," Hadeon said drily, gesturing for me to step out into the hall. He used his shadows to close the door, and I watched mutely as the tattoos crept down his arms, extending from his fingertips.

A shiver danced down my spine as I wondered exactly what those fingertips and shadows were capable of.

Heat washed over me in a rush, and I had to force myself to turn away before Hadeon could read the thoughts that were undoubtedly playing across my face.

It was going to be a long-ass night.

Chapter Thirteen

DINNER WAS EVEN WORSE THAN I THOUGHT IT would be.

It was bad enough that the entire half-naked court was gawking at me. Some of them looked on in what could only be described as awe, even going so far as to whisper their thanks for the sacrifice I didn't remember making. But most of them were impossibly smug, visibly gratified to see a collar around the neck of their enemy's princess.

Then there were the lady elves.

If I got one more perfectly toned ass in my face while one of them found an excuse to squeeze between Hadeon and me, leaning into him and exposing their admittedly impressive assets, I might just figure out how to call on my isos after all.

Hell, maybe that was the real purpose behind this whole charade. Hadeon was hoping that if I got irritated enough, I would set someone on fire.

I told myself it was only irksome because of the constant

edging into my personal space, even though I knew my reaction outpaced that minor inconvenience by a long haul. But the other possibility... That made even less sense under the circumstances.

Even if something deep inside was screaming that the king did not belong to them, my annoyance was ridiculous, because he didn't belong to me either.

I didn't even want him to.

I took a long sip from my glass, hoping the dry blue wine that tasted like some sort of magical wintry sangria would help calm my irritation. Of course, the glass was empty right in time for another busty, perfectly toned elf to make her way between us.

"Your majesty, there were more reports of wraiths along the border," Leda, the soldier from the first night, crooned as she thrust out a bare hip perilously close to my face.

I gestured to one of the servants, motioning to my glass, and they skittered to the kitchens, hopefully to grab more.

While I waited, I shoveled in a bite of roasted meat that reminded me of my favorite carnitas tacos. Another forkful let me soak in the savory and sweet blend of the pork — delicately, this time, lest I wind up eating on the floor on top of everything else. Though, perhaps that would be preferable.

Nyx, at least, seemed to be enjoying herself. She was happily chewing on a bone I was mostly certain came from an animal and not an elf, though she did keep shooting disdainful glances at the scantily clad parade in front of Hadeon.

It felt like solidarity, and suddenly I wished I could feed one of them to her.

"Thank you for reporting, Lieutenant," Hadeon told Leda with a terse nod, only glancing in her direction long enough to dismiss her.

Her shoulders slumped incrementally, and Celani snorted what might have been a laugh.

"Is there always so much entertainment?" I asked under my breath.

She leaned over to respond, hiding her grin behind her wine glass, but Hadeon cut in.

"Are you entertained, Feralinia? And here I thought I heard a distinct note of...displeasure."

His shadows stretched toward me before he reined them back in, and I glared at him.

"Well, your company would have that effect on anyone," I said reasonably, still too quiet for the rest of the table to hear.

He made a noncommittal noise in the back of his throat. "I think Lieutenant Leda would disagree."

My fork stabbed into my plate with an audible clink, and Hadeon chuckled.

Fortunately or unfortunately, the elf from my memory chose this exact moment to interrupt. He was just as eerie as he had been then, his pale eyes giving him a decidedly undead feel.

"I'm sure Princess Phaedra was saddened to hear about the loss of her citizens today," he said with a smug glance at my general chest region.

I sat up straighter in my chair. I had no real connection to Phaedra's home, but the fact that he wanted to bait me with anyone's death was reason enough to hate him.

At his side, Captain Xanth smothered a smirk — barely — and I added him to my list of douchebags.

A list that, honestly, included nearly everyone in this room by now. I would take the carnivorous three-headed dog over most of these soldiers.

"It's Ember, actually, and I'm afraid I haven't yet heard the news." My tone was all false congeniality.

Fortunately, the servant returned at that exact moment, refilling my glass with a fresh bottle of blue wine, before adding to Celani's and Xanth's glasses as well.

I picked up my drink, taking a small sip while I waited for the creepy elf to respond.

"We hardly need to discuss that here," Kallius cut in quickly, sympathy apparent.

I appreciated the sentiment, but I had no desire to look weak in front of anyone here.

"No, please, Colonel Aereon." I pulled his name from the memory Phaedra had thrown at me earlier, taking a chance that his rank hadn't changed. "I'm sure we'd all like to hear the riveting tale of how my people lost their lives today. Tell me, did they take your soldiers with them?"

Hadeon shot me a sideways glance that I ignored, focusing instead on the Colonel's reddening cheeks.

"Your time with the humans has made you even more... interesting," he sneered.

A bitter laugh escaped me. "Here I thought you found me plenty interesting before."

Shadows crept toward me, possessively wrapping around the base of my chair just before scooting me to the left until I was right next to Hadeon. I sighed, taking another sip from my glass.

"I'm quite certain the princess isn't interested in the brawls at the border today," Captain Xanth cut in smoothly, for all the world as though he hadn't been the one suppressing a smirk just a moment ago.

But now he was looking at his king, appearing properly chastised.

"Oh, I'm quite certain I am interested," I argued flatly.

"Yes, do give your report, Colonel." Hadeon's voice was ice.

Whatever amusement he felt when he was taunting me about Leda had disappeared. Now, he wasn't so much as glancing in my direction. Even his shadows were coiled close, tense and irritable as the rest of him.

Was he upset with the colonel for baiting me? Or me for responding?

Was I supposed to play the part of docile prisoner?

Nyx growled softly, and the blood drained from Aereon's face. He cleared his throat, looking at Hadeon when he spoke.

"There was only a border brawl, your majesty, as the captain mentioned. Three soldiers from the Sun Court stumbled across the river, but we...dispatched them."

Heat bloomed in my cheeks, and memories of Phaedra on a battlefield poured to the forefront.

"Casualties?" Hadeon inquired.

The colonel hesitated. "Two."

"Which is why you've been instructed not to engage the Sun Court," Celani snapped from my right. "The wards have been allowed to remain in place for a reason, to minimize losses on *both* sides."

Anger flashed in Xanth's eyes.

"Surely you don't intend for the colonel to allow our enemies to invade?" he spoke up in defense of his superior.

"We have plenty of enemies in the Never Court, Captain," Celani observed calmly. "If your men are so bored that they seek out more, or so incompetent that they can't safely defend our border against *three* soldiers, perhaps a reassignment is in order."

A muscle worked in Xanth's jaw, but he only nodded, shooting a wary glance at the king. And Nyx.

"It won't happen again, General," he said calmly.

Aereon dipped his chin in assent, though color mottled his face.

Conversation picked up again in stilted, awkward exchanges. Kallius leaned across his sister, speaking to me under his breath.

"To answer your question earlier, no." There was a hint of mischief in his eyes. "It's usually quite boring. But you always did bring out the dissension in people."

I shrugged. I didn't mind if my presence made assclowns like Aereon show their true colors. "I'll take that as a compliment."

Celani huffed out what might have been a laugh. "Of course you will."

Not for the first time, I wondered about who Phaedra had been. If I would have liked her. If I was similar to her, this warrior of a princess who sounded like a bit of a nightmare in her own right. Her presence haunted me even as it was beginning to intrigue me.

Hadeon glowered on my left, and I suspected I was not the only one haunted by something tonight. Whatever had happened to piss him off, it wasn't ebbing away.

Just when I thought this night couldn't get more fun, I had a furious shadow king to contend with.

Chapter Fourteen

HADEON ESCORTED ME BACK TO MY ROOM IN A strained, palpable silence that danced between us like his shadows, ominous and always waiting in the periphery. Though I should have left it alone, curiosity was a relentless hag, and I couldn't quite stop myself from prodding at him.

"Was an evening of putting your pet princess on display not as fun as you wanted it to be, or have I done something to offend his majesty?" I asked just before we got to my door.

His shadows flared around him, a sure sign of his ire. He whirled on me, and I stood my ground, tilting my chin to look at him.

"You called him Colonel Aereon."

I blinked at him, nonplussed. "Is that not his name? Should I call him master, or something else appropriately subservient for a captive speaking to a high-ranking member of your court?"

Hadeon's thunderous expression didn't shift. "Yes, that is his name. But how did you, little Ember, know that?"

The blood drained from my face. I hadn't wanted to let Hadeon know that I was getting any memories back at all, unsure if they would give me something useful. But also because some of them were more confusing than I wanted to think about.

The question was why he cared.

"You're angry because I had an instinctual reaction from the remnants of Phaedra's soul?" I hedged. "What difference does it make to you?"

He stiffened but didn't back away.

"I like to know where I stand with my enemies."

If I hadn't been so fixated on his features, and if I didn't have the benefit of whatever bit of Phaedra I carried around, perhaps I would have missed it — the barest tightening of his lips before he spoke, the only tell he had.

He may not have been outright lying, but he damned sure wasn't telling the whole truth. I stepped closer to him in challenge, never breaking his gaze.

"Is that all we were? Enemies?" Whether or not he had been the person in the bathtub in my memory dreams, I wasn't an idiot. There were layers of hatred here that had nothing to do with a long-standing enmity between our peoples or a personality clash.

His lips parted, his eyes blazing in warning. "Do you still want to pretend you remember nothing?"

I raised an eyebrow with far more bravado than I felt with his breath ghosting across my skin. "I don't have to remember anything about her life to know that you're lying."

A muscle clenched in his jaw. "I have never once lied to you."

"Of course not, because I was the only liar in our relationship." My tone was equal parts questioning and sarcasm.

"You still are," he growled, his shadows wrapping around my wrists in a rapid, fluid movement and pinning me to the smooth stone wall. "But tell me, Feralinia, what is it that you so desperately want to know?"

All rational thought fled my mind.

In that moment, all I could think was that the things I wanted — *needed* — to know were not things he could tell me. Like what his lips tasted like, and how his shadows felt when they were caressing rather than restraining, and if the inexplicable pull I felt toward him was real or just the phantom echoes from another woman's soul.

I wanted to ask if he had ever been in that gorgeous tub with me, or if even that had just been a demented form of Stockholm syndrome, another way for him to treat me like something he owned.

In the end, I either wasn't brave enough to ask what I wanted to know or didn't want to risk letting on how many of the memories I was privy to. So I met his stare solidly.

"Why do you hate her so much?" *Why do you hate me so much?*

If there had been heat in his gaze before, it was gone now, replaced by a glittering rage so encompassing I wasn't sure I wanted the answer to that question after all.

"Because," he said, his voice low, deadly. "She broke a promise to me, and it got someone I love killed."

The ice in his eyes spread to me, freezing me straight to my core.

The few pieces I had been able to put together about Phaedra's life had told me she wasn't just some simpering princess, but an actual warrior.

But this...

Had she really been responsible for someone's death off the battlefield? Was it an accident, or did she do it for some sort of revenge? Jealousy?

I was still reeling when the shadows disappeared from my wrists. The king was gone half a second later, leaving me alone in the hallway with all my questions and a guilt rooted within my soul.

MY DREAMS that night had a frantic, nearly desperate quality to them, like Phaedra was trying to tell me something.

First, I dreamt of the battlefield again, bathed in its usual crimson hue. I was in her body, as always. Only this time, I felt her terror. Her resolute need to protect her people. A golden-haired elf stood next to her as she raised her hands in front of her, bright light emanating from them.

"Don't," he begged. "Phae, you'll burn yourself out."

"But you'll live," she said simply. "Go, little brother, or this will be for nothing."

Then he left, his expression shattered, while she let loose a light that decimated the battlefield, charring the Moon Court soldiers into blackened corpses. The few who tried to run were also caught in her unearthly blaze. And why wouldn't they be? Any who escaped would go after her family.

The scene changed to one where Hadeon sat on his onyx throne, the moonlight an unearthly halo around his dark hair. He looked down on her with an indecipherable expression.

Though his features were unchanged, his eyes looked younger somehow, not half as bitter as they were now.

"So this is the Sun Court princess we've heard so much about. Feral little thing, aren't you?"

Titters rippled around the throne room, but Phaedra's gaze didn't waver from his face. Her limbs were shaking, and I could feel her weakness like it was my own, just as I could feel her refusal to falter in front of him.

"Tell me, did you enjoy senselessly murdering my people?" he asked casually, as if he were inquiring about the weather.

She lifted her chin higher. "It's actually considered an execution when I do it," she said evenly. "And I wouldn't go right to senseless. To me, it made plenty of sense."

He tilted his head, arching a single navy eyebrow, and the scene changed again, this time to the clearing we had gone to train. Over and over again, Hadeon threw shadows at Phaedra while she refused to budge.

"I won't help you learn my people's weaknesses," she said, pushing herself up off the ground and dusting off her white gown. "Or mine."

Hadeon's shadows expanded around him in a way that was familiar, but she didn't cower.

"I would almost think you had no weaknesses," he said, a strand of darkness reaching for her.

She knew better than to feel proud at his jab. Sure enough, he wasn't finished.

"But everyone has a weakness, and I will find yours." The shadow pushed a stray hair behind her ear, both gentle and ominous.

Something in her chest finally quailed, her heartbeat picking up speed.

Was this how he broke her? Slowly, over time?

Then the vision shifted once more to the two of them in a dark forest, a wounded puppy with three heads blinking up at them. Before I could glimpse anything more, a familiar wall of shadows drove the scene away.

Usually, I would wake up, but tonight, flames chased the shadows, insistent and furious. When the image cleared, I — she — was in a bed. This bed, if the mural on the ceiling was any indication.

It had been easier to separate myself from Phaedra in the other dreams tonight, but now we melded as one. This vision was more solid, almost forceful, like she was pushing it toward me...or fighting to keep me anchored in it.

Darkness covered my eyes, so I couldn't see anything, but I could feel *everything*. My hands were restrained against the headboard by what felt like cool silk, something I could tell I welcomed. Someone pressed a searing kiss against my mouth before the lips trailed along my jaw, down to my neck, igniting a fire that burned straight through me.

One strong hand gripped my thigh, the thumb teasing slowly upward, while the other hand played along my curves.

The mouth moved downward, teeth grazing along my collarbone while silken strands of hair trailed along my skin, adding yet another sensation. I arched into the body that pressed over mine.

"More."

"So impatient, Feralinia," a familiar voice growled as the mouth lowered to tease along my navel.

I tugged at my restraints enough to direct a small jet of firelight at his shadow in retribution. He chuckled darkly, and the sound reverberated through my body. His teeth grazed along my skin while his hands explored in tantalizing patterns.

Stars exploded in my vision as he furthered his ministrations. Cool tendrils caressed my sides, traveling in an arc from my shoulders down to my thighs.

It was all too much and exactly enough. A strangled cry escaped me at the precise moment a burst of light eliminated the darkness, removing any unreasonable shred of doubt about the identity of the man.

I saw the shadows that bound my wrists and played along my skin, the navy hair that spilled onto my chest.

And the perfect, chiseled face of the king.

Chapter Fifteen

I SPENT THE NEXT MORNING TRYING NOT TO THINK about the dream, about whether I had witnessed some fairly epic hate sex or if they had been in some kind of real relationship.

About Hadeon's hands, tongue, or teeth on my skin.

Still, I couldn't help but notice that Phaedra had chosen a moment that answered at least two of the questions I had the night before. What Hadeon's lips tasted like — darkness and wine — and what his shadows felt like when they were caressing my skin — silk.

Did she answer the third question as well? Was the pull I felt just her memories of the admittedly good time he had apparently shown her on more than one occasion?

I tried to remember how she felt in that scene. It was obviously clouded under a haze of ecstasy and something nearer to defiance closer to the surface, like whatever part of her soul or her memory was showing me that scene in spite of...his feelings? Mine?

But underneath all of that, I could have sworn I felt something deeper. That didn't mean he reciprocated, though, and I still wasn't sure who she had gotten killed.

I was out of sorts when I went to training, both because of the dream memories and all the unfamiliar pent-up energy that came along with them. Phaedra had gotten a hell of a climax. That only made one of us.

Not that that was anything unusual where I was concerned.

Hadeon seemed off this morning as well. At first, I thought it was just my perception as I tried very hard not to look at his face. Or any other part of him.

But as the day stretched on, it was clear our argument last night was making him even more closed-off than usual, and even more surly.

Halfway through the morning, a preternaturally harmonious bark startled me out of the meditation I was halfway mastering by now.

"I told you to stay, Nyx." Hadeon sighed, leveling her with a stern expression.

The cerberus shot him an unimpressed look, all three of her heads clearly annoyed as she settled on the ground next to us.

"You knew she wouldn't stay away for long," Celani commented, stepping aside to give the canine a wide berth.

"How did she even get here?" I asked, looking around the field. She certainly hadn't ridden a baztet.

"Through moonbeams," Kallius offered. He, too, kept a respectful distance from the cerberus.

Of course. Why hadn't I thought of that?

She was like some sort of underworld version of a My Little Pony, except a cerberus who ate people when the mood struck her. This world never got less strange, shadowy sexual encounters notwithstanding.

"It's probably time for a break anyway," Celani said with a sideways glance at a very agitated Hadeon.

"Indeed," he muttered, heading toward the picnic area.

Once again, everyone laid out food, taking turns filling their small plates with what was essentially a charcuterie layout. Hadeon was distracted, staring off into the distance as he absently brought food to his lips.

And I was distracted watching him, in spite of my very best efforts.

Which is why I didn't immediately notice when a massive head butted in next to me to steal my entire plate of salami.

"Nyx," I scolded without thinking, shoving the head away on reflex.

We all froze, Nyx included. Slowly, I turned to look at the cerberus, steeling myself for my impending demise.

Surely, Hadeon would step in if it came to that, present terrible mood or not. Instead of looking like she wanted to devour me, though, the cerberus looked...chastised? Letting out a small whine, she crossed her paws and laid all three heads down on the ground, silver eyes flitting back and forth between me and the clearing.

Hadeon looked at me for the first time since we took off on his baztet this morning.

"If you don't tell her you aren't mad, she'll be impossible all day," he said in a long-suffering voice, gesturing toward Nyx.

I blinked, sure I misheard him. He wanted me to reassure the extremely deadly creature, who may or may not have wanted to devour me on more than one occasion, that I wasn't mad at her because I had hurt her feelings?

Hadeon let out an impatient huff, and I reluctantly turned to the giant, sulking dog.

"I'm not mad, Nyx," I said uncertainly. "You're fine."

Three sets of puppy-dog eyes looked over at me dubiously, reminding me of the tiny, wounded version of her I had seen in my dream last night.

"Really," I said more softly. "Here." I reached out to take the last salami from the plate, breaking it into three equal pieces before tossing them her way.

Kallius groaned a protest, snatching up the rest of the cheese like he was afraid I would offer that next.

But Nyx was thrilled. She happily snapped the meat out of the air piece by piece, like she was showing off.

"Good girl," I praised her, still unsure.

She looked pleased, her enormous tail thumping against the ground hard enough to make the entire clearing tremble. Hadeon, on the other hand, scowled even more fiercely.

"Let's get back to work, Feralinia."

I froze for the second time in as many minutes, trying to keep my breathing even, my features calm. After last night, that word, that *name* did things to me I tried very hard to ignore.

Hadeon narrowed his eyes, peering at me like I was a particularly vexing puzzle, and I cleared my throat.

"Sure." The word was softer than I wanted it to be.

My easy acquiescence only increased his suspicion, if the twist of his lips was anything to go by.

Celani and Kallius were unnaturally quiet, with none of their usual banter or conversation. The entire mood in the clearing had shifted, and as usual, I was left wondering if it was something I had done or if they were lost in memories of a princess who had been dead for longer than I had been alive.

AN HOUR into the next segment of training, Hadeon made a somewhat abrupt choice to leave. Celani moved to follow, but he shook his head.

"Kallius can come, and Nyx...will do whatever she wants. You can see the princess back to the castle."

They departed quickly. When it was only Celani and me — and Nyx — I found it even harder to concentrate. My eyes kept flitting to the fiery court, thinking of the battle scenes in last night's dreams and the blatant hatred I felt from the Moon Court last night at dinner.

"Your people despise me," I finally said. "Is that because of the war?"

She raised her eyebrows. "You know about the war?"

More than I wanted to. Not as much as I should.

"Just that there was one," I answered.

She nodded, then gestured toward the cliff that faced the Court of Fire and Sun. She sat on the ground near the edge, and I followed, looking out at flame-colored mountains and golden fields. Nyx settled next to us, seemingly content to stay here rather than go back to Fengari Palace with Hadeon.

The hairs rose along the back of my neck. I wasn't precisely afraid, but I was definitely wary of her presence without Hadeon here to rein her in if she got snacky.

"Yes, there was a war," Celani pulled me back to the present. "Humans, as I understand, don't live very long, but elves have long lives and longer memories."

"And I killed the people they loved." I thought of Merikh, Xanth, even stupid Colonel Aereon. Maybe it wasn't just a bias on their part. Maybe each of them had a real reason to loathe me specifically. "So they hate me."

"Some of them," she conceded.

I appreciated that she didn't bother to sugarcoat it.

"But not you?" I asked, watching the way the sun shone brightly on Phaedra's home, wrapping its rays around the mountains and valleys and saturating them in the sunlight that so often escaped the Moon Court.

As close as it was, it certainly felt like another world.

When I glanced back at Celani, there was a hint of a smile at the corner of her lips.

"Oh, I did." She let out a dry laugh. "I was the one who brought you in the first time."

I tilted my head, surprise furrowing my brows.

She leveled a look at me. "I am the king's general. Is it so shocking?"

When I considered it, hadn't he sent her after me the second time, too?

"I guess not. But you don't seem quite as visceral in your hatred of me now. What changed?"

Emotions played across her features, almost too quickly for me to read. Contemplation, remorse, sadness. Her violet gaze held mine searchingly before she squared her shoulders. Then she was back to being the stoic general.

"You did, I suppose." She shrugged. "You aren't her. And I don't believe in holding someone to something they don't even remember."

Her phrasing was pointed, her tone even more so. I thought of the many times she had intervened in subtle ways between Hadeon and me.

"You mean like the bargain Phaedra made with Hadeon?" I pushed. I was blatantly fishing now, but it wasn't like he was ever going to tell me.

I braced myself for her offense, but she only quirked an eyebrow as if to say, *nice try.*

"You don't call him by his title." She settled back onto the plush aquamarine grass.

The subject change didn't escape my notice, but I took the hint.

"Should I?" I demanded. He damned sure didn't call me by a title.

Celani shrugged, though there was something heavy in it. "She never did, either."

I considered that, wondering if my omission of his title was because of her or just because the idea of calling someone *King* was so foreign to me. My eyes skated across the landscape, resting on a gilded castle that sparkled in the distance in a kingdom that was almost mine.

"Can I ask you something?"

"You can ask," she said with a half smirk.

But she might not answer; I knew the implication. Still, I found it easier to talk to her than I had anyone since coming here, an ease in our interactions even though she had been the one to kidnap me — twice, apparently.

Maybe I really did have Stockholm syndrome.

"Is Phaedra's family... Are they alive?"

"They are." Her tone was carefully even, like maybe she knew how hard it was for me to ask, or to hear the answer.

I took a breath, looking up at the golden constellation hanging in the sky between the two courts, the one that was inked into nearly every inch of my skin.

The one Phaedra must have stared at while living in a strange limbo between her prison and her home.

"Are they looking for...her?"

She studied me again in her calm, assessing manner. "Would you want to see them if they were?"

I thought about her brother, the elf with the golden hair, and the rumbling voice I suspected belonged to her father, the gentle murmurings of her mother.

Then I thought about how the girl they wanted to see was dead, and I didn't even have her memories to comfort them with. I wasn't a warrior or a princess, and I sure as hell didn't know how to be anyone's sister, let alone remember how to be a daughter.

I was just an orphan who happened to house some fragment of their dead loved one's soul.

And even if there were more, even if I had more to give them, it would still feel like a betrayal of the family I had once upon a time.

My mother had been so obsessed with the one child she had been able to bear that she had not only traumatized us all with a very uncensored video of my birth, but had recorded what felt like every minute of my life after.

She was a photographer, though, so it was natural. I had always felt I got my artistic nature from her. And my temper.

Then there was my father, who was a professor of philosophy. He had been quiet, reserved, and given to daydreaming, but he adored us both. I always assumed I got my strong adherence to ethics from him, as well as the empathy I had been prone to before the world took most of it from me.

What did it mean, if I was no more than Phaedra reborn? That they weren't really my family? Were there no genetics at play, only isos? Was that why a woman who had tried for a decade to conceive had only ever managed me?

Worse than all of that, I wondered if I would have meant as much to them in light of the truth. Would they have loved me less if they had known that on some level, I was never really theirs?

When the silence had stretched on too long, I finally cleared my throat, giving her the answer I suspected she already knew.

"No," I said simply.

Sure enough, she nodded, like the response was expected. But there was no judgment in it, only understanding, if I could call it that.

"Then don't torture yourself with questions," she said in her no-nonsense way. "Hadeon is taking care of it."

Of course he was. He had probably been fielding messages since I got here. I should have been infuriated at the audacity, but instead, I couldn't help but feel just the slightest bit... relieved.

Maybe even grateful.

Chapter Sixteen

ANOTHER WEEK WENT BY WHEREIN I SHOWED NO sign of any isos at all.

Hadeon kept his distance at the palace, but was relentless at the training grounds. It brought to mind Phaedra's memories from before — the way he pushed her endlessly and she refused to give anything back.

Unfortunately, I was not her. And I would give anything to call to life whatever dormant isos still hummed in my veins just to make him back off.

It didn't help that my nights were filled with dreams and memories I would rather not have. Every night, images chased each other through the two versions of my life. No matter the life, they always ended in Hadeon's bed, in his arms, wrapped in his shadows.

It made my fragile grip on my temper, my sanity, so much more tenuous, even without Hadeon hurling his shadows at me over and over and *over* again. Sometimes they just surrounded me in a cocoon of darkness, and sometimes they knocked me on my ass.

He lifted his chin in what I now recognized as a warning that he was about to strike, and I sensed this would be another of the ass-knocking variety. I was already tired and at the end of my rope, but I refused to give him the satisfaction of asking for a break.

So I stood my ground, bracing myself.

It turned out to be entirely unnecessary, because Celani stepped between us, holding up a hand.

"A word, your majesty," she said, gesturing toward the tree line. There was deference in her posture, but her voice was hard.

Hadeon took an irritated breath but nodded.

"Nyx, stand guard," he ordered before storming across the clearing.

The giant dog let out a low whine, her heads angled toward her master as she watched him walk away. It was the first time I had been alone with the cerberus since she insisted on following us for training. Even Kallius wasn't here; he had gone to face some trouble at the border of the Never Court from the threat Hadeon had neglected to expound on days before.

Nyx stretched her massive body, letting out three individual yawns before stalking forward, erasing the distance between us. The gentle light of the moons reflected off her runes, giving them a subtle sheen.

I swallowed as she approached, unsure whether or not I should be afraid. Her giant body towered over mine, and I stared up into a set of gray eyes as her middle head blocked my view of the sky.

I had been watching her closely ever since she didn't eat me for shoving her head, and she really didn't seem to mean any harm. At least, not to me. Where I had seen a hungry monster before, now I just saw a puppy desperate for attention.

It didn't make me naïve. I knew I would always be one wrong move away from being her lunch, but I didn't think she was intent on it anymore.

Her middle nose came in close, taking a giant sniff before the one on the right did the same. Then she nodded meaningfully toward Celani and Hadeon.

I hesitated, trying to read her before the head on the left nodded as well.

"You —" I began quietly, looking back and forth between the elves and the cerberus. "You want me to go to them?"

Nyx snorted, a small gust of wind soaring from her nose and blowing back my hair. Her runes glimmered brighter, catching the moonlight, and the sharp lines of her body turned almost...transparent.

She nodded toward the faint shimmer that appeared behind Hadeon's back, and the elves' voices were suddenly clearer.

"Your way isn't working," Celani said, sounding more than a little impatient.

My eyes snapped up to meet Nyx's, trying to make sense of what was happening, when I recalled Kallius's explanation that she could travel through moonbeams. I darted a glance between the two places on the field, realizing she had opened a sort of eavesdropping portal.

"I could hardly have foreseen a life on Earth making her even more difficult," Hadeon forced out, his voice pulling me back to their conversation.

"Thank you," I mouthed the words to the giant dog, certain she understood them.

"Like you wouldn't be, under the circumstances," Celani retorted. "You're pushing her too hard and in all the wrong ways."

Hadeon scowled, his shadows flaring in exasperation.

"What is it you suggest?"

There was a pointed pause. "I want to take her to the temple."

"Of course you do." His voice was dark. Ominous. "Because it's not like we need her alive or anything."

Something in my stomach twisted in response.

"Xanth sent scouts to the area yesterday, and they reported no wraith activity. Besides, it's clear you're not going to take her." A hint of censure edged her tone.

"Don't sound so offended," Hadeon scoffed. "The goddess knows perfectly well why I don't patronize her temple."

His shadows expanded again, and his hands fisted at his sides, but Celani only shook her head.

"You'll have to get over that someday."

"Agree to disagree." He lifted one muscular shoulder in a shrug that was far more casual than the resentment burning in his gaze.

"About *that*, sure, but not about *this*." Celani sounded resolute.

Several heartbeats passed before the king let out a growl. "Fine. Do as you will. Just bring her back reasonably intact."

Sweet nothings like that must have been how he wooed Phaedra back in the day. I couldn't even be offended, not when I was grappling with a mix of fear and excitement at the idea of going somewhere that wasn't the palace or the training grounds.

And in spite of the way I had been avoiding it up until now, I couldn't deny a small bit of curiosity at this glimpse into Phaedra's past that had nothing to do with brooding kings or warfare.

I WAS GETTING USED to traveling by mystical jaguar, but I was in no way prepared to find two baztets saddled and ready to go at the stables instead of just one.

Kallius was back at the battlefront, and neither of these baztets belonged to Hadeon.

Celani watched me impatiently, her silver hair blowing back from her face with a gust of wind as she climbed up onto her mount, gesturing between me and the other.

The jaguar yawned, its teeth shining under the golden moon. I took a step back and shook my head.

The general grinned and leaned forward in her saddle,

patting her creature's neck and doting on it like it was just a kitten.

"Listen, Ember, as much as I'd love to cozy up on a baztet with you, it's hard for me to be on my guard at your back. Besides, you have the hang of it by now."

I furrowed my brow, pointedly blinking up at her.

Did I have the hang of it?

I balked for several more seconds before feeling the eyes of the entire courtyard fixed on me, like they, too, were waiting to see if I would grow a pair. Finally, I shook my head, stepping forward.

I grabbed hold of the pommel, slipping my foot through the stirrup before hauling myself onto the saddle. I barely had time to finish securing the lap belt before Celani urged her baztet into a run.

They were just taking flight when my mount grew impatient and sprinted off to join them.

My fingers trembled as I grasped the reins in one hand and the pommel in the other, holding on for dear life as the baztet's wings began to flap. The crisp air rushed over my face and whipped my hair behind my head like living flames.

A rush of adrenaline flooded my veins when the baztet vaulted straight up into the air. Momentarily, I lost my balance, my stomach twisting, sliding back in my saddle. I risked a glance behind me to watch as the ground disappeared far below us.

Panic seized me. I threw myself forward, wrapping the reins around my wrists and using my thighs to grip her sides like that might keep me from plunging to my immediate death.

Then I realized some part of me was missing Hadeon's firm body at my back, the way I knew his shadows would catch me if I fell, and I scowled.

To hell with that.

I wasn't some simpering princess who needed a king to save her. Who couldn't function if he wasn't around.

"Yes," I finally called out to answer Celani. "Yes, I do."

Maybe. If not fully now, I would have the hang of it by the end of the day. Celani gave me an approving nod.

The wind blew around me. It danced in my hair and whipped at my cloak and gown in a way that made me want to let go just a little. To cede control to the elements, and to fly wherever my baztet wanted to take me.

There was something about being solo in the air, something that made me feel like freedom was just another flight away.

There was no freedom for me in the Moon Court. Not with my collar and my warded room and my constant guard — the eyes that always watched me no matter where I was in Fengari Palace — but it was hard to remember all of that while the wind roared in my ears and the rest of the world was so tiny and far beneath my feet.

Celani was content to let me fly. She kept a careful distance, allowing me to feel out my baztet, to have a little fun as we dove down to the sparkling river, soaring above it for several long seconds before taking off again to race up through clouds.

Finally, we fell into place next to Celani and her jaguar. "This is Misti, by the way," she said, leaning back in her seat to play with a black-and-blue spotted tail.

She seemed more relaxed up here. Did she love flying, or just being away from prying eyes and expectations?

I nodded my head, looking down at the giant cat that seemed to be tolerating me. "Does this one have a name?" I asked, pointing to my baztet. The creature growled in response and I was almost certain it understood me.

"Comet," she said, and a purr immediately rumbled through my baztet.

I repeated the name, eliciting the same response.

"So why are we going to the temple?" I asked, scratching Comet behind the ears.

She had only told me that we were leaving, and I hadn't asked why. I wondered what she would tell me of her conversation with Hadeon, but also was genuinely curious what the reasoning behind this was.

Celani pursed her full lips, her posture going rigid for a moment before she answered.

"Your isos comes from the goddess. It stands to reason that being closer to her might help you access it, or at least understand it." She sighed. "Besides...Phaedra would have wanted to go pay her respects."

There was something in the way she said her name.

"Two years was a long time for her to be here without any friends," I ventured, shamelessly leading her. "She must have been really alone."

Celani darted a glance at me. "She wasn't. Not always. She

had...a pet, of sorts."

"But no friends?" I pushed.

A knowing gleam lit her eye. "Do you really want to know? You usually don't like to hear about her life."

That was true enough. It filled me with an odd disconnect, outside of the endless infuriating sense of déjà vu. It didn't matter, though, because the moment a smirk touched her lips, a memory hit me.

Celani walked into my room, holding a bottle of silvery, swirling wine in one hand and two glasses crisscrossed in the other.

"You're going to drink this, then you're going to tell me whatever it is you've been trying so badly to hide." She set the bottle and glasses down. "Celestial hells, how did you survive at court when your face shows everything you think?"

"Believe it or not, the people of the Sun Court aren't constantly trying to kill each other."

"No, because you're too busy trying to kill us."

"Harsh. But yes. That. Still, there's something to be said for inner kingdom loyalty."

Celani sighed. "You know how Hadeon's mother was. Give him time, and he'll get there with our court."

"I know he will."

Her eyes narrowed, her head tilting. "Do you?"

I could practically feel Phaedra's cheeks heating. "I'm just saying that he's a...decent king."

"Is that all he's decent at?" Celani waggled her eyebrows.

"Just...shut up and pour the wine."

The sound of laughter echoed as the vision went black.

All of that happened in a single blink, like a waking dream. I opened my eyes to find Celani waiting for my answer.

Maybe it was the memory or maybe it was the slightly guarded look in her violet eyes, an expectation I wasn't sure I could handle but couldn't quite bear to disappoint either.

"Yes," I said firmly. "I want to know."

Did she hear what I wasn't saying? That I wanted the truth from her, and not just about this? That I was willing to give her her own space to remember or grieve the friend she lost?

Her smirk widened, something in her eyes that said she did understand those things.

"I wouldn't go right to friends," she lied. "But I grew to tolerate you, I suppose."

"Her," I corrected quietly.

Space was one thing, but the distinction was important.

The smile fell from her lips, turning to something more like concern. "It doesn't have to be a bad thing, that you're like her. Yes, she was feral at times, but she was also funny and passionate and brave as hell."

"Maybe the problem is that I'm not like her." Something about the pretend freedom of being in the air allowed me to give her a small touch of honesty.

"Yes, you are," she said earnestly. "You don't have to be the same person if you don't want to, but I would have known your soul for hers even without the prophecy. Or the hair."

I didn't know what to say to that, so I said nothing. Celani seemed content to let us fly in a companionable silence that was probably awkward only for me.

It may have been a mystery how Phaedra fell into whatever the hell she shared with Hadeon, but I didn't wonder at all why she had been friends with Celani. It felt like I knew Celani's soul nearly as well as she knew mine.

WE FLEW for well over an hour before reaching the temple.

It was somehow exactly what I expected, but also so much more.

Massive sandstone columns rose up to create a tower that cast a shadow over the three courts it was connected to. There were three distinct bridges over water that shifted from silver to gold to gray.

The water from the Never Court looked toxic, like it was slowly poisoning the rest of the lake. I thought back to Hadeon's words about how the wraiths and whatever infection they brought with them wouldn't end in the Never Court. It would spread to the rest of Aelvaria, then go even farther.

The gray, bubbling waters seeping from that side of the lake made that threat feel all the more tangible.

"Are you ready?" Celani asked, stepping up beside me to cross the bridge.

I nodded, shifting my attention to the temple that towered above us. Sandstone walls and columns reached up toward the sky, and smooth steps led us to a large, rounded wooden door.

As soon as we stepped through the entrance, I knew there

was something different about this place. Even if I hadn't known Phaedra had been here, I would have felt it.

I had expected a place that was too quiet, too still, even eerie, but this temple was brimming with life, almost like it was excited I was here. There was a charged quality to the air, a warmth and energy that permeated the space.

Sure footsteps brought me toward the southern part of the temple until I hit a wall. It was smooth like marble but radiant like stained glass in the full light of the sun. Red mountains formed the backdrop, but at the center was a massive golden tree with its leaves and branches stretched out toward me in invitation.

By instinct or some weird form of soul muscle memory, I reached out a hand to the glowing stone at the center of the tree.

It flared to life as soon as I came into contact with it, a light stretching up from the roots, even brighter as it reached the trunk and the trees. Then, the wall swung open to reveal a vast section of the temple that must have been reserved for the Court of Fire and Sun.

The room was warm, cast in hues of red and orange.

Smooth white marble benches waited in the center of the room, while golden columns stretched up to a domed ceiling painted with images of golden warriors like Greek gods.

A barrage of memories assaulted me, like I was seeing a holographic video play out around me.

First there was a girl with bright blue eyes and long flaming hair, the strands disheveled and sparking as she sprinted through the room. Laughter pealed through the air, hers and that of a slightly deeper voice.

I turned to find a boy, around eight, with golden hair and bronze skin and a mischievous grin, also running. An older boy followed, more subdued but laughing all the same.

Then a woman, a soft smile on her lips, warm like the sun after a cold dip in the lake.

"Children, what have I told you about running in the temple?"

"The goddess doesn't mind!" the girl said. "She told me so."

"I'm sure she did, little firestorm," the woman replied in a placating voice.

Tears stabbed at the backs of my eyes, which must have been some magic of the temple, because I didn't cry, ever, let alone over a family that was never really mine.

A massive man entered at last, whatever he said in his booming voice swallowed by the raging inferno of his beard. Literal fire surrounded him, and his features were far sterner than the woman's.

But his arms were gentle as he scooped up the little girl and sat her on his shoulder. Then his eyes were on the oldest boy, a severe expression twisting his features as he stared down at his son.

"You can't expect to rule a kingdom if you can't get your sister to behave for five minutes, Elion," he said.

The older boy nodded gravely, but the younger one snickered. "Does that mean *you* can't rule a kingdom, Papa?"

A bright laugh escaped the woman, and the scene faded away, another apparition taking its place.

A beautiful woman stood in front of me in a long, golden gown that contrasted her olive skin tone. A gilded tattoo on her arm formed the shape of the same tree that was on the door of the temple, but it was the amethyst waves framing her delicate, heart-shaped face and violet eyes that stood out the most.

She was the woman from my hazy memories at the casino. The one who slid my cat ears back into place and told me everything would be better soon. I swallowed hard, my eyes narrowing as I studied her more closely.

Her full lips tilted in a sad smile.

"I am no apparition, child." The voice sounded like autumn leaves rustling in the wind, like waves crashing gently against the shore and snow falling on a wintry mountain. It sounded like *life*.

"Abba," I whispered. The name came from the recesses of my mind, from Phaedra's mind.

"I have missed you," she said, her violet eyes softening as she stepped closer.

"Have you?" I asked, even as I felt the truth of her words.

She nodded. "You know you were always one of her favorites. And mine."

She meant the goddess, and she sounded earnest, but the words struck a painful chord.

"Then why did you want me to die?" I couldn't help but demand. "Why did you let me be taken by *him* instead of returned to my family?"

I hadn't realized that these questions were eating me alive until she was here, in front of me. All of Hadeon's anger at the goddess must have been contagious because I felt it too. The resentment. The betrayal.

Her features softened, her lips turning downward as her eyes filled with sadness, and I felt the echo of a pang in my chest like it was my own. Maybe it was, for that matter. There was certainly a bitterness that felt like it was coming from deep inside my soul. Phaedra's soul.

"I cannot speak of that which I have seen, either in your past, or in your future, little one. But you will know in time."

"That's very helpful, thank you." I didn't bother keeping the sarcasm from my tone.

The smallest hint of a smile graced her lips again. "The goddess will forgive your impertinence because this life has been short and you are far too weary for such a young soul. Besides, your influences cannot be helped."

There was a sardonic edge to that last sentence, one that told me she referred to Hadeon.

"They could have been," I added after a moment, glancing at the space where the memory of Phaedra's family had stood.

If I was going to be ripped from my life, it could have been by people who wanted me and loved me. Abba shook her head, her amethyst waves falling over her shoulders.

"Everything has happened as it needed to."

I wasn't sure if she was placating me or *seeing*. She looked away, perhaps listening to someone I couldn't see.

"My time here is at an end," she sounded disappointed. "Tell the shadow king that he will not prevail if he allows old grievances to rob him of his faith in that which he knows to be true."

Then she was gone, and Celani's voice was echoing in the cavernous chamber instead.

"Ember?" She said the word like it wasn't the first time, and still, it took me too long to react to my name.

Because for the space between heartbeats, it didn't feel like mine.

"Yes?" I asked.

"You just...froze," her eyes widened as excitement emanated from her. "Did she come to you, then?"

"You knew that she would?" I wasn't sure if it was a question or a statement, but Celani nodded regardless.

"I hoped. She always liked you."

"So she says," I muttered.

I took another glance around the chamber, full of shades and impressions of memories I could barely touch, voices that were familiar and foreign, a happiness and sense of self that didn't remotely feel like mine, and all of a sudden, there was nowhere I wanted to be less.

"Can we go now?"

Something must have shown on my face because Celani didn't argue or even ask why. She only nodded, an inscrutable look passing over her gorgeous features.

"Sure, Ember. Let's go home."

I didn't have the heart to correct her again, not when we both knew I had no home. Not in the human realm anymore, not in Phaedra's court, and sure as hell not in Hadeon's.

Chapter Seventeen

I PUSHED OPEN THE DOOR OF THE TEMPLE, INHALING the fresh air as I practically ran down the sandstone stairs. I squeezed my eyes shut, forcing my mind to stop racing through every single memory that had assaulted me within those walls.

It was too real. All of it.

My pulse pounded against my temples as I struggled to separate the visions of Phaedra's family, the achingly familiar love of her parents, and the all-too-real voice of the priestess.

"Ember." Celani's voice broke through the torrent in my mind, concern etched it. "Are you —"

I turned to look at her when she didn't finish her question. Her violet gaze was blown wide as she stared just over my shoulder.

Dread pooled in my stomach, my muscles going rigid, almost as if my body already instinctively knew what was standing behind me.

But that was impossible. Right?

Hot, acrid breath caressed the back of my neck, the scent of rot and death overpowering my senses. I braced myself, slowly turning around only to come face to face with a wall of solid darkness.

It was nothing like Hadeon's silky absence of light. These shadows were tainted, emanating unadulterated evil.

They were static and frayed, the air rippling around them like their touch was pure poison.

"Shadow wraiths," Celani muttered the words under her breath, and my mind instantly recognized them as true.

Images of a battlefield raced through my mind. Broken soldiers lay unmoving, consumed by a black obscurity. The sharp snapping of teeth filled the air, punctuated by the cries of the dying as the wraiths devoured everything in their path.

This was what had been near us in the forest that first night I was here.

Swallowing hard, I followed the jagged, mutated darkness that twisted into the shape of a feral dog standing on its hind legs, nothing like the original image of wraiths that my imagination had conjured.

These were far more real, and somehow more terrifying.

Bright green eyes bore into mine as the monster stretched its lips over broken teeth. Bile rose in my throat as another wave of putrid breath washed over me.

Every instinct in my body told me to run as fast as I could, but fear kept me rooted to the spot.

I knew this creature — this shadow wraith — or Phaedra

had, at least. I also knew that my chances of survival were next to none. Panic took hold of me, and my lower lip trembled.

"Don't move," Celani cautioned, and I heard the faint sound of steel scraping against her sheath.

The wraith's green eyes flicked up at the sound, narrowing on the general. My fingers went to the black bracers at my wrists, gliding along the small handles of the daggers like they might somehow save us from this monster.

"When I give you the word, I want you to run back into the temple. You'll be safe there until Hadeon comes," Celani whispered.

I resisted the urge to look her way, afraid of drawing more attention to myself. Even if I had time to unsheathe my daggers, I had no idea how much they would help against this...thing.

Celani took one step closer, then another, until I could see the silver point of her spear in my periphery. And it was shining.

The creature hissed and backed away ever so slightly as she stretched the weapon out again like she was trying to steer it away from us. The closer the tip of her spear came to the monster, the brighter the weapon gleamed with golden-white moonlight, and the wraith hissed in warning.

The smallest spark of hope kindled inside of me. If she had any more weapons like this, maybe we could get away. Maybe we would survive. Emboldened by the general, I quickly drew my daggers, holding them at the ready, just in case.

Celani tapped her spear against the ground, the light growing brighter as ringing filled the air. The wraith slammed its claws over its ears, shaking its head back and forth before letting out an otherworldly wail.

There was movement on my left, then my right, a thick, cloying odor wafting from both directions. Celani cursed under her breath. I risked a glance to find two more of the wraiths flanking us on either side, and I bit back a curse of my own.

"What do we do?" My words were barely a whisper, but the monster in front of me twisted its head to stare at me once again.

"*We* don't do anything. You run, and I kill every last one of these celestial-damned beasts," Celani growled.

Everything that came next was a blur of movement and gnashing teeth.

Celani lunged at the wraith closest to me, her spear growing even brighter as she stabbed at the mass. It went through the static darkness, but green smoke appeared where a wound would have been.

Another horrifying scream pierced the air and rattled my bones, and my stomach twisted in response.

Without thinking about it for too long, I aimed the dagger in my right hand at one of the wraiths, gripping the hilt the way Kallius had taught me, and used all of my strength to throw it.

The steel caught the moonlight, flickering like a shooting star as it spun, hilt over blade. The wraith dodged the hit, shifting from its corporeal form into a dense black cloud.

A lump formed in my throat as the dagger fell to the ground and the wraith's green eyes locked on me.

"Go, now!" Celani shouted, forcefully shoving me backward.

She twisted her spear through the air, slicing the beast. Static sparked from the place where her spear connected with its shadows, and that ringing sounded again.

I stumbled, nearly tripping over my own feet to get out of her way. Three wraiths converged on her, blocking any chance for her to escape.

Her spear moved through the air faster than I could track, her body ducking and darting out of the way of their attacks like she was dancing instead of fighting for her life.

She was grace incarnate, and if I had doubts before about why she was chosen to be general, they were completely gone now.

Then she did something unexpected. I hadn't seen her use her isos yet, but I had no doubt what this was. She leapt into the air, landing on the ground with her knee and fist.

The air shifted around her, and the wraiths moved slower than before. Then they were moving up. Like gravity itself had reversed.

Celani took advantage of the moment, striking blow after blow while they could do nothing but float in the air, suspended in whatever form they had been in, and take each hit.

I inhaled slowly, trying to steady myself and reach for that fire I felt the first day. Right now would be a great time for some of that damned isos to make itself available to me.

Straining my muscles and clenching my fists, I dug deep,

begging whatever god or goddess was listening to give me something, anything to help.

Heat sizzled through my veins, my tattoos flickering for half a heartbeat. A spark appeared at my fingertips before abruptly dying out again.

Son of a —

I tried again, and again, my desperation climbing as I stood by and watched Celani fight the wraiths.

When her isos wore off, they crashed back against the ground, their rage and desperation fueling their movements as they charged her.

"Get. Out. Of. Here," she shouted again, blocking another strike.

Green eyes locked on mine, and panic rose in my chest. Celani focused her attention on that wraith, distracting it so I could escape. So I could run away like a coward.

Logically, there was nothing I could do to help, no isos I could call on. I suddenly hated myself for that, for not trying harder to find a way to access my only real means of defense. Now that it could mean the difference in whether Celani and I lived or died, I could do nothing.

I couldn't just abandon her, but I didn't want to distract her either. I backed away, trying to see if there was any clear path to hurl my dagger.

Only a few feet from the steps, a dark cloud blinked to life in front of me. Another wraith appeared out of nowhere, baring its teeth as it blocked my only means of escape.

I tumbled to the ground, quickly pivoting to regain my footing before trying to sprint away.

Blinding pain clouded my vision as the wraith slashed at my back, knocking me down once more. A scream wrenched its way out of my throat.

I turned around just as the wraith lunged again. I watched as its mouth swung open, its teeth clamping down on my forearm. An eerie growl rumbled from its chest as its rotting teeth dug into my flesh.

Panic clawed its way through my chest, choking out every rational thought. I plunged my dagger into his side, kicking and trying to claw my way free of the monster hovering over me.

Small clouds of green smoke sprang to life wherever I landed a blow, something I could only imagine was this creature's blood. But it wasn't enough to stop him. Or slow him down.

I was getting nowhere. My final dagger was virtually useless, and the wraith quickly knocked it away. The monster pinned me to the ground, its teeth sinking further into my flesh as a growl tore from its throat.

This was it.

This was how I died.

I closed my eyes briefly, offering up another silent prayer, this time that my death would come quickly and that Celani would escape. That this pain would end.

When I opened my eyes again, it was to a bright flash of orange light. Heat seared into my left side as a ball of fire soared toward us.

The wraith hissed and screamed when the light connected with its arm, its jaw relaxing long enough to let me go.

I scrambled away, holding my bloodied arm to my chest, watching in awe as the fireball swarmed around the wraith with a vengeance. The flames licked at the monster's head and torso and legs, setting fire to each place it touched.

The wraith stumbled back on the steps of the temple, growling as the ball of fire rained down on it with a relentless fury. Finally, the nightmarish creature disappeared in a hiss of green smoke.

I crawled backward, turning in the direction where I knew Celani was still fighting. Her movements were slower than before, her strength visibly flagging as she fought two of the three wraiths. Blood stained her silver hair crimson and dripped down over dark-brown skin and violet eyes.

I cried out a warning as one of them moved behind her, its claws wrapping around her arm as she raised her spear high into the air. The beast squeezed and wrenched her closer, its jaws snapping right in front of her face.

She let out a cry as her weapon fell from her grip. Before it could hit the ground, she bent her knees, her feet kicking the wraith in the chest as she tried to get away.

Then the spear struck the ground, and that frequency sounded again, sending a loud ringing through the air that forced the wraith to stumble back, dropping the general in its confusion.

Half running, half limping, I made my way toward her. I didn't know what I was doing, but I couldn't stand by and watch her die.

The fireball appeared at my side again, pausing mid-flight to look at me. There was something curious in its gaze, as if it were asking a question. Maybe I was crazy, or maybe it was my desperation speaking, but I found myself begging the damned thing.

"Please," I said, my voice hoarse. "Help her."

Two amber eyes blinked within the flames before it darted forward, swirling around the wraiths long enough for Celani to grab her weapon again.

Judging by the way her eyes widened in horror, she wasn't nearly as relieved by the flame's arrival as I had been, but she took advantage of the distraction, fighting alongside the fireball to defeat the monsters.

Celani twisted in the air, bringing her spear straight down through the middle of one of the wraiths. Its scream shook the earth before it disappeared into a green mist just as the other one had.

Then another sound pierced the air, reminiscent of a bird's screech. The final wraith had somehow grabbed the fireball, choking the flames from the creature even as it scorched and burned the wraith's dark, shadowy flesh.

Celani panted, her shoulders rising and falling as she took one final swing toward the wraith. Before her spear could make contact, the creature turned toward me, narrowing its beady green eyes in my direction and disappearing in a cloud of smoke.

The small mass of fire fell to the ground, its flames snuffing out with a hiss to reveal gold and white spotted wings. One of them was bent at an odd angle, bright red blood staining its feathers.

I raced forward as Celani stumbled to her knees next to it,

barely reaching her side before I did the same. The animal turned its head toward me, a pitiful caw escaping its beak, and I didn't hesitate before reaching out to help it.

"Get away from that thing," Celani barked, her words laden with pain and panic.

She tried reaching for me, but I moved just out of her grasp, something about the animal calling to me.

"It's just as dangerous as the wraiths," she panted, wiping the caked blood from her brow.

"No, it just saved our lives!"

There was nothing ferocious about the animal, especially without the flames surrounding it. With the round face and beak of an owl, four legs and paws like a cat, and the tail of a lion, it was like some sort of little magical fire griffin.

It had saved us, and now it was hurt. Badly.

"Ember," Celani hissed my name in warning, using her spear to help her stand. "They kill for sport. We are lucky that the wraith took it out before it could turn on us."

She raised her weapon, pointing the steel tip toward the defenseless animal. Something primal reared up inside of me, and I moved between her and the bird, but I stumbled.

My vision swam for a moment before I blinked it away. Now that my adrenaline was crashing, exhaustion must be setting in.

Before Celani could stop me, I leaned forward, my arm seizing in pain as I scooped up the little fire griffin, cradling it to my chest.

"It's not hurting anyone in this condition, and I'm not

leaving it here to become prey to any more of those..." I stopped as my vision swam. "Monsters," I choked out.

Nausea pooled in my stomach, twisting my insides into knots. My legs gave out, and I lurched to the side. Celani caught me by my injured arm, causing pain to explode along the limb like my veins were on fire.

"By the Goddess!" she gasped, her gaze finally locking on to the bite mark. "We have to get you out of here."

There was no more arguing after that, and no more attempts to make me leave our fiery savior behind. There was only her urgency and an odd feeling of familiarity as she threw my injured body over Misti's back to fly us both back to Fengari.

Guess she wound up cozying up to me on a baztet after all.

Chapter Eighteen

I BARELY REGISTERED MISTI'S ROUGH LANDING, OR Comet's growl as he flew in right behind us, or even Celani's desperation as she called for the soldiers to come help us.

A whimper sounded in my arms, followed by a soft purr, and I remembered the little flame griffin. With what little strength I had left, I pulled the creature closer to me, burying my face in its feathers as I tried to focus on anything but the pain.

My breaths were shallow, and a foul taste coated my tongue. I shivered as rough hands lifted me from Misti's back, pulling me from the saddle. My bones rattled at the impact of my feet against the stone bricks, and pain seared up my spine.

I glared at the soldier, noting the scar that ran from his indigo eyebrow down to the dimple in his chin. His expression almost looked apologetic as he helped me find my balance again.

At least until the creature in my arms let out a caw. Then

he was skittering backward, cursing under his breath. Several other voices followed suit, each silver-cloaked elf around us practically tripping over their own feet to get away from me.

I heard Celani's voice and tried to focus on her words, only making out a few of them before my thoughts slipped away again, following a glowing green thread to the darkest corners of my mind.

I fought against the tide. I didn't want to go there. Not back to the wraiths and the smell of death.

Shaking my head, I forced my focus back on the conversations around me. Anxious voices muttered incoherent words, but the panic and anger I heard were enough to glean what they were talking about. The wraiths...

Another wave of agony lanced through my arm, my vision swimming. My knees wobbled just as a roar ripped through the courtyard, its force practically shaking the ground beneath my feet. Or maybe that was my precarious balance.

I teetered sideways, the world turning on its side. Black shadows appeared, supporting me just before I hit the ground.

Another voice registered, deeper this time, and closer. I blinked as strong hands pulled me into a warm chest, solid arms cradling me like I was something delicate — the touch a stark contrast to the angry voice that boomed through the courtyard.

It was dark, but I could swear a concerned face stared down into mine, familiar in its intensity and starlit gaze.

I blinked and it was gone.

Maybe I imagined it. Maybe I was already dreaming.

Hadeon would never look at me like that. I didn't want him to.

Exhaustion settled into my bones, and the pain in my arm and back faded to a dull ache.

"Are you injured?" the voice rumbled from Hadeon's broad chest, but the question wasn't directed at me.

It was Celani who answered.

"Minor contusions," she said. "My armor kept their teeth away from me."

There was a long pause, or maybe I drifted off to sleep again, only waking at the deep voice closest to me.

"I told you it was dangerous," Hadeon hissed, his angry words a contradiction to the gentle way he held mean and the way his shadows traced a delicate line down my face, tucking a strand of hair behind my ear.

"It was supposed to be clear. Xanth reported just this morning—"

Another growl tore through the room, and the pain in my arm intensified. Heat swelled in my arms and against my stomach, comforting before it began to burn.

There was more shouting, accompanied by hurried movements and the sound of footsteps running through hallways.

Images of the wraiths filled my mind, gnashing and clawing and tearing through my memories. I wasn't sure when I started trembling, but soon I was convulsing. The heat disappeared from my arms, and all coherent thought fled me.

All I saw were rippling specters, jagged edges of broken teeth and the cries of a thousand dying soldiers.

And then there was nothing but darkness.

I SLIPPED in and out of consciousness, of dreams — or a tangle of memories — belonging to both Phaedra and me, though it became increasingly difficult to differentiate between them. Strong hands lifted my head, replacing the damp pillow beneath my neck. Soft caresses smoothed hair away from my face, and a low, familiar voice muttered vicious curses, though his tone was laced with concern.

Pain radiated throughout my body, coursing through my veins like acid, eating away at my bones. I could smell the rancid decay of the wraith's breath, feel the acrid heat against my face and down my back.

A cool cloth dabbed my forehead, down my chest, and over wounds that were too hot. Too sticky and putrid.

My skin hurt at the slightest touch, and I would both sweat and shiver at the same time. It reminded me of being a child at home with chicken pox, my mother's cool hands applying calamine lotion. The memory mixed with one of a different virus, a sick, restless boy in bed next to me, and a woman singing calming lullabies to us both.

I had no control over where my mind went, or when, or whose life I was remembering or if it was nothing more than my imagination at this point.

I heard Phaedra's name whispered in the dark. There was a desperation in the baritone. Desperation and something far more primal.

Then I heard *my* name, again and again, like an echo in a music hall or in a dark cavern.

Ember.

Ember.

You are not doing this. Not again.

Pain ricocheted through me. The hurt and misery raked its way through my bones as I grieved everyone all over again. It was too real. Too much.

Then the images shifted. It was warmer, brighter. I saw Phaedra's reflection in a gilded mirror. Watched as she traced the lines of a shadowy collar around her neck, smirking up at a man in challenge.

Celani's voice pulled me in a different direction. Her tone was chiding, and she laughed as Phaedra winced under a steady needle inking the skin on her hands. *For a royal, you're handling this with very little grace. Toughen up, princess.*

I saw her parents. Her brothers. I heard the laughter of her friends and saw her mourn them as they were slaughtered on a blood-stained battlefield.

I saw crimson-colored mountains and golden sunsets. I felt her anger, her fear as she stood face to face with the king of her enemies. Saw the way she fractured under his touch. The way she fought him. The pleasure she drew from him.

Forever is a long time to bargain with. Hadeon whispered the words against her lips. I tried to cling to that memory in particular before it danced just out of reach.

I felt it all. For hours or days, my mind raced through a thousand lifetimes, floating in and out of dreams and distorted memories like some cruel biography playing out in my mind on a never-ending loop.

Strong arms wrapped around my frame, pulling me into the crook of theirs, molding me to the shape of them.

There was searing heat, flames that raged around the room. Phaedra's power? Mine? Another cry of pain, the hiss of water, and the smell of smoke.

Smooth fingers traced the curve of my cheek. A gentle but bitter laugh. The soft, lyrical whine of a dog just before an all too familiar pain spasmed, dragging me back into the darkness all over again.

MY EYES BURNED, and my mouth was dry.

It took several tries to clear my vision, and several more to make sense of my surroundings. The room was dark, shafts of light from the golden and silver moons streaming in through the long windows.

My blurry vision tried to make out the shapes on the ceiling, the stars that danced there. Not stars, I realized after a moment, but candlelight.

I tried to swallow, but my throat was full of sand, or maybe shards of glass. It scratched and burned until I managed a cough. There was a blur of movement to my left, followed by a whisper of sound before a glass of water appeared in front of me.

"Drink, Feralinia." Hadeon's voice was quiet as he held out the glass.

I blinked again.

The dark, swirling shape hovering above me wouldn't come into focus.

My lips parted, a harsh breath wheezing past them as I inhaled. I tried to sit up but my body was leaden. I needed to be upright, but the words refused to form. Somehow, Hadeon understood anyway. He set the glass back down on the nightstand, leaning forward on his chair next to the bed.

Shadows swam in the air around us, and pillows floated toward me. Hadeon used them to pull me closer as he gently stacked the pillows behind my back and beneath my arms, his moonlit gaze fixed on mine, carefully searching for...something.

There was something different about him. Something less guarded, less formal, less *something*.

I scanned the sharp lines of his face, the set of his jaw, his fathomless midnight eyes. Then I realized his usually perfect hair was wavier, like he'd been running his hands through it, which was only possible because, for a change, there was no thorny crown winding around his brow.

Without it he looked...not softer, necessarily, but younger maybe. More approachable.

As soon as the pillows were in place, Hadeon gently rested me against them before quickly removing his hands. He brought the cup back in front of me, holding it to my lips and reissuing his command.

"Drink."

I took a slow sip, carefully letting the water skate across the veritable desert that was my mouth. Once I'd had my fill, he removed the cup.

"I lost my daggers," I said through chapped lips.

I wasn't sure why that was the first thing that came to mind, but it felt important to my muddled brain. A muscle ticked in Hadeon's jaw, and he dipped his head in a subtle nod.

"I'll get you better ones."

Something in me rebelled at that, but I didn't want to look too closely at why.

I averted my gaze, unsure of what my expression revealed to him, and even less certain I wanted to read into his. Slowly, the rest of the room came into a hazy sort of focus, and my lips parted.

It took me a moment to register what was wrong. The ceiling mural was different from the one above my bed, the blankets several shades darker.

Blinking again, I turned my head slowly to take in the massive space.

Nyx slept in the corner on a bed obviously made for her. A balcony wrapped around three walls to reveal an endless expanse of stars, and there were gilded beams on the ceiling, looping around white marble pillars that stretched down to the floor. Candles floated in the air, casting faint golden light on the elegant alabaster furniture and the midnight curtains.

This was not my room, but I recognized it all the same. I knew that to my left was a door leading to another glorious bathroom with moonflowers and star lilies growing on vines along the wall. I knew the heady scent of the oils and soaps that were stored there as well.

Somewhere in the long-forgotten part of my consciousness, I knew this room better than I knew my own. Better than I knew my apartment back on Earth. Better than any other place I had ever been.

And I knew it belonged to Hadeon.

Chapter Nineteen

THE NEXT TIME I WOKE, I FELT FAR MORE LUCID. Hadeon sat in a chair by the fire, staring into the flames. There were also three giant heads weighing down the bed next to me, and three sets of eyes looking irritably at...

"You let him stay," I said, examining the sleeping fire creature that seemed to be the cause of Nyx's ire.

Hadeon narrowed his eyes, a muscle working in his jaw, but when he spoke, he sounded bored.

"Yes, well, what's one more feral creature in my castle?"

Nyx growled, and Hadeon shook his head. "I wasn't referring to you."

She didn't look mollified as she let out a gust of air, a small growl escaping with it.

"Besides," he sighed as he turned back to me, "I couldn't very well get rid of your namesake."

My head was still fuzzy from sleep and stupidly, I asked, "It's called an ember?"

Hadeon looked far too satisfied. "A feraline."

Of course it was.

I tried to shake off the rest of my sleepy haze long enough to glare at him, but with lucidity came the memories of the wraith attack. I sat up with a start, regretting it when my wounds pulled.

Hadeon's shadows raced over to gingerly push me back to the pillows, pressing against my shoulders.

"Celani?" I remembered her saying she only had minor contusions, but I wasn't sure how much of the conversation I could trust.

"Is fine. Her armor protected against the malice — the infection that the wraiths leave behind," he clarified. "So it was just a few minor injuries she had to heal from."

Remorse flitted through his midnight gaze, gone just as quickly as it came. "They weren't supposed to be there."

It was probably as close to an apology as he ever came.

"I know."

He narrowed his eyes, and I remembered that I only knew that because of my eavesdropping. I opened my mouth to lie and tell him Celani mentioned it, but he was already shooting a sideways glance at Nyx.

She scooted closer, like she was planning on hiding all seven hundred pounds of herself behind me to avoid his disappointment. I couldn't help but smile, and Hadeon looked away like the sight of me happy bothered him.

Silence fell, heavy and unwieldy. The reality of our situation set in, the extreme awkwardness of being in his room — in his bed.

"Why am I here?"

"There isn't a cure for the malice that spreads from the wraiths, but I can siphon it with my shadows. It takes time, proximity, and it's a process that has to be repeated several times to be effective."

That explained why we were in the same room, but not why I was in his. He could have come to mine, or there were guest rooms. I doubted it was for his comfort, seeing him sitting stiffly in the chair.

Still, I wasn't sure how exactly to respond to that, how to tell the shadow king, *I still hate you for taking me captive, but thank you for saving my life, even if you had an ulterior motive.*

"But why am I *here*?" I pressed, feeling singularly inarticulate in my exhaustion.

"My isos is strongest here," he said, gesturing vaguely to the high, open balcony that flung shadows all around the room. It must have faced the same direction as mine — I could see the same constellation framed perfectly by the arches of the doorway.

Again, I felt the sharp pull of recognition, even stronger than before. I was intimately familiar with this room, and I couldn't see him allowing someone he was...*casual* with into his private space.

"Was Phaedra injured often by the wraiths?" I asked.

Though part of me genuinely wanted to know, I was at least half baiting him, curious what he would let slip about how much time I had spent in his room and why.

He met my stare for a long moment. Each particle of air between us was charged like a thousand bolts of lightning. The corner of his lips pulled up into a knowing leer that had my mouth going dry.

"Not particularly," he purred. "Why do you ask, Feralinia?"

The bastard was playing games, which I realized was hypocritical of me to be upset about when I was doing the same. I matched his smirk with one of my own.

"No reason. Just curious. And tonight?" I asked, more tentatively.

His Adam's apple bobbed, but his expression was neutral.

"As I said, proximity and repetition." He sounded almost offensively unhappy about said proximity.

All right, then.

Silence stretched between us again, with only the soft purrs of the feraline to break it. For several stilted moments, I tried not to stare at Hadeon, or notice the casual way he tucked his long hair behind his pointed ear, exposing the multiple piercings there.

When his gaze caught mine, my pulse spiked, and I quickly glanced behind him at the open balcony instead.

Another awkward moment passed before the even more embarrassing interruption of my stomach growling. Heat rose to my cheeks.

If I expected Hadeon to say something placating about how long I'd been asleep or offer me the out of healing working up an appetite, I would have been disappointed. He did neither.

Fortunately for us both, I always expected him to display

varying degrees of douchery and was therefore not disappointed when his grin only widened.

I cast about for a change of subject and abruptly remembered Abba's message for him, wherein she essentially called him a stubborn ass. He had made his dislike for all things pious evident, so I watched him carefully as I broached the subject.

"Abba sent a message for you."

He went still, as I suspected he would. "Did she? What did the great, omniscient priestess want me to know that she couldn't tell me herself?"

I knit my brow, belatedly wondering why she hadn't come herself. Surely she didn't think he would listen more if it came from his enemy.

"She said, 'Tell the shadow king that he will not prevail if he allows old grievances to rob him of his faith in that which he knows to be true.'"

A muscle clenched in his pale, chiseled jaw. "I see she is as helpful as ever."

Though his response was flippant, I got the feeling he knew exactly what she was referring to. Before I could work up the nerve to prod him about it, though, my stomach growled again. Quieter this time, but no less mortifying.

"Is it nearly breakfast?" I asked, my desire for food outweighing my stubbornness at playing into his satisfaction.

"Dinner, actually."

He said nothing else, and I gritted my teeth, preparing myself to ask if he planned on providing said dinner when the door pushed open and a servant came in, carrying a silver tureen.

The elf gave the feraline an even wider berth than he gave Nyx. I almost felt sorry for him until he shot me a disapproving look, probably for being in his precious king's bed.

I gave him a wide, false smile, and settled against the silky black pillows, leaning into the comfort I felt in this space rather than shying away from it long enough to irritate the servant.

Hadeon's expression didn't change, but his eyes did shift with what I could have sworn was amusement.

I tried not to notice the way it lit up his face, or the swooping feeling inside of me at the sight. I tried not to notice anything at all.

And I failed, quite admirably.

ONCE I WAS FINISHED EATING, Hadeon directed me to his bathroom, watching my steps carefully to be sure I wasn't going to keel over. I was determined to put on a brave face for the trek, not wanting to lose that bit of independence or privacy.

I braced myself as my legs wobbled and my vision blurred. It was only slightly disorienting to walk again after being in bed for so long, but I tried not to let Hadeon see that as I crossed the distance from the bed to the dreamy bathroom.

It wasn't much closer than mine, but he didn't seem to

want me away from where his isos worked the strongest. If I was being very honest, I wasn't sure I wanted to go either.

It was safe here. Secure.

Whatever his reasons, whatever our convoluted history, I knew Hadeon would work to keep me alive. For all the crap I had given him about not caring one way or another if I lived or died, I knew now how much bluster had been in those threats.

My recent brush with death left me on edge, more than I would have expected, like the part of my soul that remembered dying the first time was even more terrified to go back there. To leave this world again, to plunge into...nothingness, or wherever Phaedra had waited in the years before I was born.

So I didn't complain as I helped myself to Hadeon's rather glorious shower. Where I had my epic bathtub, he had a shower big enough for at least ten people, open to the stars and with a steaming waterfall.

Another familiar tree grew in the corner, its branches arching up through the water as it cascaded over delicate white and blue flowers. It added a sweet floral note to the shower, their oils softening my skin and hair as I stood beneath them.

I was too weak to stand long enough to fully enjoy it, but I at least got to wash the grime and dried sweat and blood from my skin, and wash my hair with soap that smelled more familiar than I wanted it to.

There was a towel already laid out on a stone bench in the dry corner of the room, along with a fresh nightgown.

Finally, when I was dried and dressed, I shuffled back to the bed. Hadeon was lying on one side of the generous mattress, but I couldn't honestly stop to care when I was less than two steps from collapsing.

"Will you never learn your limits?" he growled.

"Eff all of the way off," I muttered back, sinking against the smooth pillows of what I now could feel was a freshly made bed.

I couldn't help the small contented sigh that escaped me. I was so tired, and it was so comfortable. Besides, it smelled nice, familiar, like home. A small distraction from the pain from my arm and back.

"Are they what you want me to fight, then?" I asked after a moment, trying to imagine going up against the wraiths again. To imagine a scenario where I would be strong enough to fight them.

Hadeon scoffed. "No. You will be providing light to intensify my shadows so that *I* can fight. While you are on a baztet, high in the sky and far away from them."

The part of me that remembered being a warrior wanted to protest, but the part that was lying in bed injured after unsuccessfully attempting to fight off a wraith couldn't argue.

I opened my mouth to respond when white-hot pain lanced through my back, stealing my breath and stilling my tongue. It raked over my bones with sharp talons. For a moment, I wondered if my skin was splitting open, if there was acid slowly devouring me.

Hadeon leaned forward, his long, navy hair spilling onto my face as he studied me. "Where does it hurt?"

"My back," I gasped. "Burns."

I swallowed down bile and gritted my teeth. My breaths

were strained and when I closed my eyes, all I saw were green toxic clouds and blackened teeth.

He nodded sharply before his shadows washed over me and into me, like a cooling bucket of water. The room went black, but I wasn't afraid of this darkness. It was comfortable. Soothing. At least, until they started tugging deep inside me, like a scalpel digging into an infected wound.

"Breathe, Feralinia," Hadeon instructed firmly.

So I did, one hitching, stilted inhalation at a time, until the pain finally subsided.

Green curls of smoke stretched out from my body, dissipating into the protective shadows. I watched as Hadeon's isos smothered what I assumed was the malice he'd mentioned before.

When he was finished, his shadows lifted and I could see the rest of the room, including Hadeon's expression. For a fraction of a moment, something akin to dread was etched across his features.

Then it was gone, replaced with his usual arrogant air.

"The malice?"

He nodded once, his shadows slinking back into his skin, returning to the dark tattoos along his shoulders and collarbones. "It will be a few days before it's out of your system."

He settled back against the pillows, and I couldn't suppress my shock when he held his arm out in an unmistakable invitation.

"You'll heal faster," he said simply, though I noticed he looked up at the gilded ceiling rather than at me.

I wanted to believe that I was desperate to get better or

that I was in too much pain from my injury to care, but if I was desperate for anything, it was the feeling of being nestled safely against the muscular chest that looked far more inviting than it should.

It was all the more reason to say no. I knew that. Stockholm syndrome or Phaedra's memories were taking hold of me, I told myself. It was easier than admitting that the glimpses I got underneath Hadeon's mask were more than just intriguing. They were intoxicating.

So with all the lies I couldn't tell myself right on the tip of my tongue, I slid across the silky sheets and into his arms.

Maybe I would have been okay if it had only been companionable, or rife with sexual tension, or any of another thousand shallower emotions. If I hadn't fit perfectly under his arm. If his mountain scent didn't overwhelm my senses and tug at a visceral response that didn't feel like it was from any lifetime but this one.

As it was, tears stabbed the backs of my eyes. I took a shallow breath, trying not to inhale his scent, but still calm myself.

His arm pulled closer around me in what was surely just a coincidence, and somehow between one ragged breath and another, I managed to sink into sleep.

But it was neither peaceful, nor dreamless.

Chapter Twenty

Two more days passed wherein I mostly stayed in Hadeon's bed, which made a total of eight days since the attack. Eight days that I had spent sleeping next to my... enemy? Captor?

The lines were becoming more blurred by the day, but I knew I was in trouble when he casually announced he was going out for the day and my heart skipped a beat in my chest.

No.

I was not allowed to start using the untouchable, condescending king who held nothing but secrets and sarcasm as some kind of prickly security blanket.

"All right," I said, ignoring the small bit of panic that rose in my chest.

He examined my face before gesturing to a box the servants had just brought in.

Moonlight reflected off of the midnight lid, highlighting the faint dusting of silver embedded in the smooth material.

I carefully removed the lid, my fingers frozen as my eyes raced over a stack of blank paper stained caramel with age, pots of ink with different-colored lids, and multiple quills.

Some had metal nibs like the one I'd tried to use as a weapon. Others appeared to just be feathers from various birds. Or baztets... I lifted the gleaming black feather with silver strands, holding it under the candlelight.

Underneath the others, though, was something even more familiar to me. Several sharpened sticks of charcoal.

When I met Hadeon's gaze again, his expression was decidedly closed off.

"I thought you might need something to keep yourself busy, lest you and that feraline of yours destroy my room." It was a lame excuse, but I didn't call him on it. Not when my hands were itching to sketch the skyline and the gilded arches of Hadeon's balcony framing the golden constellation.

"Wise man," I said by way of thanks, keeping my own expression neutral and my tone flat.

My heartbeat still hadn't slowed, but at least there was excitement along with the edge of anxiety now.

"Nyx will stay here as well," Hadeon said, like he knew exactly what worries were plaguing me.

I frowned, darting a glance between them. The canine usually jumped at the chance to follow him around, but she didn't even look tempted. Her three heads were splayed out on her bed over her giant paws, her ears standing at attention as she watched our back and forth.

"Why isn't she going with you?" I asked.

Hadeon said nothing, his moonlit gaze meeting mine

briefly in a way that was answer enough. It clicked then. How she had insisted on following us to the training grounds. How she had slept in the hallway just outside of my door.

That first day, she had leapt at the chance to kill Merikh, not because he threatened Hadeon, but because he had hurt *me*.

It hadn't been an order from Hadeon, but his permission that sent her leaping forward to devour him.

I thought back to Phaedra's memory of swampland and a small, injured puppy with three heads and the most beautiful bright gray eyes. Celani's words came back to my mind, telling me that I had a pet.

"She's not your cerberus, is she?"

His Adam's apple bobbed once before he shook his head. "No, she's not."

"She's mine," I said, looking into three sets of puppy eyes.

Nyx's tail wagged, and she stretched and came to rest her heads on the corner of the bed. I tentatively reached out a hand and rested it against her fur. Her eyes flitted closed and she let out a low whine.

"I think she prefers to believe that you are hers," Hadeon countered quietly.

I looked up at him, more questions than answers after his revelation.

Like why he had kept my dog for fifty years when he claimed to hate me. Why nothing between us felt as simple as hatred or lust, or captives and captors.

Why every single dream I had was invaded by his perfect, scowling face.

Nyx whined and pressed harder against me as if she sensed my turmoil, and I broke whatever silent staring contest Hadeon and I were having.

He left without another word.

NYX LOOKED up at me once Hadeon was gone. For the first time since I met the cerberus, I recognized some of the emotion in their depths.

The way she looked at me with pure adoration in her eyes, the way she always hovered close by, like she was waiting for me to acknowledge her, all the while treating everyone else like they were some disposable snack... All the signs had been there.

I ran my fingers along the ice-colored markings on her fur, tracing the whorls and lines until the pattern felt all too familiar and memories tugged at my mind.

A much smaller Nyx curled up in my lap, even though she weighed nearly as much as I did, as I rubbed a salve on an injured ear. Her left head nuzzled into my chest, the middle one tucking under my arm as if she could disappear inside of me.

Hadeon's deep voice muttering something about his castle being overrun with wild things while I pointedly ignored him.

I saw glimpses of memories where Nyx used her ability to open portals between moonbeams to allow me to eavesdrop.

The way she followed me everywhere. Even straight into battle. The moment I left her behind.

Swallowing, I pushed that last memory away, unwilling to follow it any further tonight. Not when the wraiths were still so fresh on my mind.

Instead, I lay my head against Nyx, breathing her in while I allowed her steady pulse to calm my own. She smelled like a campfire on a snowy night, and it helped banish some of the terror threatening to edge in.

After a moment, the air felt clearer, the images of wraiths faded, and I slowly felt safer in my skin.

Finally, I looked down at the small box on the bed, deciding to give my mind an outlet. I hadn't drawn anything since that day in my room where I inked every memory of my life on Earth onto paper.

I took the box of art supplies out to the balcony. Then, I glanced between the cerberus and the wall that separated Hadeon's room from mine.

"Do you mind?" I asked, gesturing to show her what I wanted.

If cerberuses could smile, I would swear that's what she did. All three of her mouths popped open, her soft cheeks pulling up at the corners revealing rows of glimmering teeth.

Suddenly her eyes morphed from gray to a glowing silver as she opened a portal to my room.

I stepped through to grab my phone and earbuds, willing to sacrifice the slowly fading battery for a little music.

After popping in the earbuds, I turned on my phone and hit play and "Villain" by *NEONI* came on.

Nyx and I made our way to the balcony, and I chose a spot on the smooth stone floor to sit. Nyx laid right behind me. She leaned her back up against mine and kept guard over the room — mostly over the feraline, who she watched with sharp eyes.

Her hatred of the fire griffin made more sense in light of our history — or jealousy, more accurately.

For his part, the owl-cat-baby-fire-griffin prowled the balustrade, completely uninterested in the cerberus. Though the tip of his tail ignited every so often when I paid too much attention to Nyx instead of him.

He was still injured, but over the past couple of days he had allowed me to give him tinctures and treats while Hadeon used shadows to wrap his wing. The king was the only choice after the feraline had set fire to one of the maids and singed Celani's hair when either tried to help.

At least Hadeon could snuff out the flames before they did too much damage, much to the creature's unending irritation. I was beginning to see what Celani had said before, that they were vicious creatures as well as opportunists.

The feraline would wait for the perfect moment to burn someone when they were least expecting it. He lulled them into a false sense of security before going up in flames to scare the living hell out of whatever unsuspecting soul was nearby.

Well, everyone but me.

Since bringing him home, he had been oddly attached to me, intent on dampening his flames when I risked petting him. It shouldn't have made me like him, knowing that I was the only one he tolerated, but I would be a liar if I said it didn't endear me to him more.

Once he found a suitable place to perch on the railing, he began preening his feathers, casting periodic judgmental glares at Nyx's proximity to me.

I couldn't help but be amused at their little feud, just like any territorial cat and dog back on Earth. Only, you know, magical and deadlier.

Leaning more into the cerberus, I picked up my charcoal and began sketching the creatures until my fingers were stained black and images were slowly coming to life on the parchment.

Soon the first page was filled with small details, the feraline's speckled feathers, his pointed ears and long flaming tail. Nyx's large eyes, the gentle slope of her middle snout, the details of the runes that covered her right head, and the delicate, scarred ridges of the ears on her left head.

Then my sketches drifted skyward, the way they always seemed to, and I began drawing the golden constellation that hovered just outside of the palace, the same design that was etched into my farthest memories and was the basis for every tattoo I had ever designed.

I was so focused on the smallest details, my fingers aching as I traced and sketched, that I didn't notice when Nyx stiffened behind me, or register the sound of Celani's footsteps over the music blaring through my headphones.

I startled, the charcoal breaking in half as I pressed it too firmly against the paper when she stepped into view.

"Interesting subject matter," she remarked, leaning against the giant pillar to my right. Or at least I assumed that's what she said as I read her lips.

"Knock much?" I griped, and she laughed.

I quickly removed my earbuds, shutting both them and my phone down to conserve as much of the battery as possible.

"I did knock," Celani answered, crossing her arms. "You just didn't hear me, and your guard here clearly didn't care if I was a wraith."

Nyx growled in response, and the general took a step back.

"Apologies," she said, holding her hands up in surrender. "I was teasing, but I can see that's not appreciated right now."

Nyx let out three indignant huffs of air, and I shot Celani a smug grin.

"How are you feeling?" she asked after a moment. She stared down at my arm, her violet eyes softening as she took in the array of tooth-shaped scars.

"It's fine," I said, shrugging. I ignored the way the movement tugged at the tender skin. "It's better than it was, for sure."

I had taken the bandages off this morning to allow the skin to breathe. The bite marks were healing, but they still looked fairly disgusting. The wraith's jagged teeth had torn through the tattoo of a comet soaring past the same constellation that lit up the sky just behind her.

"What's it called?" I finally asked, in an attempt to change the subject. I gestured toward the golden stars.

I didn't want to dwell on that day, or the days since where Hadeon had poured every ounce of his energy into pulling out the malice that the wraith had infected me with. Fortunately, Celani was wonderfully insightful, and didn't press me.

Instead, she pursed her lips, her gaze darting from me up

to the sky. "That is Ahvi," she said evenly. "It's a relatively new constellation. Only appeared within the past century."

That didn't sound possible, but I didn't question it. Nothing about this place should be possible, and yet...

"Does it mean anything?" I asked, watching as the largest star in the center flared to life, shining brighter as if it knew we were talking about it.

"In the ancient lunar dialect, it means something like 'incandescent sun'—" Celani began before the feraline cut her off with a loud caw.

It seemed he had only just noticed her presence, or only just decided to care. Either way, his tail was igniting as he stalked forward.

The rest of his body lit up, flames threatening to burst to life along his feathers as he stared her down.

She backed away immediately, and I couldn't help but laugh at the mighty general being afraid of such a small creature.

"Ahvi." I said the word more to myself than anyone else, but the feraline halted his movements, pausing to nibble at the fur on his paws. I considered the meaning of the word as I studied him for another long moment. "I think it suits him, don't you?"

Celani rolled her eyes, her tone full of exasperation as she slid down next to me on the floor.

"Of course, you've decided to name him," she said before letting out a small bark of laughter. "But yes, it's fitting. Promise me I can be here when you tell Hadeon."

I ignored the way his name twisted something inside of me

but once again, Celani didn't press me on it. Instead, she chose that exact moment to ring for an early dinner to be sent up.

Things between us were easy, comfortable. And not only because of her history with Phaedra, but because it felt like she understood me, Ember, and respected me as someone separate from her old friend.

Dinner arrived on more platters than the two of us could ever hope to devour, laden with meat stews, fluffy flatbreads, and roasted vegetables smothered in savory sauces.

There were desserts, too, cakes and tarts and an array of fruits covered with a sweet white cream.

Celani eagerly filled her plate, devouring her favorite foods first before demanding I do the same. We curled up in front of the fireplace, our stomachs full of desserts and wine before we even began eating anything resembling protein.

Our conversations drifted along various subjects — everything from the mundane to her letters from Kallius at the border, to her least favorite captains, to our mutual adoration of chocolate cake.

Even to why some of the paintings moved while others didn't.

"It's an isos," she explained. "There is a family of artists who can infuse isos into their paintbrushes, something that is highly sought after, as you can imagine."

I could imagine, and it had me wondering if the same isos could be infused into a tattoo machine. The idea of moving tattoos and all of the possibilities they presented distracted me for several long moments.

Everything about this felt familiar. The food, the laughter

and conversation, it all pieced something together inside of me that I hadn't allowed myself to realize was missing, and broken.

It made me miss Isa and Ivy, but for the first time in weeks, I didn't feel guilty for enjoying my time here. Not when I knew they would have loved Celani too.

Hours passed, and we had finished our second bottle of wine when I finally decided to bring the subject back around to the general's cousin.

She hadn't questioned the fact that I was staying in his room, or made any comment on our newfound alliance, and I didn't know if that had something to do with his history with Phaedra, or if it was as clear-cut as Hadeon had made it sound.

Proximity and repetition and whatnot...

"So," I began, my voice more curious than anything as I tried to downplay my eagerness for an answer. "Is this normal? To need to be so...close for someone to heal you?"

I took a sip of my wine, allowing the blue liquid to infuse me with more confidence than I felt.

"I mean, should I expect to have to bunk up with the king of the enigmatic and surly every time I'm injured?"

Celani barked another laugh and shook her head.

"Not unless you're dealing with malice. Though, it is different for you because you're—" She forced a cough, her eyes darting away from me before she continued. "Because you're from the Sun Court," she finished.

My attention snapped toward her, but hers was suddenly focused on the wine dregs in her chalice. I was sure that hadn't been what she was about to say, but I knew she would clam up if I called her on it.

Several more hours passed and eventually Celani drifted to sleep in the chair by the fire. I climbed into Hadeon's bed, but my restless mind refused to turn off and it wasn't until early morning when his shadows gathered by the door that I finally felt like I could breathe again.

I didn't speak as he stepped closer, casting his shadows over me the way he did whenever he was scanning me for more signs of malice.

"You should be sleeping, Feralinia," he said, the moonlight catching on his fair skin as he looked in my direction.

Then he turned his attention to his cousin, gently waking her up and sending her back to her own rooms to sleep.

He was quiet as he removed his cloak, tossing it on Celani's vacant chair before he crossed the distance to my nightstand. The heady scent of bergamot and snow washed over me, but it was tinged with something else, something that my mind rebelled at.

Hadeon silently placed two gleaming daggers on the polished wood, and I immediately registered the faint scent of wraiths.

My eyes flicked up to meet his, but he was already turning around, quietly announcing his need for a shower before disappearing behind the bathroom door.

My breath caught in my throat as I took in the onyx hilts and the silver blades. The ones that matched the bracers he had given me. The same ones I had lost when the wraiths attacked.

I stared at them in the dark, my mind racing as I considered what this meant. Was that where Hadeon had been all day? Did he find them while doing something else? Or had he gone to hunt them down after I said I wanted them back?

I didn't have anything resembling an answer by the time he emerged from the steaming bathroom, his long hair slick with water and a fresh pair of trousers resting low on his hips.

He climbed into the bed, tucking himself in next to me. Warmth spread from his body to mine, and it wasn't long before his breathing evened out and sleep pulled him under.

I followed shortly after, too many questions swirling in my mind, ones I wasn't sure I wanted answers to.

Chapter Twenty-One

THE NEXT DAY, KALLIUS CAME TO BREAKFAST WITH Celani. We ate on Hadeon's balcony at a small table that overlooked the shimmering lake at the base of the mountains.

It was a welcome change in routine when I was beginning to feel stir-crazy. Though I loved Celani's calm nature, and I was at least used to Hadeon's darkly protective presence paired with his sardonic humor, Kallius was a breath of fresh, chatty air.

He talked a bit about the warfront in his easygoing way, after a glance to Hadeon and the king's response of a subtle nod. Was I inner circle now that I had been injured? Or was it just glaringly apparent that I would never leave this place?

Not that Kallius revealed much, but he did tell a few amusing stories about the soldiers, things that made them all feel so much more...for lack of a better word, *human*, than the ethereal elf warriors appeared in my mind.

"Oh, and Eros requests leave for his mate journey," he threw in casually.

Hadeon tensed, then nodded. "Granted."

There was a slightly strained pause before Celani spoke up.

"A bit young, isn't he?" she said, taking a sip from her coffee mug.

Kallius shrugged. "But you know Eros. He's determined."

"What's a mate journey?" I asked.

Hadeon's midnight eyes fixed on Celani, who looked back with something almost like defiance before she turned to me.

"The goddess *blesses* some of us with soulmates." She stressed "blesses" like she was bracing for an argument.

Sure enough, Hadeon made a bitter sound in the back of his throat which she didn't deign to acknowledge.

"How do you know?" I asked, resting my fork on my plate. "If you have one, I mean."

Kallius darted a glance between his cousin and his sister, but she didn't seem to feel the hesitation that kept the other two elves silent.

"She puts a marking on your skin to lead you to them," Celani said evenly.

"Like a...map?" I asked, my gaze flitting to the icy blue runes on her skin. "Or a clue?"

"Of a sort," Kallius answered, gesturing casually toward the sky. "It's a constellation. And their marking will be the same pattern of stars, but the mirror image."

"It's said the brighter the constellation, the stronger the bond," Celani added.

She wasn't looking at me anymore. Instead, she appeared

lost in thought, eyes boring into the few crumbs left on her plate.

I couldn't help but wonder if the silence that fell over the table was because each of them was thinking about their soulbound, if they had one, or if they knew who their mate was yet.

Admittedly, I was more curious about one of them in particular. The one who was looking at his food with far more attention than it deserved.

"So you journey to find them?" I asked with all the nonchalance I didn't feel. "It sounds like a bit of a crapshoot."

I had no idea how following star marks worked, but surely it would lead you to a whole city full of people you would have to sift through.

"That's why it's considered a journey," Celani said. "Usually, elves wait until they're older, since it can take both time and patience. And because going too early...could be unfortunate. Having a match doesn't necessarily mean you'll be able to make a relationship work with them."

"No, but it means you'll be twice as upset when it fails," Kallius muttered in response.

She gave him a look, and he shook his head. "Sorry, sis, but you know I'm with the king on this one. It's only a blessing if it works."

"All relationships take work, but there's value in knowing someone could be perfectly compatible with you, as long as you're willing to try," she insisted.

I remained slightly hung up on the logistics of this. Or at

the very least, distracted with them. "What happens if you both leave at the same time?"

"Then you hope fate intervenes and you meet in the middle," she said.

"Or you miss each other, and you spend your entire lives miserable and empty and searching," I countered.

The words rang with an uncomfortable amount of truth, and I wished I could take them back, especially when Hadeon and Kallius both studied me.

Celani groaned, taking the attention off of me. "Not you, too!"

Kallius laughed and responded with a comment about me being on his side. They continued to banter back and forth, but I wasn't really listening.

I was busy trying to keep my eyes on breakfast, on Nyx, on anything but the familiar constellation burning in the night sky.

The one I had inked on every spare surface on my skin, as if it belonged there.

The one that shone brighter than all of the rest.

As SOON AS Hadeon left to hold court, I stripped down in front of his bathroom mirror. Painstakingly, I turned in every direction I could get to view my exposed skin.

There was nothing.

At least, not that I could see under all of my tattoos.

Peering closer, I examined the golden lines, each hidden constellation I had drawn into my skin.

From the moons and suns scattered all over, to the flowers and vines, the mountain range, and butterflies, even the individual feathers of the phoenix on my back. The Ahvi constellation was in each one, in the shape or lines or shading, so it took me studying each mark twice before I found it.

Seven stars along my collarbone, just a shade darker than the glowing, golden ink of the branch there, easily mistaken for shadows.

I leaned up against the mirror, as close as I could get, peering at each individual star to be sure I wasn't imagining it, even though I *knew*. Didn't it make sense, the way that constellation had called to me?

The way I had never been truly attracted to anyone in my human life. I thought I was just dead inside, but recent encounters disputed that theory.

I was so focused on my appraisal, stewing in the shock that wasn't quite shock, that I nearly fell off of the smooth marble sink when I heard the door shut.

"Feralinia?" Hadeon's deep voice intoned.

Damn it.

I scrambled to the floor, throwing my dress back on, then opened the door like I had been casually using the bathroom instead of scrutinizing my body for signs of a soulbond I wasn't ready to think about.

"Yes?"

"Put your shoes on. We have a meeting."

I narrowed my eyes at him. "With who?"

"You'll see."

I glared, but curiosity won out over stubbornness, and I slipped my feet into my combat boots and haphazardly tied the laces just in time for Hadeon to shadow us away.

I kept thinking I would get used to it, the way that he overwhelmed my senses every time he wrapped us both in darkness, but I never did. Even after several nights in his bed, waking up pressed against him, breathing him in, his name on my lips from one of Phaedra's memories, this particular method of travel still rattled me.

The moment I was enclosed in his shadows, my nerve endings caught fire, igniting my core. I took shallow breaths, as I always did, trying to ignore his overwhelming scent. It didn't help.

His presence itself was overwhelming.

As soon as we landed, I stepped away from him under the guise of surveying our new surroundings. The unfamiliar room was circular and covered with giant gilded frames that showcased otherworldly settings.

The images moved and for a second, I thought they were paintings made with the same isos as some of the pieces throughout the palace. Then I looked closer and realized that wasn't it at all.

They were moongates. Portals into other worlds.

I froze, taking it all in. There had to be at least thirty gates placed around the room, maybe more. I scanned them all, wondering if I would see anything familiar, anything that called to me, when light flickered to my left.

Heat radiated from a black iron frame. Four scaled

serpents devouring each other wound around the image of a dark room with an onyx throne. Torches of pure lava floated in the air, and in the center of the room was an hourglass filled with black and red sand.

I wanted to take a closer look when I realized Hadeon was standing in front of the one next to it.

It was a circular frame made of thorny vines and gilded flowers. But instead of a scene playing out in the center, there was just a faint swirling of light, like it was a video call searching for a signal.

"This is more like the window I create with my shadows, only it goes to a fixed location. You cannot move through these."

"So what are we doing here?" I asked, more than a little disappointed that this wasn't the Grand Central Station of moongate travel.

"Waiting, apparently," he responded irritably.

Finally, someone on the other side cleared their throat. "They're fetching her now."

Hope surged in my chest. Her? There was only one *her* I wanted to see.

"Ivy?" The question came out in a quiet breath.

He nodded, and my heartbeat picked up in my chest.

Was this her doing? The last time he showed her to me, he'd mentioned that she was just as unyielding and insistent as I was. That she'd been asking for me.

The creaking of a door sounded, and I couldn't help but freeze. A few words were murmured until Hadeon finally huffed.

"Is the girl finally here? For the love of Terrea, just put her in the mirror." He seemed...less than happy about this meeting.

I glanced at him, and he only shook his head, muttering the word "fae" like a curse, so low that only I could hear. Maybe he was irritated by them, but it felt like a bit more than that. His shadows flared protectively around me, like he was worried I would try to make a break for it through the moongate even though he had said I couldn't.

Or like he was worried they would take me.

Before I could think about it too much, Ivy was there. Her hair was brighter than it had been on Earth, hanging over the shoulders of what looked like a thin, lacy, golden nightgown.

Relief flooded my veins, so potent I was practically bowled over by it. My friend was alive, and she was safe. In a world where Ember was being steadily eclipsed by the ghost of a dead princess, there was one person who remembered me. I opened my mouth, but no sound escaped.

Hadeon helpfully solved that problem, speaking up in a lofty tone. "Do you not provide clothing for your pets, or does she choose to wear her sleeping garments during the day?"

That was rich, when he had left me with only a nightgown more than once, but I got the distinct feeling he was intentionally giving me a moment to gather myself. So I didn't call him on it...too much.

Shooting a weak glare at him, I finally found my voice. "Leave Ivy alone. She just likes to be comfortable."

That was true. Though her colored cheeks told me it was an accident this time, I remembered her most often in sweatpants and soft shirts. Then, because she had always brought out the joker in me, I couldn't help but add, "Not all of us like to dress like an extra from the *Lord of the Rings* every time we leave our room."

He raised an eyebrow, and I gave him a look that hopefully conveyed a desire for space to talk to my friend without him looming two inches from my back. With a tightening of his jaw, he shadowed a whole two feet away.

Show-off.

I looked back at the mirror to see a faint smile tugging at Ivy's lips, darkened by the nostalgia that brimmed in her eyes.

"Thank God you're all right," she gasped. "I've been worried ever since I realized this wasn't some prank you were playing on me. I told you and Isa that we shouldn't have gone to that party!" She rolled her eyes, then abruptly stopped. "Wait. Isa! Is she okay?"

Was she?

I swallowed hard, knots twisting my stomach.

Kallius had walked her back to her room, but knowing Ivy had been taken also, I wasn't as confident that nothing had happened to her as I wanted to be. Reluctant to launch into the entire explanation, I gave Ivy the simplest answer I could.

"As far as I know," I said sadly. "She wasn't with me."

"She must be so worried," she responded.

My stomach sank. She didn't know about the effect of coming across the portal, that all of Earth had forgotten us.

I looked at Hadeon, half hoping he would say something to contradict my understanding, to say he had only been lying to taunt me, but he only stared back as if to say it was my choice whether to tell her the truth.

And there was no choice. Not really. She deserved to know.

Squaring my shoulders, I faced Ivy.

"She doesn't remember us," I told her, shaking my head in remorse. "None of them do."

Ivy didn't have many more friends than I did, but she had liked Isa, and she had been close with Stan from the gym. So I forced myself to expound.

"Not her or Stan or anyone," I continued. "It's part of the isos — the magic — surrounding who we were."

She took that news far better than I had, only nodding stoically, though a darker emotion passed through her eyes. There was no disbelief. No accusations of lying. I felt down-right unreasonable by comparison.

Then again, my news had come from Hadeon at his peak assishness, and hers had come from a friend.

"Are you okay?" she asked.

How to answer that?

Oh, not bad for being wrenched away from my home and drowning in memories of a past life and being held captive by a stranger who isn't, quite. But I was certain she already felt the sting of at least two of those things, and I wasn't ready to touch on the third. So I put on a braver face.

"I'm okay," I told her. "Better than being dead! Are you? I've been worried."

"About the same as you." She smirked, and I knew she understood all the things I hadn't said.

It didn't alleviate my concern for her, knowing she was likely hiding any danger she was in just as surely as I was.

"Maybe soon, the two of us could visit and remember them," she suggested.

Remember them in lieu of them remembering us. It was something, at least.

Before I could respond, another voice cut in.

"Okay," a woman said as the moon-screen went black. "They got to see each other and know they're okay. Now we have High Court business to attend to."

Then the sound was gone, too. And so was Ivy.

My stomach lurched, my hands reaching for where she had just been. For the second time, I didn't get to say goodbye to my friend.

Hadeon shadowed us out without another word, and I tried not to wonder when I would ever see Ivy again.

If I would ever see her again.

Chapter Twenty-Two

THIS TIME WHEN HADEON TOLD ME WE WERE TO dine with the court, my stomach wasn't quite the bundle of nerves it had been before. I couldn't say the same for my levels of irritation.

I knew what to expect this time. There would be an endless parade of bosoms at the dining table while leering eyes or disdainful scowls were fixed on every single move I made.

Before dinner, Hadeon left to take care of some business with Kallius and Celani. He made sure to cast a pointed look at the daggers on the nightstand before fixing his glare on me.

"Make sure you wear them," he ordered before sweeping from the room.

I considered his words as I showered. I had worn them every day since he returned them to me, only bothering to remove them when I went to bed for the night.

Was there something about this dinner that had him

worried? A threat inside Fengari that he was certain I would need to arm myself against?

As soon as I emerged from the shower, I slipped the black bracers over my arms, securing the daggers before attempting to dress.

My maid came in soon after, her cautious aqua gaze flitting between Nyx and Ahvi as she took her time to style my hair and apply cosmetics.

It was clear that she approved of Nyx barely more than the feraline. Between her muttered curses and scornful glances, there was no attempt at concealing her thoughts on him being here, with me, in the bedroom of her beloved king.

Though, to be fair, I couldn't fully be sure if her "rodent of the Sun Court" comment was directed at the feraline or me.

For his part, Ahvi was becoming more docile by the day. He only really tried to set her on fire twice. The third time was more of a warning when she stepped too close to his makeshift nest. That felt like a win.

When she was satisfied with my general appearance, she moved to the armoire to pull out my gown for the evening while I deliberately did not think about how my entire wardrobe was slowly migrating to Hadeon's room.

This dress was similar to the last one I wore to a court dinner, if not a little more revealing. Delicate stitching and jewelry held together swaths of black silk that were translucent if you stood too close.

Once again, the design carefully highlighted the tattoos covering my skin, crisscrossing over my breasts down to my hips, revealing my lower stomach.

Elegant gold beading accented the waist of the dress, dripping down over my navel, while delicate chains pooled over my shoulders and linked up to the collar around my neck. The chains were connected to sheer mesh sleeves that cascaded down past my wrists, doing nothing to hide the new scar on my arm.

I supposed that didn't matter, not when word had already spread through the palace about the attack. They would all likely be looking for the mark, anyway.

When Celani arrived to escort me to the dining hall, the maid practically sprinted from the room. Ahvi was on her heels, his eyes glaring and his tail aflame.

"I see your evening has been more exciting than mine," she said with a grin.

Her hair was braided back on one side and fell in sleek waves on the other, just over her brow. Her eyes were lined with white, and the tips of her lashes looked like they were dusted with snow.

The gown she wore was similar to mine, only hers was an ice-blue color that highlighted her runes and silver hair, a striking contrast to her dark-brown skin. Instead of daggers hidden in bracers on her wrists, her exposed thigh glinted with a garter full of pristine silver blades.

When she noticed where I was looking, she cast me a rueful glance before flashing an array of various weapons on her other leg.

"We're hosting a few of the outlying captains tonight, along with their families."

There was something in her voice that told me she left a lot unsaid. Unease prickled along my spine, but I squared my shoulders.

Celani led me downstairs and into the great hall. This time there was no hiding behind Hadeon's shadows as the doors swung open. Instead, Celani linked her arm in mine, her full lips tilting up in a wide smile as she marched us forward.

A hush fell over the room like a blanket of snow, and all eyes followed us to the head of the table.

Hadeon's chair was empty. I scanned the room, searching for those familiar moonlit eyes. Kallius spoke with the odious Colonel Aereon, several familiar soldiers present nearby.

But there was no sign of the shadow king.

I told myself that the nervous twisting of my stomach wasn't because I couldn't find him, but because there were so many people in the dining hall tonight, even more than the last dinner.

That made sense. The other was stupid.

Celani's steps slowed whenever we passed a group of elves. She waited to move on until they noticed her and dipped their heads respectfully toward their general, and by extension me.

One by one, she acknowledged each soldier, never letting go of my arm. She commended their efforts in the war and was outwardly polite, but refused to leave until they also greeted me with a modicum of respect.

Servants rushed around the room, refilling wine and water goblets before setting down trays of food on the long table. They covered them with gleaming silver cloches that kept the food warm until it was time for us to eat.

When Celani and I took our seats, she made sure that I

took the one directly next to Hadeon's massive black chair at the head of the table, while she took the one at my right, just as she had last time.

Then she gestured for the servants to fill our glasses. Before I could reach for mine, she took it instead, bringing it to her lips and taking a long sip before handing it back to me.

The room halted.

If there were crickets in Aelvaria, I would have been able to hear them with no difficulty. Every set of eyes locked on to us, like she had just committed some major faux pas. Or I had, if the accusation in their glares was anything to go off of.

"What the hell was that?" I asked under my breath before taking a drink from my now less-full glass.

It wasn't that I didn't mind sharing, but the move had been intentional, somehow.

The corner of Celani's mouth tilted upward before she lifted her own glass and drank from it. She spoke from behind her chalice, as low as I had.

"A gesture of protection," she said carefully, before glancing around the still-gawking guests. Her expression was challenging as she met their gazes.

An uncomfortable laugh bubbled past my lips.

"Aren't I already under Hadeon's protection?"

"Yes." She gave me a small dip of her head, relaxing back in her chair. "But now you're under mine."

I wasn't sure why that was more impactful, and my confusion must have shown, because she expounded.

"Usually, the only person under the protection of the general is the king." Her violet eyes met mine meaningfully.

Before I could ask her what that meant exactly, or why she would make an exception for me, Hadeon's voice rang out. I slowly turned my head to find him glowering at his guests.

A shiver raced up my spine as I watched his thundercloud gaze harden on all of them. The air shifted under the weight of his anger, and the elves seemed to be bracing themselves against it.

Had something happened between the time when he left the room and now? Was that why he was late?

Or was it something else? Something that explained Celani's public display of protection and Hadeon's insistence on my arming myself with the weapons I always wore?

Whatever the cause, it was soon clear I would be waiting until dinner was over to find out.

He was in the same resplendent armor as last week, his thorny silver crown a stark contrast to the dark-blue hair that hung down past his shoulders.

"Sit." It felt more like an order than an invitation, one that his people were quick to obey.

After a week in his bed where I saw the more casual side of him, the sight of him here, now, standing before his people and wielding his commanding presence like a weapon tugged at something in my core.

My gaze homed in on the taut line of his clenched jaw, the soft curve of his bottom lip, and I was overcome with the sudden and visceral need to know what he tasted like.

Not that the thought hadn't crossed my mind more than once before, but something about him here screamed *mine*.

Which was wildly...something.

Heat rose in my cheeks, and I was grateful when he spoke his second word since entering the room, the command to eat. I didn't hesitate before taking several long swigs from my goblet, trying to think about literally anything else.

Wraiths. Bloody daggers. Jerk-faced captains and colonels. Baztets. Portals. War.

Nothing worked. And it certainly didn't help that Hadeon's shadows would flare whenever anyone deigned to speak to me as the night progressed.

Just the sight of them stopped Leda halfway through the word "princess." In another instance he used them to pull my chair closer to his as Xanth demeaned the Sun Court and their lack of support in the war against the Never Court.

And finally, when Colonel Aereon dared to look in my direction, Hadeon's shadows settled over my shoulders, possessively tucking a strand of hair behind my ear like he was claiming me.

Unlike the last dinner, he didn't make conversation. Instead, he watched each elf at his table with the careful scrutiny a hawk would offer its prey, which had the added benefit of stopping any lady elves from sticking their bits in his face.

So at least I was spared the ol' ass-in-face maneuver I was privy to during the last dinner.

When his shadows gently caressed my wrists like they were checking to make sure my daggers were in place, the pieces finally came together in my mind.

The intentionality behind Celani's presence at dinner. The way she had paraded me around the room. Hadeon's extra dose of protectiveness and the way he was staking his claim. His insistence on me wearing the daggers.

He was sending a very clear message. Too bad I wasn't sure who it was for.

ONCE WE RETURNED to Hadeon's rooms, I confronted him with my suspicions.

"You think someone sent the wraiths after me."

He surveyed me for a moment while he casually unbuckled his armor. I tracked the motion of his fingers against my better judgment, transfixed by their easy, practiced movements.

When my gaze returned to his face, he was studying me with amused eyes and a cocky smirk.

"It's not a possibility we can rule out," he said, all arrogance.

To hell with that. I might have been staring, but I sure as hell wasn't the only one who had trouble keeping my eyes off the other. Slowly, without breaking eye contact, I pulled my hair over one shoulder, turning to gesture toward the flimsy chain across my otherwise bare back.

His breath caught in his throat, a quiet hitch that nonetheless resounded in the silent space.

"Can you get this for me?' I asked, turning and looking back at him over my shoulder. "The maid isn't here yet, and I'd like to change."

He narrowed his eyes, and I gave him a wide-eyed smile that was part challenge, part feigned innocence.

"Of course," he said, his voice richer and darker than it had been before.

Just as I suspected, it was an easy, familiar motion for him to unhook the chain at my neck. But if I meant to tease him, the joke was on me, because I was the one fighting for composure when his knuckles grazed along my spine.

Heat spread from the contact, awareness prickling through my veins and overflowing into the rest of my body. Goosebumps rose along my skin, betraying the feeling I was trying so hard to keep from the man who caused it.

Hadeon chuckled in my ear, and a small, strangled gasp escaped me.

Damn him.

"Will you be needing any more help tonight?" he asked.

"No," I rasped, conceding defeat in spite of myself. "I think I've got it from here."

I held the chains together, turning back around to find he wasn't half as unaffected as he was pretending to be. His pupils were blown wide, the black nearly eclipsing the navy and silver.

There was something else in his expression, though. Reservation or resistance or even anger, enough to make me remember who we were to each other.

On that last thought, I couldn't help but scan his exposed skin as I had so many times in the hours since Celani told me about the constellation. He followed my gaze, his face holding more warning than amusement.

It was a warning I knew I should heed. What would it matter anyway, these remnants of a life and love that weren't really mine?

Still, I couldn't help but meet his stare with the smallest hint of defiance. There were only so many lies I could tell myself before I sought the truth.

Whether either of us liked it or not.

Chapter Twenty-Three

THE TENSION BETWEEN US THE NEXT MORNING WAS thick enough to suffocate me.

I did my best to focus on literally anything but Hadeon as he strode through the room, shirtless and perfect, aside from the fact he was also a giant dillhole.

It helped that he seemed just as intent on ignoring me as I was him. Now, if he would just put a shirt on, everything would go a lot smoother.

When my maid finally entered, my shoulders sagged in relief. I rushed over to her, much to her surprise. With wide eyes, she watched me carefully, suspicion lining her features as she laid out my clothes for the day.

They were black, of course, but surprisingly not a dress.

"Pants?" I asked cautiously.

I didn't realize how much I missed them until the possibility was dangled before me, but I could count on one hand how many times I had worn a dress in my entire life before coming here. A couple of weeks did not make me any more enamored of flowing skirts that got caught around my ankles when I walked.

My fingers traced the thin scaled fabric. It was matte black, but with delicate silvery threads running through each scale. It took me a moment to register that it wasn't truly silver, but that pale ice-blue color that the Elven blades were made from, just like the armor Celani had worn the day we encountered the wraiths.

"Star-forged armor," Hadeon corrected from the other side of the room.

He left before I could ask why I needed armor today.

"Goodbye to you, too," I muttered.

Was my new outfit merely a safeguard because we were back to training? The clearing wasn't as protected as Fengari.

I didn't focus on that for long, heeding my maid's direction as she led me to the bathroom to get ready.

With a small amount of apprehension, I allowed her to slip the skintight pants up my legs, along with the long-sleeved tunic that came down to rest on my upper thighs.

There were a few laces to adjust around the shoulders and hips, which she took care of within seconds before looping the sleeve over my middle finger and wrapping my bracers and daggers around my wrists.

Then it was time for the matching boots. They came to my knees, lacing over the front of my shins, with thick soles and steel in the toes. They reminded me of a much nicer version of my combat boots, only stronger.

Though the reason behind the new shoes was likely

ominous, a smile tugged at my lips when I walked with the confidence of someone in footwear that could break a bone.

She was just braiding back my hair on the sides and pulling it all up into a high ponytail when Hadeon returned.

I made to follow her to the door, assuming that we were headed to the stables, but instead, Hadeon tucked me against him with his shadows and whisked us both away. My heart was pounding in my chest for reasons that had nothing to do with fear by the time we landed in an unfamiliar clearing.

A moongate stood in the center, a line of soldiers on either side. They eyed me warily, but greeted their king with respect, stepping back to give him more space.

He nodded, then led us both to the moongate. I shot him a questioning look, stopping just short of arguing with him outright in front of the men.

"I'll explain on the other side," he said quietly.

I was torn. A belated explanation was more than he usually offered, and there was the slightest bit of hesitation in his gaze, like he was waiting for me to say I didn't trust him enough for that.

But after several nights in his bed, the daggers, and the way I had watched him exhaust himself to pull the malice from my body, I was reasonably certain that I did trust him with my safety. Besides, if I didn't go willingly, I had no doubt he would find another way to get me there.

So I dipped my chin in assent, taking a step forward.

My jaw dropped when we emerged.

A wall of mist stretched up as high as a mountain in front of us. Through it, I could make out the slight shape of sharp

rocks and decrepit trees, but everything beyond the mist felt...
wrong.

We were in the Never Court, or very close to it.

Unease twisted my stomach as I stared into what felt like
death. There was no movement on the other side of the wall.
No life or sound. Nothing.

Then Hadeon was pulling me away with his shadows
again, until we were standing in a barren valley past the wall of
mist. My skin crawled as I looked around, the fog thinner here
than at the border.

The feeling of unease and smell of death intensified once
we were fully inside the Never Court. Everywhere I looked,
there was destruction. Rocks tumbled down the mountains,
the ground was cracked and split, and some places gave way to
sinkholes.

There were barely any leaves on the trees, their branches
breaking or already broken and lying on the ground by their
roots.

I blinked and a memory of this very valley crawling with
wraiths hit me. Wave after wave of black static and green
smoke where elves fell at my side. I blinked again and they were
gone.

The valley was empty.

"This was the last place she was before she died," I said
quietly. Hadeon had told me that much, but I could feel it,
too, now that I was here...that same desperation from my
dreams in that split second of memory. Terror of losing something that meant everything to me. Resolution.

Fear clawed up my throat, and it was an effort to breathe

evenly.

"You get memories when you're awake as well." Hadeon's voice was carefully neutral, even if his eyes were suspicious.

I looked at him sharply. "How do you know about the dreams?"

"You talk in your sleep."

The intimacy that knowledge suggested had heat rising to my cheeks, mostly because I knew exactly what kind of dreams I had been having. I didn't want to think about what I might have said in the early hours of the night with the star of said dreams a couple of feet away.

"So why are we here?" I didn't bother with subtlety when I changed the subject. Besides, it was the most important question at hand.

"Celani says your isos flared when the wraiths attacked."

"A bit," I admitted, not sure where he was going with that.

"So we're going to try to recreate that." He waved his hand, and I felt the collar around my neck dissipate.

My heart faltered, knees weakening at the idea of facing the terrifying creatures again.

"You. Bastard."

I had barely finished the word before a wraith stepped out of the shadows, stalking toward me. Hadeon tensed but made no move to intervene. Shaking and internally cursing Hadeon, I held my hand out. A feeble light flickered to life then died just as quickly.

"Hadeon." It was a mix between a demand and a plea.

He looked over at me, eyes widening with enough surprise to make me realize I had never actually called him by his name to his face. Not that the douche canoe was actually moved by it or ceding to my unspoken demand that he get me out of here.

Yet he didn't look away, something unfathomable churning in his midnight gaze. Then, the darkness morphed behind him, and the air seized in my lungs.

At least twelve wraiths had materialized. Celani had struggled with a fraction of this.

And Hadeon was still distracted, looking at me.

Less than a heartbeat passed, but it was long enough for sheer, familiar dread to grip my insides. *Not him.*

My entire body burned with rage that was only half my own, my veins turning to liquid flame. My thoughts intertwined with Phaedra's, my ire mingling with hers until, for the first time since I landed in this strange new world, we felt like one person.

One *furious* person who was done having the people I loved taken from me.

I may have blindly followed where fate drunkenly led when I was too young and naïve to know how it would break me, how it would break him, too, but I had not died just so that the universe could take him from me now. Not like this. Not when I had clawed my way back to him from the grave itself.

Strands of my hair flowed out around me, blazing like the sun itself as I lifted my hands toward the hideous creatures. Then I released half a century's worth of fury — hers and mine — in a vast, relentless inferno.

The creatures turned to ashes on the spot.

Chapter Twenty-Four

My isos sputtered out as quickly as it had come, leaving crippling exhaustion in its wake.

With the magic gone, so too was the overwhelming presence of Phaedra and her memories and her rage.

Hadeon stared silently at me over the smoldering remains of the wraiths, like he was waiting to see if he needed to step in to dampen my isos. Before either of us could speak, another creature formed and his shadows attacked without him even turning around.

My lips parted. Of course my intervention hadn't been necessary. But I had panicked, and Phaedra's consciousness had fed off of it, all because —

"You baited me," I spat.

He didn't deny it. "You needed to feel how it worked, what motivated it."

Did he know I would step in to protect him? Was he using

whatever the hell was between us against me, or had he assumed the fear would motivate me?

Both ideas brought fresh rage coursing through my veins, enough to give me the strength to stay standing.

I shook my head, too furious to speak. "Take me back."

He surprised me when he didn't argue, only shadow-whisked me back to the moongate. A short walk and another shadow travel had us back in his rooms.

I pushed away from him as soon as we were there, shaking my head. Nyx and Ahvi both greeted me, but I was too angry to do much more than give them a quick pat in response. Finally, I walked out onto the balcony, hands gripping the railing while I tried to find the smallest bit of peace.

Of course, my eyes landed on the freaking constellation.

Ahvi.

Its brilliant, golden orbs mocked me as they twinkled obliviously in the sky.

I felt Hadeon's presence behind me, because I always did, because why wouldn't I, because he was my —

I spun around to confront him only to find him inches from me, his chest heaving. He parted his lips to speak, but I didn't want to hear what he had to say, didn't want one more convoluted comment from him, didn't want to hear a name on his lips that I wasn't sure would feel like my own, no matter which one he decided to utter.

My eyes met his, and I shook my head, just the barest half an inch to the left and back again. He closed his mouth but didn't retreat. Didn't move at all.

A thousand lifetimes passed in the next moment. A

phantom of his breath on my lips. Lightning and fire and shadows all existed in the space between our fractured, weary souls.

And *oh* how I would have died all over again to blame him for what happened next, but I knew in the very essence of my being that *I* was the one who leaned just the slightest millimeter forward.

Then his lips were on mine, tasting, devouring, consuming me whole. I couldn't think or breathe, but I didn't need air anyway when I could have subsisted entirely on him for this lifetime and all the ones that came after.

His kiss wasn't gentle, his hands even less so as they clenched around my waist. His thumb dug into the hollow inside my hipbone and squeezed until I let out a gasp. I ran my hands through his hair, raking my nails along his scalp and tugging on the strands more forcefully than I needed to.

He was angry, and I was furious, and this was the closest I had come to being alive — to being whole — in my entire mortal existence.

I pulled back just long enough to look into his starburst gaze, and suddenly I was looking into his eyes from exactly this angle in exactly this spot on the balcony on an entirely different night.

"I TOLD you not to come back," he growled.

"And I told you that you may command this kingdom, but you do not command me."

The smallest smirk tugged at his perfect lips, though it

didn't erase the warning in his eyes. "Here I thought you rather enjoyed that."

I shrugged a single slim shoulder. "Only on my terms."

"As everything is, my feral princess." His features turned serious again. "It's too dangerous."

My chin lifted, my entire stance going rigid in challenge. "We had a deal. My soul for yours. Forever."

"Don't make promises you can't keep." He sounded softer, closer to pleading than I had ever heard, then or now.

"I can keep this one. I will." That much was true. Abba had sworn it.

He leaned into me like he was inhaling my very essence, lips ghosting along my skin. "Promise me."

"I promise."

"I mean it, Phaedra." His tone rang with command, and awareness prickled through my body even as defiance stirred in my veins. "Promise me you won't do anything reckless. That you'll stay off the front lines, with Nyx. That you'll stay safe."

"I promise," I repeated.

BUT EVEN IN THE MEMORY, I knew it was a lie.

I blinked the vision away as a thousand little things came back to me, a thousand things that I had been denying since I arrived.

The pull I felt toward Hadeon. His fury over my getting someone he loved killed. The fact that he kept a stray dog Phaedra had adopted for fifty freaking years after she died. The stupid constellation across my skin and my mind and my soul.

Stepping back from him, I held my hands up like a physical barrier between us.

"Show me."

He didn't pretend to misunderstand. He only pulled off his jacket, turning so I could see the midnight tattoo running along the top of his spine. Of the Ahvi constellation as it appeared from this balcony. The exact opposite of the one on my collarbone.

Memories clouded my vision, accosting me, but I tried to shut them out long enough to focus.

"Were you ever going to tell me?" I demanded.

A muscle worked in his jaw. "As I said, it isn't the blessing Celani believes."

That was a no, then. I had tried like hell not to care these past couple of weeks, but I knew I had failed when his words landed like a kick to the gut.

Whatever else I doubted, I knew in every part of my soul that Hadeon had loved Phaedra. Maybe she had been easier to love, that version of me who was brought up with a home and a family, firmly grounded in her role as a chosen one and a warrior and a princess and the sure knowledge that there was a soulmate out there waiting for her.

She wasn't twisted by the doubt of having her entire world ripped away, the hard edges of never being able to trust another soul.

I had gleaned enough from her memories to know that, despite the war she fought in and the choices she was willing to make, there had been a kind of purity to Phaedra that was entirely absent in me.

I have known you to be many things, but weak was never one of them.

Of course he didn't feel like it was a blessing that the woman he loved died only to be replaced by a broken, entirely too human version of herself.

And I... I wasn't sure what I felt, how much of these feelings were even mine, whether I craved Hadeon's taste and feel because of memories from another life or a bond I had no say in.

Either way, it all felt like a story that wasn't mine, that never really would be.

"No." I finally responded. "I can see that."

He opened his mouth to respond, but another voice cut in.

"I'm so sorry to interrupt," Celani said.

She did sound sorry. That made one of us.

I was more than ready to be anywhere else, anyplace but on a balcony full of Phaedra's memories and mine, with a king who spent far too much time in both, where I could still smell the night sky on his skin and still feel the tremble in my limbs from the wraiths he had manipulated me into fighting.

"What is it?" Hadeon asked, turning to face her.

I was prepared to be grateful for her distraction when her next words knocked me on my ass.

"Someone is here for the princess."

Chapter Twenty-Five

I FOLLOWED CELANI DOWN THE WINDING STAIRS toward the great hall.

Apprehension crept along my skin, curling in my gut. Whatever residual exhaustion from using my isos I felt had been chased away by Hadeon's soulmark and a stranger showing up to see me, especially when Celani was so on edge about it.

She hadn't explained who was waiting, but the stiff set of her shoulders told me she wasn't happy about their presence.

Her fingers gripped the handle of her spear, her dark-brown skin paling.

Kallius waited just inside the door, his broad frame blocking my view. As soon as he heard us enter, he shook his head, turning to meet my gaze.

"Em, you don't have to —"

I didn't hear whatever else he said. Not when my eyes

locked on a set of blue-and-golden ones that were more familiar than they should have been.

A tall, handsome man stood on the other side of the room. His long, blond hair glowed like a halo as it cascaded over his shoulders, highlighting the golden buttons of his forest-green jacket. A thousand memories flitted through my mind at once.

Laughing through the temple with him. Sneaking out of a golden palace late at night and running through the golden fields of the Sun Court. Climbing the Mitera Tree, then begging the goddess for forgiveness when we inevitably broke one of the branches.

The pain in his eyes when I sent him home from the battlefield and offered myself as sacrifice instead.

His brow furrowed slightly as he studied me, his expression carefully guarded.

"Leander," his name slipped from my lips.

His eyes softened, and his shoulders sagged in relief.

I wasn't even aware that I was running until I had flung myself into his arms, tears stabbing at the backs of my eyes when he scooped me up into a hug.

The familiar scent of cedar and smoke washed over me. It didn't matter that this was Phaedra's brother or that the memories belonged solely to her, because for a brief moment, he belonged to me, too. Once again, Phaedra and I didn't feel as separate as I wanted to keep us.

When he let me go, his hands came up to grab either side of my face, his fiery eyes searching mine.

"It is you," he said, his mouth twisting into a wide grin.

"They say you're called Ember now," he added, and something inside of me started to fall.

"Yes," I said softly, and he nodded.

"Well, it suits you a hell of a lot better than Phaedra ever did."

Relief weakened my knees, so potent I felt another unwanted prickling behind my eyes.

"Prince Leander." Hadeon's voice filled the room, and Leander sighed.

He slung his arm over my shoulders, lifting his proud chin to face the King of Moon and Stars.

"I could ask how you snuck past our borders, but I imagine you won't tell me anyway," Hadeon said, unamused.

Leander winked at me, and I surmised this was something Phaedra would have known. It was interesting that she had never shared it with Hadeon, but their relationship made little sense to me, even now.

Hadeon stood between his cousins, his muscled arms crossed over his broad chest. His eyes were solely fixed on the man at my side, intentionally avoiding looking at me.

"I wouldn't have needed to come if you had agreed to let us speak with her," Leander said, and there was a note of challenge in his tone.

Hadeon arched a navy eyebrow.

"And if she had wanted to contact you, she would have. Her leash is not so short."

I grappled with anger at Hadeon and guilt because it wasn't a lie. I hadn't wanted to contact them.

Leander's sharp inhalation told me that the comment had stung, but he offered a reassuring smile that I didn't deserve.

"It's not..." I trailed off as I tried to explain. "I just didn't know —"

Leander pressed his lips to the top of my head. "It's fine, sis. Really. I can only imagine how overwhelming it all must have been." His words were little more than a whisper, meant just for me.

"So," Hadeon interrupted, pulling our attention back to his side of the room. "Now you've had an opportunity to see her, see that we haven't sacrificed her to the goddess, or fed her to one of our baztets..." He gestured casually toward the door. "Feel free to leave and report back to your parents."

Leander's muscles tensed, his eyes narrowed on Hadeon.

"You surely don't expect me to leave before I've had a chance to catch up with the sister I've spent fifty years mourning."

Hadeon opened his mouth, and I knew what he was going to say before he even spoke. For whatever reason, he staunchly objected to Leander being here, but I couldn't stand the idea of my brother — it was impossible to think of him as anything else — leaving so soon after he arrived. His presence was an unexpected bit of comfort when it felt like everything else was falling apart.

I caught Hadeon's gaze, letting him see the resolve in mine.

"I never ask you for anything," I said quietly.

It was true. He gifted me things when he saw fit, but I hadn't outright asked him for any of it. Not my freedom, not more quills or ink. Hell, not even pants. But *this* — this mattered to me.

Hadeon studied me, holding my gaze for several heart-beats. A muscle worked in his jaw, and he turned back to my brother.

"You may avail yourself of a guest suite. But if you leave, Prince Leander, you do so alone. Do not forget who she belongs to."

The first time Hadeon had ever said those words, I had assumed he meant as his prisoner. Now, I wasn't sure what he meant, but I was sure that bringing it up in front of my brother was wholly unnecessary.

My fingers twitched, irritation rising inside of me like the tide. Even Celani blinked pointedly in his direction. Hadeon didn't give anyone a chance to respond before he turned on his heels, his shadows trailing him as he swept from the room.

Kallius glanced between the four of us before following his cousin.

Leander was the one to finally break the silence. "It's nice to know that he's just as affable as ever."

THOUGH LEANDER technically had his own room, we visited in mine, at Hadeon's insistence — delivered through Celani, of course, since we still hadn't spoken. He had only paused long enough to put my collar back on, much to Leander's irritation, before sweeping out of the room.

"Probably because of the warding," Leander said. "He doesn't want me to abscond with you in the night, and this room is locked down."

"You can sense that?"

"You don't remember much, do you?"

"Bits and pieces," I admitted. "It comes to me sometimes more than others."

It was easy to trust him, to talk to him in a way I hadn't been able to with anyone else. Whether that was because of our shared childhood in my first life or the advantage of having more memories when I met him, I wasn't sure.

Maybe it was just his easy acceptance, the way he blithely called me Ember without judgment or expectation. Even now, he wasn't disappointed that I didn't remember things. He only nodded, launching into an explanation.

"I can sense the remnants of isos, and I imagine it works a lot like our father's power. He has flames, but he can also leave eternally burning fire as a ward around important things. The king's shadows can exist independently of him, like in that collar." He gestured, his lips pursing.

"It's to dampen my magic — isos — because it was a bit out of control," I found myself defending.

"Indeed," Leander agreed a bit too amicably. "Because why wear a ring or a tiara when you can wear a collar."

So everyone knows who you belong to.

"Yes, well. He's also an ass, so there's that."

Leander let out a chuckle. "Well, he's not an ass you have to stay with. You could come home."

There was that word again, with its murky connotations.

I shook my head. "For now, I need to stay."

"Need to, or want to?" Again, the question was without censure.

What had Phaedra told him in their past lives? It wasn't a stretch to assume he knew something of her relationship with Hadeon.

"I told him I would help him with the wraiths, so let's go with need," I hedged.

Leander nodded, not surprised at my mention of the wraiths, which confirmed my theory that it wasn't only the Moon Court they were attacking.

I waved my hand airily. "Anyway, I'm sick of talking about him."

Sick of thinking about him. Sick of wanting him and hating myself for it.

"Tell me about you. About our family." Again, I noticed how easy it was to feel the truth of the possession in that statement. Something about using my isos, getting more memories, having my brother here — *kissing your soulmate*, a voice in my head interrupted.

Regardless, it was getting easier to think of that past life as mine, or maybe it was just getting harder to differentiate them.

Leander gave me a knowing look, but he complied. Over the next several hours, he told me stories about our family, about our kingdom. I listened and lost myself in the distraction of it, but I didn't miss the way he skirted around one glaringly important issue.

"And the war?" I prompted.

He blew out a breath, golden eyes studying me. "Which one?" he asked, the words tinged with bitterness.

Sadness flooded my veins, empathy for him, for my past self, for all of it.

"Is that all we knew?" I shook my head "All we were?"

"It certainly felt that way sometimes." His face darkened at the memory, an indication of the years that didn't show in his smooth skin.

It was strange to think that he had lived longer than I had, my little brother now technically older than I was. Though I wasn't sure how to calculate my age now, with over forty years in Terrea and another twenty and change on Earth. Wherever Phaedra's soul had been in the interim felt stagnant, unmoving.

"The war with the Moon Court, then," I said. "I remember battlefields and killing, but I don't remember why."

Shadows passed through his eyes, dimming their golden light. Was he envisioning the same thing I was, the moment where I told him to leave me?

"I'm not sure any of us really knew why. The queen of this court, she was..."

"Vicious?" I guessed, something stirring in my mind.

"To say the least." He stretched out his legs, and Ahvi gave him an irritable look for shaking the couch. "She wanted power, and she hated our court. She had already turned her own into a bloodbath, then she came for us. Centuries into a bloody border war, someone finally took care of the queen, but the damage had been done."

"What happened to her?" I asked.

His voice got quieter. "No one knows for sure. One day, the queen was conscripting a soldier into her personal service — a notoriously bloody job, one with a short lifespan as well as rumors about why she only had young, attractive males in her service. The next, the queen was dead, Hadeon fought for his right as king, and the soldier's sister was appointed as his general."

Celani. Remembering her spear, her impressive isos, and her generally protective nature, it was not surprising to think she might have committed regicide to keep her brother safe.

"So the queen died, yet the war raged on anyway?" I asked, my hand absently scratching Nyx's head.

Leander had either seen my cerberus before or was just given to fearlessness, because he hadn't shied away from either of the dangerous creatures taking up residence in my rooms.

"There were discussions of ceasefires. But yes, it went on until..." He trailed off, that haunted look passing his face again, and he didn't need to finish his sentence.

"Until I was taken."

He nodded.

All along, I had wondered why Hadeon had kept me alive that first time, whether it was out of spite or ownership, and how early our relationship had turned physical. It had crossed my mind that he felt some kind of pull toward me, had known I was his soulmate or had been unable to stand the thought of me dead.

But was it just a political maneuver, holding me hostage? If so, it worked, by the sounds of it.

For all I tried to steer the conversation away, somehow it always came back to this, to him. To us.

"And the other war?" My words were barely a whisper.

"The other war was...insane." He swallowed, reaching out a hand to touch Ahvi's head like he could take comfort from the flaming beast that had tried to bite him more than once. "It only lasted two weeks, but it decimated the ranks. You came back, insisting that Hadeon wasn't responsible, but our father swore he was. The creatures were made of shadows. He thought you had been brainwashed here, that Hadeon was setting a trap for our family, so he wouldn't even consider fighting in a united front."

That matched up with the first dream I had here. *This is Hadeon's doing.*

"So you were fighting there, and I came back here?"

Leander nodded, blinking back a sheen of tears. "I thought my place was with our people, but I should have come with you." He squeezed his eyes shut, fifty years' worth of unspoken remorse bleeding from every pore of his being. "If I hadn't, maybe you would have —"

I held up a hand, refusing to let him take the blame for a choice I made, one the goddess had all but required of me.

"Stop," I ordered. "It wouldn't have changed anything. The prophecy was set. We didn't know it then, but it was always going to end that way."

"Then I could have been by your side," he insisted.

"It wasn't like that. I went alone." I didn't remember everything about that day yet, but I knew that much.

I had sent Nyx to Hadeon, and I had gone with Abba alone.

Leander's face grew even more pained, and I held my arms out like I vaguely remembered doing when we were kids. He knelt by my chair and I wrapped my arms around him, giving him the kind of comforting hug I had only given a handful of times in my human life.

"I'm here now," I assured him.

It seemed ridiculous now, how many times I had worried that those words would be a lie, that I would have to fake my affection for the people who had loved Phaedra.

Whether it was her memories or the genetics that once tied us together or the appreciation for everything he had been in the short few hours since he trekked into the enemy's kingdom alone to find me, there was nothing fake about the love I felt for my brother now.

Chapter Twenty-Six

WE WERE AWOKEN FAR TOO EARLY BY AN ANGRY knock at the door.

I blinked away the sleep from my eyes, trying to make sense of where I was and why the bed was so cold. Empty. It took a moment to register the fact that the familiar mural on the ceiling was different from the one above Hadeon's bed.

Because I wasn't in Hadeon's room. I was in mine.

Something twisted inside of me as I remembered the hours I'd spent tossing and turning before exhaustion finally pulled me under, even with Leander's comforting snores from the couch in front of the fire where he had passed out mid-conversation.

It shouldn't have been so hard to sleep without Hadeon.

After yesterday, I shouldn't want to sleep next to him. Yet, I was apparently a masochist.

Another loud knock pulled me from my thoughts before the door swung open to reveal the elf in question.

Hadeon's expression was impassive, but his shadows danced furiously behind him, betraying his foul mood. It wasn't necessary — I would have guessed that things were off just from the fact that he knocked at all.

He glanced between me and Leander, who was sprawled out with a sleeping Ahvi tucked under his arm.

Something flitted across Hadeon's features before he quickly stamped it out.

"We need to train," he said flatly.

Leander gently set Ahvi on the floor, and the feraline's tail flared to life in displeasure. Then my brother casually stretched, his grin widening as he met the king's hardened gaze.

"Excellent," he said. "When do we start?"

Celani's head appeared in the corner of the doorway, her eyes flitting back and forth between her cousin and my brother.

Hadeon blinked. "Your presence isn't required, but you're welcome to sequester yourself in your own rooms until we return."

Leander laughed. "I assume this is about her isos. Tell me, Shadow King, do you really think you're the best one suited to teach her how to channel fire? I think I'll come."

Shadows curled around Hadeon, stretching out like talons before he reined them in again.

"We'll be taking baztets," Celani added, as if that were a deterrent.

But Leander only rubbed his hands together in a display of excitement.

"Excellent, I've always wanted to try riding one."

I got the impression my brother was a bit of an adrenaline junkie.

Celani shook her head, trying to disguise her amusement by looking back toward the hall. Hadeon, however, was far from entertained by the exchange. He was terse when he spoke again.

"Be ready in twenty minutes," he said, turning to leave the room.

My friend sighed as Hadeon passed her to head into the hall. Ahvi took a step forward, his eyes locked on her as his tail went up in flames.

"I swear to the Goddess if you even *try* to set me on fire, I will throw you from this balcony," she vowed.

The feraline tilted his head like he was considering her words.

Finally, he sauntered away, curling up next to Nyx on the floor, much to the cerberus's dismay.

Celani looked at me next, exasperation heavy in her gaze. "Must all of you be so..." She gestured toward Leander and me. "Court of Fire and Sun-like?"

Leander ran a sun-kissed hand through his long blond hair. "I'd say it was in our nature, but I would think that was rather obvious."

He winked at my friend then, and she rolled her eyes.

"You have not changed in fifty years, Leander Onassis," she observed, shaking her head like she wasn't sure whether that was a good thing or not.

"I think you'll find that I've changed more than you real-ize, Celani Leskaris," he said, his eyes heating slightly.

I glanced back and forth between the two, the tension in the air suddenly far more uncomfortable than I was prepared for.

"That's General Leskaris, to you," she corrected before turning her attention to me. Her expression was carefully neutral as she continued speaking. "Kal and I are coming, too. He's overseeing training with his men, but he'll meet us there soon. I'll grab us coffee and breakfast to go?"

"Please." I smiled at her, and she nodded, shutting the door behind her as she left.

I searched Phaedra's memories but couldn't come up with a single explanation for whatever that was.

"Are you going to explain?" I asked lightly.

"A different story for a very different day, after several very strong libations," he said. "For now, let's just get ready, shall we? Wouldn't want to keep your precious king waiting."

With that, Leander went back to his rooms to change, and I got ready in mine. He met me back at my door, and together, we trekked to the courtyard for what was sure to be an inter-esting afternoon.

CELANI, Hadeon, Kallius, and Leander stood around me on the field, their eyes fixed on me like I was the evening's entertainment. Which did nothing for my nerves. Performance anxiety, that's what this was.

Where I had been able to easily call my flames yesterday with the wraiths, right now, I was like an eighty-year-old man on a date night without his Viagra prescription.

I squeezed my eyes shut, calling to mind the wraiths and remembering the way they lingered just behind Hadeon. I focused on the fear I had felt, followed directly by waves of anger when I realized how he'd baited me.

Something sparked to life, writhing under my skin like it was trying to break free. I didn't try to block it, instead allowing the feeling to fuel me, flowing through me like a raging, living river of fire.

Distantly, I registered the sound of shouting voices. At first, they were encouraging, excited. Slowly, they morphed into something more cautious. Then, there was fear.

My eyes snapped open. Through a haze of flames and smoke, I caught sight of Kallius and Celani taking several steps backward, their expressions concerned as they tried to cover their faces from the bursts of fire that exploded from me.

"Feralinia." There was a warning in Hadeon's tone, one I couldn't heed and wasn't sure I wanted to.

I closed my eyes, relishing the feel of heat washing over me. A dam had broken, and power was flooding me in a frantic, desperate way. As if the isos had been waiting for this moment. As if it had missed being used as much as my body had missed using it.

When I opened my eyes again, though, it took me a moment to realize what was wrong. I wasn't standing on the field anymore. Instead, I was floating, rising higher in the air as the heat emanating from my body increased.

Hadeon watched me carefully, his shadows growing and expanding as if he were waiting to use them. Leander was the only one who didn't look afraid. Instead, he watched me with the smug expression of someone who was more than proud.

My flames grew. A bright burst of light traced under my skin, stretching from my stomach down to my toes and up to my throat.

My skin itched, and my head ached. Exhaustion was settling deep into my bones, but its weight couldn't bring me down. I floated higher and higher.

I was too hot. It was too much.

My pulse raced, my thoughts running wild. If I couldn't stop the flames, couldn't rein them in, would I hurt my friends? Would I set fire to the mountain? Would I burn myself up until there was nothing left but ash and smoke?

Hadeon's churning gaze met mine. With a flick of his wrist, shadows sailed toward me. They fought against my flames for long seconds before a collar was once again around my throat, and the heat inside my veins started to die down.

His darkness wound around me, dousing the remaining flames before gently bringing me back to the ground.

I drifted like a feather into his waiting arms. One heartbeat passed, then another with his hands cradling me and his midnight gaze locked on mine. He said nothing as he set me on my feet, not removing his hands until he was certain I could stand on my own.

My eyes remained on his, but Hadeon looked away, his expression shuttering as Leander approached.

"I didn't realize things were this bad," my brother said, his hands stroking my face.

The smug expression he wore earlier was long gone, replaced instead with a simmering anger. His focus snapped from me to Hadeon, and he practically growled when he spoke. "You should have sent for us."

"I had it under control," Hadeon said flatly, his fingers still wrapped gently around my arms.

Leander let out a bitter huff, his blue eyes sparking as they shifted to amber.

"Of course you did," he seethed. "What were you going to do? Wait until she got herself killed? That is your style, I suppose —"

Shadows flared around us, blocking out the starlit sky. Hadeon's expression remained completely blank, but his voice was a freshly sharpened blade, deadly and precise.

"Funny," he said. "I could have sworn when Celani took her prisoner from her own unguarded border, she was alone, weakened, on a blood-soaked battlefield while you ran away like a child. Only one of us was *willing* to let her sacrifice her life for theirs."

Leander's grin was feral, and flames danced even brighter in his fiery blue eyes.

"No, she never trusted you enough to tell you the truth about what she was doing, did she?"

Hadeon's chest heaved, his shadows snapping forward like the gaping, starving maws of vipers.

"Enough!" I cut in before they tried to kill each other. "Both of you. None of those accusations are fair, and I will not let either of you wield me as a weapon to hurt the other."

Celani and Kallius were close by, swords in hands as if they had been ready for the argument to come to blows.

It was Leander who stepped back first. He crossed his arms over his chest, his head tilting back to breathe in the sky and the rising sun.

"Fine," he said after a breath, his gaze flitting down to meet mine as it turned back to a more normal shade of blue. "But you need to speak with our father."

Hadeon stiffened but didn't try to argue, even as my stomach twisted into knots.

Nevertheless, I nodded. I hadn't been ready to see them before, but Leander wasn't wrong. If I wanted to control my isos, I needed to talk with people who had magic similar to mine.

"All right," I said after a moment. "I'm ready."

THOUGH WE HAD AVOIDED direct interactions since the tense moments at the clearing, I wasn't half as surprised as I should have been when the shadows in my room rearranged themselves in the shape of a sexy, brooding king.

It struck me now that I had never been nearly afraid enough of the power he exuded with every step he took, never truly felt unsafe with him. Maybe what we were to one another should always have been obvious.

Hell, maybe it had.

His gaze raked over me, entire lifetimes seeming to pass in the moments between when he entered and when he chose to speak.

"I've arranged for you to meet with your family," he said at last.

"Why didn't you before?" I asked, already suspecting the answer.

"You didn't want to see them."

"I didn't want to do a lot of things," I reminded him.

He scowled but didn't respond, and I knew he wouldn't. It was just one of the many things he was content to leave unspoken, the small ways he protected me, even if some of them were selfish.

"You aren't half the villain you were so determined to make me think you were."

He stepped closer, his shadows settling around us in a way that anyone else would have found ominous. Instead, my isos flared to life, practically begging to come out and play with his.

I stuffed it down, needy bastard that it was.

"You clearly haven't gotten all of your memories back," he said.

I sifted through the things I knew and had put together since our perilous conversation on the balcony.

"I don't need my memories to know that for someone who claims to hate Phaedra, you do a lot for her."

My gaze slid to Nyx, who was happily snuggled up in the corner of the room.

"You think everything I've done is for *her*?"

I met his gaze, forcing myself to stand my ground. "You don't even know me."

Hadeon stepped closer to me, overwhelming my senses like he always did. His eyes blazed, the shadows stretching around us both until we were cocooned in the darkness that called to me so much more than it should.

"That's where you're wrong, Feralinia," he purred. "No matter what name you go by, in a different body, in a different world, with a different accent and different memories, I would know you every time. Every version of you across space and time and circumstance."

The air between us was charged with energy, weighed down by all the tension we refused to surrender to. I was acutely aware of the bergamot scent of his shampoo and the even cadence of our breaths just slightly too controlled to be natural.

"That doesn't change just because you fight with daggers instead of a spear or spend your time sketching instead of setting things on fire."

He was so, so close to me now, his low, impassioned voice ghosting along every exposed inch of my skin, thicker than his shadows and twice as deadly.

As much as I wanted to keep my pride, the truth came spilling out anyway, siphoned from my being the same way he had pulled the malice out of my veins.

"Then why are you so bitter that we're still soulmates?" I demanded, leaning into him in spite of myself.

"Aside from your obvious feelings on the matter?" he asked, tilting his head to growl into my ear. "Because whether you go by Phaedra or Ember, you are the woman who broke a promise and left me to grieve for half a celestial-damned century without so much as a goodbye. That is not an experience I'm eager to repeat. Not even for you."

He stalked away while I tried to process that rather than preferring one version of me over another, it was every version of me he hated. Loved. Whatever the hell it was he felt.

"I'll meet you downstairs," he said, turning without giving me a chance to respond.

Which was fine. I didn't know what I would have said anyway, to any of it.

Chapter Twenty-Seven

THE EVENING SAW US BACK IN THE ROOM OF NOT-quite moongates where Hadeon had brought me to speak with Ivy. I still didn't quite understand how they worked, and why you could walk through some moongates, but not others. Leander said it had something to do with the type of metal chosen for their frames, that some ore was more conductive of teleportation isos than others.

It made as much sense as anything else, I supposed.

My brother escorted me toward a golden frame with a lion's head at the top. The image moving in the center was of familiar red mountains glowing under the haze of a brilliant sunset.

The picture shifted in and out of focus, twinkling like a mirage before a booming voice broke through the silence.

"Phaedra?" My father's voice cracked.

His broad frame filled the moongate as he stepped in front

of it, his amber eyes locked on to mine. He brought one hand up to cover his mouth, the other pressing against the painting, right where I was standing.

A fissure split my chest, carving me in two.

"Papa," I whispered, choking back the emotion rising in my throat.

Half of me yearned to step through the gate, to fall into my father's arms and cry, letting him comfort me just as he had when I was a child. The other half felt like that was a betrayal to the parents who raised this version of me, the ones I had mourned every day since I was ten years old.

Did loving Phaedra's family mean forgetting about mine? That Ember's father didn't matter, because he was dead and this one was alive?

Nausea churned in my gut, and I took half a step backward, trying to ignore the pained expression that tugged at the king's sharp features. His golden brow furrowed in confusion, but he stayed silent, watching for what I would do next.

I had said I was ready for this, but I wasn't at all prepared for the feelings that came with seeing my parents. Hadeon glowered in the corner of the room, and I turned, allowing myself to take a small bit of comfort in the presence of his shadows, even if he was a bastard most of the time.

Then the gentle hum of my mother's voice drifted through the moongate. I turned back in time to see her join my father. Her blue eyes bored into mine, sparkling with unshed golden tears.

She hadn't aged a day since the memory I saw in the

temple. Her tan skin was smooth, her red hair pulled back in a long, elegant braid. A golden crown with a diamond-studded sunburst rested on her head.

The same contradictory feelings warred within me. How was I supposed to juggle these lives, these emotions, and remain true to both versions of myself?

It had been easier with Leander. I hadn't grown up with siblings, but my parents...

"Mama, Papa," Leander began, casually wrapping his arm around my shoulders. "*Ember*," he emphasized my name in a pointed way, "has had some trouble controlling her isos since returning to Aelvaria, so we thought we would reach out to see if you have any advice."

He said it all so easily, as if this were the most normal conversation in the world to be having with his parents and once-dead sister via magical FaceTime from the palace of their oldest enemy.

My mind started to spiral until I heard a third familiar voice.

"So this is where you ran off to," Elion commented guardedly. "I should have known."

He stepped into place just behind my parents. His regal features were drawn but as unreadable as always. His long copper-colored hair was tucked behind pointed ears studded with rings, and his golden eyes glinted like the sunrise.

He kept his attention fixed on Leander, and I tried to ignore the intentionality behind it, like he couldn't bear to even glance in my direction.

"Yes, yes." Leander's response was heavy with exasperation, his blue eyes meeting mine as he winked. There was something comforting in the gesture. "But back to the matter at hand. How do we help Ember control her isos?"

My parents spoke in hushed tones, their worried glances flicking up to mine every so often. I got the distinct impression that this wasn't something they had ever heard of before. Elf children developed their isos slowly and over time so they would know how to control it.

The idea that I couldn't surely seemed barbaric.

"Has she tried a bloodstone?" Elion asked after several uncomfortable heartbeats.

I searched both my memories and the ones of Phaedra I could access, but I couldn't remember ever hearing anything about that before.

Leander arched an eyebrow in exasperation, bringing his sun-kissed hand up to pinch the bridge of his nose.

"You could ask her," he said pointedly, casually gesturing toward me.

Elion took a deep breath, as if the idea of speaking to me was a great burden he hadn't been prepared for, and I internally winced.

"Ember," he drawled, his golden eyes finally meeting mine. "Have you tried using a bloodstone?"

I shook my head.

"Of course she hasn't," Hadeon snapped. "No one has used them in over a century."

"No one has gotten this much power this fast since then either," Elion countered.

Hadeon's shadows flickered in irritation, but his expression was thoughtful as he deliberated.

"Anyone want to maybe take a second to tell the humanoid what the hell a bloodstone is?" I said.

My mother — *the queen,* I mentally corrected — sighed, pity softening her delicate features.

"A bloodstone is a type of stone hewn from the heart of Terrea. Because it comes from a place of raw isos, it acts as an amplifier for your power, as well as a control...a funnel, of a sort," she explained, her gentle voice a balm to my burned soul. "But they are rare, as you can imagine."

"Yeah, your precious shadow king's mother hunted them all down ages ago so that no one could dare become more powerful than she was," Leander muttered.

Darkness bled through the room in warning, but the corner of Elion's mouth quirked in amusement.

"Not all of them, brother," he said, moving his hands behind his back. "It just might take a little while to locate some."

I nodded like I understood, when the reality was, this was all far too much information for me to continue processing.

"But don't you have a captain with amplifying isos?" Elion asked, his attention fully fixed on Hadeon now. "Xanth, was it?"

Hadeon's lips tightened, his fingers twitching at his sides.

"I will not dignify that with a response when you are clearly fishing or spying on my court after we agreed to a ceasefire."

Elion's gaze sharpened, and he tilted his head to the side.

"Whereas your never-ending well of information on our court is nobly acquired."

Hadeon looked almost impressed with Elion, and didn't bother to argue.

Once my brother and the King of Moon and Stars finished their pissing contest, Elion left with the excuse of needing to deal with court matters.

The rest of us stood in uncomfortable silence until my parents finally decided to launch into the questions that had been bubbling inside of them.

For what felt like hours, I fielded inquiries about my time in the Court of Moon and Stars, the treatment I had received, the circumstances by which I had been returned to Aelvaria, and even a few questions about my life on Earth.

All the while, my mother shed golden tears and my father insisted on calling me Phaedra. It wasn't easy with them the way it had been with Leander, but the longer we talked, the more it felt like pieces of me were clicking further into place.

Whatever part of my soul was Phaedra's, the part that belonged with them, welcomed them eagerly. That didn't stop me from being grateful for Hadeon's intervention when their questions drifted toward my return to the Court of Fire and Sun.

My father scowled at Hadeon, his once comforting tone burning like the hottest part of the flame when he was forced to address the king of the Moon Court.

"I trust you will remember your place —" He was cut off as the moongate sputtered and froze, like a video-call with a bad connection and then they were gone.

Hadeon didn't explain the abrupt ending, but the quirk of his lips told me he was responsible. Wordlessly, the three of us wound our way through the palace until we were back in my rooms.

It didn't escape my notice that Hadeon refrained from shadowing me this time, just as he kept his distance physically. It was just as well. Even though my body and soul longed for him, it was an added complication in a situation that was already a mess.

At least, that's what I told myself with every tense step back to my room.

LEANDER AND I had dinner sent up. He nobly refrained from commenting on the way my eyes drifted in the direction of Hadeon's rooms every so often.

I couldn't tell if I actually missed the bastard or if it was only Phaedra's soul crying out for its mate, but the conflict between us made me feel like I was burning up from my isos all over again.

I shook the thought away, forcing myself to lift my spoon to my mouth and pretending the savory stew didn't taste like ash on my tongue. Questions swirled around in my head like a whirlpool, tumultuous enough to drown me if I didn't do something.

Leander studied my expression in concern.

"What is it?" he asked, resting his hands on either side of

his plate as if he was no longer as ravenous as he had claimed to be just a few minutes ago.

I met his blue eyes, several thoughts coming to mind at once, but the question that found its way to my lips wasn't the one I was expecting.

"Why were Hadeon and I a secret?" I asked.

Every memory I had gotten had made it clear we kept our relationship from the public.

He sighed, a weary sound absent any surprise, confirming that he had known about us.

"Peace was still so fresh," he started, then furrowed his golden eyebrows. "And relative, considering you were here as a captive."

My fingers went up to trace the shadow collar around my neck, and Leander tracked the movement.

"Matches between the courts were unheard of, and there were a lot of simmering feelings on both sides." He swiped a hand over his face, his expression hardening. "Then Valandril came along and everything went to hell, anyway."

Memories crashed in. The name was like a trigger, and suddenly I was in a dark room, holding hands with two other women. I stared into a cruel face, warped in pain and fury as roots wound up around him, slowly devouring him.

Valandril.

A creature of nightmares and ruin.

The images dissipated, like Phaedra hadn't meant to let them in, like she didn't want to go back to that moment any more than I did. She didn't want to remember that pain.

"What did he do?" I asked, rubbing the palms of my hands

at some long-forgotten injury that had existed on both of them.

Leander's features went slack. He pushed his plate forward, his mouth twisting in disgust. When he spoke, it sounded heavier, burdened by years of war and death.

"He was the king of Isramaya," he began. "The kingdom of the vampires. I don't know exactly what happened, but we've heard rumors that in his greed, he stole from the Life Tree on Sacred Mountain."

My eyes went wide. Celani had explained that Sacred Mountain was the kingdom designated for the goddess herself. The tree was the source of all life and power. It was what filled Terrea with isos.

"He planted its root in the Shadow Mountains that split his kingdom," Leander continued grimly. "And when that happened, evil spread through the world like a plague. You said you've seen the wraiths, but what came before them was much worse. Monsters of shadow and malice that tried to devour Aelvaria just appeared one day out of nowhere.

"They consumed the Court of Mist and Memory in less than a week. They would have destroyed the rest of the kingdom too, if it hadn't been for..."

He trailed off, his blue eyes squeezing shut.

"If it hadn't been for the prophecy, and the sacrifice," I said, and he nodded solemnly.

There was a long, stilted silence where I grasped at something to say before finally realizing there was nothing. There were no words for the death that relentlessly haunted us both.

As much as I could remember, anyway. Phaedra held on to

most of those memories like a vise-grip, and she was refusing to cede anymore to me tonight.

But I had a feeling it was coming. All of it.

Chapter Twenty-Eight

I WAS RIGHT. THAT NIGHT, THE DREAMS CAME FOR me in full.

In the twenty-six-ish hours that had passed since I kissed Hadeon, I got an influx of memories, but they were sporadic and disjointed, out of order and hard to pin down.

Seeing my parents must have broken what was left of the dam, though, because tonight...tonight I saw everything.

Worse, I *felt* it.

First there was my childhood. I saw my early life as the slightly feral princess of the Sun Court. The way my magic was different, stronger, even then. Though my parents loved me, they hadn't known what to do with me. Their bewildered looks and exasperated sighs formed the backdrop of my childhood. In the periphery, Leander helped me sneak in stray animals while Elion stoically looked the other way, the corners of his lips tilting upward.

Then I was crying because someone at court had been

mocking me, and Elion was smoothing a stray curl, though his serious expression didn't shift.

"I'll always protect you, little sister," he said, marching away to enact his vengeance on the person who dared upset me.

Was that why he had looked so devastated when I saw him earlier? Did he feel like he had failed? Remorse flooded me, but my mind had barely begun this journey.

Next, I saw Abba visiting through the years. I begged her to tell me who my soulmate was, to explain how to follow the constellation.

"You're so impatient, little one," she chided gently. "The goddess yet has plans for you."

"Is it true that since it's brighter, he will love me even more?"

Her smile faltered. "It's true that your bond will be stronger."

"Why do you look sad about that?"

She placed a hand on my chin, nudging it upward. "You'll have to be just as strong, my child. Stronger even than your bond. Stronger than the love you have for one another."

"I could be strong if you'd tell me where to find him," I said in a singsong voice.

At that she laughed, the sound like wind chimes on a breezy spring day.

"If I told you where to find him, you wouldn't appreciate him in the same way."

Then the scene changed to one I was familiar with. The battlefield. The moon elves were on our land, threatening our people. My brother was at risk, then my family after that. So I sent Leander away, using the last bit of my isos to keep the people I loved safe.

Minutes or hours or seconds later, Celani picked her way through the corpses like a Valkyrie of pure vengeance.

"Not so deadly now, are you, Princess?" she sneered.

"Touch me and find out," I bluffed.

She wasn't deterred, hoisting my limp, burnt-out body over her shoulder and carting me on a baztet back to the king. I knew I should be afraid, but my eyes were fixed on the sky... on the golden stars that lit the exact path we took to Fengari Palace.

Then I stood in front of Hadeon, defiant even as his unearthly beauty stole my breath away. His eyes cut into me like twin icicles, devoid of warmth, and yet I was captivated by them.

Surely, the goddess wouldn't be so cruel. Wasn't I her chosen? Her favored? Abba had said she loved me. I had spent my entire life trying to be worthy of the male out there waiting for me.

Everything I had done and all the lives I had been forced to take and the lifetime I spent feeling restless and out of sorts, all the while believing I had someone who loved me on the other side of a constellation. Someone who understood me. Someone I could love in return.

Not this — whatever the hell this was.

Was this what Abba had meant when she said to be stronger than our love? That I would have to avoid it? That giving in would be the end of me?

It sure as hell felt that way.

So I demanded dresses that covered my collarbones without saying why, and he, to my everlasting surprise, complied. I refused to show him my isos, and he didn't torture me for it. I returned his every jab with one of my own, and he never once punished me for the impertinence.

He wasn't doing anything the way he was supposed to.

I thought it would be easy, stopping myself from falling in love with a monster, someone who hurt me. Too bad he didn't hurt me; he killed the people who tried. And he wasn't a monster. He was just a king who was doing his best to undo the damage his mother had wrought.

On the outskirts were memories with Celani and Kallius, the friendships formed in spite of my best efforts, and the way I started to see us all as two sides of the same coin rather than enemies. Those were softer, integrating with what I knew now, but weren't where my mind wanted to focus tonight.

The day we found Nyx in the clearing came next.

"Hadeon, we can't just leave her here."

He gave me a dubious look that clearly said he disagreed. "If you want a puppy, I'll get you one that won't eat you."

"That's very generous of you," I deadpanned.

Hadeon shrugged a single shoulder. "Never let it be said that I am not a gracious master."

"Hadeon." My tone was more demanding this time.

With a great, long-suffering sigh, he wrapped the tiny glowing cerberus in his shadows and carried it with surprising gentleness all the way back to Fengari. Where it promptly peed on his shoes.

"Has anyone ever told you that you're more trouble than you're worth?" he muttered.

"That wasn't nice." I cooed at the three-headed puppy. "He didn't mean it."

"I wasn't talking to the cerberus."

Visions flitted by too fast for me to follow after that, showing me how, day by day, I tried with everything I had not to love him.

And day by day, I failed.

He wasn't perfect, by any means. He was ruthless and driven and operated with a morality that tended more toward black than gray. Yet with each sardonic comment that had my lips turning up, each time he showed the compassion that neither his mother nor his barbaric court had managed to rob him of, I felt my resolve slipping.

The next time the memories slowed down, we were having breakfast on the balcony. My collar was gone. Celani was in the doorway, requesting permission for one of her soldiers to embark upon her mate journey.

He scoffed. "On her own head be it."

She nodded and left, then I turned to him with narrowed eyes.

"You don't think the soldier will find her mate?" I asked.

He shrugged like it was nothing, but something stirred behind his eyes. "I think she'd be better served if she didn't."

I blinked, trying to stave off the sinking feeling in my gut.

"Right, because who wants to find someone who is suited for them in every way when they could just be alone and miserable?" There was a bite to my speech I couldn't quite quell.

A muscle twitched in his jaw. "According to who? I don't need the goddess to tell me who I'm compatible with. I'm sure I can figure that out all on my own."

I sat forward, gritting through my teeth, "It's not about some passing compatibility. It's about finding the other half of your soul."

He gave one of his infuriating shrugs. "So you say. I'm not convinced it even exists in the capacity so many elves insist upon. And even if it does, I'd just as soon go without."

It was like the air was stolen from my lungs, my heart struggling to find the will to beat.

"You don't have a soulmate mark?" Had I really been wrong this whole time? Was it like he said, and I only convinced myself based on some fleeting attraction.

He raised an eyebrow. "How invasive, even for you."

I recognized a dodge when I saw one, especially after months of dealing with him.

"So you do?" I pressed.

Emotions flitted across his features before I could read them, then his blank mask returned. "What I have is a healthy enough self-interest to avoid intentionally tracking down someone who will be little more than a liability in the end."

Maybe he was right. Maybe it was a liability. It sure as hell felt that way, like I was breaking into a thousand pieces at little more than his unknowing rejection. I fought to keep my features steady.

"Yes, you're certainly not short on self-interest," I spat.

"I'm only surprised you don't appear to be short on cowardice either."

"Feralinia." He growled the word like a warning, but it was one I had no desire to heed.

I shook my head. "Has it ever occurred to you that you could be stronger with another person or is it so impossible to you that you might not be perfect in every single way?"

His eyes flashed with fury as his perfectly wrought control finally shattered, his shadows flaring out around him. "Do you have any idea what being my soulmate would entail?" he demanded. "What someone would do to that person just to weaken me out of spite or vengeance or a play for power?"

I leapt to my feet, my breakfast forgotten. "Then I suppose you'd better hope whoever the goddess chose for you is a hell of a lot braver than you're turning out to be."

With that, I spun to leave, ignoring the rare, gobsmacked expression he wore. In the year I had been here, I had never once left the breakfast table, never stormed away, never all but ceded an argument the way I was doing this one.

But if I stayed here another moment, tears would race down my cheeks and my humiliation would be complete. Bad enough he didn't want me. I wouldn't give him my pride along with my heart.

Of course, no sooner had I walked into my room than the shadows shifted to reveal the king, who had exactly no sense of privacy.

"You can't just walk away in the middle of a conversation," he growled as I turned my back on him.

"Oh? Apologies, your majesty. Are you going to collar me

again?" It was a chore to keep my voice clear when there was something permanently lodged in my throat, but I tried.

Celestial hells, I wanted him to leave. I was so, so close to crumbling.

Instead, he closed the distance between us, his solid footsteps barely echoing on the ground behind me.

"I might if you test me," he purred.

My mouth went dry. Stars, if the problem wasn't that I might want him to, in the twisted, broken part of my soul that would forever belong to him whether he damned well wanted it or not.

He brought a hand to my shoulder, turning me to face him with a gentleness I had no power to resist.

His eyes darted to my lips, then back to my eyes, which I knew were blazing bright blue with the intent I couldn't seem to hide, and the sheen of tears that was even more telling.

"Feralinia." He said the word like a question. A demand. A breaking.

I couldn't say anything at all.

"You know," he murmured, his voice full of resignation and wonder and just the slightest bit of awe. "You truly are more trouble than you're worth."

Then he leaned toward me, giving me everything I was foolish enough to need so badly from him.

Our lips met, and the world imploded. Entire galaxies perished and were born during nothing but the feeling of his mouth finally, finally on mine.

Time lost all meaning. I explored the way he tasted, while he laid us back on my bed, his shadows balancing us both. The memory didn't linger the way I selfishly wanted it to, skipping ahead to his lips skating down to my neck, my collarbone. He shoved my dress out of the way to give himself access to my skin.

Then he paused, his lips on my skin, eyes meeting mine.

"How long have you known?" he whispered.

"No longer than you have." Because there was no way he hadn't felt it, this inexorable pull between his soul and mine.

What had started as something frantic slowed, time moving in the solid thumps of my heart while I waited for him to deny it, to deny me, to tell me all over again how little he wanted any of this.

Instead, he lowered his mouth to the constellation, pressing kisses more tender than I would have believed him capable of against each of the seven stars.

"I thought you didn't want a soulmate," I choked out.

"I want you," he responded.

"Even if I'm a liability?"

"Not *if*," he said darkly. "But yes, Feralinia." He moved his lips down, his hand skimming up my thigh.

"If you can be brave enough to face down everyone who will try to take you from me, then I can be brave enough to let you."

"Don't kid yourself," I said, gasping as his hand slid higher. "You don't *let* me do anything."

He chuckled, a dark promise. "We'll see about that."

The memory sped up again, racing through months of hiding our relationship until we determined peace was stable enough to risk it. Of late nights and languid mornings and me moving into Hadeon's room while he told his servant he wanted to keep his property closer. Of Nyx growing older and more enormous, evenings on the balcony with Celani and Kallius, flying on a baztet, Hadeon praying at the temple because he said even he knew enough to thank the goddess when she gave him everything.

I saw the night I all but proposed to him, offering him one of the bargains he was so fond of dangling in front of other people.

"My soul for yours," I said.

His chin dipped, his interest piqued. "I think you get the raw end of that deal."

"Well, there's a catch." I leaned up to capture his mouth with mine. "It has to be forever."

"Forever is a long time to bargain." He murmured the words against my lips.

"That's a chance I'm willing to take," I assured him.

Then word came in the night. Valandril had struck. The Court of Mist and Memory was overtaken by shadow creatures. My father blamed Hadeon while the latter prepared for war.

"You have to go back, where you'll be safe," he insisted.

"All right," I agreed. Not for my own safety, but because it was the only way to convince my family to ally with him. But it didn't work. My father wouldn't be swayed, even when his own kingdom was under threat.

Abba came to me while I was in the gilded halls of Illios, the Sun Palace, looking sadder than I had ever seen her.

"There may yet be a way, but it may require more than you

are willing to give." She squeezed her eyes shut. "More than we have any right to ask of you."

I tossed my head in defiance. "There is no price too high if it saves him."

From her expression, I knew what that price would be. I knew what it cost her to ask me. I knew what it would do to Hadeon if I accepted.

But I would be damned if I let him die.

Still, there was a chance, so I went back to the fight for the court that had become my home alongside the person who had become my world. Leander made me a portal even as his uncertain eyes pleaded with me not to go.

"Your place is here," I told him. "Don't worry about me."

Don't come with me when I will not be coming back, is what I really wanted to tell him. He threw his arms around me one final time before closing off the space between us, and I went to face my soulmate.

Hadeon was predictably furious until I made him a deal I had no intention of keeping. I promised him I would stay safe, knowing it was a lie. And again, it was worth it to keep him alive.

Anything was worth that.

Then we were at the battlefront in what the people were starting to call the Never Court. The black monsters attacked, but Hadeon and I stayed at the top of the mountain, fighting from a distance like I promised. I cast enormous beams of light that intensified Hadeon's shadows, and we took them out in droves, but their number was endless. For each monster we killed, two more rose up in its place, each controlled by the

Vampire who had taken it upon himself to rip everything we loved from us.

Desperation gnawed at me from the inside out. I would sacrifice my limbs or my life, but I could not lose Hadeon.

"I have to get closer," he said.

"It's not fair to ask me to stay behind," I protested. "You know that."

"I have never claimed to be decent or fair," he growled. "But I will damned well hold you to your end of the bargain."

I could tell him I had a way out of this, but he would stop me. Abba's power was waning from battling Valandril. Hadeon would fight to the death to keep me safe, no matter my own wishes. He was who he was, and I loved him for it.

But there was no place for the truth between us now.

"All right." I leaned up and pressed my lips against his for what I knew would be the last time. "I'll stay with Nyx like I promised."

He turned to go, and I called after him.

"I love you, Hadeon," I told him. "Not because of a mark on my skin or a promise from the goddess. Because of everything you are."

Remember that, I silently begged. *Remember who you are and live on anyway.*

"And I love you. If anything, in spite of the mark on my skin and the promise from the goddess." His lips tilted up in a dark smirk. "Stay with Nyx," he repeated.

I nodded, unwilling to let my last words to him be a lie. And for a while, I did stay with Nyx.

Until Abba came for me.

Then the last memory played. The Sacred Temple. A tree of life that was dying. A captive Vampire who was clinging to life. A prophecy. A golden chalice. A sacrifice willingly made. A vow offered along with my isos.

"By the shadows of the starswept sky and the embers of the dawn, I offer my life in exchange for theirs." Then a whisper. "Mortem pro amore." *Death for the sake of love.*

And finally, I understood why Abba looked so sad when she told me that our bond would be stronger, what she had meant when she said I had to be stronger than our love.

Because all I wanted was to run back to him, to spend the rest of this life with him for however little or long we had left. But I wanted him to live more.

The golden stars, the constellation that had been created just for us, the love I waited a lifetime for. All so that when the time came, I would be willing to make this choice.

Not for my people or the world, but Hadeon.

For the other half of my restless, wandering soul.

Chapter Twenty-Nine

I WASN'T SURE IF I SHOULD BE GRATEFUL THAT Leander was in his own room or not. My thoughts were a mess.

On the one hand, my soul had finally merged with Phaedra's. I could recognize on an intrinsic level that we had always been the same, just as I was the same person I had been as a child, even if I knew different things now and had different experiences.

On the other hand, I now had two lifetimes' worth of grief to carry around. It clawed at my gut, a sentient, ravenous beast I tried to satiate with the golden memories of my families — human and Elven both — and with the few untainted memories I had with Hadeon.

It was strange. Now that I understood the customs here, I knew we had been whatever this world's version of *married* was. Did that mean we were estranged now? Divorced?

The tumultuous maelstrom of feelings and memories

eventually dragged me out onto my balcony, where my unwavering gaze landed on the brilliant constellation that had started it all.

And ended it.

The hours ticked by in a barely discernible lightening of the sky, something I only noticed now that I remembered my two years of experience with the Moon Court's sluggish dawn.

I wasn't as surprised as I should have been when he found me on the balcony. Or rather, I wasn't as surprised as I would have been, before I had Phaedra's instinctive understanding of who he was.

Hadeon's shadows heralded his presence, as they always did. Tendrils of darkness that expanded and reached for me before he could command them to return. His control wasn't as flawless as he would have let the amnesiac version of myself believe.

But then, neither was mine.

It took everything I had not to turn to him, bury myself in the hard planes of his chest and beg for his forgiveness. Not to call upon the sparks of my isos and set him on fire for the way he had acted since I returned to him.

The urges were equally strong within me, right up there with the fracturing I felt in every part of my being when I remembered him telling me that what we had wasn't worth the pain. That *I* wasn't worth it. The soulmate he had never wanted to begin with, back to torment him in another life.

Though I was certain he had come to fetch me for training, he stopped short when he saw me.

I felt his appraisal, felt the moment when he decided not

to speak and instead walked with sure, measured steps to the railing. He stopped several feet away and stared out at the Ahvi constellation like he, too, hoped it held the answers to all the problems we couldn't solve.

Wasn't it supposed to?

Maybe Hadeon had been right all along, and our bond never was a gift. Maybe it was only ever a sacrificial lamb created for the slaughter, one we fattened with each touch, kiss, and promise that brought us closer to being willing to watch the world end for the sake of one another.

Finally, I turned to look at him. For a fraction of a second, I took the opportunity to observe him, broad shoulders tense as his massive hands clutched the railing. His face was even more perfect than it had been in the memories, like the years had honed it into something more real and even more beautiful.

But his eyes were haunted when he tilted his head toward me, wounded by the demons I had cursed him with.

He held my gaze for an interminable moment.

"You remember," he said without inflection. It wasn't a question, so I didn't bother to answer.

"Did you see that in my dreams?" I asked.

That was another thing I understood now that I had my memories: we could enter one another's dreams. That was why the shadows so often eclipsed my dreams, when Hadeon got sucked in.

Though even in my first life, we hadn't been entirely sure how much of that was voluntary.

"No." His deep voice was quieter than usual. "I saw it on

your face just now. You haven't looked at me like that since... before."

Like someone who understood him? Loved him? Resented him for reasons beyond kidnapping and collaring me?

"Perhaps I would have, if you hadn't been such an ass since my return." The words lacked any real heat.

I was more tired than angry, more confused than furious.

He shrugged, the movement graceful even with his tense shoulders. "That would have only worked in opposition to our mutual needs."

"*Your* needs," I corrected quietly.

"Also yours," he bit out. "I thought it would be helpful to at least let you build up your isos before you went gallivanting off to die again."

I chewed my lip, frustration curling my fingers around the cold stone of the railing.

"It wasn't as simple as you're making it out to be." Like I chose to run off and leave him for fun.

He grunted a noncommittal response, and I didn't press him. It was an argument neither of us was prepared for. Hell, I didn't feel prepared for any part of this conversation.

Just when I thought we were going to table the rest of our substantial issues, he took a breath to speak.

"How long?" His tone was calmer than the storm swirling in his moonlit eyes.

"What?" I furrowed my brow.

"How long did you know what you had planned?" A muscle worked in his jaw, his features going colder. "How many times did you look me in the eyes and lie to me before running off to do the goddess's noble bidding?"

Oh. That.

It was remarkable how quickly we were having this fight after I got my memories back. Hadeon must have nearly given himself an aneurysm biting his tongue for as long as he did. Fifty years of frustration and questions.

No wonder he was angry when I arrived at court.

Still, I was exhausted, having barely come to terms with these memories before he was demanding answers from me.

"Not long." I sighed. "Less than a week."

Even as I said it, I heard how it would sound to him. An entire week I could have prepared him but chose not to.

"Did you know you would return?" He pinned me with his gaze, scrutinizing me for signs of a lie.

Did I know I would come back to him in this lifetime? Abba had promised me that our souls would find each other one day, but I had, admittedly, assumed it would be in the afterlife.

I let out a slow breath, staring out at the seven glowing stars that always seemed to be mocking me.

"No," I admitted.

He scoffed, the sound bitter in my ears.

"But," I added, "I knew that if I didn't go, you would die, and that was enough for me."

Hadeon grimaced, looking out at the sky and away from me. "Well, as long as you're secure in your convoluted reasoning, far be it for the rest of us to question you. Just pray to the goddess you love so much that you never have to be on the other side of that decision."

His exhale formed a cloud in front of him, one that brushed against the wards surrounding my balcony.

"If you have your way, that will hardly be an issue." Because we would never be together to begin with. "What was it you said? That given the choice, you would just as soon I never returned?"

I didn't realize that I was giving him a chance to take the words back until he didn't. Instead he turned to face me, doubling down.

"At least then I could have grieved without you here hurling salt in the wounds you created."

My lips parted on a furious gasp. "If you wanted to grieve in peace so badly, why did you collar me and keep me by your side?"

There was the barest heartbeat of hesitation before he answered. "Because I needed you, as you know perfectly well."

"To fight the wraiths?" I baited him in spite of myself. "Lie to yourself, but don't lie to me."

He leaned closer, his lips inches from mine.

"Why would I lie at all when you tell enough for the both of us?" he growled.

Then his darkness engulfed him, and he was gone before I could tilt my head up and succumb to the desire he ignited in my soul. A frigid breeze brushed up against my heated skin, soothing me like the shadows I didn't want to admit I missed so much.

Had the goddess known the way Hadeon would react

when she put me in a position to abandon him? Was that why our bond was stronger, some last-ditch effort to make him love me enough to overcome the hurt my sacrifice had caused?

Looking at the spot on the balcony he had all but stormed away from, I couldn't help but wonder how her brilliant plan was working out so far. Maybe Abba was right. Maybe Hadeon was rubbing off on me.

I pushed myself off the railing, stuffing all my feelings, new and old, down where they belonged. For better or worse, the war wasn't over, and we had work to do.

Chapter Thirty

CELANI CAME TO ESCORT ME TO TRAINING LATER that morning, a raised eyebrow the only indication that she knew something had changed.

I shot her a sideways glance.

"You put on a good soldier face, you know." My tone was dry, but I knew she recognized the hint of humor in it.

Sure enough, the corner of her mouth tilted up. "I *am* a soldier, you menace."

I exhaled a laugh. At least this was one uncomplicated thing...or, less complicated, I amended. The last few weeks couldn't have been easy on her, even aside from the way she was constantly torn between Hadeon and me.

"I'm sorry," I said with more seriousness.

Celani's violet eyes narrowed — in suspicion or confusion, I wasn't quite sure. "For what?"

I hesitated, taking a moment of comfort in the familiar soft pad of her measured footsteps, the confident set of her shoulders. How would it have felt to have those small, random pieces of her when she didn't remember me?

"How hard it must have been for you to pretend, to see your dead best friend and treat me like a prisoner," I finally answered.

"Don't flatter yourself," she muttered, blinking rapidly.

The corner of my mouth pulled upward. "Of course not. Kallius is obviously my best friend."

She aimed a punch at my arm, like I knew she would. And my efforts to dart out of her reach failed, like I knew they would.

"Ow," I said.

She rolled her eyes. "You need to build your muscles back up. This is getting pathetic, even for you."

We walked for a while down the hall while she chewed on something she obviously wanted to say. Finally, when we rounded the corner, making our way down the second set of stairs, I lost patience.

"What is it?"

She leveled me with a look out of the corner of her eye. "I liked it better when you didn't remember me." Couldn't read her, she meant. "Human Ember was nicer than you are."

I shrugged, both because I knew she absolutely had missed me and because there was probably some truth to that. Now that I felt more complete, Phaedra's memories and Ember's melded as seamlessly as my childhood with my adult life. So while I felt like Ember, the pieces of Phaedra that came from her life as a princess and a warrior felt stronger now. Less distant.

"You're trying to distract me," I pointed out.

She sighed. "I'm only wondering if all this magnanimous understanding applies to my cousin as well."

I stumbled over the next marble step, glaring at her as I regained my balance.

"The one who has acted like a bastard since my return, you mean, or the one who told me again mere minutes ago that he wished I'd stayed dead?"

Celani winced, the expression incongruent on her stoic features. She waited the span of several heartbeats before responding more quietly than before.

"You don't know what it's been like for him."

It was strange, the possessive rage I felt that someone else knew a part of Hadeon I didn't, had experienced years with him that should have belonged to me. Even when that person was my friend and his cousin, there was an unreasonable surge of jealousy that she knew him then and would know him in the future he was trying so hard to push me out of.

That feeling was easier than the relentless storm of guilt and pain and longing and hope and agony that was threatening to pull me under.

I wanted to ask more questions, but I needed to hear answers from the source. And not today.

So I took a deep breath, squaring my shoulders. *Princess. Warrior. Survivor.*

I could still be all of those things.

"Let's just focus on training," I said once I was sure I could control my expression and my voice. "At least that's one thing that should be easier now."

I HAD SPOKEN TOO SOON about training.

As it turned out, my physical muscles were not the only ones that weren't strong enough in this life.

Though I understood the concepts behind using my isos now, the reality of controlling it was...somewhat less easy.

It didn't help that my isos wanted nothing more than to go meld with Hadeon's, like a shameless flirt throwing themselves at their crush again and again.

My firelight was trying even harder than before to escape, and I wasn't sure I had the strength to rein it in much longer.

I wondered if it was my memories or the escalated tension between Hadeon and me that was causing me to burn so much hotter than usual.

"Let it go," Hadeon ordered, his voice a resonant baritone that ignited my fire even more.

"Gladly," I muttered, letting out a breath and releasing my tenuous hold.

Flames burst forth, straight toward Hadeon in a powerful thread that would have been dangerous to anyone else. Of course, he easily smothered the fire with a wall of darkness before putting the shadow collar back on me.

Leander looked impressed in spite of himself.

"She still needs the bloodstone," he commented.

Hadeon nodded, a single, sharp dip of his defined chin. He reached into his vest pocket, pulling out something small made of the same pale, shimmering blue as his crown and my daggers.

A ring.

My breath stalled in my throat.

Logically, I knew it meant nothing. Here, there were no wedding rings. No weddings at all — or marriages, really. Elves were private beings, and a couple's commitment to one another was between them. It was up to them to divulge whether they were soulmates, or how long they intended to be together.

Nevertheless, the sight of Hadeon looking at me over a ring in his hand stirred things in me I had no desire to confront in the light of our most recent conversation.

He frowned, catching on to the sudden shift in my mood, and I cleared my expression.

"A bloodstone," he explained. "I don't know where the former queen hid the rest, but this one was in the palace vaults. It's smaller than I would have preferred, but it should at least help you temporarily regain control."

He stretched out a hand, and I snatched it from him, unwilling to lose myself in the feel of him sliding the metal along my finger.

"Thank you," I said, my tone terse enough that Leander and Celani both raised their eyebrows.

Ignoring them, I put the ring on, choosing my right hand and my middle finger, as far away from symbolism as I could get.

The crescent moon curved from just below my middle knuckle to the base of my finger. In the center was a star, studded with tiny sparkling pale blue gemstones. The band wrapped from the outside curve of the moon to the center of the star, leaving a gap in the middle so that both pieces seemed to float independently on my hand.

I forcibly averted my gaze just in time for Hadeon to wave away my collar. A torrent of isos flooded me, just as it had before. This time, though, I didn't have to struggle to hold on to it.

Where the collar dampened my power to the point that I barely felt it in me at all, the ring acted more as a funnel, giving me a single, central point to stem the flow instead of trying to hold back a deluge from my entire being.

Tentatively, I let it go once again. A jet of fire streamed out, more refined and easier to control than before. I directed it with a twitch of my fingers, and it swirled in graceful arcs between Celani and Leander.

Inevitably, of course, my isos eventually gravitated back to Hadeon. It danced around him like it was showing off, and something akin to pride crossed his features when he nodded.

"Again," he commanded. "This time, try to break free of my shadows." His deep timbre curled around me just as surely as his shadows did.

I tried not to think about the gentle way they caressed my skin or the darkness that encased the two of us, blocking Leander, Celani, Kallius, and even Nyx from view. Tried not to think about the heady scent of bergamot and snow that filled my lungs. Tried not to remember the way he tasted like Elven wine.

I shook my head, focusing my thoughts on the isos flowing through my body instead.

I could feel the bones of the mountains beneath my feet, the veins of raw power that flowed from Terrea's core into me, and the distant tug from the Sacred Tree as she fueled my power.

Without the distraction of controlling my unruly power, the bloodstone opened me up to a new understanding of my magic. I could feel the isos in the air around me, in the ground beneath me, in the heat of my fire.

And I could feel it surging from the King of Moon and Stars. Pulsing from him like a raging inferno.

No wonder everyone was terrified of him.

I would have known that Hadeon was goddess-blessed from the sheer volume of power that coursed through his veins, even without being told.

That power called to mine, like it wanted nothing more than for my flames to come out and play, like they belonged to him as surely as I did. Like my isos was his. And his was mine.

"Feralinia." Hadeon's baritone rumbled through me, heating me from the inside out. Literally.

My skin began to glow, the tattoos gleaming like Celani's runes. My long fiery waves flared out around my head, licking at Hadeon's shadows like real flames. A purr of approval settled over me, and I resisted the urge to shiver.

Once again, flames ignited at my fingertips, and a pale white light shone beneath my black scaled armor. It illuminated the space between us until I could finally see Hadeon's midnight eyes and the flecks of silver like stars.

"Well done, Feralinia," he said. "Now give me more."

No, you give me more, I wanted to say.

More than a stupid nickname with the refusal to move past a fifty-year old grievance. More than a single kiss that was everything and not nearly enough.

Instead, I increased my flames, turning every bit of my frustration into that bright beam of pure, white light. It wasn't as powerful as it had been in the past, but neither was it burning me up from the inside out.

"Call it back," Hadeon ordered.

That, too, was easier than it had been before, but remained a challenge. By the time I stemmed the flow, sweat beaded on my brow and my lungs were burning.

Hadeon took one look at me, dipped his chin, and said, "Again," in that obnoxiously calm voice of his.

So I did.

Maybe if I burned off some of the isos brimming underneath my skin, it wouldn't long for him so much.

Maybe then, I could pretend to be just as unaffected as he was.

BY THE END of the day, I was spent. Magically, physically, and emotionally.

I sank on to the small sofa in my room, my hair wet and steaming after my bath, but Leander stretched out his arms to pull me back up.

"Come on, sis."

I shot him an incredulous look. Now that I had my fire back, I was more than a little willing to burn him where he stood for suggesting anything other than a nap.

"I don't want to go anywhere," I said flatly.

He pursed his lips in concern. "I can send for dinner, and we can eat on the balcony."

I pulled a plush blanket over me, cocooning myself in it like the sad, tired burrito I was. "Not hungry."

"Well, I'm starving, and you need to eat." He sat next to me, moving some of the blanket so he could see my face better. "Come on, Em. What's your favorite food?"

I rolled my eyes dramatically, and sighed. "It doesn't matter, because there are no tacos here. Only brooding soul-mates and mysterious goddesses and war and powers that burn you."

"And family," he said quietly, his blue eyes boring into mine.

"And family," I confirmed, more warmth in my tone.

Gently, he peeled the blanket off my shoulders and tugged me to my feet. "There's got to be a kitchen around here some-where. I'm sure we can figure something out for...tacos."

Those could and should have been famous last words. But I could probably use a distraction, and there was something wholly entertaining about making Mexican food in whatever fancy Elven kitchen Fengari boasted.

Reluctantly, I exchanged my nightgown for a tunic and pants. Several had been added to my wardrobe since Hadeon noted my preference, not that I noticed or cared that he was oddly considerate along with being an asshat ninety-eight percent of the time.

At the very last moment, I grabbed my cell phone, deciding that a night of taco-making deserved some music as well. Even if my battery was at a lamentable twenty-seven percent.

We opened the door to my room to find Celani standing guard in the hallway. She eyed us with suspicion, and Leander rolled his eyes.

"I'm not going to abscond with her, *General*. We're just going to make tacos."

"Tacos?" Celani repeated the word in bewilderment.

"They're like...sandwiches," I explained badly. "But made in pockets of very thin bread, and the insides are all mixed up."

It didn't sound half as appetizing as I meant it to. By the look on Celani's face, she agreed.

"They're delicious," I added, somewhat defensively. "And pair well with Elven wine."

Sort of. In the way that tacos paired well with everything. Celani tilted her head, looking appropriately intrigued, when Helpy Helperton chimed in to assist.

"Besides," my brother said. "Ember is sad because she got all her memories back and the king is being exactly the same as he always is, which is to say—"

"I see," she cut him off with a glare. "All right, then. Tacos it is. Let's go."

So the three of us left with Nyx in tow. Ahvi would likely be furious when he returned to an empty room, but it was his fault for deciding to go out hunting what I sincerely hoped were animals and not people.

We went all the way down to the lowest level of the palace, a floor I had never visited in this life or Phaedra's.

It was well past dinnertime, so there were only a few servants in here who Celani ordered out as soon as we arrived, leaving us alone in the biggest kitchen I had ever seen.

"Best not to take chances," she said darkly, her eyes resting on me and Leander both.

I nodded, taking in the space around us. Cool, gray stone walls rose above dark wooden cabinets. There was a massive stove lining the far wall, and cast iron pans hung from the ceiling next to the torch light.

In the center was an island with a large sink. Several shelves underneath housed bowls, plates, and canisters of cutlery.

It was even more overwhelming than I imagined, and I suddenly wondered if Leander had taken up cooking in the time since I died, or if he was just a hopeless optimist.

One glance at his wide eyes and the similarly uncertain expression he was trying to hide, and I had my answer. The staff probably would have been helpful...but maybe not, given their feelings toward us. In any event, I wasn't sad to have their judgment sent elsewhere after the day I had already had.

But we were here now, so we may as well try to figure it out.

Nyx guarded the door, her massive frame barely fitting inside the kitchen doorway, while Leander, Celani, and I split up to search for ingredients.

I called out a list of things for them to watch out for,

something that had all of us laughing by the time I realized they had no clue where a container of flour might live.

It took nearly an hour to search the larder and cabinets for the things I could only assume we needed. Mostly, I procured food ingredients while the other two procured booze and appropriate glassware.

Leander poured us each a glass of the wine Celani found as I grabbed the leftover roasted meat that tasted like carnitas, along with several vegetables that seemed like they would be at least mediocre replacements for salsa.

Despite her prowess slicing through her enemies on the battlefield, Celani's vegetable chopping skills were sadly lacking.

However, she was better than Leander, who dropped half of the food on the ground while he distractedly watched whatever we were trying to do. Though, I noticed he mostly watched Celani, and I doubted it was for instructional purposes.

"This looks like flour," I said to my brother, after sifting through multiple bags of unmarked white and brown and yellow powder.

"Sure." Leander shrugged.

"We could just ask the staff," Celani suggested from the island.

Leander made a humming sound in the back of his throat. "We could have, before you ordered them away. Besides, I doubt they would come back with the way they all fled at the abject horror of not one but *two* Sun Court members in their midst."

I nodded. "This is true. Leander was just the icing on their Sun Court cake of hate."

"Besides, I'm not sure they'd be exactly thrilled with the mess we've made so far," my brother said with a gesture toward the disheveled larder and the multiple pans and plates scattered all around.

Celani and I nodded, a silent agreement that we would figure this out for ourselves.

We had just finished prepping all of our ingredients when Nyx let out a low whine, moving to the side to allow Kallius through the kitchen door. Her giant puppy eyes were filled with more than a little jealousy that she couldn't be closer, but I didn't particularly want cerberus fur in my food, no matter how much I loved her.

"We're cooking, brother," Celani said just a touch too happily. She had the drinking part of cooking down, anyway.

"Is that what you're doing?" he asked, his tone dubious.

"You can't judge when you don't know anything about tacos," I told him, before sipping from my glass.

It tasted like autumn and berries and Hadeon's lips.

I took several more gulps, trying to dislodge the thought, when Kallius met my gaze. His eyes danced with amusement.

"I can judge when you, apparently, don't know anything about kitchens. Have any of you ever set foot in one before?"

Leander shrugged. "I mean, I'm a prince, so, I feel like my answer is obvious."

Celani followed suit, though she looked decidedly irritated about it. "General, little brother." She pointed at her chest. "People just bring me my food, or I eat rations."

Kallius turned to me. "Surely you —"

"Have absolutely been in a kitchen," I assured him with a confident dip of my chin. "In America. On Earth."

He blinked in disappointment, like all the hopes he had in me were crushed with those words.

"All right then," he said briskly. "I'll set up over here, if you can — no, Ember, do not light the burner with your very volatile magic, please and thank you. I will do that."

I brought my hand back to my side with a little harumph. He continued to bark orders at us while I went through the arduous task of trying to remember the art of tortilla making. Isa was so much better at this than I would ever be, but I was determined to make *Abuela* proud.

Another bottle of wine, an explanation of who Ruelle was, how their music blared from the speaker on my phone, and several burned corpses of what could have been taco shells later, we had something close to workable.

The kitchen was filled with the appetizing scent of chili and garlic, pork, and salsa, along with the cozy aroma of freshly grilled tortillas.

Maybe that's what drew Hadeon. Or maybe he just followed the pull of my isos the way I had so badly wanted to do with his.

I was certain I would have noticed his presence earlier if my senses weren't dulled by the wine. As it was, by the time I looked up, the shadow king already leaned in the doorway, having edged Nyx farther into the hall. His massive arms were crossed as he watched us destroy his kitchen with a vaguely confused sort of horror.

"Do I even want to know?" his low baritone inquired, and I shook my head, pausing the music.

"Probably not." I said as I checked on the simmering meat on the cast iron, adding a pinch of salt and what tasted like cumin to the pan. I wasn't sure the food needed any more seasoning, but I was eager to do anything that didn't have my attention slinking over to Hadeon.

He made no move to join us, but he didn't leave, either. And for all he said that he didn't want anything between us, and wouldn't risk it, the look in his eyes while he watched me wipe flour from my forehead as I threw a few more tortillas together said something else entirely.

At the very least, it was not the expression of someone who was ready to throw in the towel on whatever convoluted relationship we had.

Celani went over to him, handing him a glass of wine while Leander joined me at the stove.

"I've missed you," my brother said. "This. The kind of ridiculousness that sets Elion's carefully coiffed hair on edge."

I huffed out a laugh. "His hair is not coiffed."

"Metaphorically, it is," he insisted.

Fair.

"I've missed this, too." And I really had.

Even on Earth, it had always felt like something was absent. I knew most of that was probably the whole fractured soulmates thing, but it was this, too, the sense of family I had with each person in this room.

As a child who could never quite settle, I wondered if part of that was missing the siblings I should have had.

"Do you think you'll come home, then?" he asked more quietly, while Celani explained tacos even worse than I had in the background, and Kallius fretted over the tortilla I had forgotten to flip.

Home.

I thought of the word, trying to pair it with blazing mountains from my memory or even the skyline back home. But it was no use. All I could see was a sea of stars and a three-headed dog and a breakfast table on a balcony that overlooked a silver waterfall.

Not that any of it mattered.

It would be more than I could bear to stay here while Hadeon kept me at arm's length indefinitely. Besides, there was no place for me here after we fought the wraiths.

My eyes drifted to his to find them already trained on me. He released a breath, turning to go like he couldn't stand the thought of staying another moment.

Leander followed my gaze to the now empty doorway, wholly unsurprised when I murmured, "I'm not sure yet."

Chapter Thirty-One

I woke up the next morning with my first hangover since entering Terrea.

Between all the wine, the tacos, and the general aftereffects of realizing this palace and its infuriating king were more of a home to me than I had ever known, my head was throbbing and my stomach more than a little precarious.

After rubbing the sleep from my eyes, I slowly sat up in bed, careful to lean against the headboard for support.

Leander didn't look much better than I felt.

He was asleep, his mouth hanging open while his arm was casually thrown over his head to block the dim light of the stars.

I tiptoed around the room, leaning down to scratch Nyx's ears. She flopped onto her back, her eyes drifting shut again.

Ahvi was carefully nestled in his fireproof bedding on the balcony instead of cuddling with Leander this morning. He let out a purr when I ran a hand along his feathers, even though he refused to open his eyes.

After showering and dressing in the thin, long-sleeved armor I usually wore for training, I slipped toward the door on silent footfalls. As soon as I twisted the handle, however, Nyx portaled next to me.

Her massive middle head nudged the top of mine, her large puppy eyes betrayed that I had planned to leave her behind.

"All right, girl," I whispered. "Come on."

It was early, but I was in dire need of coffee and maybe some leftover tacos to soak up the wine still sloshing in my stomach. Otherwise, I might end up hurling on Hadeon when he dragged me back to the training grounds. So Nyx and I crept through the halls, past the quiet bedrooms and down the stairs to the kitchens.

It took a little convincing — and several apologies for the state we left the kitchen in — before the kitchen staff finally consented to not pitching my precious leftover tacos, allowing me to eat them for breakfast instead. I enjoyed my tacos with a side of purple pomegranate seeds.

Though none of us were about to become fast friends by any means, the servants at least appeared as if they hated me a little less. Or maybe they were just growing used to my presence in the palace.

Either way, they left me alone with nary a glare cast in my direction while I sipped my coffee and filled my stomach.

I was on my final bite when a familiar voice pulled my

attention to the door. Hadeon stood there, his navy brows furrowed in slight confusion as he studied me.

A servant rushed forward, placing a steaming mug of coffee into his waiting hands, then handing him a small plate of eggs, bacon, and fruit.

I shoved the last morsel of taco into my mouth, wiping the salsa from my chin. I had only ever seen him eat on his balcony, so his presence here was unexpected to say the least.

Though the staff didn't seem especially shocked to see him.

"Sometimes it's faster to come by on the way to training."

I nodded. He took a deep breath, perhaps having some internal debate. Finally, he rested his plate across from mine before taking a seat.

"I would have thought you had your fill of my kitchen last night," he commented airily. "If this is going to become a new habit of yours, I should warn my servants accordingly."

I shrugged as he lifted his fork to his full, waiting lips.

"I think we've come to an understanding," I said, picking up my mug and taking a sip.

He tilted his head in question, so I expounded.

"They have agreed that I can have tacos whenever I would like, as long as I let them do the cooking, and never ever allow Leander or Celani into the larder unsupervised again."

Hadeon's lips pursed in slight amusement, but he focused on his meal once again.

"You never said why you're awake so early," he added after a long silence.

"You never asked."

Hadeon's moonlit gaze flicked up to meet mine, and my heartbeat stuttered.

Was this how we were doomed to spend the rest of our lives? Dancing around truths and volleying with quips and banter, never knowing if a simple question would beget a simple answer, or if it meant so much more.

I didn't want to be the girl who overanalyzed and obsessed and pined. I didn't want —

Before I could continue that thought, a loud bell rang and Hadeon's shadows flared in response.

The ceramic cup slipped from my hands and clattered to the floor, shattering into tiny, jagged pieces.

The servants looked to the king in alarm, and Nyx let out one of her unearthly howls, the three pitches clashing unharmoniously with the clanging of the bell.

"What is it?" I yelled over the cacophony.

The sound rattled my bones and vibrated the air in my lungs. I made my way over to the cerberus, placing my hands over two of her ears to try to mute some of the ringing.

Hadeon didn't answer. Instead, his shadows swirled, flickering in and out of focus like they did just before he was about to shadow travel.

"Go to your rooms and wait for me to come for you," he said in between the chimes of the bell. "Nyx, take her."

To hell with that.

I shot an apologetic look at Nyx before making my decision.

Just before he could whisk away, I grabbed his arm, my

boots grinding the broken pieces of the cup into the stone floor.

His midnight gaze bored into mine, his jaw set in a hard, determined line. I cut him off before he could speak.

"Either you take me with you, or I follow you with Nyx."

He studied my expression for all of two heartbeats, a thousand emotions winking in and out of the stars in his eyes. Finally, he nodded. His hands wrapped around my waist, and we disappeared into darkness.

When we materialized, it was in a large, open room in one of the towers. Round stone walls led up to a massive bell in the center of the ceiling. Momentum propelled it back and forth, the loud clanging even more deafening here.

Gold and silver moonlight streamed in from the open windows, illuminating a table covered in maps and what looked like chess pieces. A war table.

Celani was already here. Kallius, too, along with Aereon, Xanth, Leda, and a handful of faces I didn't recognize.

Hadeon flicked his wrist, his shadows stretching out to grab the bell and silence it in a single move.

"Where?" he demanded.

Celani moved one of the chess pieces to the map on the left, and I took a step forward to get a closer look. It depicted the entire court and beyond, from the southernmost tip of the Parapeto Forest in the Never Court to the peaks of the Diamante Mountains in the north.

Red lines represented the border of the Sun Court, and green lines edged the border of the Never Court.

There were several chess pieces near a glowing orb at the

base of the mountains on the map. That's where Celani pointed.

"Just outside of Vasi," she said. "They've breached the Borderlands again; they're too close."

Hadeon's hands clenched into fists that he pressed against the table. Tension bled from each of his pulsing shadows.

"How many?"

Celani sighed, setting her jaw. Her eyes steeled as she said, "Last count was twenty-seven wraiths, but my soldiers report there are more at the border, trying to get through."

Several muttered curses hissed through the room, and my stomach twisted.

"How in the celestial-damned hells did twenty-seven wraiths breach our borders as far as Vasi?" Hadeon's roar shook the room, but he didn't wait for an answer.

Instead, he began issuing commands for different captains to rally their troops as quickly as possible. He ordered others to ready safehouses and the great hall to receive the elves who would seek refuge and need healing.

The room cleared quickly, and Hadeon rounded on me.

"I can help." I attempted to head off his refusal, but he shook his head.

"Yes, you can," he snarled. "By staying here."

"Hadeon —"

Another growl cut me off. "You cannot reliably manage your isos, and I do not have time to debate this with you right now."

"I have the bloodstone," I argued. "And you're right about

the time constraint." I moved to stand closer so he could shadow us both to the baztets.

He stopped in his tracks, finally meeting my eyes. "Feralinia. Do you honestly not understand that it will be impossible for me to focus on my people when you are in danger?"

I went still in spite of myself, not only because of his words, but because of the single moment of blind panic that flashed through his starburst gaze before he smothered it with indifference.

Hadeon might be a master manipulator when he wanted, but he was telling the truth about why he wanted me to stay here.

"And what of the danger to you?" I asked quietly.

He brushed me off. "That number of wraiths does not pose a threat to me."

Logically, I knew that was true. He could take out a dozen wraiths in a single strike. It didn't quell the visceral need I had to be with him, to make sure he was safe, but he was right. There was no actual cause for me to go.

These were his people in danger, and it wasn't fair of me to go if I would be in the way, no matter how much that rankled at me.

I felt the echo of his own panic building in me, the unreasonable terror that one of them would get the better of him, that something would happen and no one would have his back because he was busy protecting theirs.

Celani will be there, I reassured myself.

"You will come back to me," I ordered.

I wasn't even entirely sure what I meant. Come find me when this is over, so I know that you're safe. Come back to me, period.

Electricity crackled in the heavy air between us, charged with all the things we both refused to say. Then he nodded once before disappearing in a swirl of darkness.

It took everything I had not to follow him.

NYX CAME to get me shortly after they left. She whined gently as I paced the room, moving forward to press a massive head against my back. I turned and wrapped my arms around her, taking whatever comfort she was willing to give.

Eventually, she beamed us back to my bedroom where Leander was waiting for an update. I filled him in as much as I could before pacing again.

With Hadeon and the others gone to fight, I stood on my balcony and watched for them to come home, for any sign of the fighting, even knowing I couldn't see the village from here.

Of course, there was nothing.

No distant sound of snarling wraiths. No shouts of pain or the ringing frequency of star-forged weapons. Only rolling blue hills and luminescent trees, framed by gray mists.

It should have been a good thing. It meant that I was safe. Leander was safe. The people who lived and worked at Fengari were safe.

I could do nothing but wait and pace the small balcony, and wait some freaking more.

My hair expanded the more I moved, sparking and casting the room in hazy orange. The Ahvi constellation shone in the distance, each star a glimmering reminder of all the things I wasn't sure I would ever get to have.

I may have been the goddess's chosen, but it sure as hell felt more like a curse these days.

Though each tick of the clock was interminable, in reality it was a surprisingly short amount of time before they returned.

I was still relentlessly pacing my room while Leander made occasional comforting small talk when Celani's familiar knock sounded at my door.

It took everything in me not to rush to the door for news.

And as much as I needed to make sure my friend was safe, when I wrenched open the door, I couldn't lie to myself well enough to ignore the tidal wave of relief that crashed over me when Hadeon stood on the other side, next to his cousin.

"You're all right," I breathed.

He nodded, all the calm he was pretending to feel belied by the frantic way his eyes searched my form, like he wasn't sure he would come back to find me unharmed, or to find me here at all.

How many people had he seen die tonight?

"Everyone else?" I inquired, a bolt of fear going through me when I realized one of our number was missing.

Celani dipped her chin in confirmation. "Kallius is with the troops, but he's uninjured."

I breathed a sigh of relief, stepping back to allow them into the room.

"How many wraiths were there?" I asked, shutting the door behind them with a click.

Leander poured Celani a glass of wine, wordlessly handing it to her, then, with somewhat more reluctance, handed one to the king. The joviality he usually displayed was muted, his eyes dark with understanding of what it means to be suddenly called into a battle where the people under your protection are being slaughtered.

It was strange for me to realize that, I, too, had a unique understanding of that situation.

"More than we expected. Forty, at least," she answered, downing the contents of her glass in three long swallows.

Leander immediately stepped forward to refill it.

My lips parted. From my memories of fighting the more powerful monsters that Valandril had created, I knew that number didn't present a problem for Hadeon, even on an overcast night when the shadows weren't as powerful.

But for ordinary soldiers, it would have been impossible. The villagers would have been decimated.

I frowned, trying to put together the pieces. "Is it normal for them to attack that way?"

I combed through Phaedra's memories of what it was like to fight Valandril's monsters. The panicked heartbeats in between breaths as we fought hordes that never seemed to end.

Was that how the wraiths were, too? Were we doomed to face another full-scale war that would end with the deaths of thousands? At least then, there had been a way out, but now...

Celani shook her head. "No." She took a breath as if to say more, then let it out.

I narrowed my eyes at her. "What aren't you saying?"

She looked to Hadeon, who hadn't said a word, though his glowering presence took up the entire room. Whatever she was searching for, she didn't find, because she turned back to me with pursed lips.

"It's just interesting timing for the increase in attacks," she commented.

"Because I'm here?" I directed the question at her, but I looked to Hadeon for confirmation.

His lack of denial was response enough, and guilt gnawed at my insides.

"Usually they appear in pairs, at most threes or fours," Celani explained. "But never a full-on assault on this side of the border. That's why we've been able to hold them back for so long."

"I don't understand how this keeps happening," I said. "All of the malice was supposed to disappear when Valandril did."

I had given my life to take it with me to the grave, and now his monsters left behind their demented spawn to terrorize our people.

"Not everything Abba promised you?" Hadeon jeered after taking a sip of his wine.

Behind his taunting there was the smallest hint of what might have been sympathy, on literally anyone else.

"Abba only promised me one life that day," I bit back pointedly. "And she delivered."

343

He opened his mouth to argue, but Celani rose from her place on my sofa, physically standing between us to explain.

"The ones Valandril created did die. These might be similar, but they're different, too. They feel different, somehow. As far as we can understand, Valandril's monsters left a taint on the Court of Mist and Memory that allowed these things to be born."

"So how many could possibly be left if you have been killing them in droves for half a century?"

"We don't know, exactly," she hedged.

"Thus the plan to dispose of them en masse," Hadeon supplied.

Which was where I was supposed to come in, except that Hadeon had made it clear I was still very useless to them all.

"Why does it seem like you don't think that's a viable option?" I demanded.

Celani took a breath, deliberately ignoring Hadeon in a way that told me this was information he hadn't planned on sharing. "Because whatever or whoever is creating them, they keep multiplying. There seems to be no end to them."

Chapter Thirty-Two

THE NEXT DAY, WE RETURNED TO LIFE AS NORMAL. Or whatever sense of normal I had come to expect in the past few weeks.

I went back into training with a new sense of urgency after Celani's ominous words last night and the subsequent dreams of bloodstained battlefields set to the sound of the Vampire King's painful screams.

For nearly a week, we worked harder than we ever had to call on my isos, to channel it and control it, pushing it to its limits.

Hadeon and I continued our careful routine of dancing around things we refused to say. If we weren't training on the mountain, we largely kept our distance.

Or we did right up until it was time for the weekly court dinner, where I was forced to sit at his side while he played the role of possessive owner. His shadows flared around me when he pulled my chair in closer to his, or tucked my hair behind my ear while the rest of the table pretended not to watch.

At least my brother was having an easier time of it than I was. Despite their rampant prejudice, he managed to charm half the table in a way I had failed to do with twice as many opportunities.

Then again, he had always been better with people. Even as a princess in the Sun Court, I had spent a solid half of my time offending the nobles with my forward-thinking ways.

At night, I spent time with Kallius, Celani, and Leander, the latter of whom was trying and failing to train Ahvi to be just a little less fire trigger-happy.

In fairness, the feraline was still a kitten, and he mostly only set Hadeon on fire these days, which bothered Leander not at all.

With each passing day and the reality of the coming battle looming before us, it was getting impossible to ignore the concept of *after*. After I lent my isos to get rid of the wraiths. After I had a reason to stay here.

Hadeon might have said he wasn't letting me go back when I had no memories, when he was trying to pretend we were something else entirely to one another, but I knew that wasn't true anymore.

He wouldn't risk a war to keep me prisoner, which my father would most certainly launch if he thought I was truly being held captive again.

Besides, I would just as soon set myself on fire than stay in the Moon Court as some sort of half-neglected pet for the stubborn-as-hell shadow king who was supposed to be my soulmate. So Leander's question about whether I was going back to the Sun Court followed me around, dogging me the way Phaedra's memories did.

The dreams hadn't stopped now that my memories were back. If anything, sometimes they felt stronger, like I was more present.

Tonight was no different.

Shadows slid along my skin like silk, chased by Hadeon's smooth lips. He trailed a line of kisses down my collarbone, along my constellation, then in between my breasts.

I arched against him, making needy, demanding noises, and he brought one hand up to my breast while his mouth moved lower. He stopped at the navy lace underthings I had worn with him in mind, skating his lips along the fabric. His tongue darted under the lace and a gasp escaped me...just in time for a familiar darkness to blot out the image.

My eyes flew open. Every part of me was hot and aching and increasingly furious.

Wrenching the covers off, I stalked toward the hall. Leander was back in his own room tonight, which meant, fortunately or unfortunately, there was no one to stop me from storming over to Hadeon's room.

Nyx whimpered when she spotted me leaving. Her tail wagged, and she got to her paws like she was about to join me, but I shook my head. This was not a social visit. Or one that would last long.

Not bothering to be subtle, I flung open Hadeon's door.

He didn't bother to feign surprise to see me. The sight of him sitting up, bare chested against his dark sheets with disheveled hair and an arrogantly raised eyebrow was almost enough to make me forget why I had come.

But not quite.

"Stay in your own dreams," I ordered, my voice more breathless than I liked.

"Wish that I could, Feralinia," he growled, running a hand over his face. "But yours are rather...forceful."

A flush rose in my cheeks. "It's not like I can control them."

Hadeon narrowed his midnight eyes and pursed his lips.

"Indeed. I was merely being helpful, obscuring them from us both." Then he tilted his head in mock confusion. "Though, you don't appear to be grateful for my intervention."

I clenched my jaw. Was I the only one this was difficult for? I looked away, all the fight and arousal leaving me in a single whoosh of air.

"Would distance help?" My tone was flat.

Would it help keep our dreams from mingling? Would it help this hurt less?

Hadeon's features tightened, his eyes sparking with warning. "Distance?"

I swallowed, sticking out my chin with a resolution I didn't quite feel. "Leander asked when I was coming home."

It was strange, remembering the way he had reacted to my use of that word when I came here. What I now recognized as offense had flitted across his features, and I knew why.

Home.

You need to go home, he had demanded when Valandril came. *It isn't safe here.*

This is my home now, I had insisted. *You can't take that back.*

But he had. And for what?

"You aren't leaving." It was an order.

My hands dropped to my sides, frustration and defeat creeping into my bones. I couldn't do this anymore. I couldn't keep punishing us by living on the other side of a wall neither of us wanted or was willing to tear down.

"You need to make up your mind, Hadeon."

His gaze heated, two burning silver stars flaring to life at the sound of his name on my lips.

"I won't stay here as your captive, and we both know you don't want me to stay as anything more."

Darkness erupted around him. For the span of several heartbeats, he stared at me unblinking.

"I won't force you to stay," he finally said, his words like a knife to my gut.

Because he damned sure wouldn't ask me to, either. Memories from Phaedra's lifetime came to the forefront, a softer version of the king before me, still jaded and dark but full of a hidden optimism for his court, and full of an infinite amount of love for me.

"I am sorry for what I had to do," I told him, turning to go. "But I'm not sorry you're alive."

His scoff rang out behind me. "You miss the point entirely. The issue is not what you did. It's that you would do it again."

I spun back around. "Yes, I would, because I had no

choice. No choice but to go, and no choice but to hide it. More was at stake than the two of us."

"Is that so?" His voice was hard. "If it was isos the goddess needed, I could have taken your place. Valandril could have been defeated, and the world saved, you along with it."

The blood drained from my face, even knowing that hadn't been an option. "It didn't work that way —"

"But if it had?" he cut me off.

Seconds ticked by, my chest rising and falling with each breath. All I felt was a blind panic imagining a world where I lived and Hadeon died.

"Not so easy to be on the other side, is it, Feralinia?" The gentle taunt scraped my insides, hollowing me from the inside out.

"Easy?" I echoed. "Do you think it didn't destroy me to leave you that day? Do you think I didn't feel your absence even in my time on Earth?"

Hadeon rose to his feet, rage overflowing.

"Do you think that a few passing years of feeling lost is the same thing as trying to live every day with the loss of half of your soul, your only vestige of hope a vague prophecy from the same celestial-damned goddess who ruined your life to begin with?" His deep baritone rumbled through me.

Ruined his life? What happened to thanking the goddess for giving him everything?

"If you want to know who is ruining your life, Hadeon, you don't have to look so far." I gestured toward his entire self. "The goddess gave us another chance. You're the only one who is hellbent on wasting it."

His face contorted in offense, but I didn't care. All at once, I felt it again, the sharp, stabbing pain of rejection. The same crushing disappointment as when I first realized that my soulmate would just as soon never have found me.

Then he had kissed those fears away, had thanked the goddess he barely deigned to acknowledge for me. I had found peace in his shadows, and belonging, two things that didn't come naturally to me.

Now I had this.

Anger kindled within me, blazing bright enough to match his own, so I barreled on.

"I would think that if you had missed me that damned much, you might have been glad to have me back instead of punishing me for things I didn't even remember."

A disbelieving huff of air escaped him, and he stepped closer to me.

"You think the problem is that I didn't miss you enough?" he growled. "You think that I didn't sleep in the bed we had shared every night and think about the cocky little smirk you give when you get the last word or how your eyes blaze like the center of the sun itself when you're angry?" He took another step, and I backed away, retreating more from the raw emotion in his tone than his physical presence.

"You think I didn't dream every night about the way you feel with your body writhing against mine, the way you sound when you're begging me not to stop? The way you taste when you're right at the edge of breaking?"

Heat spread through me, equal parts desire and shame, but he wasn't finished.

"I missed you every day, Feralinia," he all but shouted. "Then your precious Abba came to tell me where to fetch you from when the portal opened, but she neglected to mention that you wouldn't remember a single damned thing about our lives together. So there you were, looking at me like I was a stranger and begging me to send you back to a life that was never yours to begin with."

"Did you want me to remember?"

"I saw the benefit in sparing us both the unnecessary entanglement, given what happened the first time around."

I squeezed my eyes shut, trying to gather myself.

You don't know what it was like for him, Celani told me.

No, I hadn't understood. Maybe I hadn't wanted to understand, to come to terms with the damage I had done when I made the only choice I could. I hadn't wanted to accept the truth: that day had broken us both in ways that couldn't be fixed.

"All right, then," I finally said, opening my eyes in time to see him swallow in what might have been remorse. "I guess that answers my question."

Then I turned and walked back to my room before he could see me cry. This time, he didn't try to stop me.

HADEON DIDN'T TRAIN the next day.

There was no real risk of me burning out with my bloodstone and the control I had now, or so Celani explained as she led us up to the clearing. My brother worked with me until sunset, quieter than he usually was.

It was like he sensed how badly I needed to exhaust myself.

"Do you want me to stay?" he asked as he and Celani walked me back to my rooms.

I mutely shook my head. I just wanted to be alone, the way I was apparently destined to spend the rest of my life. I fell asleep bracing myself for memories of Hadeon, but it was another familiar face who shared my dreams that night.

Ethereally serene features framed by amethyst waves greeted me as soon as I closed my eyes. She studied my face for several long moments before her expression fell.

She smiled sadly. "You're in pain, my child."

In spite of the circumstances, I could feel my unhappiness mirrored in her chest. A surge of affection for her rose up in me, the face that had guided me through my childhood, even if there was a latent vestige of betrayal as well.

Still, the choice to die that day had ultimately been mine.

"I always knew there would be consequences," I said softly.

It was pointless to blame her or the goddess now.

I had known from the moment I walked away from that battlefield that Hadeon would despise me for it. I just hadn't known I would have to return to face his ire. For all the accusations I flung at him, maybe I was the coward.

"You have never been that," she said with a shake of her head, having seemingly heard my thoughts.

I wrapped my arms around myself, feeling smaller than I

had in a long time. My bones were soaked in bitterness, in defeat.

"Was it always going to end this way?" I couldn't help but ask. "Is that what you have Seen?"

Abba stepped forward, her golden gown flowing out around her in the misty haze of my mind.

"I don't See everything, child." She pressed a gentle hand to my cheek. "I See possibilities, and even the goddess cannot See through the malice in the Court of Mist and Memory."

That wasn't an encouraging thought.

Abba smiled as she forced me to meet her eyes.

"I know that in every story in which you found your soulmate, you then went on to make this sacrifice. But it hasn't ended yet," she said gently. "There is more of the prophecy yet to be fulfilled."

I recalled the caramel-stained scroll that he produced that first morning, the way the bottom was ripped, the barest hint of inked words staining the frayed edges.

Even Hadeon hadn't known what it said, and though I had my memories back, though I could viscerally remember Abba reading the prophecy as it was fulfilled, my mind had somehow blocked out her final words.

"Oh, good," I shook my head. "Because that's worked out so well for me thus far."

Abba's expression was pained, but she recited the ending anyway, starting with the last line I knew. "In fifty years, eight heiresses will return, to bring peace to all lands that burn. The lines of fate have been spoken, on the night The Veil shall reopen."

Each word stirred something deep in my memory, something I had heard once before, murmured just as I succumbed to death, and forgotten. Or intentionally obscured.

"Thus far, I have only brought dissention to the lands, burning or otherwise," I commented, nonetheless chewing over the words in my head.

She shook her head. "As I said, child, this is not yet an ending."

"Why are you telling me this now?" I asked, frustration seeping into my tone. "Or rather, why didn't you before?"

She sighed. "Because you deserve that which was promised to you as a child."

"I don't understand."

"You will."

I loved Abba with the long-forgotten part of my soul, but the more recent part of me was sick to death of her vague warnings and promises that had all led me here.

"Is that why you came, then?" I asked running a hand through my long hair. Small cinders fell from my fiery waves, disappearing as soon as they hit the floor.

She smiled like she knew exactly how irritated I was and wasn't remotely bothered by it.

"No. I believed it would bolster you to know that your story isn't over, but I came tonight to deliver a message."

"From the goddess?"

She nodded.

"For Hadeon again?" I clarified. "Because I'm fairly certain he didn't actually listen to the last one."

A smile tempted the corner of her mouth and she shook

her head like she had expected that very thing to happen.

"No. This one is for you." Her eyes glowed brighter, her expression far away. "You must go to Thalassa Village tonight. Someone is waiting for you, from your past life and this one. She needs your help, and the goddess desires you to grant it. You are not the only one who has yet to fulfill their destiny."

Someone from my past life and this one? Was it Ivy? Or had I crossed paths with one of the other eight?

Abba's features returned to normal, and she gave me a last smile, reaching out to smooth my hair from my forehead as she had so many times when I was younger, and more recently when I was at Fairy Bar, under the influence of Elven wine and completely unprepared for what was to come.

"It was a fitting name your mother on Earth chose," she offered quietly, watching the cinders from my hair dance along her skin.

"The remnants of a dead star?" I said, recalling Hadeon's words when I arrived.

Phaedra meant star in the ancient language, so it *had* been fitting in a macabre sort of way.

"Yes and no." She smiled softly again. "The embers of a fire smolder and burn long after the flames are gone. They are endlessly resilient, and they represent hope, not death. Ashes are dead, but embers can be coaxed to life again and again."

Then she was gone.

And in spite of myself, whether it was her words or the hope of seeing someone who might understand just a little of the insanity of my life, I did feel just the slightest bit better.

This wasn't over yet. Any of it.

Chapter Thirty-Three

I awoke shortly after Abba left my dreams. Every instinct I possessed screamed for me to sneak off to Leander's room, to coax him into helping me sneak out of the palace.

Then I heard Hadeon's voice in my head, telling me I continued to miss the point. I saw the betrayal that lingered behind his eyes when he asked me how many times I had lied to him. Maybe he would have stopped me then, but had I even given him the chance?

It hadn't seemed worth the risk. And, if I was being very honest, I hadn't thought I would come back here to face the consequences of that choice. As angry as I had been earlier, I saw where things had gone wrong.

Was he right when he said that history was doomed to repeat itself? Was the problem less about circumstances, and more that we had built our relationship on the burial ground of the pieces of ourselves we hadn't fully come to terms with?

And when it came time to exhume the bodies, neither of us was prepared.

With more questions than answers — as usual — I found myself creeping into the hallway for the second time in as many nights. Instead of going left to Leander's rooms, I turned right, traipsing the familiar path to Hadeon's.

Nyx whined behind me, her silver eyes looking up at me hopefully. When I nodded, her entire body shook with excitement.

I didn't bother knocking. Instead, I twisted the crescent-shaped door handle, letting myself and my cerberus into Hadeon's bedroom.

"Feralinia?" Hadeon shot up in bed, scanning me from head to toe, far more surprised to see me than he had been last time.

His bare chest gleamed under the weak shafts of silver moonlight, his sleek midnight hair sliding over his bare shoulders where his shadow markings pulsed and shifted along his skin.

"Abba came to me," I said quickly, ripping off the bandage before I lost my nerve.

His shadows flexed.

"What did she want?" If he hadn't been so tired, maybe he would have hidden it better, but I saw the exact moment fear flashed behind his eyes.

He really was so damned stubborn, pretending we still had a choice now, like refusing to be together now would keep us both from breaking if we lost one another again.

But I hadn't come here to fight about that again. At least, not yet.

"She wants me to go to Thalassa Village and says there's someone waiting for me. I think it's one of the other girls from the prophecy."

My thoughts went to Ivy again. If there was a chance she needed me, I wouldn't hesitate. Even if it was one of the others, I needed to see it through.

Hadeon's lips twisted. "And of course you want to go, regardless of your own safety."

I took a deep breath, having already anticipated his bitter reaction. If I was being honest, I wasn't even sure I blamed him for it. So I didn't push back.

"I was hoping you would come with me," I said softly.

Hadeon opened his mouth then closed it, like that wasn't the comment he had been expecting. Which was fair, since Phaedra wouldn't have given him that choice in the past.

I wasn't his captive, but it was his kingdom, and he was the stronger fighter, especially since my isos refused to come back in full force. We both knew he could stop me if he wanted to, and I was taking a chance that he might do just that.

But change had to start somewhere, and so did trust.

He held my gaze, scrutinizing me to see if I was playing a game.

"Thalassa is hours away by baztet," he observed noncommittally.

Hope flickered to life in me.

"I know." I tried not to sound too eager.

He nodded once. "When are you supposed to arrive at this meeting?"

"Tonight."

A muscle ticked in his jaw, his shadows curling into him like he was physically holding them back from caging me here.

"Very well." He sighed and stood. "We'll bring Nyx, but leave your uncontrollable beast at home."

I couldn't help the small smile that spread across my lips, or the teasing in my tone when I responded.

"And here I thought you'd want to come."

He stepped away from the massive bed to head to his wardrobe, but not before I saw the corners of his mouth tilt upward in a tiny grin.

It felt like a victory, all things considered. Like the barest hint of possibility.

WE WERE silent as we flew over the snow-capped peaks. The blue and silver valleys gleamed like a field of gemstones beneath the stars, stealing my breath away.

Every so often, I caught a glimmer of light as Nyx appeared somewhere beneath us, appearing then disappearing in the shafts of moonlight.

A faint blue line shimmered on the horizon. The longer we flew, the more distinct it became, until I could make out a vast ocean.

Memories niggled the back of my mind, trips to Lake

Michigan and its white sand beaches with my parents mingling with images of glimmering golden shores hidden behind crimson mountains.

The memories twisted and spun through my mind until a sense of ease began to spread through my bones. It wasn't just the shoreline ahead that felt familiar for a hundred different reasons, but this specific one tugged at long-forgotten memories.

I blinked, and a battle unfolded behind my eyelids. My vision danced between fighting monsters, to being tangled in sheets with shadows at a small tavern inn. We had been to this small coastal village before...close to the end.

Suppressing a shiver, I forced the thoughts away, along with the pain they brought with them.

Hadeon's baztet swooped lower, soaring over Ourania Bay just outside of Thalassa Village.

Nestled at the base of the bay was a longship made of dark wood. The golden moon lit up two square sails with a flaming sword and runic symbol. A menacing figurehead graced the bow, carved into a tangled mass of snakes.

Hadeon stiffened behind me, his arms going rigid as he clenched the reins in his fists.

Nothing about the ship was familiar. Back in the Court of Fire and Sun, we hadn't bothered to travel past our shores, let alone cross the border into the other Courts. It was rare to have visitors from other kingdoms.

My stomach churned and adrenaline coursed through my veins. There was a part of me that felt uneasy with not knowing who the ship belonged to, but there was another part that hoped it was Ivy.

I had never seen a fae ship like that, but then, I had never seen one from the other kingdoms, either.

I leapt from my baztet once we landed, leaving Comet in the sleepy hands of the stablemaster. My feet prodded me forward while Hadeon reluctantly followed a single step behind me.

The cobblestone road glittered with sea spray, and the air was a mixture of salt and citrus; brine and the sweet azure fruit trees that only grew along the coast.

Nyx appeared a moment later, one of her massive heads nudging me needily. The few hours of separation hadn't been very kind to her.

I pressed my head against hers, scratching her gold-tipped ears. I wasn't sure if waltzing up to strangers from another kingdom with a giant cerberus would undo everything we had come here for, but fortunately, it was Hadeon who had to break the news to her.

"Stables," he ordered flatly.

She let out a low, harmonic whine, but he pointed to the place we had just left the baztets. Nyx looked to me for confirmation, and I kissed her cheek.

"Sorry, girl. But I'll come back for you as soon as I can."

All three of her heads hung low, sadness filling her puppy eyes as she trudged toward the stables instead of coming with us.

I would have felt worse for her if there wasn't something pulling me in the opposite direction. I didn't know what I was looking for, but I could feel a tug inside of me, pulling me forward, like fate was guiding me by a single, fragile thread.

Fate or hope, or maybe both.

Hadeon followed me silently until we came to the entrance of a familiar door. A wooden sign above it had an engraving of a mermaid and read *The Sulking Siren*.

I took a breath, bracing myself as Hadeon pushed the door open. Though I knew better than to get my hopes up, I couldn't help but scan the room for a familiar set of green eyes and strawberry-blonde hair.

My stomach sank as several sets of eyes met mine, none of them belonging to Ivy.

Then, I registered one in the far corner of the room. Tucked away from the rest of the tavern patrons was a round table filled with unfamiliar faces with suspicious expressions etched into their decidedly un-elflike features.

Hadeon let out a sigh of frustration. He muttered the word "mages" under his breath, his distaste evident with each elongated syllable.

While the rest of the bar had a mix of skin tones and hair colors, all of them with the distinct blue undertone that belonged to the Night Court, the mages looked...almost human.

It didn't help that the points of their ears were wrong. Not just wrong, but very obviously fake, like the kind I had seen people use in cosplay back on Earth.

One of them — a woman with auburn hair and a face dusted with delicate freckles — stared at me curiously.

There was something familiar about the way she balanced

the glass in her hand, or maybe it was the strange, unnatural point to her fake ears that reminded me of a cat's, but suddenly, my memories pulled me back to the casino.

I stared at a reflection similar to hers in the bathroom mirror. Music thumped through the walls, not half as irritating as it became later.

I hadn't been drugged yet with the Elven wine, but a few shots early on had me nursing a solid buzz. My mind took note of our matching costumes as she fixed her headband in front of the sink. I must have said something aloud, because her attention flitted to me, her gold-flecked gaze sizing me up before lingering on the dagger in my boot.

Then I blinked, and I was back in The Sulking Siren.

I had no doubt this was the woman Abba had sent me for. And while I couldn't help but wish she were Ivy, curiosity had me crossing the room before I could stop myself.

The loud scrape of her chair scratched along the ancient wooden floors as she pushed back from the table. Several quick steps had her meeting me in the center of the room.

"I know you," she said under her breath, her hazel eyes carefully assessing me.

"I was in Las Vegas," I answered. "At the casino."

There was a long, stilted silence where I registered some movement around us before the room fell dark with shadows that I had a suspicion were waving threateningly.

She took a step back, glancing toward the exit before meeting my eyes again. Her breaths were even, but her posture told me she wanted nothing more than to run.

"Am I supposed to believe it's a coincidence that we're

both here?" she asked, cracking the knuckles on her right hand.

"No," I said as a tall, handsome man strode up behind her. He glanced between her hand and me, and I wondered if it was a signal of some sort, or if he just sensed her anxiety.

His features were stern, hardened. There was a runic tattoo lining the side of his neck, peeking out between the strands of his long, dark hair.

His gaze was inscrutable as he studied me. He had just parted his lips to speak when the shadows around us grew darker. I didn't need to turn around to know that Hadeon had joined us.

I didn't acknowledge him. Instead, I addressed the woman from Vegas, answering her question with a shake of my head.

"Abba sent me here," I added. "To help you."

Twin scoffs slipped from both males, and it was an effort not to roll my eyes.

The woman's gaze sharpened. She shifted on her feet, her focus on me. "Help with what?"

"I don't know, exactly," I answered honestly. I had been too caught off guard to ask Abba more when she came to me in my dream, and I was really starting to regret that now as the entire room stared.

Unease snaked through my veins as I darted a glance around the tavern. Despite the late hour, there were several elves lingering in their cups. Some of them were lost to wine, while others glared in our direction.

When I spotted a small, empty table on the other side of

the room, I gestured toward it. "Maybe we could talk over there? Or somewhere a little more private?"

"That table is private enough," the brooding mage behind her said in a flat tone.

Hadeon's shadows retreated by a fraction. "I couldn't agree more," he added icily.

"Maybe we could let these two finish their measuring contest on the opposite side of the room?" I suggested, and the corner of the woman's mouth eased up into a smile.

She looked at her companion, holding a silent conversation I couldn't follow before turning back to me and nodding.

"Sure," she said. "I'm Adira, by the way."

I wondered if that had always been her name, or if she had slipped into the demands of her past life with an aplomb I still hadn't quite managed. I realized belatedly that I hadn't gotten to ask Ivy, either.

Maybe I was the only one clinging to the twenty years I had spent on Earth, but even now, I couldn't imagine going by any other name. Besides, it was a way to honor the parents who had raised me and loved me for as long as they could.

"Ember," I told her in response, following Hadeon to the table.

We sat on old chairs made of hardened blue branches while Hadeon threw a sheer wall of shadows up around us. They stretched from the floor to the ceiling, just next to the floating candles that lit up the room.

The wall was just enough to divert attention from us and muffle the sound. I nodded my thanks, even as Adira and her companion shot the darkness suspicious looks.

The man sat up straighter, staring us down. "You claim Abba sent you, but you didn't know our names or what we needed, or have any information at all?"

"Kage," Adira admonished quietly.

"It's a fair question," he said, shooting us a challenging look.

Hadeon's shadows grew. "If you know anything at all about the priestess, surely you know this is hardly out of character for her, but by all means, if you require no assistance..."

He gestured toward the door, and I sighed, resisting the urge to press my fingertips to my temples.

"She told me to come here, but that was all. I do want to help, and frankly, your fake ears won't do you any favors here when you look like you're from the wrong court," I said bluntly.

Both of their hands twitched self-consciously.

"I know it's a frustrating place to be," I went on in a softer tone. "But you need my help whether you want it or not. And I'm here, offering, so why don't you just come out with it?"

They exchanged another look before coming to some sort of unspoken understanding.

"I don't know what happened to you," Adira began tentatively. "But I assume our stories are similar. Fell into a vortex in Las Vegas that spat me out in Terrea, facing a whole, you're not actually human, thing."

"Only to realize the war you died for hasn't ended?" I hazarded a guess.

"Something like that," she said, running her fingers along the tattoos on her hands. "There's a curse on Magiaria. Kage

—" she stumbled over his name, shooting him a grim look. "Kage's parents are under a sleeping spell that no one else can seem to remember. They don't know how to counteract it, or who cast it in the first place. And with them gone, there have been...issues."

"To put it lightly," Kage scoffed.

A muscle ticked in Hadeon's jaw. "What kind of issues?"

"The kind that will lead to war against my people," Kage responded bitterly. "Against all of the mages."

My thoughts drifted back to Valandril and his monsters, then to the Never Court and the wraiths. Were all of the kingdoms dealing with world-ending threats? Is that why we were brought back?

"That doesn't explain why you're here," Hadeon said after a beat, sensitive as ever.

"Hadeon," I hissed.

He only shrugged. Kage shot him a death glare while Adira's fingers ceased trailing along her tattoos.

"We need something that we can only get here," she admitted.

"There it is," Hadeon muttered. "I presume you had plans to steal it and sneak away?"

She met his gaze solidly, something I had seen few people manage. It raised my respect for her by several measures.

"You should assume I'll do whatever it takes to break this curse."

"What is it you need?" I asked before Hadeon could say something else ass-y.

Her voice was lower when she spoke again, her eyes scanning the tavern like she wanted to be more than certain no one was listening.

"We were combing through an old grimoire and we found a flower. It's supposed to be for memory, and we think it could help. It's called *anamisi*. It loosely translates to memory, or —"

"Remembrance," I added gravely. "The flower of remembrance."

I gave in to my stress at last, bringing two fingers up to massage my temples and wishing Abba had offered up this little detail when she told me to come here.

"You know it?" Adira perked up, her gold-flecked eyes studying mine closely as I nodded.

Before I had all of my memories back, I wouldn't have, but now, alarm bells clanged in my mind.

"It's rare," I demurred, exchanging a wary glance with Hadeon. "And it can only be found in the Never Court."

Adira dipped her chin. This wasn't new information for her.

"Fifty years ago, that would have been easy —" I started to tell her.

"Still a breach of the laws in our kingdom," Hadeon interjected unhelpfully.

I continued like he hadn't spoken. "Well, it would have been eas*ier* to get to, but now..."

I trailed off, trying and failing to not think about what waited for them on the other side of the border.

"We'll manage." Adira's words sliced through my thoughts. "We've made it this far."

I shook my head again. "You can't just *manage* with the Never Court. You would never make it past the wraiths."

"We have defenses," she said, a note of desperation lining her tone. "And I have my magic —"

"It won't be enough."

I couldn't stop my thoughts from racing through what I knew about this brand of wraith. They weren't like the monsters I had battled before, but according to Hadeon, Celani, and every other elf soldier of the Moon Court, they were just as deadly.

Without knowing them, or how to fight them, there was no way the mages would survive the trek. It was impossible.

At least, for them it was. I thought about how easily Hadeon had taken care of the wraiths at the borderland. He could shadow us in and out at will.

If he would. But I knew how he felt about putting me in danger, and it didn't seem like something he was likely to offer.

I couldn't very well volunteer him. I could volunteer myself, if I was willing to undo whatever small bit of progress I had made by telling him I was summoned here to begin with.

"I don't have a choice," Adira said.

My stomach twisted into knots when I saw every ounce of the resignation and pain I had felt in both of my lives reflected in her gaze.

My eyes danced from her to the male next to her. I thought of the way she hesitated on Kage's name before saying it was his parents who needed the remedy.

How many times had it felt like I was brought to this

world just to face one more hurdle after a lifetime of uphill climbs?

If I was right, if it was *Kage* she was so desperate to save, that was a feeling I understood all too well. I had died for it once before. Hell, maybe she had, too.

Was that how we were fated to repeat this life? An endless cycle of sacrifice and grief because we were the only ones who could save those we loved?

Regardless of Abba's insistence that I find Adira, and the Goddess's desire to see Adira fulfill whatever destiny she had in store, I would have wanted to help her — to find a way to break this cycle for her, for me, for all the women who sacrificed their lives to save this world.

Slowly, I turned to face Hadeon. When his eyes met mine, they brimmed with something I couldn't begin to read as he studied my features.

I was utterly unprepared when he spoke up.

"Yes, you do," he intoned. "We will retrieve the *animisi* for you."

I wasn't sure which part to be more shocked about, his offer or his use of the word *we* instead of *I*.

Was he only honoring the promise of help I had already given her?

Or, somewhere under all of his cold looks and sardonic distance, was he remembering a time when he and I would have given anything for the choice he offered her? For a way out.

Chapter Thirty-Four

WE STAYED FOR A WHILE AFTER THAT TO JUST TALK. Adira had so many questions and hadn't yet gotten all of her memories back. I listened as she explained what she remembered of our sacrifice, and filled in whatever gaps I could.

She wanted to know about my family on this side of the portal and the one I left behind, as well.

For far too long, she had also been an orphan, but she didn't have an Isa or Ivy to help ease that sting of loneliness. Even now, she was alone in Terrea, with the exception of Prince Kage and his band of thieves.

But there were gaps in their memories, too.

Because of the curse on Magiaria, there was so much that no one had been able to explain to her, things that Kage and his people had forgotten.

Like the prophecy.

I handled that part as delicately as possible, the very

mention of Abba or the goddess bringing out a deep-rooted anger in Hadeon and Kage both.

Begrudgingly, I found myself grateful for the information that Hadeon had meted out when I first arrived. Maybe he hadn't told me everything, but at least I hadn't gone in completely blind.

Then again, no one had put a collar on Adira, so perhaps *grateful* wasn't the word I was searching for.

It was late when we finally trudged upstairs to our room. Well, I trudged, and Hadeon glided like someone who would never lower himself to something so plebeian.

At least some of my human nature had stuck with me.

When the door shut behind us, I forcibly wrenched my attention away from the single bed and all the memories it held, turning to face Hadeon.

His features were inscrutable, but there was a guarded set to his shoulders. He raised a single eyebrow under my assessment, a question.

"You pretend not to care, then you offer to go into the Never Court for a stranger."

Hadeon's muscles went rigid. "I didn't offer for her sake."

Of course he hadn't.

Stars help me, my entire body thrummed with want. Being this close to him and seeing the bed we had once shared, not out of safety or obligation, but out of love and passion. Seeing the barest hint that he cared so much in spite of everything that had happened, in spite of his best efforts not to... It was intoxicating and excruciating.

"Still," I said quietly. "You could have stopped me from going instead of volunteering to help."

"And you could have snuck away in the night with the assistance of whatever goddess-given isos your brother refuses to divulge," he countered in a deep tone.

He had taken note of my olive branch after all, and it mattered to him. It wasn't much, but it felt like the smallest step toward something hopeful.

In spite of that, or because of that, I was in no way prepared to join him on the bed just yet. So instead, I poured myself a glass of blue wine and stepped out onto the small balcony while he was in the lavatory.

It was a relief to realize the Ahvi constellation was on the other side of the inn. For once, I didn't have the golden stars taking up all of the space in the sky and my mind, just the slivers of the contrasting moons hanging high in the sky.

It wasn't long before Hadeon joined me, his shadows announcing his presence as usual. They stretched toward me like they wanted to close the distance between us nearly as much as I did. Then they curled back into him, which was for the best.

Touching him would be a mistake. Letting his shadows slide along my skin and leaning into the comfort of his darkness when it would all just be temporary...even more so.

He walked on sure, measured footsteps to the railing, standing several feet from me.

"You should get some sleep," I told him, a dismissal as much as a plea.

He didn't look at me when he responded in an even tone, "I could say the same to you."

"I'm not tired." It was a lie.

I was *exhausted*.

The memories, the crushed hope that I would see Ivy, the uncertainty surrounding Hadeon, and the constant effort of resisting my draw to him, it was all consuming me as surely as the electricity that zapped between our bodies.

"My mistake." He didn't bother to make the words sound genuine.

I turned to look at him, giving him a taunting smile more casual than any part of me felt.

"Where's a phone when I need one?" I teased. "If I had gotten a recording, I could play it on a loop, even let it replace my music while I make tacos or draw. You, admitting you were wrong, over and over again into the wee hours of the night."

He chuckled, the sound caressing my skin as surely as his shadows did. Or had, in our other lives.

"I admit when I'm wrong," he blustered.

A snort escaped me, inelegant and entirely human. "And you say I'm an unconvincing liar."

"I don't think I've ever said that," he said, the levity leeching from his features.

No, that had been Celani.

I sighed. I didn't want to argue with him. Not only was I too tired, but...maybe I owed him a real apology, rather than miniscule gestures and terse conversations where we danced around the truth.

Maybe it was past time.

"I'm sorry," I said plainly.

His gaze snapped to mine, widening in enough shock that it was almost offensive. Deserved, though. Neither Phaedra nor I had ever apologized to him for anything.

I cleared my throat, holding his cautious stare. "I should have taken my chances with telling you the truth. If it was the goddess's will, she would have found a way to make it happen. I don't think...I don't even think that was the real reason I didn't tell you."

He leaned down, resting his arms on the railing. His shoulders rose and fell as he took a deep breath, as if he were bracing himself. The air between us was so, so fragile, like it was spun from glass and the wrong word could shatter it into a thousand irreparable pieces.

"Then what was?" His quiet words skated along the tenuous space rather than breaking it.

"I was just...terrified." Tears stabbed at the backs of my eyes as I forced myself to go back to the night where Phaedra clung tightly to the most traumatic thing she had ever endured. I couldn't tell if she was trying to save me from that pain or if she just couldn't bear to relive it herself, but even now, I didn't have the memories in full. I knew, though, how it had almost broken me.

How it still did.

"I didn't know if I'd have the strength to leave you because you were right." My voice was barely above a whisper. "If the tables had been turned, I would have wanted us to go together.

I would have done anything to die by your side, and I knew at the first sign of resistance, I would cave to your choice. That I would damn the entire world to avoid hurting you."

I forced myself to meet his eyes again, knowing there were tears pooling in my own. He deserved to see this, the way I had suffered — if only for a brief time — for the decision that had ruined his life. He stared back with clear bewilderment and no small amount of pain radiating from his infinite gaze.

"In the end, only the thought that you would live, that you would heal, that the goddess would find a way to take care of you, gave me the strength to go."

I tried to blink away the tears, but only succeeded in causing them to cascade down my cheeks.

"And then you died alone." He sounded...destroyed.

"Not alone. I had the women," I said, gesturing vaguely toward the door. "And Abba."

"What comfort," he said sardonically.

A watery laugh escaped me, in spite of myself.

"It was to me, you ass."

Silver moonlight highlighted his smirk, and maybe it was the wine. Maybe it was seeing another woman in my shoes, fighting for a man and a world she barely understood. Or maybe it was just time.

Regardless, I found myself sharing more truths than I had originally intended.

"That's why it means more than you know that you're willing to help her now, whatever your motives. She died by my side, whether she remembers it or not. She deserves a long life, with the person she..." I trailed off, not wanting to turn this conversation into anything it wasn't.

"Who's to say she'll get that now?" he demanded, his words soaked in bitterness like cherries in a bottle of brandy. "You can't think the goddess is watching out for her."

Guess we were having the conversation, after all.

"I do think that. I think that she's paid her dues, and that there is happiness waiting for her somewhere down the line. Peace." I turned to face him, letting my gaze linger on the exquisite outline of his defined jaw, the silver starbursts in his moonlit eyes, and I willed him to listen to the rest of what I had to say. "But even if I didn't believe that, even if I thought she was going to lose him tomorrow, or he her, I would still believe that it was worth it to try."

In my first life, I was a hopeless romantic. My second life, full of emptiness and longing for the soulmate I didn't consciously remember, had not lent itself to that trait. Now I was somewhere torn between the two.

I did believe that it was worth it to try, but I was not the same person who could fight for a love that Hadeon refused to believe in. Which was why I met his eyes solidly before tacking on, "As long as he's trying, too."

A muscle jumped in Hadeon's jaw. "Maybe he doesn't know how. Maybe that's a skill he lost along with half of his soul."

I moved closer to him until I was standing only inches away, our breaths mingling in a single white puff of air against the cold night sky.

"Then I suppose he'll have to decide if it's worth learning

again." With that, I spun on the balcony and headed inside to get ready for bed.

Hadeon didn't join me for hours.

DARKNESS WASHED over me in a soothing blanket, shutting out the heat that seared in from the window panes.

"Aren't you supposed to like the sun?" Hadeon teased.

"No one likes the sun when it's roasting them like a pig on a spit," I shot back, nestling in closer to him and his cooler skin.

Distantly, I knew this wasn't right. That it had been freezing when I went to bed, even if my isos kept me from feeling the cold.

But something else was wrong. I couldn't see most of Hadeon, or feel him. Instead, I saw myself framed through his navy hair, like a camera angled downward from the top of the same bed I had fallen asleep in.

From his perspective, I realized.

"How ever did you survive life at the Sun Court?" he demanded.

"With great difficulty," I whined.

In truth, I had always preferred the colder contrast to my heated skin. Yet another thing that set me apart from the rest of my court.

"Now make yourself useful," I said, smirking up at him while I gestured to his shadows.

"As my Feralinia commands," he drawled, encasing me fully in his shadows.

I breathed a sigh of relief, one that quickly turned into a sigh of pleasure. It was strange, hearing it through Hadeon's ears. Feeling his surge of arousal at the sound, his body's response when I arched against the shadows that had gone from sheltering me to restraining me against the bed.

"And here I thought you said I was in command," I purred.

"Of course, Feralinia. Just tell me to stop," Hadeon said in my ear.

"Bastard," I said. Even without being in my head, I knew full well I wasn't going to tell him to stop. And so did he.

His teeth grazed my ear, and I felt his restraint, felt the way he wanted to consume me, body and soul, until we both caught fire. His intense need to be inside of me, to make me safe and *his* every minute of every day. I arched against him again, naked curves pressing into the hard planes of his chest.

Every part of me was ablaze with the intensity of my desire, heated contrast to his dark, cool shadows, but oh how Hadeon loved to play. He ran his shadows along my skin, alternating the silky sensation with the way my skin burned for him until I cried out for more.

Grinning, he captured my mouth in his in a kiss that was more incinerating than the blistering sun had been, moving his hand to toy with the scrap of lace that was the only clothing remaining between us.

"And now?" he growled.

"Don't you dare."

Self-satisfaction mingled with the molten desire flooding his veins as he ripped the fabric like it was nothing in his powerful hands. A whimper escaped me, and he nipped along my jaw, down my body, between my breasts, stopping just below my navel.

I made a sound of protest, straining to indicate that I wanted him now, without the teasing and the foreplay he was so fond of. I was fond of it, too, but not tonight.

"You can't expect me to skip my favorite part," he said with mock chiding.

Then his mouth was otherwise occupied, and my protests abruptly halted. He glanced up to admire the view of me, arms stretched above my head, back arched, lips parted in pleasure...

And suddenly, I was flung from the dream.

My eyelids flew open — my real ones.

It was, in fact, warm in this room again, but only because I was plastered against Hadeon, my skin on fire, his shadows trailing along my side and wrapping around my wrists.

I felt the moment he jolted into consciousness, mostly because he pulled his shadows back. They went reluctantly, like they were disappointed to leave, and damn if that didn't make all of us.

Even Hadeon was breathing hard.

I moved away from him, trying to pretend I didn't notice that his breathing wasn't the only thing that was...well. Anyway.

"What was that about forcible dreams?" I said, unable to resist taunting him after he had been such a royal asshat about my own.

"I'm going to shower," he grumbled.

I bet he was.

"I hope it's a cold one," I shot back with a wicked grin.

It was easier to tease him than to acknowledge how badly I needed a cold shower myself.

Or how much I missed being wrapped in his shadows, in every single way.

Chapter Thirty-Five

It was a silent trek out of the inn. Any reprieve the joking mood or the sexy dream had offered was quickly snuffed out as Hadeon explained everything I would need to know about the wraiths.

Unlike the monsters we had fought in the past, Hadeon had gathered that the wraiths relied on their hearing to see, like sonar. So we would have to be completely silent as soon as we crossed the border.

As we ate our breakfast, we discussed every plan and contingency plan until he was reasonably certain that we had more than one way out if things got too dangerous.

We moved through the streets toward the stables, and I tried not to think the worst.

If something happened today, it would end like this, with too many unspoken words and an ever-growing tension slowly choking us like the frayed edges of a noose around our necks.

Nyx nearly knocked me off my feet as soon as we

approached the stables, her large puppy eyes warring between accusation and relief.

I tried to reassure her while Hadeon had the stablemaster fetch his baztet. We were only taking one today in an effort to attract less attention from the wraiths. His mount Vega was stealthier than Comet.

I would leave them all behind if I could. The baztets. Nyx. Especially Nyx. I hated the idea of taking her with us, but I also knew we couldn't stop her from following, lest she catch the next moonbeam and appear at the worst possible time.

Dread pooled in my stomach as we took off, flying higher and higher into the air until Thalassa Village was little more than a speck in the distance. Vega soared through the clouds, letting out a low growl as we crossed the border between the Moon Court and that of the Never.

Mists shrouded the ground below, the temperature dropping the farther into the court we went. I suppressed a shiver as we dipped between crags and the moss-covered cliffs and karst towers.

I wasn't cold, exactly, but it felt like we were flying into a tomb. Which made sense, since Hadeon had told me there was no isos here anymore. Normally our own isos replenished from the elements, but whatever taint was in the Never Court would block us from rebuilding our power as long as we were here.

Hadeon stiffened, bracing himself as he used the reins to guide Vega lower into the darkness. The fog was so thick, we could barely see more than a few meters in front of us.

Even Vega's glowing runes didn't provide enough light to see by.

I could use my isos to clear some of it away, but that would undoubtedly call too much attention to us. The wraiths' eyesight was weak, but even they would notice a blazing beacon in the sky. At least Vega's light mimicked the faint outline of stars, much easier to overlook than the veritable beacon mine would provide.

We passed another jagged karst formation — tall, limestone rocks sparsely covered with dense thickets of greenery between old wooden bridges and stairs that led to ruins.

The air was thick, reeking of stale, algae-covered water and decaying trees, like we were flying directly into a neglected terrarium. Once we were low enough, the mist thinned so we could make out the ruins of old villages and battlements, all of them abandoned and crumbling.

I held my breath as I scanned the ground for signs of movement — wraiths or otherwise.

I knew not to really hope for the latter. Valandril's monsters had destroyed everything before I went to Sacred Mountain, but a small part of me held on to the barest hint of hope that there was something left.

That maybe when this was all over with and the wraiths were dead, it could be the Court of Mist and Memory again.

The lower we flew, the more that hope died.

Nothing moved here. Not the wind. Not animals or forgotten elves. Not even the shadows, which was odd...

Had the wraiths made their home near the border? Had

they drained the court of all its isos, and that was why they were trying so hard to breach the Court of Moon and Stars?

I wasn't sure if that thought should fill me with dread or hope... If the wraiths were all at the border, this could be over quickly. But if the isos was gone, did that mean the *anamisi* were, too?

And the elves? Had some of them sought refuge in the other kingdoms, or had Valandril wiped them all from existence? It was hard to believe anyone could be in hiding, surviving in this place.

Hadeon directed Vega to a small peninsula along the coast where there was a little less mist to combat.

He didn't speak as we dismounted, pulling treats from the satchel to reward Vega for getting us this far. Then Hadeon silently removed our bags before sending his baztet up to circle the skies until we returned, far away from the wraiths.

Nyx appeared within seconds, and I raised a finger to my lips, ordering her to be silent. She crept forward, eyes aware, body tense and alert as Hadeon handed me my bag.

I took it with a nod, watching as he threw the other over his broad shoulders. When he tied his long navy hair back into a knot at the nape of his neck, I intentionally avoided looking at the golden tattoo peeking out above his shirt.

After scanning our surroundings, he pointed toward the shoreline in the distance, a silent request for Nyx to portal us there. The cerberus shimmered, her eyes bright as she called on the wan shaft of moonlight on the other shore.

Half a heartbeat later, we were farther into the Never Court than I had ever been.

WE CONTINUED in a stop and go pattern, shadow-traveling to a new spot before breaking to do it all over again. Hadeon and Nyx took turns transporting us, depending on how much moonlight she had access to.

It was important for him to conserve as much of his isos as possible. At least until we knew if the wraiths really would be a threat.

At the third stop, we landed next to a dry riverbed across from a small group of wraiths. My heart stuttered in my chest as their green eyes locked on us, preternatural howls piercing the air as they scrambled toward us.

Nyx growled, her massive jaws snapping just before Hadeon whisked us all away.

The deeper we went into the Never Court, the more difficult the jumps became. I drew in a breath, feeling the atmosphere seep into my lungs. Humidity clung to my skin until it dripped down my face and back.

I felt empty. Wrong. It wasn't just that the air was thick and cloying. Each breath labored with too much death, too little oxygen... It was that there really was no isos here.

No connection to the Life Tree that powered Terrea. No goddess to call on. No Abba.

There was nothing but the remains of a world that had long since died.

Tension continued to mount as we took longer breaks between jumps, our isos slowly suffocating. Each mile felt like a hundred until exhaustion settled over me like a weighted blanket.

With each stop, my doubt grew like poisonous vines, choking out what little hope I had left.

I had known this wouldn't be easy, but I didn't think it would be impossible. Abba wouldn't have called me here if I couldn't help Adira. She wouldn't leave us with no way out.

Eventually the sun was directly above us, limiting Nyx's ability to portal us forward. Some of the mist dissolved under its rays, making it a little easier to see farther ahead of us.

Hadeon's shadows had just begun swirling when I heard it, the gentle hum of the flowers.

I stepped away from the shadow king before he could carry us away again. He froze, his eyes narrowing before they widened in recognition.

Anamisi was rare long before the war that destroyed the Court of Mist and Memory, prized because of both their magical properties and their music. Their music changed with their environments, morphing from something as gentle as a lullaby to the crescendo of a symphony.

My gaze tracked the sound through the mist-shrouded trees just ahead of us. It was greener here, somehow.

Maybe there was a last thread of isos that refused to let go, or maybe it was just the first place we had been that still had access to sunlight to help the plants thrive.

Some of the trees even had leaves, their branches standing tall, even as rot ate away at the bark.

I sucked in a small breath, reaching out to grab Hadeon's arm and pointing. Something sparkled on the forest floor, and when I strained my eyes, I could make out a cluster of pale green flowers.

Hadeon went rigid when he spied them, his isos expanding protectively around us. His full lips silently formed a warning as his shadows formed the shape of a giant tree.

I nodded solemnly, understanding exactly what he meant.

A dryohp.

We had discussed the possibility of running into the brutal, sentient trees back at the inn, but the longer we traversed this dead kingdom, the more I'd doubted their continued existence.

I had never seen one in person and wasn't eager to face it now.

When we were children, Leander had always sworn the Mitera Tree in the Sun Court was one of them — an ancient protector of the forest, a tree that would come to life to defend the flora and fauna under its protection.

Each time we risked climbing the giant golden and extremely sacred tree back home, I wondered if she would come to life.

Fortunately for us, she never did.

I swallowed hard, carefully scanning the valley for wraiths and moving roots and branches, anything that would signal a tree monster that would prevent us from collecting the *anamisi*.

It seemed clear. It seemed easy.

That should have been our first warning.

Hadeon released his shadows, keeping them low to the ground. The seconds crept by like hours as the shadows skimmed over the pumpkin-shaped fruit that the flowers grew from.

They hesitated over several before recoiling away from some taint or rot that I couldn't see from here. Finally, Hadeon's shadows flared excitedly, wrapping around one of the pumpkins.

He waited half a heartbeat before plucking the entire thing from the root. Adira hadn't said which part of the flower was the most important for her potion, and we couldn't be too careful.

Before he could bring it back through the trees, though, an angry shriek pierced the air, loud enough to rattle my bones and teeth.

My blood went cold, and Nyx stepped in closer, her heads bowed low as she stared in the direction of the scream.

It wasn't the same roar of the wraiths, but that wasn't a relief. The sound might alert them, might call them to us.

Another scream rent out of the tree closest to us. The branches shook, bark sloughing off as it ripped its roots free from the ground. Its branches stretched forward like claws as it spun around to face us, and there was no hesitation as the creature lunged in our direction.

The dryohp was massive. Most of its body had been hidden beneath the ground, but now it hovered above us, casting long shadows over Nyx's heads.

The knot in the center of the trunk opened like a gaping mouth that continued to howl in anger.

In the span between heartbeats, Hadeon dropped the fruit on the ground, throwing up a wall of shadows to block the dryohp from reaching us. The muscles in his arms tensed as he braced himself for the impact.

The force sent Hadeon flying backwards, his feet sliding over the crumbling ground as he strained to hold his isos in place.

The dryohp wailed again, fighting against the hold.

Nyx let out a growl, leaping forward with a vicious set of barks that shook the tree, and it turned its attention on her.

Panic clawed at my throat as I called on my isos.

Before I could light a single flame, the dryohp's leaves began to glow a bright shade of emerald that spread their light through the surrounding mists.

Then the leaves were flying through the air like bullets. They sliced through the safety net of Hadeon's shadows, headed straight for Nyx.

The ground hissed with each hit, the leaves eating away at whatever they touched like they were made of pure acid. Solid rock, grass, whatever happened to be in their way melted into nothingness.

Including a patch of my cerberus's fur.

She howled at the same time a furious cry escaped my throat.

Anger fueled my isos, my flames flaring brighter as I focused my attention on the tree. Fire burst from my fingertips, licking at the air around me.

I took a deep breath, exhaling and sending them forward at the center of the dryohp's trunk, right into its mouth.

Another scream pierced the air, this time from the ancient tree as it convulsed beneath the flames.

Hadeon's shadows intensified under the light of my isos, and he picked the creature up and hurled it toward the cliff just beyond the small copse.

"Help Nyx," I cried over my shoulder before darting forward to grab the *animisi* fruit, tucking it gently into the satchel at my side.

"Ember," Hadeon's voice was a deep growl, and I whipped around to face him.

He had barely used his voice since we entered this place, but the necessity of that had probably gone out the window with the dryohp.

Nyx was alert at his side. Tufts of her fur were missing, and her left head was bowed, but otherwise she seemed okay.

But that wasn't Hadeon's problem. His gaze was fixed firmly behind me. My stomach sank as realization set in.

I didn't need to turn around to know what he was looking at, especially when a dark mass of static blinked into existence behind him. Its sunken green eyes shone hungrily as it tilted its canine head back and forth, sniffing at the air.

Fury surged inside me, mingling with desperation as another wraith appeared at its side, then another, and another.

Soon we were surrounded by ten, twelve, forty static shadow wraiths.

I took a slow, even breath, my eyes carefully scanning the forest as even more appeared.

Logically, I knew Hadeon could take them out with a single blow, but I also recognized the look on his face. The worry twisting his expression as he glared at the ones surrounding me and the twenty feet or so of distance that separated us.

A guttural growl sounded just before hot, putrid air blew through my hair. A long, mangled snout sniffed at my head, then my ear and cheek. The heavy scent of rotting flesh smothered my lungs, and it was an effort not to gag.

At that, Hadeon lost hold of his carefully honed control. His eyes hardened, and without moving, shadows grew and stretched around him like a storm cloud, writhing and ominous.

In the blink of an eye, the wraith at my back arched and imploded into a cloud of green mist. The shadows moved faster then, striking through the wraiths before they could take a single step forward.

Soon, we were surrounded by green clouds and the smell of a thousand decaying bodies.

I breathed in through my mouth, climbing to my feet to try to escape the scent that clung more intensely to the ground where they had died.

Still, I could taste them on my tongue, feel them as their remains coated my lungs and stung my eyes.

I hadn't even had time to call on my isos to help him this time. It was over before it began. Adrenaline spiked in my chest, my heart galloping too fast to measure.

But it *was* over, and now we could —

A thousand unearthly screams split the air, cutting off the thought.

The ground shook beneath our feet and the leaves on the

remaining trees trembled and fell from the branches, like the entire forest was bracing itself for whatever came next.

I scrambled toward Hadeon and Nyx, barely reaching them as the air grew thicker, the scant isos flowing through my veins snuffed out like the wick on a candle.

My stomach twisted and sank as hundreds of wraiths flooded the forest, encircling us en masse.

A curse slipped past my lips as Hadeon wrapped his arms around me. The fog grew thicker with each new wraith that joined the furious army, their lips pulled back over their blackened teeth.

The scent of death hung heavily in the air, choking out every last ounce of oxygen until I was gasping for breath.

Then they were moving, all of them at once. A wall of wraiths racing toward us.

I tried summoning my isos again, my ring glowing faintly as a flicker of light sparked to life in my hand. Before I could cast it, gentle shadows surrounded me. Hadeon tugged me in closer to his side, something like desperation at each point of contact as he whisked us away from the battle.

We landed on the karst just above the forest. Stones slipped beneath our feet as the ground crumbled and threatened to give way. Nyx scrambled to keep her footing, her frame far too large for this ledge.

A small whine slipped from her throat just before Hadeon's shadows swallowed us again.

I blinked and we were on a more stable cliffside. I clung to both the shadow king and my cerberus, my breaths shallow.

Another disembodied scream sounded, even closer this

time than it was before. We looked down in time to see hundreds of wraiths pouring from a hole in the mountain just beneath our feet.

The mines...

It took me longer than it should have to realize where we were. But streaming from the mouth of the Zoferi mines was a river of death and darkness racing to where the rest of the army had been.

I met Hadeon's midnight gaze, recognizing the same shock that I felt.

It was as if the mountain itself was creating them, spawning this never-ending horde of monsters.

Hadeon's brow had furrowed like he was trying to figure the same things out.

Was this their home? Where they hid? Was this the source? And if it was, did that mean it could also be their end?

The continuous torrent of wraiths shook the mountain, cracking the ground beneath our feet. This time it wasn't Nyx scrambling for purchase, it was me.

Hadeon caught me just as a stone broke free from the ledge. It slid downward before tumbling from the cliff, banging against every single rock and ridge along the way.

The wraiths froze all at once. Their massive wolfish faces turned at the same time, their haunted eyes locked on to our hiding spot above them.

Cool shadows surrounded us, enveloping me like a cloud as Hadeon whisked us away once again.

We stopped only long enough to make it back to the peninsula where Vega waited.

He was pacing along the shore, his shoulders hunched and ready to fight until he spotted us. He practically bounded over to meet us, dipping low to help us into the saddle, clearly just as anxious to leave this court behind as we were.

Nyx whined, her head shaking back and forth like she was trying to dislodge something from her ear.

She couldn't portal like this, could she? My heart dropped, panic sweeping through me as Hadeon quickly secured the seat belt across our laps.

It was too far. Too much for her.

"No," I began to say, as she let out another whine. "We can't —"

A cloud of darkness raced over the ground. It was headed right for us. I tried to unhook the belt and scramble back to Nyx, an unreasonable voice in my head telling me that I could protect her if I stayed.

And then Hadeon was spurring Vega around, swooping back over to Nyx. He placed a shield of shadows between her and the wraiths.

"There, Nyx." He gestured to a single shaft of moonlight peeking in several feet away.

With a final roar, she jumped toward it, then she was gone in a single, brilliant gleam of silver. It was too soon for relief, though, even as Vega carried us higher away from the eerie shrieks of the wraiths below.

Hadeon's arms wrapped around me tightly, as if he were making sure I was still in his lap. As if by sheer force alone, he could keep me here, keep me safe.

Too many emotions raced through my mind. My eyes burned, and my breaths were coming too quickly.

When we crossed the border, silver and gold blinked into existence below us. I watched her appear and disappear a few more times before I could take my first real breath.

Closing my eyes, I rested my head in the crook of Hadeon's neck, placing my hands on his muscled forearms, my fingers digging into the thin armor there as I tried to center myself.

It was over now. And we were safe. All of us.

We had the flower, and we were safe.

Chapter Thirty-Six

THE RIDE BACK TO THE INN WAS TENSE. My heartbeat finally slowed about halfway there, allowing me time to process the implications of everything we had seen.

We knew where the wraiths were being made now. It was the only explanation for why so many of them had poured out from the mines. A shiver ran down my spine as I recalled how many there had been.

How if they wanted to, they could easily overtake our borders and sweep through Aelvaria like a plague.

So what was stopping them? Were they just waiting for the right time? Or were they simply driven by instinct instead of thought?

Either way, it was clear that we needed to make a move. And maybe, with enough power and the right soldiers at our sides, we could cut them off at their source.

I thought back to memories I had of Hadeon and me fighting the first time around. There would be no standing on a cliffside now. I would need to be in the center, strengthening his shadows for the final blow.

Something I was sure he would take well.

Snow whipped around us. The closer we got to our destination, the thicker it became. A storm was blowing in, because of course it was.

When we reached the inn, we stopped long enough to give Adira the flower. Hadeon hovered right next to me, but I couldn't bring myself to want more space when I was just as shaken as he was.

Adira looked at me, concern behind her brash façade. "Something happened."

I didn't bother to deny it. I nodded, my eyes burning.

Nyx hadn't yet arrived at the stables. And now I was second-guessing whether or not I saw her traveling beneath us. Questioning whether or not she ever made it off of that peninsula.

"My cerberus," I said, and her eyes widened. "She was with us. She's hurt."

I couldn't keep the worry masked, and I hated myself for sounding so weak, but Nyx was *mine* to protect.

"I might be able to help with that," Adira said, turning to face Kage. "Grab a vial of the ravi draught." She paused, turning back to me. "A cerberus, like...?"

"Like the three-headed dog of the Underworld," I supplied. "Yes."

She nodded, though her brows were still raised like she was struggling to believe it. "This is our strongest healing elixir, but fair warning, it reeks like hot ass and cat piss."

Kage glowered as he stepped forward with the vial.

"These potions are not easy to come by." He held the vial out, examining the eddying liquid under the stopper. "What will you give me for it?"

Adira and I locked eyes, before she turned to glare at Kage. "Seriously? Don't be an ass."

"You want a trade?" Hadeon's voice was dangerously low.

Tendrils of shadow snuck around me, climbing up to pluck the *animisi* out of Adira's hands.

"Sure, let's trade," he growled. "We have something you need, and you have something we need."

Kage's lips flattened, the gaggle of mages behind him looking just as irritated by this turn of events.

"For the love of —" Adira groaned, snatching the vial from Kage to hand to me.

As soon as it was in my hands, Hadeon gave her back the *animisi*.

"Thank you," she said, looking down at the humming flower with obvious relief. "And I'm sorry your pet was hurt. The draught will help, though."

"I really appreciate it." The wind howled outside of the window, whistling through the glass panes. Once again, my thoughts drifted to Nyx, wondering if she was back yet.

"You should go," I added after a beat. "Before the storm really rolls in. Somewhere you'll be safe."

She scoffed. "I'll let you know if I find such a mythical place in my travels." Then her voice softened. "But thank you. We'll leave now."

I realized that I was sad to see her go, though I barely knew her. She was a remnant from my life before, one of the few people in the world who understood a unique part of my life, who remembered reality TV and smartphones and playlists and tacos.

On impulse, I reached out to put my arms around her. She tensed under my touch, but reluctantly returned my embrace.

"I hope you find what you're looking for, and I hope that one day you find peace," I whispered.

It felt impossible right now.

"I hope the same for you," she said, her tone implying that she didn't think it was any more likely than I did.

I pulled back. "And if we ever take care of this threat..." *without dying*, I amended internally.

"If we manage to stave off this war..." she said with a dark half smirk.

"Maybe we'll meet again one day," I finished.

She nodded and was off, her mages following close behind. Kage darted a final look over his shoulder, dipping his head as he scanned us both.

It was likely as close as we would get to a goodbye from him, but I was fine with that. We all had been burned by this life and the last, and I really did wish them well.

No sooner had the door shut behind them than a flash of silver light appeared through the window, followed by several whines of pain.

Nyx.

I ran back through the door of The Sulking Siren, practically throwing myself at her.

There were burn marks all over her. Patches of fur missing

where open wounds continued to bubble and dissolve, the dryohp's acid slowly eating away at her.

I yanked the stopper from the vial, my eyes burning at the terrible scent. She was going to hate this, but I didn't care if it saved her life.

First, I poured a little of the draught on the worst of her wounds. She whimpered and scratched at the ground beneath her feet. Slowly, the acid burned away and her skin knitted itself back together.

I poured the rest of it down her throats, apportioning an even third for each.

The draught was slower to respond this way, but it was clear that it was working as the gouges on her paw and ear disappeared and the cut on her tail repaired itself seamlessly.

Relief washed over me in waves, and I threw myself at my cerberus, wrapping my arms around her neck.

Even Hadeon's shoulders relaxed. His shadows wrapped around her, scanning her for any other injuries before he reached out to run a hand over her head.

She was going to be all right.

Eventually, the snow picked up in intensity, forcing us all to seek shelter. We escorted Nyx to the stables before making a run for the tavern. I thought about Adira and the ships navigating through the storm. The winds weren't bad enough to be dangerous, but it would be unpleasant to say the least.

I hoped she was safe.

"I really do hope we see them again one day." Truthfully, I wouldn't mind seeing all of them one day, the seven women who had shared my fate.

"I hope we meet again someday as well," Hadeon muttered, his lips pursed in thought.

I narrowed my eyes at him. "You do?"

"Indeed," he drawled. "Especially considering she absconded with my favorite dagger."

I blinked up at him, a laugh bubbling out of me in response. Between the physical, magical, and emotional exhaustion weighing me down, I couldn't help but find it hilarious that the shadow king was just robbed.

"And you just — what?" I prodded. "Didn't notice or sense it with your many shadows?"

He shrugged noncommittally, and I bit back a small smile.

"Her dagger was worthless against the elves, let alone the fae or the vampires."

"Then why not just let them bargain for it?"

"Her companion irritated me."

Of course he did. "Still, it isn't like you to care so much."

I was mostly teasing, but his features turned serious. He wiped the snow from his hair and armor before he responded.

"She reminded me of you."

"Because of her flaming red hair, or because she, too, is witty and capable?" I pressed on our way up the stairs, even though I could tell from his tone that the comparison wasn't likely to be positive.

Sure enough, Hadeon fixed me with a grim expression. "Reckless and in over her head."

I sighed. We were having this conversation now, then.

Before I could respond, he gestured for me to go back to the room. He followed me up, each footstep as ominous as the shadows that flared from his body. The whole way here, they had wrapped around me like it was an instinct even he couldn't force them to disobey.

Or perhaps he hadn't tried very hard.

I tried to brace myself for the talk we needed to have.

No matter how he felt, Hadeon's need to protect me was ingrained in his soul. And as much as I wanted to curl up into his shadows and lose myself in that protection, that wasn't an option for either of us. Not before, and not now.

"You know I have to go," I said once he closed the door with his shadows. "That's why you brought me through the portal to begin with."

Arguably, I hoped that at least part of it was also the whole I-was-his-dead-soulmate-returned thing. Even Hadeon wasn't big enough of an ass to leave me in the human realm for another fifty years just to be petty. He wasn't likely to admit that right now, though.

"When I assumed you would have your memories and the skills that went with them," he shot back.

That stung a little, but it wasn't unfair.

"I have one of those things, and I'm...working on the second. It's no different from when you took me to the borderlands or when we went to get the flower just now."

"Yes, because that worked out so well. And it is different because of the wards," he said darkly. "Didn't you feel them?"

"That was never my strength," I reminded him.

"They won't allow me to shadow in or out of those mines." Hadeon's jaw worked in frustration.

My mouth fell open. That wasn't something I expected to

hear. Shadowing had never been a problem for Hadeon. Even when it came to Elion's wards, which were arguably the strongest of anyone I had ever met, they had never been a match for Hadeon's shadows.

"Then we'll have to fight our way in from the outside." I spoke calmly, like I didn't know damned good and well the argument we were about to have.

"No," he growled. "We won't."

And there it was, the stubbornness I had expected.

"You need me for this." I squared my shoulders, meeting his eyes defiantly. "And even if you didn't, I wouldn't walk away and leave both of our people to suffer the wraiths when I can help stop them."

It was only half the truth, something the warning in his eyes told me he suspected. I would go into those mines for the same reason I went with Abba all those years ago. For my court, yes.

But mostly for Hadeon. *Always* for Hadeon.

"You aren't ready, and the bloodstone limits what you can do," he countered. "We'll wait if we need to."

"There isn't time, and you know it. They're already getting bolder. How many more people will we let die?" Let alone the fact that I didn't trust him to wait for me.

He would sooner risk his life and his people in those mines than me, even now. Whatever else was between us, that I knew.

"And when you can't channel the isos you need?" he demanded.

"Then I'll take off the bloodstone and go all light-bomb on them," I shot back.

He clenched his jaw. "And burn yourself out doing it."

I shrugged, like that didn't worry me as well. "You'll be there with your favorite shadow accessory if I can't rein it in."

He paused, considering, before he opened his mouth to argue again. This time, I cut him off.

"I'm going, Hadeon. I won't lie about it, or sneak off in secret, but I will go." My isos flared to life, a beacon of determination.

Something shifted in his expression. His shadows stretched out toward me, and for once, he didn't rein them back in. They twined around my ankles, my wrists, soft and cool like liquid silk with all the strength that was uniquely Hadeon.

"And what makes you think I won't just restrain you, Feralinia?" His words were a whisper, a promise, spoken in the limited air between our bodies.

Visions of last night's dream, along with all the others, flooded my brain. The heat in his eyes was unmistakable, a fiery answer to my own. But it was more than that.

There was a surrender there, too. A breaking that had been slowly building from the moment we escaped the wraiths.

"Don't make threats you don't intend to follow through on." I wasn't even sure which threat I was referring to.

The obvious one, to keep me in a cage, one I hoped he wouldn't stoop to. Or the unspoken one, the line I so desperately wanted him to cross. In a lightning-fast move, his shadows pressed me up against the wall.

"And what if I do intend to follow them through?" He erased the space between us, his senses invading mine, surrounding me.

"Then you know what's at stake." I swallowed hard, a wave of emotion crashing over my chest while heat flooded my limbs, making its way toward my torso, then lower.

"Everything," Hadeon breathed, the gentle scent of wine cascading from his breath to my lips. "It always is with you."

"So make your choice."

It took everything in me to infuse my words with a bravado I couldn't even begin to feel. If he walked away now, I would crumble. I would dissolve into a nothingness that even the goddess could never piece back together.

But this was an all-or-nothing deal.

Hadeon leaned down, his knee parting my legs. Delicious heat flooded the space, and it was an effort not to writhe against him, to add friction to the place I so desperately needed it.

"There is a never a choice when it comes to you." Hadeon's voice was a low murmur in my ear, chills racing along my skin in between each word. "I lost you once. I could have lost you again today, and it would have destroyed me all over again. The damage is done, Feralinia. You're mine in every life, whether I want it or not."

"That's not good enough." I turned my head slightly away from him before I caved. "I might have played the part of your reluctant soulmate before, but you either want this or you don't. I won't be the inevitability you torture yourself with."

Every part of my body — and my soul — longed for him, but not like this. Not without something more.

"You are an inevitability, and you do torture me. But in the unlikely event that we survive the oncoming wraiths, it is not so you can go back to the court that was never home to you," he declared, his knee moving upward.

A hiss of air escaped my lips, and I tried to look away again, but Hadeon's cool fingers gripped my jaw, gently adjusting my chin until I was facing him.

He waited until my eyes locked on his before continuing.

"If you need to hear me say it, then let me be clear. I need you in my palace, terrorizing my kitchen staff with your messy cooking and everyone else with your slew of feral creatures. I need you challenging me at the breakfast table and sparring with me on the hillside." He moved closer, speaking the last part against my lips. "I need you in our bed. On our balcony. In your bathtub and my shower and everywhere else I can feasibly have you, every day, for the rest of our lives, as long as the stars-forsaken goddess wills that to be."

"You said *we*," I whispered, needing the confirmation that he wasn't going to keep me from this fight. *In the unlikely event that* we *survive.*

A muscle ticked in his jaw and his hands clenched, but his voice was firm. "I have no intention of losing you, Feralinia. Not again, not by circumstance or choice."

I heard everything he wasn't saying. It wasn't quite a compromise because he had basically just told me point-blank that he would die before letting me die. But he also acknowledged that he couldn't keep me like his pet and allow me to fight only at his whims.

It was the best I would get from him, and it was enough. Because I had no intention of losing him either.

This time, wherever we went, we would go together.

My gaze flitted from the starbursts in his midnight eyes down to his parted lips. I darted my tongue out to dance across the seam of my mouth, and a low growl rumbled through him.

My chest rose and fell against his, and he shifted his knee, coaxing a gasp from my lips.

His shadows tightened around my wrists like they were begging me to move, begging me to break the hold the silence had over us all. Heat ignited in my core, burning its way through my body until actual flames lit up my eyes.

Hadeon's mouth twitched in a knowing grin as I finally leaned into him, erasing the distance I had been desperate to close for a lifetime.

His mouth moved against mine as he breathed a sigh of relief over my lips. I moved my tongue out to taste him.

Another growl rippled through him at my eagerness, and he forced his shadows to drop me, his strong hands sliding in to support my weight. His fingertips dug into my skin, his lips skating across my jaw before moving down to my throat.

I gasped, wrapping my arms around his neck before winding my fingers through his long navy hair.

Each touch was desperate. Hungry. Relentless.

I pulled his hair back, forcing his mouth to meet mine again. I bit his lower lip and tugged it into my mouth. I traced the skin with my tongue, sucking and biting as he brought my legs around his waist.

His hands caressed my body, each plane and curve. There was too much fabric between us. Too much separating me from the smooth lines of his body.

"Admit you were never going to leave," Hadeon growled, rocking his hips and causing more of that exquisite friction I was so desperate for.

"Admit you were never going to let me," I breathed.

Silver starlight burst in his eyes, his fingers digging deeper into my skin, simultaneously eliciting both pleasure and pain. Another gasp hissed past my lips, and Hadeon swallowed it when he crushed his mouth against mine.

Then we were leaving the wall. A low whine escaped me when he broke off the kiss, setting me down on my own two feet once again. Before I could argue, though, his shadows slid around me, working in time with his fingers to unlace my armor.

First, he rid me of the fitted tunic, taking his time as he unveiled each new inch of skin. His lips laved praise on my stomach, his tongue sliding up between my breasts as his thumbs traced tantalizing circles.

He took his time, slowly kissing every single constellation on my body, each mark that told the world I belonged to him. He worshiped those constellations with his lips, his tongue, his teeth.

My fingers laced through the strands of his hair as he dipped down to his knees, his dexterous fingers working on my trousers next. As soon as they were off, along with the boots that took an unfortunate amount of time to unlace, his hands went back to exploring my body.

He traced the hardened muscles of my thighs before bringing his hands up to cup my backside. He anchored me in place, pressing kisses along my inner thighs, moving upward until he found the place he had been looking for.

My head flew back, my fingers gripping his hair even tighter as I allowed him to hold me in place, memorizing each dip and curve, each place he had revered a lifetime ago.

I gasped, shaking as the cool night air contrasted with the heat of his tongue. Shivers racked me, the sensation almost more than I could stand.

Then he was moving me toward the bed, the backs of my knees hitting the mattress as he sat me down.

My panted breaths were ragged in the silence of the room, growing faster as I watched him slide out of his armor. He was finally bare before me, carved from moonstone and marble. Every inch was perfectly sculpted, like the goddess had taken more time with him, so caught up in the mastery of her work that she forgot he was supposed to be mortal.

A breath lodged in my throat as I stared, speechless. My memories had not prepared me for this. His long navy hair swept over the swirling tattoos on his shoulders and collarbone, ending at the defined planes of his torso.

My gaze trekked downwards, appreciatively taking in the ridges of his abdomen that dipped down into a *V*.

Flames danced in my eyes, igniting from my fingertips and singeing the blankets, as I took in his length. That hunger grew inside of me, an aching deep in my core that craved him. Only him.

"I need you," I whispered, my tongue tracing the seam of my lips as I met his eyes again.

Hadeon's pupils blew wide with a desire as strong as mine.

His shadows slid underneath me, lifting me enough to line me up with the pillows in the center of the bed. Then he was hovering right above me.

His eyes skated over my face as his hands eased around my wrists, pinning them above my head. Expectation pebbled my skin, and I held my breath, waiting.

His name escaped my lips, the sound unrecognizable in its desperation.

A low growl rumbled through his chest in response, and then we were one, fused together as surely as our souls were. I gasped, my head falling back on the pillow while I savored the rightness that clicked into place now that we were together again.

Hadeon's eyes were locked on my face, studying my expression as he pushed me to the brink of pleasure.

This was right.

Perfect.

Our bodies danced to a rhythm that only we could hear. He grew more desperate, and my hips rose to meet his as I pushed back against the hold of his shadows.

I needed to touch him. Needed to run my fingers through his hair and scrape my nails down his back as I came undone.

As if he heard the thought, Hadeon released me, pressing against me until his chest rested fully against mine. My fingers dug into his shoulders as tension coiled through me, tightening until I was sure I would burst.

Stars burst like fireworks in my vision as a scream slipped out of me. Waves of pleasure washed over me. Blinding me. Drowning me.

A growl ripped from his throat, rattling the glass-paned windows as his shadows stretched to fill the room with darkness. Hadeon didn't stop until we were slick with sweat and gasping for air, until every muscle in my body was spent.

We lay in bed for hours, clinging to each other in the darkness until desire roused us once again. I didn't need to sleep, eat, or breathe. All I needed was the other half of my soul as we made up for all the time we had lost.

Chapter Thirty-Seven

THE STORM HAD PASSED BY LATE MORNING.

There was a part of me, a tiny one, that wondered if the blizzard that came out of nowhere was the goddess's doing, something to force Hadeon and me away from the world for just a little while longer.

Now that I knew what we were up against, I doubted we would have many opportunities to hide away.

Maybe that's why there was an urgency in everything we did. There were no slow explorations, no subtly whispered affirmations. It was like every touch and kiss was an expression of what-if.

What if I had never come back to you?

What if we lose each other again?

What if I was wrong, and all of this was just so I can sacrifice myself over and over in a cycle for eternity where these fleeting moments are all we'll ever have?

I wasn't sated when morning came, but at least the pervasive wrongness that had dominated both of my lives since the day I went with Abba was gone, a sense of rightness in its place. For however long I had left, Hadeon was mine, as he was always supposed to be.

For now, we had a war to fight, and it was one I intended to win.

"You know what we have to do," I said when we were securely in the air on the baztet.

Hadeon was no one's fool. He realized what the sheer volume of wraiths meant, what it would take to make a dent in their defenses without burning ourselves out before we could reach the inside. Or rather, *who* it would take.

We needed the Sun Court.

He sighed in resignation, but his shadows caressed me, half a century's worth of need and want reluctant to be pushed to the side after a single night.

"Yes, Feralinia. I know." Bitterness coated his tone. The years had only made the relationship between my family and him more contentious, not less.

"We can't win without their help." I had gone through every version of a battle plan we could have, and I knew Hadeon had done the same. And reached the same conclusion.

"If they agree this time." That was fairer than I wanted it to be.

They had said no before, but this time, Leander was here.

"They will agree," I insisted. *Hopefully.* "It's your people we have to worry about. They won't want to work with the enemy."

"They'll see reason," he said with a note of finality.

Or he would make them, he meant.

One way or another, we would both do whatever we had to do.

SURPRISING NO ONE, Hadeon's methods tended more toward manipulation than force. He called a council meeting as soon as we returned, including Leander, then presented the facts as we knew them.

"Will we be able to take on that many?" Leda asked.

"Not with our numbers," he confirmed.

Several sets of eyes slid to me, then my brother. Captain Xanth reared back in outrage.

"You can't be suggesting we fight alongside —"

"I would suggest you not finish that sentence when you're speaking about my soulmate." Hadeon's words fell like the drop of a guillotine.

Silence descended in the room. The blood drained from Captain Xanth's face.

Hadeon and I had discussed this on the way here. We weren't hiding this time, whatever the consequences. If something happened to us, I would damned well not be remembered as his enslaved princess.

I studied the reactions in the room, from revulsion to acceptance. Of course, Leander didn't flinch. He had known from the last time around, but even if he hadn't, he would have put on a show of support for me.

Celani sat straighter in her chair, daring anyone to comment.

No one did.

"That still doesn't answer the question of whether they will come," Leda bravely interjected. "Or how we will face this threat even if they agree. The time it would take for them to march here, let alone all the way to the place you describe..."

I exchanged a look with my brother, who raised a dubious eyebrow in response, as if to say, *Do I have to*?

"Trust has to start somewhere," I whispered.

I hadn't even told Hadeon what my brother's power was. The king was my soulmate, but I wouldn't spill my brother's secrets without his permission. I knew what I was asking of him, to set aside generations of enmity and accept this court as our allies. I let a hint of pleading enter my eyes, desperately hoping he was willing to trust the Moon Court long enough to overcome our real enemies.

My brother did not disappoint.

With a dramatic sigh, Leander waved his hand. At first, nothing happened. Then a portal opened...to a very familiar location.

Kallius laughed, while Hadeon looked skyward like he couldn't believe the things he had to put up with.

"Really, brother?" I asked.

Leander gave me a smirk, reaching through the portal to pluck one of Hadeon's quills from the nightstand by his bed.

"Does that answer your question about how we'll move the armies?" he asked with no small amount of arrogance.

Leda nodded, still a bit in awe. Hadeon pursed his lips.

"And mine about how you continue to sneak into my court."

Leander shrugged. "It should be a relief. We could have invaded at any time, as you see. Just as you could have dismantled our wards." It was a guess.

I hadn't revealed the extent of Hadeon's skill with wards, but his shadows did give him an intimate knowledge of how to build and take them down.

"The trust is already there, however unacknowledged," Leander finished up, meeting the eyes of each person at the table.

Not everyone was convinced, including Xanth, but it was as good as we could get with this amount of time.

Now we just had to make my family say yes.

WE STOOD on the dais in the middle of the circular room. Gilded frames lined the walls, moongates that allowed us to communicate with each of the kingdoms.

I swallowed as I stared at the one in front of me, watching familiar red mountains glittering beneath the midnight sun.

My stomach twisted, and I clenched my fists as Hadeon waited patiently to open the call. His expression was neutral, but his shadows undulated in irritation.

This was the last position he wanted to be in. Vulnerable and waiting for my father to turn his back on the Moon Court and the wraiths all over again.

But he was willing to try. And that meant everything.

We had made a choice not to have Leander portal us there because not only was that kind of distance taxing on his strength, but we thought my family would take it even less well if the "enemy" appeared in their midst.

Not to mention how little Hadeon liked the idea of being in my father's palace, at his mercy.

Leander took a step closer to me, casually slinging his arm around my shoulders.

"They won't bite," he said playfully. "Well, Elion might, but I'm sure it will be fine."

I didn't have that same confidence. Ever since we left the council room, the two versions of myself had been at war.

One half wanted to start this conversation off with accusations about the past — to threaten and beg and do whatever the hell I needed to in order to make them do things differently. The other wasn't entirely sure where to begin or how to speak to a family I hadn't known for fifty years.

But dragging my feet wouldn't make it any easier. We might as well get it over with.

"Okay," I breathed, and Hadeon took my cue to connect our moongate to the one in Illios palace.

There was a faint humming sound as the portal between our kingdoms opened enough to allow whoever was on the other side to see through to ours.

Several long moments passed until my parents came into

view. My mother's mouth curved in a tentative smile while my father squared his shoulders, his eyes crinkling at the corners.

"Phae-mber," he said awkwardly, my mother's elbow catching him in the ribs before he could offend me.

The gesture was so casual it sent a pang through me. Then Elion stepped into the frame, and that pang only strengthened. He canted his head, his golden eyes assessing me carefully.

"I see you found yourself a bloodstone," he said drily, eyeing my ring.

I nodded. "Thank you for the suggestion."

Elion's gaze narrowed slightly.

"You're different," he said flatly. A muscle worked in his jaw before he added, "You're...you."

My eyes burned, and I dipped my chin once. Of course Elion would recognize me, recognize the part of me that was fully his sister once again.

A thousand memories darted through my mind. Images of Elion's rare smile, his protective stance when someone at court challenged or insulted me, the indulgence he always showed me, even when he was trying to be firm.

Warmth unfurled in my chest, bolstering me for what I needed to say.

"We need your help." I shifted my gaze to my father, knowing his reaction would be strongest.

"We?" the sun king demanded.

Hadeon stepped out from the shadows, standing at my back with his arms crossed over his broad chest.

"Yes," he ground out. "We."

"Now, now," Leander cut in. "Before this becomes the emotional reunion we've all dreamt about, give us a chance to explain."

Our father continued to glare at Hadeon like he hadn't heard Leander speak. Centuries of hatred reddened his bronze cheeks while dark wisps of shadows swirled angrily behind me.

"You expect us to believe that the shadow king will not betray us at his earliest convenience?" he spat.

Hadeon might have held his tongue, but his shadows did the talking for him, encasing us both in a protective shield.

"He can't hurt her, Father. You know that," Elion said, bringing his finger and thumb to the bridge of his nose.

My father glared at Hadeon. "I know no such thing."

My mother gave him a flat look. "You do know, because you know perfectly well that she's his soulmate."

My lips parted, but no one, not even my father, showed a single hint of surprise at her declaration.

"You knew?" I gasped.

"Why do you think he wasn't waging a war to get you back?" my mother asked softly.

Truthfully, I had wondered if it was because he didn't want me back exactly as I was now. Something inside me eased at the knowledge that he did want me, would have fought for me if he had believed for a moment that I was unsafe.

"That doesn't mean he can't betray the rest of us," my father pointed out.

"No, but it means he won't." Leander was uncharacteristically serious. "And if you can't trust him, trust Ember."

My father gave me an assessing look, as though trying to

decide whether he could do that very thing. Would he always have wondered, or was it my name, my time as a human, that had made him consider?

Then again, he hadn't listened the last time I told him.

Before I could point that out, Elion spoke up again.

"She died for this argument once before, Father, and I will not stand by while she is forced to make that choice again." He fixed his gaze on me, looking me in the eye for the first time since I returned to this world. "I failed you then, little sister, but this time, I will be there to keep you safe."

Hadeon's shadows cupped my shoulders protectively like they resented the implication that he couldn't keep me safe, but I had eyes only for my family. Golden tears swam in my mother's eyes, and I could have sworn my father had to swallow one too many times before speaking.

"Very well, my daughter." He said the words slowly, as if they cost him. But he looked at me solidly when he asked, "What is it that you need?"

Chapter Thirty-Eight

I<small>N THE END, MY FATHER DECIDED</small> <small>THAT HE AND</small> Elion would come with the army while my mother would stay behind to protect our people, in case the worst were to happen.

With her ability to weave sunlight into corporeal objects, she was every bit the warrior they were, but someone had to stay behind. Hadeon looked meaningfully at me when my father pointed that out, and I accidentally let a burst of fire lick from my palm to his bare bicep.

He didn't so much as flinch, his shadows creeping in to shield him like I knew they would. A smirk pulled at the corner of his lips, and he didn't try to hint at me staying behind again.

Though the darkness in his eyes told me he wanted to.

I couldn't pretend I didn't understand how he felt, either. I could barely breathe at the thought of something happening to him, then my brother made it clear he had every intention of coming into the mines with us.

"You said you can't bring an army into the mines," Elion pointed out in his no nonsense tone.

"We can't," I confirmed.

"Then you need as much of the goddess's isos as you can get. You might be her favorite, little sister, but she was hardly stingy with the rest of us." His lips tilted up in a display of arrogance I knew was earned, and still, my stomach sank.

I had just gotten them back. Leander would only be opening the portal, but Elion...

"We would be grateful for your assistance," Leander chimed in like the traitor he was.

Hadeon nodded, though he looked as if it physically pained him to do so. Realistically, there had been no question of whether to ask them. It wasn't just that we needed their help. It was their war, too. The Sun Court was farther from the wraiths, but even they had fended off the stray attack. That would only get worse if we failed.

We knew the wraiths wouldn't stop until they had devoured all of Aelvaria, and even then, they would keep going, just as Hadeon had told me so many weeks ago.

So there was no real argument to be made, even if it killed me.

We ended the mystical FaceTime call and headed upstairs where the others were waiting. Hadeon let out a low sigh, his shadows moving over my skin in a way that was decidedly less protective and more...demanding.

Sensual.

Enticing.

Celani only smirked at him, presenting a bottle of wine.

"Have your fun later," she said. "You know it's tradition."

Memories flooded my head of the night before the last battle. There had been the same knife edge between hope and despair, an endless sense of waiting that we quelled with a bottle of Elven wine and a mountain of banter.

At least this time, Abba hadn't asked me if I was ready to die again. Actually, she had been oddly silent since I went to see Adira. Not that it was unusual for her to dip in and out of communication, but I had assumed I would hear something about the Mage girl.

A popping sound pulled me out of my thoughts.

"Busting out the celebratory wine in anticipation of our victory? I like your style, General." Leander grinned.

Celani leveled him with a flat look, pouring the bubbly drink into several glasses.

In some ways, Aelvaria wasn't so different from Earth. The wine was a lot like champagne, only it wasn't quite as carbonated, and it was lightly flavored by the blue melons that were so popular here.

I lifted my glass, and they all stared at me with some confusion.

"It's a toast," I said.

"Like where you burn your bread?" Celani's brow furrowed.

That had been another culinary project that hadn't gone exactly as planned, due in large part to my unpredictable flames. Hadeon made a small sound of amusement in the back of his throat, and I lifted my head with what little dignity I could muster.

"No. It's where you raise your glass and say what you're drinking for. Like..." I thought for a moment. "To not dying tomorrow. Again."

Hadeon scowled when I drank, but reluctantly followed suit at my prodding.

Kallius raised his glass tentatively, unconvinced this made sense, but announced, "I'll go next. To victory over the wraiths."

Celani laughed, drinking before she raised her own wine. "To more of Ember's human delicacies when this is all over."

That was a fitting description for tacos. I nodded my approval, drinking.

Leander's features turned impish. "To the look on Elion's face every time Hadeon touches his little sister."

We all drank.

Finally, I looked at Hadeon, who let out a sigh. But the barest corner of his mouth tilted up, and he looked only at me when he said, "To the future we deserve."

We all drank again.

We did deserve this. We deserved more than this, but I would settle for a handful of years without having to look over my shoulder, without worrying that Hadeon or my friends and family would be ripped from me at any moment. We deserved a small bit of peace, and that's what I was going to fight for.

ANOTHER HOUR of Hadeon's shadows tracing maddening, teasing circles along my skin under the table was all I could tolerate. It became a game between us, where he sent me pointed looks that said, *this torture can end any time you like*, and I tried to hold out.

"Feralinia," he taunted, his pupils blown wide with desire. "Is something the matter?"

I narrowed my eyes, but I was fairly certain the heat emanating from my gaze in no way resembled anger. His nickname for me reverberated in my soul, equal parts comforting and enticing.

I loved our family, but if this was my last night in this life, I wanted to spend it in Hadeon's arms. In his bed. Wrapped up in his scent and his shadows.

Knowing it would make him unbearably smug, I abruptly got to my feet, not bothering to give an excuse they would see right through.

"We're going to bed now," I announced.

Leander made a face, and Celani laughed.

"Is that the very expression you were toasting Elion for earlier?" she teased my brother.

He tipped his drink to her in confirmation. The sound of their laughter cut off as Hadeon shadow-traveled us back to his rooms.

"Was there something you wanted, Feralinia?" he growled in my ear.

I lifted my eyes to his, peering up at him through my lashes. Now that we were here, I could drag this out a little longer, to torture him the way he had tortured me.

"Of course not," I said airily.

Then I casually unhooked my dress from the back of my neck, letting it fall to the floor. My breasts were bare, only my silvery lacy thong still intact, tied in the back with a little bow.

"Did *you* need something?" I asked, all false nonchalance.

Hadeon's eyes darkened, his expression going slack as he took in the bronze curves of my body, lingering over the golden tattoos in my skin, dipping between my breasts. He paused at the lacy scrap of fabric I had worn with him in mind.

His shadows crept along the floor and wound around my ankles, holding me securely in place.

Hadeon stalked toward me with slow, purposeful foot-steps. He stopped directly in front of me, close enough that my mostly nude body was pressed against his coat. It was a cool contrast to my flushed skin.

He put a hand on my cheek, his thumb caressing just under my lip while he leaned down to speak in my ear.

"Now that you mention it..." His teeth scraped along the lobe of my ear while he wrapped one hand around my thigh and dragged the other down to my neck.

A gasp escaped in spite of myself, but I couldn't even care that he was winning this game of ours when my entire body brimmed with need for his. I crushed myself against his coat, and his shadows pulled me back against the wall.

There was nothing gentle about his touch, but that wasn't a bad thing. I didn't want soft kisses or tender caresses.

I wanted him to claim me. To own me. To command my body with his until we were desperate for air.

"Did I say you could move, little Ember?" he asked, pulling back in punishment like he had plucked the thought from my mind.

I parted my lips to protest, but another shadow wrapped around my mouth, cutting off my words. He raised an eyebrow, daring me to dissipate it with my flames if I didn't want to play this way.

And *damn him*, I did.

I wanted to cede control to him for this night, to pretend that I could exist here, under his protection. That he could control the outcome of tomorrow for us both. I needed it.

We both did.

His lips curved up in pure arrogance as his thumb dragged a single, featherlight touch from my collarbone to my breast. A strangled sound threatened to escape me, muffled by the silken shadow.

He chuckled, and the sound did nearly as much as his touch to undo me. Then he stepped forward, skating his lips along the skin of my neck, hovering over my collarbone like he had a lifetime ago.

His tongue slid along the tattoo, tracing each branch like he knew them intimately, like he had studied them in spite of himself for every moment I had spent in this new existence with him.

At the same time, his hand worked to undo the bow of my undergarments, his fingers grazing along the curve of my backside before he let them fall to the floor.

I didn't move, knowing he would stop if I did, but staying still was agony. Perfect, irresistible agony that I planned to repay in full. Only when he worked his way down my body did I finally protest.

He pulled back to look at me, and I made sure he was watching when I very pointedly lowered my eyes to his own very obvious arousal.

"Feralinia..."

I looked at him in challenge, and his shadows fell away from my mouth, loosening their hold on my upper body until I could gracefully sink to my knees.

When my wrists were unbound, I worked on removing his clothes, then worshiped his body with the same enthusiasm he had shown mine. He was equal parts reverent and commanding, grasping my hair and dragging his thumb along my lips until he was close to breaking.

Until I was, too.

Then he pulled me to my feet, trapping me against the wall once more and entering me in one smooth motion. I wrapped both of my legs around his waist while ecstasy overtook every molecule of my being. The stars themselves rose up in me, each joining pushing me further over the edge of an explosion I couldn't contain.

My tattoos blazed golden, and his shadows expanded to fill every bit of space in the room, my heated skin eclipsed only by the intense, overwhelming feeling of his body against mine, inside mine, like we were the same. Not just two halves of the same soul, but melded together in an unbreakable, undefinable way, with no beginning and no end.

Finally, I shattered, the flames of my hair fanning out around us both in the split second before darkness engulfed us completely.

He didn't bother setting me back on the floor, which was good since my trembling legs wouldn't have held me. Instead, he carried me back to the bed, pulling me on top of him and pressing a kiss against my forehead.

For several long moments, I laid against his chest, listening to a heartbeat that raced in time with mine as we caught our breaths.

"I was promised forever, Feralinia." Hadeon's baritone rumbled through his chest. "And I intend to hold you to that bargain this time around."

It was equal parts domineering and tender, a declaration of love and an order to stay in this life with him.

I sat up to get a better look at him, staring down into the canvas of stars in his eyes and watching our entire future play out in his gaze.

"And I intend to keep it," I responded softly.

I hoped like hell I would be able to.

Chapter Thirty-Nine

I STOOD ON THE BALCONY, MY EYES FIXED ON THE Ahvi constellation. It was brighter this morning, nearly as golden as one of the pregnant moons next to it.

Both of Aelvaria's moons were fuller than usual, closer to our atmosphere, like they were weighed down with the same dread that filled the Courts beneath them.

I crossed my arms, my fingers drifting up to the mark on my collarbone, tracing each line, each star in a silent prayer.

"Feralinia." Hadeon's voice was a low purr as he stepped behind me.

He wrapped his arms around my waist, his fingers splaying on the bare skin of my stomach as he pulled me against him. I closed my eyes, breathing him in like he was my last chance for fresh air.

Hadeon exhaled, his warm sigh sending shivers across my skin.

"What are you thinking about?" he asked, his lips trailing

over my shoulder while his fingers drew tantalizing circles along my ribcage.

My chest seized, my stomach twisting as I turned to face him.

Stars danced in the midnight canvas of his eyes when he stared down into mine. His gaze was heady as he took me in, searching my face for the answer.

I stretched my hands up, wrapping them around his neck so I could outline the constellation that marked him as mine.

"Tell me we'll make it through this. That we'll come back...together."

A muscle in his jaw ticked, and his fingers dug into my skin a little more.

"Why don't you ask your goddess or Abba?" he retorted, arching a navy eyebrow.

I rolled my eyes. "Be serious for a moment."

He swallowed, his gaze roaming from my lips up to my eyes, before landing on the sky above us.

A knock on the door saved him from answering. I wasn't ready for this moment to end or for everything that would come next, but fate apparently wasn't willing to wait any longer.

Nyx leapt up off the floor, rushing toward the door as Hadeon followed. She was pouting about being left behind today, so she was on edge and hyper-focused on every noise.

Even Ahvi was a little more subdued than usual, and I wondered if he would stay behind, too, or if I would be as terrified for him on the battlefield as I had been for Nyx before.

He had no real reason to follow me, so I was hopeful he would stay. I needed him to stay.

I couldn't risk anyone else.

Once I had slid into my robe, covering myself fully, Hadeon opened the door. Celani waited on the other side, a solemn expression etched into her delicate features. Her hair was pulled away from her face in warrior braids.

"The troops are ready, and Leander is waiting for your word to open the portals to the Sun Court." Hadeon nodded, gesturing for her to come inside.

"Have you decided who you're leaving behind to guard Fengari?" She swallowed as she braced herself for Hadeon's decision.

It wouldn't just be someone to guard the palace. It would be the person who would protect the court from the wraiths if the worst happened.

Hadeon's chin dipped, and Celani braced herself.

"You know it has to be him. Kallius is invaluable on the battlefield, but aside from you, he's also the only one I trust to stay behind."

Celani flexed her fingers at her side but nodded.

"Understood," she said coolly. "Do you want to tell him, or should I?"

Hadeon's shoulders sagged. That wasn't a conversation that was going to go smoothly. Denying Kallius this battle and the chance to protect his sister's back was going to be difficult to say the least.

"I'll take care of it," he said. "Once Ember is ready, I want the two of you with Leander to greet the Sun Court. We need to be ready to move as soon as their last soldier comes through that portal."

Celani's fist came up over her chest, the sign of respect among the Moon Elves. Then her violet eyes flitted over to meet mine, her gaze softening a little.

"No secret missions for the goddess that we don't know about?" she asked, her words halfway between teasing and concerned.

"Not this time. I'm with you."

She nodded once then spun on her heel, leaving us alone once more.

Hadeon's shadows swirled as he watched me from over his shoulder.

"If you change your mind, Feralinia," his deep voice rumbled through the room, "I will follow you in death, down into the very depths of hell and I will drag you back kicking and screaming if I must. Goddess be damned, I will not let you go again."

I swallowed, tears burning at the back of my eyes.

"Promises, promises," I whispered.

THE COURTYARD WAS FILLED with soldiers.

Silver, star-forged armor and weapons gleamed under the light of the moons as they lined up in formation. The thrum of expectation filled the air while everyone prepared for what we could only hope would be our final battle.

All morning, Leander had been opening portals around the Moon Court, while Kallius and Captain Xanth directed every capable soldier through.

Celani and Colonel Aereon filled each of the regiments in on what we were about to do, making certain they had access to the star-forged weapons that actually stood a chance against the wraiths.

Then they explained that we wouldn't be the only ones fighting.

Murmurs sounded throughout the ranks as they were told that Sun Court soldiers would be joining us. This was going to be one of the most difficult parts, making sure our soldiers didn't go to war with each other before we made it to the Never Court.

The sun was just beginning to rise when my brother finally opened another large portal to the Sun Court.

Elion waited on the other side, his gold-tipped scythe glittering brighter than the armor covering him from head to toe. My father stood next to him, only slightly uncomfortable as he stepped through the portal.

Leander strained his isos, stretching the gateway between our kingdoms wide enough to reveal the thousands of soldiers at their backs. Their expressions were somber as they followed their prince and king into the court of their enemies.

Elion said something to the soldiers that I couldn't quite hear, and in almost perfect unison, all of them turned to face me.

A low gasp rang out through the soldiers, whispers

spreading through the ranks as each of them took a knee. They removed their helmets, bowing their heads in my direction.

My chest tightened, and on instinct, I raised my hand in the air forming a fist before crossing my two middle fingers — a sign of royal approval that I hadn't made in a lifetime.

The soldiers cheered, and in the distance, I registered my father's proud smile. He guided the men into position while Elion marched directly toward me.

My older brother's golden eyes hardened as he reached down into the satchel at his waist before carefully removing a delicate tiara.

I blinked several times, my gaze locked on the burnished gold leaves, leaves I had only ever seen grow on the Sacred Tree. They flickered, sparks igniting at the edges as they stretched toward a diamond-studded starburst in the center.

The goddess had blessed the Mitera Tree so she would never shed her leaves unless she wanted to, just like the dryohps in the Never Court.

The fact that they were here on this crown meant she had either given them to Elion willingly, or he'd somehow stolen them.

But that wasn't even the most remarkable part. Right in the middle of the starburst was a rarity — a fire crystal.

A bloodstone.

Leander let out a low whistle as he joined us.

"And you pretended not to care." He tsked, nudging Elion with his shoulder.

Our brother didn't bother looking at him. His gaze flicked

from the tiara down to the moon-and-star ring around my finger.

"I suppose two bloodstones is a bit excessive," he said drily. "But since this one is already attuned to our bloodline, you'll have to make do. Unless, of course, Leander has a sudden desire to wear a tiara."

"I would look great in a tiara," Leander fired back in mock offense. "But our sister here needs all the help she can get today. Still a little more human than elf if her waning isos says anything."

Elion's mouth twisted in disgust, and Leander barked out a laugh.

The corner of my mouth twitched upward as my younger brother took the tiara from Elion. He made a show of examining it before shrugging and placing it on my head.

Power flared to life, my veins alive with isos that was begging to break free. I gasped, feeling the full effects of the fire that had been blocked all this time.

A rush of heat flooded my body, racing under my skin like a heat wave. When I opened my eyes, Elion was staring at me, pride evident in his gaze.

"That's better," he said, scanning my hair that was well and truly flaming, and my tattoos that glowed so brightly I practically lit up the field.

I shivered, savoring the feeling of being whole again. Of being powerful.

Leander tilted his head to the side, studying me.

"It's a little understated for my taste," he sighed. "But now that I know you're willing to hunt down bloodstones for your siblings..."

Elion just shook his head, continuing to ignore him.

Our father approached next. He cast a glare in Hadeon's direction as he and Celani spoke with the Moon soldiers, then he pulled me into a hug. It was warm and unexpected and a thousand other things I couldn't quite name.

It took a few startled heartbeats before I could think clearly enough to return the gesture. I wrapped my arms around his back, settling against his broad chest the way I had as a child. A small piece of me, of both Ember and Phaedra, felt another piece of my soul click into place.

"I have missed you, little firestorm," he whispered into my hair before pulling away.

His expression was stoic again, but I saw the emotion dancing behind his eyes.

And I realized just how much I had missed him, too.

THE ENTIRE COURTYARD was collectively holding its breath.

Hadeon stepped up beside me, his shadows wrapping around us, like they were primed and ready to whisk us away if things went sideways.

Leander moved to the center of the armies, iridescent light blooming and cracking around him like fragments of broken mirrors. It moved and spun until a kaleidoscope of color lit up the field.

Our plan was simple. As simple as plotting the demise of hordes of wraiths, using the people I loved most in the world as the battering ram.

Elion would escort us to the entrance of the mines, but no farther. From there, my father would accompany Xanth, Hadeon, and me inside.

Between us, our isos allowed us the best chance of getting past the wraiths to find their spawn point while the entirety of our armies stayed behind to fight them off.

Our numbers were the only advantage we had, but I couldn't shake the feeling that it might not be enough.

Once Hadeon gave the signal, Leander pushed forward, the light growing brighter, the air thinner, until a gateway into the Never Court opened.

There was a stilted moment of silence, a brief calm in the storm as mist stretched forward, dissipating under the sunlight of the Moon Court.

Shadows shifted on the other side, slowly at first. Then one by one, green eyes blinked into existence, widening in fury as they tilted their heads to examine the portal.

That was when the screaming started.

Unearthly wails pierced the air as a group of wraiths darted forward. The Moon soldiers immediately struck their shields with their swords. A loud ringing filled the air and the wraiths crumpled under the sound.

They pressed forward, pushing the wraiths back with each

strike of their star-forged weapons while we looked on, waiting for our chance to strike.

A halo of fire bloomed around my head, brighter and hotter with the assistance of the bloodstone Elion had given me. Light pulsed in my hands, behind my eyes, my isos begging me to set it free.

"Not yet, Feralinia," Hadeon said, though his shadows were whipping around us, clearly just as eager.

We waited, watching as our armies charged into the fray, listening to the sounds of a thousand battle cries and the screams of the wraiths. Celani led the fight, her star-forged spear little more than a silver streak in the air as she brought it down again and again.

The weapons from the Sun Court flamed to life, each scythe and sword slashing through black static in a storm of fury.

Light bent around the wraiths, confusing them long enough for our regiments to divide them, slowly picking off one section at a time. Gravity shifted as Celani slammed her fist against the ground, sending a wave of wraiths up into the air.

Flaming arrows shot through the sky, piercing the creatures over and over until they dissipated into the mists.

My fingers danced at my sides, and I shifted my weight back and forth, wanting nothing more than to join this battle, to utilize the isos that was finally at my fingertips.

The line moved forward, and we inched closer to the portal. It was a waiting game, one none of us at the back of the line had much patience for. Boots marched over dead ground, drumming a steady beat as our soldiers moved deeper into the Never Court.

Finally, a loud whistle pierced the air — the signal that it was our turn.

Our small group fell in line, moving into the space the armies had carved through the center of the horde.

Blood-curdling growls reverberated in the mist as we stepped through the portal. Black teeth snapped, claws slashed through the air. The wraiths were furious, moving forward like a raging tide, destroying everything in their path.

Dust rose from the ground, swirling through the mists enough to cloud our vision even further. Everything was murky, blurry, and disorienting, and the wraiths used that to their advantage.

From the other side of the portal, it had been easier to see the bigger picture. We had watched our armies succeed in decimating theirs, but now that we were here, it was harder to have perspective.

The air was putrid with the scent of sulfur and rot. Dead soldiers lay on the ground near our feet. While our armies had moved forward, killing their fair share of wraiths, the monsters flooded out in a never-ending stream of darkness from the mouth of the mines. Whenever one fell, another would take its place.

Something about our presence infuriated them even more. They were suddenly desperate. *Incensed.*

They swept over our armies in a wave, filling the gaps between soldiers as they surged toward the portal.

My breath caught in my throat, and I whipped around in

time to watch as Leander closed the gate between our courts so that the wraiths couldn't use it to their advantage.

So many soldiers were waiting on the other side, but he couldn't risk letting the wraiths through.

His blue eyes softened in the split second he met my gaze. He had just enough time to mouth the words 'To our victory' right before the portal disappeared.

Without access to the isos in the Moon Court, it was already harder to breathe. All around us, our soldiers were beginning to slow, their isos dwindling each time they called on it.

Three Sun soldiers fell to my left, their screams slicing through me as the wraiths descended on them in a flurry.

Hadeon and I acted at once. Shadows streamed from him, encasing the bodies and casting them out of harm's way while I cast fire into the wraiths.

It engulfed them, swallowing them whole and burning the creatures to nothing more than green mist, their howls of pain cut off before they could really begin.

Rage flooded through me as I sent wave after wave of flames to dissolve the beasts who had breached our line. We were still conserving our power, so we hadn't yet started using them in tandem, but our individual isos was enough to cut through this line.

Hadeon was a furious storm cloud at my side, slaughtering any shadows that didn't belong to him. He didn't hesitate behind the wall of his soldiers. He refused to wait for the real battle that lay ahead of us, using his shadows to destroy as many of the creatures as he could.

As Phaedra, I had seen Hadeon in war. Watched as his shadows devoured battlefields, leaving nothing but the bones of his enemies in their wake.

As Ember, I had only witnessed a fraction of his power.

Today, he was an entirely different kind of warrior, a monster in his own right. A god of death and destruction.

His shadows sliced through the wraiths like a finely sharpened blade cutting through water. A blur of darkness pressed forward, and Hadeon's shadows pushed back, blowing them far away from the line like he was the wind and they were nothing but dust.

His isos spurred mine, charging it, fueling it, igniting something inside me that made me forget for a moment that our lives were on the line. Hours could have passed, or minutes, as we diminished the numbers of the wraiths, getting closer and closer to the mines.

When we finally made it to the entrance, Celani let out another whistle, and the armies fell into formation around the mouth of the cave.

Elion stepped forward, his face a hard line as he slowly raised his hands from his sides up toward the sky, pushing an invisible wall toward the mouth of the cave.

Light rippled and stretched as he forced his isos to create a net around the mines.

He had never used his power against the wraiths, so we weren't sure if it would work at all, let alone how long it might last. But it was better than not trying at all.

Fire poured from my hands, flames licking at the air inside the cavern and forcing the wraiths backward. They screamed and burned, their furious cries only cut off when Hadeon's obliterated them.

Colonel Aereon raced forward, using his isos to become a silhouette of smoke as he hid among the wraiths.

Confusion flickered in Hadeon's gaze. This hadn't been part of the plan. He wasn't part of the group assigned to enter the caves.

Had he just sealed his own fate?

Elion continued to work on solidifying his wards, while Hadeon and I pushed back the wraiths, slightly more cautious now that we didn't know if we were killing Aereon.

Then a flash of blue appeared. A star-forged sword sliced through the air again and again. The wraiths turned, no longer focused on their exit but on the traitor in their midst instead.

The distraction was enough to allow Elion to solidify his ward around the outside.

He muttered a prayer to the goddess, his quiet voice tugging at some long-forgotten memory in the recesses of my mind. Every moment we had spent at the temple, praying to the Goddess, whispering to Abba, begging for their assistance and their guidance.

I hoped she remembered those prayers now.

A guttural scream ripped through the air just before the wraiths focused their attention on us once again, but as they raced forward, they were met by a wall of fractal light.

The corner of my brother's mouth twisted into a feral grin as he watched their anger grow, watched as they couldn't escape.

It would make the next part of our plan harder, but would

at least offer our soldiers a fighting chance while we were gone. If they could hold off the wraiths that were lingering in the mists, the wards would at least keep the new ones from decimating our forces before we could get back.

The sound of battle continued to rage behind us, steel sweeping through the air, followed by pained cries and screams of unearthly monsters.

But that was nothing compared to what lay ahead.

Hundreds of green eyes darted back and forth, trying to find the location of the noise with their jaws snapping furiously at the wall of light.

Hadeon stepped up first, his starlit eyes meeting Elion's in something like approval. My brother glared back, arching a russet eyebrow in silent response.

"How long will the wards hold?" I called over the din of clashing steel behind us.

Elion swallowed, his mouth returning to a grim line.

"I'm not sure, but I don't think it will be long if I don't stay behind to keep it in place," he said, his golden eyes sharpening as they met mine. "The faster you get this done, the better."

That was more or less what we had planned on. Hadeon dipped his head in a solemn nod, taking a step forward. Shadows swirled around him, prepared to sweep through the wall of wraiths.

My father fell in line beside him, his isos covering them like a blanket. The wraiths hissed as the elves blinked out of existence, my father's magic hiding them in plain sight.

The monsters might not have been able to discern much in

the darkness before, but they couldn't see the elves at all now. None of us could.

Captain Xanth's lips pulled back in disgust, but he rushed to join them, unwilling to leave Hadeon alone with the sun king for longer than necessary.

I turned to follow them.

"Be careful, little sister," Elion called after me. "Stay alive this time."

I squared my shoulders, bringing my isos to my fingertips and giving him a sharp nod.

"I will." It was a fool's promise, but one I intended to keep.

Chapter Forty

I held my breath as I stepped under my father's shield. A prism of color danced in my vision, surrounding us like a mirrored dome.

Hadeon's shadows filled the space, stretching out along the ground, the walls, and the ceiling as he took out wraiths behind the ward. He chose different entry points, distracting the monsters by attacking from behind or at their sides.

Green eyes blinked, whispers of death both confused and panicked as they turned into a green fog.

We crept forward through the horde, keeping our steps light and our isos at the ready. My pulse raced, my stomach twisting into knots wondering how far we would get before they realized what was happening.

The four of us moved quietly, relying on the howls from the wraiths and the din of battle to cover our echoing foot-steps. They parted around us, confusion breaking their focus from the wards only briefly. I swallowed hard.

It was working. The plan was working.

Between my father's reflective shield, Hadeon's shadows, and the way Xanth's isos allowed him to act as an amplifier, we were quickly making our way through their numbers like an invisible cloud.

The light glowing from my father's hair and mine allowed us to see enough that I didn't need to use my isos. Yet. So I held on to it, waiting for the moment I would be able to unleash it all at once.

We were a blade, carving our way through the darkness. It was as easy as breathing.

Almost too easy.

A sinking feeling settled over me, wrapping around my bones like an anchor determined to bring me to my knees. Questions whirled around my mind in a vicious cyclone of unending doubt.

What if something more sinister than the wraiths waited at the end of this dark tunnel? What if I had misinterpreted the prophecy, Abba's words, all of it?

My isos sputtered, my hair flickering like a single flame in the wind, threatening to dissolve into a useless plume of smoke.

Taking a deep breath in, I held it for several beats before letting it go again. Then I focused on the tangible things around me: the brush of Hadeon's arm against mine as we quietly marched toward the unknown. The fire of my father's hair as he led us there. The heavy footsteps of the wraiths as they moved around us like we were a boulder in a raging river, their darkness rolling over us, but never through.

Moisture dripped from the ceiling and trickled down the walls. The air reeked of mildew and decay, slickening the stones beneath our feet, making each step more precarious than the last.

But the goddess had made me a promise.

I clung to her words like they were the very oxygen I needed to breathe.

When gifted power pays sacrifice,
Mother Terrea shall repay the price.
Blessed be her soul reborn,
Seek from where the Earth was torn.
In fifty years eight heiresses will return,
To bring peace to all lands that burn.

I QUIETLY CHANTED THE WORDS, allowing them to echo off the walls of my mind in a mantra that propelled my feet onward.

She would repay the price.

The goddess wouldn't let my sacrifice be for nothing. She brought me back so I could bring peace. So I could have it too. And I *would*.

Hadeon and I deserved that much.

THE AIR GREW COLDER AS we wound our way deeper into the mines. The farther we went, the more it seemed that the wraiths had lost their sense of urgency. They didn't rush or howl. Instead, they stood sentinel along the walls of the mines, their ears twitching each time a stray stone skittered down the path.

There was no wind or life.

There was only the heavy scent of death in the air, like the wraiths had robbed even this cold, dark place of its pulse while they ate away at Terrea's core, depriving it of its breath.

The path turned gravelly, the stones beneath our feet becoming little more than sand and dust. My boots sank in the loose gravel, my steps growing heavier.

The shield around us sputtered when my father lost his foothold, sliding forward just before Hadeon's shadows righted him. Something skipped along the path, the sound of metal clashing against stone.

The wraiths responded immediately.

Growls and the vicious gnashing of teeth echoed around us as every wraith lining the walls looked in our direction. Beady eyes narrowed, and clouds of hot breath against the cold air filled the space with the overpowering scent of festering wounds and disease.

A snarl ripped from the monster closest to us. He tilted his head curiously, his eyes locking on mine in a hazy sort of way, though he shouldn't have been able to see me. He didn't blink or look away as he closed the short distance between us. Lifting his snout high, he took a deep breath, more putrid air escaping him as he exhaled.

My mouth went dry, the hairs on the back of my neck rising as he repeated the process. I watched as he homed in on our spot in the center of the tunnel.

We could kill him.

With a single burst of light or one of Hadeon's carefully aimed shadows, we could end his life in seconds.

For several stuttering heartbeats, I weighed the pros and cons of ending him before he could call out to the others. It might draw too much attention, even with my father's shield around us like an invisibility cloak, or another wraith might take his place while we repeated the process again and again.

We needed to move forward. Our plan hinged on making our way through the tunnels unseen, and another unending wave of wraiths would get us nowhere.

My thoughts cut off abruptly as movement caught the corner of my eye.

Another wraith had sensed us, its canine-like mouth pulling back in a snarl as it studied the spot where Captain Xanth was standing. With a lightning-fast movement, it stretched out its claws, grasping at the air between us. Its talons scraped against my father's shield, screeching like nails on a chalkboard.

The sound had me clenching my teeth as my ears rang. Hadeon's shadows blazed around us protectively, and I knew it was taking everything in him not to lash out.

A howl answered in the distance, followed by another, then another. We stood frozen in the tunnel as the ground shook, and stones came loose from the ceiling and walls while we waited for the swarm.

I braced myself, waiting for them to see through the shield, but just like before, they parted right in front of my father, flooding the space on either side of us.

The wraith that swiped at our shields stepped forward again, his claws slicing through the air. We edged forward, just out of his reach, and he struck one of the other wraiths in the jaw instead.

That wraith let out a low growl, snapping its teeth at the first in warning, and my father's shoulders sagged slightly.

In relief? Exhaustion? I couldn't tell.

His isos wouldn't continue to hold. Even with Xanth enhancing him, I knew he was flagging. If we didn't find this source soon, we would have to figure out another way forward.

Dread curdled in my stomach at the thought of starting this all over again, of allowing the deaths of our soldiers to be in vain.

A small flash of blue steel caught my gaze. Near the wall of the cave, there was a star-forged sword. Colonel Aereon's. Was that what my father had tripped over?

When we grew closer, we edged toward the wall, and Hadeon scooped it up, tucking it under the shield with us.

The blade was surprisingly clean, like it hadn't even witnessed the battle we'd all been a part of before coming to the mines.

Like it held no memory of the sacrifice Aereon made for us. At least, I assumed he had died. No one could have survived that many wraiths alone, but his distraction had allowed us to make it this far.

The air grew even colder, our breaths expanding into portentous gray clouds in front of us. It was another mile deeper underground before there was a break in the narrow walkway.

I let out a long, slow exhale as I took in a vast cavern, unfolding around us like jaws of sharp, rotting teeth. The air here was worse, thick and moist as it coated our skin, the sulfuric scent so much stronger that we had to cover our mouths to dampen the smell.

Each precarious step had us ducking or weaving to avoid bumping into the cavern's teeth. Even worse were the small pools of luminous green liquid that bubbled like sulfur springs. Steam drifted above them like it was desperate to escape before dissipating in the freezing cold air.

The pools were everywhere, so close we had to walk in a single-file line to avoid stepping in them.

Everything about this place felt like the wraiths. It was soulless and empty, made from death, how I might imagine the inside of their minds to be.

I was hollow, a scrap of skin weighed down by the heavy pressure of the air. Each inhale was strained, each exhale a relief.

We crept around the fragile stalagmites, my isos creating a faint glow along the towers and walls, revealing nothing but shadows and crumbling earth.

While the creatures had flooded the tunnel, there were none in the cavern, at least that we could see, but that didn't mitigate the feeling that something was watching us — studying us carefully.

It wasn't until Hadeon's shadows glided along my skin, a reminder of comfort and life outside of this dead place, that I realized I had been holding my breath.

Stars lined my vision as a gasp hissed past my lips. I froze at the sound, my eyes widening as I waited for the inevitable sound of wraiths. I counted one heartbeat. Another. Five heartbeats. Ten.

The next sound that overtook the silence was the pop and gurgle of the green pool next to us. Black bubbles writhed beneath the toxic surface, and we watched as they oozed wisps of smoke.

Small rocks tumbled down from above, pieces of the stalactites breaking off and landing in the bubbling pools near our feet. Green liquid popped and splashed, dissolving the stalagmites growing from the cavern floor.

Xanth let out a low curse as the liquid landed on his armored trousers, obliterating the metal scales at his ankle. He jerked backward, stepping out of the safety of my father's shields.

When no wraiths immediately descended on him, I let out a quiet sigh of relief.

Once I was sure we were alone, or as alone as we could be with dread hanging over our heads like a noose and the twisting feeling that something was watching us, I tapped my father on the shoulder, motioning for him to let down his shield.

His eyes widened, his face creasing in doubt. He hesitated for several long heartbeats, watching as Hadeon called back his shadows and I let go of the firelight that had been guiding us.

Finally, he dipped his chin, his shoulders sagging as the prism of light that surrounded us slowly faded away.

That was when I felt it. A steady thrumming, like a pulse or the deep, resonant chords of a bass being strummed over and over again. Hadeon's gaze snapped to mine then toward the sound.

I followed him as he wound around the crumbling towers, searching for the source.

He stopped short after only a few feet, and I nearly collided with him. When I dipped my head around his arm, all I could see was a mass of black static. A writhing and pulsing darkness that hummed and twisted above the largest pool.

It had no eyes. No mouth or teeth. No real shape that linked it to the wraiths aside from the rough edges and the strange way their shadows rippled inward instead of out.

This was the source.

I was sure of it.

Even Hadeon looked convinced, stepping closer to examine the curls of smoke that danced above the largest of the glowing green pools that bubbled beneath it.

My skin prickled, the hairs on my arms and neck standing up as the tension in the air continued to grow.

Staring into this darkness was like watching a virus mutate under the protective lens of a microscope. This was the cancerous tumor that spawned under the skin of the Court of Mist and Memory, slowly eating away at its bones and its blood, until there was nothing left on the surface.

The giant mass of darkness shifted, the thrumming

changing to something that felt a little more familiar, if more malevolent.

An echoing heartbeat pulsed in a mismatched rhythm as the Source focused its attention on my father.

He stared back for several long moments. His expression went slack, and his eyes glossed over until I wasn't sure if he was sleeping or awake.

I whispered his name, but he didn't budge. I stepped closer, placing a hand on his shoulder, but he refused to move. There was a stiffness to his body I couldn't overcome. Then the Source shifted, its static limbs focusing on something behind me.

Hadeon.

My father finally blinked, shaking his head as he took in the cavern and the Source like he had only just gotten here. His blue eyes darted between it and Hadeon, russet brows furrowing as his lips pulled back into a deadly expression.

His eyes tracked the shadows swirling around my soulmate, and my stomach sank. Instead of the caution he had displayed on the way here, my father was suddenly furious, his movements too quick and reckless as he stumbled forward.

Accusation blazed in his eyes as he stared at my soulmate, pointing between him and the mass of static.

"I knew this was a trap," he growled, his voice not sounding like it belonged to him anymore.

"You," he said, pointing his finger toward Hadeon. "These belong to you. This was your doing."

I stepped between the two elves, my isos flaring around me as I tried to study my father's face.

It was like I didn't exist. He saw past me, through me, even when flames shot from my hair, my hands and eyes. Nothing I did could draw the attention he was so intent on giving the shadow king.

Hadeon was careful, remaining silent in an effort not to draw more attention to us. Nevertheless, he stood tall, stepping closer and shaking his head. He risked a glance at the source, realization dawning on his features.

His voice was an undertone, no more than an earnest whisper when he eventually spoke. "You know those shadows are not the same, Aithan. Right now, it's lying to you, and you need to shut out its voice."

"Papa," I said, taking a step forward. "Papa, listen."

My father's attention snapped toward me, confusion written plainly on his face. And more.

Papa's cheeks were red, but there was a pale undertone, too, like a sudden illness had settled over him. His pupils widened as he glared at Hadeon, darkness crowding out the sparkling blue of his irises. Hatred emanated from him, seeping from his pores, and all of it was directed at the king of the Moon Court.

My father's voice dripped with venom as he spewed a series of frantic threats that didn't make any sense.

Hadeon was right. This had to be the Source, poisoning his mind.

He was biased, prejudiced, and at times completely unwilling to see the humanity that existed on the other side of our borders, but this was downright unhinged.

"Papa," I said again, testing the word as I inched closer.

I took in a breath, my eyes sweeping over my father for any signs of injury. Was he going into shock?

"I warned you," Captain Xanth said. "I told you it was a mistake to join forces with them."

Hadeon's eyes narrowed on his captain, his shadows swirling in warning.

"You can see it now, can't you?" Xanth seethed. "How weak they are... How unworthy."

My isos leapt, flames shooting from my fingertips, and Xanth scowled.

"Captain." Hadeon's voice was a low growl. "You will bite your tongue."

A laugh sounded, cruel and unhinged. It made my blood curdle and my stomach twist.

I turned around to face the sound, watching a shadow slip away from the mass of darkness. The shadow flexed and pulsed with the vibration of laughter. Then it shifted, morphing into the familiar shape of an Elven warrior.

Colonel Aereon's white eyes peered out from beneath the shadows, his head tilting in my direction, though his words were addressed to Hadeon.

"Xanth is right, you know," Aereon said. "The sun king is weak. And so are his people."

He cast a disdainful look in my direction, and Hadeon's shadows throbbed in warning.

"Look how fast his mind broke." The colonel's voice was almost pitying. "Besides, it's not like he cares about you. The Source removes the filter in our minds, strips us of the lies we tell ourselves and allows us to see the truth. To speak the truth."

I shook my head, but even as I wanted to argue, I couldn't. Not entirely.

"What King Aithan said to you is his truth," Aereon taunted. "He will never see you as anything more than his enemy."

Xanth moved toward Aereon, stepping right into the darkness behind him. The word *no* slipped past my lips as his violet eyes shifted to that same toxic green of the wraiths, his body dissolving into static and shadow.

"What is this place?" Hadeon asked.

Xanth pulsed under the glowing green light of the pools, and another vicious laugh bubbled past Aereon's lips.

"It is the Source of true power. It is the creature that feeds on the Goddess's isos. A god that doesn't need her or her priestess, the one that will bring them to their knees."

I swallowed hard. *No.*

"Don't you understand?" Aereon said, taking a step closer to this Source. "Don't you see what we could accomplish with this kind of power at our fingertips?"

"The Source is ours. Its darkness calls to yours, My King," Xanth's voice sounded next.

The captain twisted his hands, and black bubbles appeared in the pools. They grew and burst until wisps of smoke were released above them. This time, instead of dissipating in the air, they transformed into menacing shadows.

Sharp teeth gnawed at the air, and emerald eyes locked on a wraith emerging from the liquid. It let out a howl that shook the walls of the cavern. Stones fell from the ceiling, crashing down into the toxic springs.

I stood frozen, my heartbeat thundering in my chest as I stared into its canine form. Its attention, however, was only for my father, who raged, light sparking at his fingertips as he swiped his scythe through the air.

His movements were clumsy, clouded by the anger that had amplified inside of him. The wraith hissed in response, but it didn't step away from the pool of malice it had grown from.

Darkness moved in my periphery as another wraith sprang to life from one of the green pools. Then another and another, until the cavern was filled with the howling of monsters and the suffocating feeling of death.

They didn't move. Instead, it was like they were waiting for a signal. Or an order.

Hadeon's dark expression told me he had realized the same thing. Right now, Xanth and Aereon were in control, and with an endless supply of wraith-making ingredients at their fingertips, we might never be able to stop them.

"Think about what we could do with this power," Aereon wheedled, his eyes pleading. Then he stretched his hands up toward the ceiling, wisps of smoke following them.

The wraiths watched with hungry eyes.

Hadeon's shadows swept over the ground, creeping along the stalagmites as they surrounded his captain, but when he tried to reach for him, the Source pushed the shadows away like a cat batting at string.

"You could be a god," Aereon whispered, his voice trembling as he stared at his king. "More powerful than Abba or the Goddess."

I swallowed hard, light surging from my skin in indignation.

"That is blasphemy," I hissed, focusing my isos on Xanth.

If Hadeon's isos couldn't touch the Source, I wondered what mine could do against it, and how quickly I could hurt Xanth before he unleashed this army on us.

Xanth let out a low, rumbling laugh, a sound that shook the cavern and caused more of the stones to crumble. Then, his eyes were on me — twin green orbs hidden inside the dark static of his skin.

He shook his head, his lips curling back in disgust as he scanned me from head to toe.

"Valandril was weak." He spat the words, and hatred sparked in my veins. "To be taken down by so little power."

He tsked, and I allowed my anger to fuel my power, shooting a ball of fire directly at him. Xanth and the Source easily shimmered out of its path, and it collided into a stalactite behind them.

There was a loud crash as the rocks fell from the ceiling, splashing into the malice pools beneath. The wraith that had been standing there hissed into a cloud of green mist.

"The Court of Mist and Memory never stood a chance," Xanth went on proselytizing. "They didn't deserve the isos they were given, and the Source saw that it was taken away."

"I will see its work complete, with, or without you, My King," Aereon added. "I will rid Aelvaria of those who do not deserve her isos. And then I will do the same to all of Terrea."

Hadeon's shadows surged, wicked tendrils sharpening into knives that were pointed directly at Aereon, while I allowed my isos to light up the cavern, my flames licking at the air with a desperation and fury I had never felt before.

Hadeon fixed him with a lethal expression, an empty smile that promised death. "Remember how weak you believe my soulmate to be when her isos brings you to your knees."

At the same time, we sent our isos flaring toward the colonel. A bright white light lit up the room, hovering over Hadeon's shadows, emphasizing them, strengthening them.

Aereon let out a tormented scream as our power connected with his form, blocking him from slinking back into his shadow self again. He writhed in pain under our isos, eventually dissolving into the worthless nothingness that he was.

Xanth howled in fury. He flicked his wrists, a silent order for the wraiths to attack as he called more from the malice beneath him.

The cavern became a blur of movement. My father regained enough of his senses to fight the wraiths back with his golden scythe while I pulled every ounce of power and heat from my ring and my crown.

The light grew, so bright it was almost blinding.

It surrounded the pools of malice and the wraiths, blocking them from moving while Hadeon flooded the cavern with shadows. With a single burst of power, they rippled from him in a wave that crashed into the wraiths in one swift movement.

Xanth howled in fury. He reached toward the pool

beneath his feet, using some invisible thread to grab hold of the green liquid before he sent it hurling through the air at my father.

A scream tore free from my throat just as Hadeon leapt in front of him. He stretched out his arms, using both his body and his shadows to shield my father from the malice.

He groaned in pain, the silver in his midnight eyes kindling to life like the deepest part of a star.

I called to the Goddess as I strained every last ounce of my isos, using it to become the white light that filled the cavern. Heat radiated from my body, melting the stones around me. Slowly I floated in the air, pure energy pulsing from my skin.

I brought my hands together, focusing that energy into light in a single beam on Xanth and the black static that surrounded him.

The pools of malice popped and boiled until there was nothing left but a whisper of green smoke.

A sound echoed through the room, curdling my stomach and rattling my bones. I wasn't sure if it belonged to Xanth or the Source, but it was pained. Enraged. Desperate.

Black static hissed and stretched frantically around the captain, like the Source was scrambling for a place to hide.

I held on to them, waiting for Hadeon to deliver the final blow.

His shadows swam beneath my light, curling around the Source and his captain.

He growled, the sound feral, echoing around and through me as he used his shadows to rip the two apart, separating them into a thousand pieces.

As soon as they were little more than flecks of dust floating in the air, I burned them into nothingness.

My vision blurred, exhaustion settling in as I sank to the ground. Though the ground was shaking, rocks crumbling and breaking around us like the entire cavern would cave in at any moment, relief crashed over me in waves.

We had done it. It was over.

I spun around, a grin plastered on my face as I searched for my soulmate.

My eyes landed on my father first. The anger that the Source had amplified in him before was gone now. Instead, his expression was twisted in something darker.

"I am so sorry, firestorm," he said, and I cocked my head in confusion.

He looked down at the ground, at a space hidden just behind a crumbling rock. My feet moved before I could even register what was happening, dread rose in my stomach.

As soon as I rounded the stalagmite, I saw him.

Hadeon was on his knees, his eyes glossed over in pain, his full lips parted in a gasp as he stared down at his hands. The pale green hue turned into something closer to onyx.

Soon, darkness coated the skin from the tips of his fingers up to his elbows, like the ash left behind after a raging fire. Or the poison left behind by pure malice.

Chapter Forty-One

"HADEON!" HIS NAME TORE FROM MY THROAT IN A single agonized breath.

No.

All around us, the mines collapsed, but I could barely move, barely think or breathe or do anything but stare at the inky malice winding its way through Hadeon's body.

Before I could even make it to his side, the familiar, cool shadows wrapped around me. They were weaker than usual, flickering, like they were struggling to hold on.

Then we were outside the mines. Barely. Close enough that tiny pebbles of debris still showered us from the bigger chunks that fell around the opening. Of course, the wards from the Source had disappeared, now that the malice fueling them was dead.

Elion had brought his down as well. The wraiths were gone, some of the soldiers still looking around in confusion, their blades in the air. Killing the Source must have eliminated

473

its monsters, but I didn't care enough to wonder about that right now.

Not when Hadeon was hurt.

The army backed away to give us some space, all but Celani, who came closer, horror on her features.

But I couldn't focus on her, or anything beyond the man on the ground in front of me.

I fell to my knees at his side.

"Use your shadows and force it out," I gritted through my teeth.

"Can't," he breathed, shaking his head.

His face was always pale, but strong, like alabaster. It was sallow now, the robustness of the color bleeding from his cheeks and leaving him a husk of who he was.

"Yes, damn it, you can," I pushed back.

Surely, he had to be able to. Tears stabbed the backs of my eyes, panic seizing my lungs and stealing my breath. There had to be a way.

"Too much," he gasped. "Not enough isos."

And he had used what he had left to shadow us out here. To save me.

"Then we'll find another way." My tone was infused with all the confidence I didn't feel, and all the desperation I did.

"There isn't one." His voice was deep, but the words came out too slow, too quiet.

Was he right? Hadeon had spent the past fifty years dealing with these wraiths, sustaining losses because of them. He had told me himself that he was the only way to fight off the malice.

I had no shadows, no potions from the mages, no way to lend him my own isos. There was no way to save him and no time to find one.

The tears streamed freely down my cheeks while I crumpled onto Hadeon's chest, listening to the slowing beat of his heart.

Elion's arms came around me, but I shook him off.

"No." I didn't want sympathy when there was nothing to be sympathetic about.

Hadeon was fine. He was going to be fine. He had to be.

His heartbeat was imprinted on my soul, the music I had lived my entire life for. It was as much a part of me as the Ahvi constellation, as my isos, as the blood that flowed through my veins.

Each beat told the story of our lives, everything we had fought for and lost. And that story was not over yet.

It couldn't be.

Hadeon's blackened hand came to gently rest on my hair, and a sob escaped me, racking my chest with searing, unending agony I would never be able to put into words.

Though I had distantly worried about him, he had always felt invincible. Untouchable. So many times, I had imagined my own death, going into whatever endless void had taken me before, but I had never let myself contemplate his.

Would I have been prepared for this if I had? Or too paralyzed with fear to try?

Was it just another one of the goddess's games?

The goddess...

"Abba!" I shouted, shooting up into a sitting position.

My hand didn't leave Hadeon's chest. The army shuffled nervously, my father and even Celani looking at me like I was cracking.

Hell, I *was* cracking. But I also knew she would come for me, so I shouted again with everything I had.

"Abba." Her name wrenched free from my throat in a blood-curdling scream. "I need you!"

When she appeared, her skin was faintly lit, her purple hair settled around her. She exuded peace, except for the tears sparkling in her amethyst eyes.

"Did you See this?" I demanded.

My hands were on Hadeon, my breaths still coming too quickly as I waited for her answer.

She shook her head sadly. "I told you, not all can be Seen, child, especially where there is that which should never have been."

She gestured to the mines where the wraiths had been, her lips pursed in sadness. But I didn't care about her explanations or her sadness. I only cared about Hadeon.

"You suspected something," I accused.

Her shoulders slumped. "It did concern me when I could See nothing at all."

"But you can fix it," I insisted.

She shook her head again, but there was the smallest bit of hesitation that time. "It doesn't work that way. Even the Goddess cannot interfere with the natural order of things."

"There was nothing natural about this!" I yelled, my body flickering with the force of my isos. "You said yourself that the wraiths should never have existed. And where the hell was your natural order when it was *my* life?"

My hair erupted in flames that sent cinders flying through the air as I met her amethyst eyes.

She parted her lips, taking a breath to explain why it was different, but I would hear none of it. Not when the love of my life, of every life, was dying. Not when I had sacrificed so much to save him.

"No," I interrupted, furious tears burning at the back of my eyes. "I have done everything the goddess has ever asked of me. I have died for her, and I have never asked for anything in return. But she does not get to bring me back from the dead and rip me from my life just to take everything from me." I gestured to my soulmate.

He was so, so pale, and so still, his chest barely moving. Another sob erupted from my throat.

"Please, Abba," I choked out.

"Elves are not immortal, child," she said quietly. "One way or another, this will end, and you will never be ready."

"One day," I agreed. "When we've had time. Time we lost. Time I gave to the goddess. But not like this. Please," I whispered again, my hand clutching Hadeon's cold, obsidian fingers. "Not like this."

I wanted to say more, to beg her or give way to the rage flooding my isos and threaten to burn the entire world to ash if he died. I wanted to say so many things, but I couldn't get the words out past the sobs that had overtaken my body.

I fell against Hadeon, listening for his heartbeat, my heartbeat, the other half of the melody that made up the only life I had ever had worth living...but it was gone.

An unearthly sound rent my throat. Firm arms closed around me, too large to be Abba's, but I didn't lean into them. I couldn't move. Couldn't breathe. Didn't want to, not in a world where Hadeon never would again.

Wetness spilled onto my hands. I looked up through bleary, watery eyes to see Abba's tears falling from her cheeks. Her hands were on Hadeon's chest, but her eyes were on my face.

Indecision flitted across her features, until she gave the smallest hint of a nod.

I froze, hardly daring to hope.

"All right," she whispered. "For the promise I made you, and the love I have for you, child."

I. Not we. Because the goddess had chosen me, but it was Abba who had loved me all my life. She had talked to me and guided me and promised me it would be worth it in the end.

She had promised me a life with Hadeon, not the handful of weeks we got to spend together that always seemed to end in death.

Relief swept through me, so palpable it would have brought me to my knees if I weren't there already.

Abba nodded again, surer this time. Looking at me, her eyes blazed with a love so bright that it became a tangible thing, igniting in a thousand colors, almost too strong to behold.

The same power flooded from her hands, directly into Hadeon's chest. Little by little, her light chased away the malice from his body until I heard it...so faint, I could have sworn I imagined it at first.

Thump.

Then louder. Steadier. Strong and rhythmic and achingly familiar. Hadeon's heartbeat.

His hands were black. His face was pale.

But he was alive.

Chapter Forty-Two

I TRACED THE LINE OF HADEON'S HANDS, RUNNING my fingers along the seam of where the inky black bled into his luminescent skin.

We were in his bed back at the palace, where we had been for the entire three days since the fight at Zoferi mines.

Since he died.

Since Abba saved him.

"Feralinia," he growled in a low warning.

"What?" I asked innocently, like he hadn't just caught me losing myself yet again in all the what-ifs that nearly took him from me.

"I'm right here," he said.

"I know." Yet my fingers anxiously crept along the jagged black lines.

"Abba told you there is no malice left, only the markings of it."

481

"You don't believe anything Abba says," I reminded him with a raised eyebrow.

He brought my hand to his lips, pressing a kiss against my palm. "But you do."

I sighed, reminding myself that he was right. Abba said he was safe, and I did believe her. She had said the Never Court would begin to heal itself, and that was already happening, too.

Leander had created a portal just yesterday showing how the tiniest signs of life were cropping up, bits of grass poking stubbornly up from the barren lands.

A familiar knock sounded at the door, rousing me from bed. Ahvi looked at the door with thinly veiled excitement, but Hadeon groaned.

"Just because your brother *can* portal back and forth doesn't mean he needs to," he complained.

I shrugged. "At least he came to the outside of the door this time."

Because there was a trauma none of us needed to relive. Somewhere right up there with Hadeon almost dying was my brother seeing my *O* face before frantically covering his eyes, muttering about how he thought Hadeon was still unwell.

Whatever healing Abba had done was effective, though. There had been no real recovery time aside from the two days we spent sleeping off the adrenaline.

And aside from the nightmares. We shared those as easily as we did our dreams. Mine were haunted by the silence that fell in the wake of Hadeon's heartbeat, the obsidian poison that spread through his body and nearly took him from me.

His were more what-ifs, scenarios where he couldn't shadow us out and the roof caved in. Where I was overtaken by the wraiths.

Where I left him alone again, only this time it was permanent, a yawning void of pain and nothingness that I felt as acutely as if it were my own.

I padded across the floor, pulling on a robe while Hadeon watched irritably from our bed. Leander was smirking when I opened the door.

"So nice to see you, sis..."

I raised an eyebrow while I waited for the punch line.

"With clothes on," he finished.

"You only have yourself to blame for that," I shot back, like the memory didn't make me want to die of mortification.

He shrugged like that was fair, scooping up my growing feraline in a way that only he could get away with.

"I actually came on official business this time." He scratched Ahvi under the chin. "Our parents want to discuss the terms of the treaty."

"Now?"

They would be here tonight, but not for peace talks.

Leander shook his head, putting Ahvi down. "Tomorrow. I can portal them back or they can stay here after..."

I turned back to look at Hadeon, who nodded tentatively. This was new, the trust between our people, but the wards had been up for too long. All it did was foster more hatred and uncertainty.

I told Leander we agreed, but he lingered. I knew why. Of

course I did. Still, I couldn't help but give him a taste of his own medicine.

"Something else you need?" I asked.

He put on a valiant show of looking casual. "Just wondering if there were any plans tonight, before..."

Before the big plans, he meant.

"I'm sure I'll be having some sort of drink, and you're always welcome to join me," I said sweetly, knowing full well it wasn't me he wanted to see.

He blew out a frustrated breath, and I relented.

"Fine. Pop back to the Sun Court for some firewhiskey, and we'll meet you downstairs. All of us," I added.

"Sure. Everyone treats the portal-maker like an errand boy," he grumbled, but he left to get my favorite drink anyway.

Which was how we found ourselves back in Hadeon's kitchen, only he joined us this time. Kallius and I made a version of barbacoa while Celani drank firewhiskey and pretended not to look at my brother, and Hadeon helpfully handed me things with his shadows.

"Those are very useful multitaskers," I commented.

He gave me a dark smirk. "So you've said."

"My ears," Leander complained.

"From what I heard, it was your eyes you had to worry about," Celani ribbed him.

He snatched the bottle from her hand and poured some of the spiced whiskey straight in his mouth. I laughed, lifting a newly rolled taco toward Hadeon's mouth.

He eyed it uncertainly. "What's the point of eating it all together like this when it can just fall out?"

I made a face at him. "You can't apply logic to perfection, Hadeon. Deliciousness is the point."

He grimaced, but dutifully parted his lips, closing them around the proffered food. It was unfair, the way he could make even eating a street taco look sexy. His tongue brushed against my thumb, and he gave me another smirk.

"Indeed it is," he agreed.

Heat flushed through me, the insatiable need I had for Hadeon rearing up the way it always seemed to. If I thought that the prospect of forever with him would make things feel calmer, I was wrong. I spent most of my time wanting to tug him by his perfect midnight locks back to the bedroom we now shared and remind him over and over again that he was mine.

Maybe it was that being with him only made me want him more, but I suspected it was closer to the silence in those missing heartbeats. Every moment with him felt precious and urgent and so, so fragile now. I wondered if I would ever feel any sort of peace in his presence, any sort of belief that this life was ours for keeps.

"So what do you think?" I asked when he had finished his taco.

"I think it's a fitting meal for a queen," he answered with a smirk.

I gave him an answering grin, but it was Celani who responded.

"Let's hope so, all things considered."

WHEN WE GOT BACK to our rooms, there were several maids and a dress already waiting. The gown was pitch black with a low V-neck and flowing sleeves that fell gracefully from a point on each shoulder all the way to the floor. The only adornments were a golden clasp at each sleeve and the tiny sparkling constellations that seemed to float on the fabric itself.

But it was the item next to the dress that gave me pause.

A crown sparkled in the low candlelight. It was carved from star-wrought silver and studded with tiny, brilliant gems arranged in the shape of constellations.

Exquisite as it was, my breath caught in my throat for an entirely different reason. I had worn tiaras in my childhood and more recently, the bloodstone crown that helped us defeat the wraiths.

But this meant something else. I was going to be Queen of the Court of Moon and Stars.

In a few short hours, I would belong to this place and these people. I would be set to rule at Hadeon's side, and finally acknowledged as his soulmate and his equal.

When I was dressed, Hadeon's eyes darkened in a way that told me it took everything he had not to order the staff out and give me a private coronation right here. His shadows played along my thighs, whispering along my skin, but he pulled them back.

"We don't want to be late," he said with a teasing glint in his eye.

Which was true, of course, but my body didn't care. I took a deep breath, stepping closer for him to shadow us to the throne room. I braced myself for the packed space and the scrutiny it would bring, but the room was empty.

Well, except for Nyx, who had promptly traveled to follow us. Since the battle, she was even more reluctant to let either of us out of her sight. The moonlight filtering in through the high windows sparkled off her three new collars, diamond studded and carefully crafted to resemble my crown.

She surveyed the room, tilting all three of her heads in confusion when she wasn't greeted with the crowd either of us was expecting.

I shot Hadeon a puzzled look.

"I wanted this moment with you first, before the masses showed up." He looked like it pained him to admit that.

Feelings would probably never come easily to either of us, but I saw the way he tried in small ways to overcome his general asshattery. At least, when it came to me.

"Any particular reason?" I pushed.

"I wanted to know what you thought of the new furniture." He smirked, looking pointedly at something behind me.

I turned, following his gaze, and a gasp escaped my lips. I had known, on some level, that I would have my own throne. But I didn't expect it to be as intimidating as his.

Where Hadeon's throne was dark and shadowy and imposing, mine looked like it was made of pure starlight. It was still fearsome in its own right, all wicked edges and elegant curves made of sparkling silver, but it was the perfect complement to his.

My feet pulled me toward the massive seat, as if by their own accord.

Feminine, graceful, powerful. This throne was everything.

"It'll do." I shot him a teasing grin, though I couldn't help running my hands along the intricately carved armrests.

Hadeon's smirk widened into pure smugness.

"Well, I did consider putting a pillow on the floor for you next to Nyx, but —" his words cut off abruptly when I sent an artful trail of fire directly at his face.

So much for overcoming his asshattery.

He blocked the fire easily, of course, swallowing it with a tendril of darkness.

"Nyx would be better company anyway," I muttered.

"Indeed." Hadeon waved a hand, gesturing for me to sit on my new throne.

I wanted to. Sort of. But something inside of me hesitated.

He furrowed his brow, studying me as I looked pointedly elsewhere.

"I assumed you were joking, but we can procure you any throne you want," he offered in an unsubtle attempt at fishing.

"It's not the throne," I said quietly. "I just..."

I took a deep breath, willing myself to be honest with him about things that weren't even easy to admit to myself. A glance at his features told me he was listening, a rare bit of concern in his starlit gaze. It gave me the confidence to go on.

"It's hard sometimes, because of course I remember being a princess and a warrior. But I also remember being an unwanted orphan. Which is not helped by the fact that your people hate me and see me as your pet." I glared at him, and he had the grace to look somewhat chastised. *Very* somewhat. "Sometimes this life feels like it was never meant to be mine, like maybe I still don't belong here."

Hadeon crossed the distance to me, placing a hand along the side of my face. I leaned into his touch, allowing myself this one small moment to be vulnerable before I would need to look strong.

"This is exactly where you belong. I know that, and our people will know it soon if they do not yet." His voice deepened on the word *our*, the emphasis a demand as much as it was a correction.

His shadows emerged to play along my body, awakening something in my soul the way he always did.

"And as for unwanted..." He leaned in, skating his lips across my forehead. "I will happily spend every night for the rest of our lives disabusing you of that notion."

Fire spread throughout my whole being, the kind that was even more powerful than my isos. The kind only Hadeon could ignite. I tried to make myself believe his words, giving myself over to the comfort of his touch. His desire.

"Just the nights?" I teased.

His dark chuckle caressed my skin. "The nights. The days. Every minute, if that's what you wish."

I did wish.

He adjusted his grip on my face, tilting my head up and bringing his lips to meet mine. Most of our kisses were heated to the point of being frenzied. This one was almost...tender, by comparison. A gentle, intimate press of his mouth on mine.

His tongue slowly dipped between my lips, slowly circling

my own. His hands and his shadows wrapped around me, cocooning me like he could shield me from my own demons as easily as he did the ones outside.

"You belong here," he growled, his breath warm and tantalizing against my mouth. "As my queen, on this throne and at my side. Always."

A shiver raced down my spine at the words, the title on his lips.

"Belonging with you isn't the issue," I told him.

He backed away, his features tightening in a stubborn frown I was all too familiar with. "This *is* your life, Feralinia, one you have earned and one you more than deserve. Not because of how you were born, but because of who you are and what you have done for our people. You have fought for them, bled for them, as a queen should."

The unwavering confidence in his voice eased something inside of me. So often, I struggled to reconcile who I had been on earth with who I had been here. But Hadeon saw all of me.

Every version. All the Embers and Phaedras across time and space and circumstances, just as he had told me.

Squaring my shoulders, I gave him a nod. Then I sat on my throne like the queen I had managed to become.

Eyes glinting with pride, Hadeon called for the doors to open.

The next hour passed in a series of moments that flew by, interspersed with those that seemed to stretch on into eternity.

Elves from all over Aelvaria were in attendance, Moon and Sun Elves both tolerating one another long enough to see their people unite under one crown. The significance of what we were doing wasn't lost on me. Our courts had been at war for far too long, and this was the first real step toward healing the rift that separated us.

Two sides of the same coin. Sun and Moon.

There was still healing to do. Especially with my father, who had taken all of the guilt of what happened in the mines upon himself since we returned.

He might not approve of my mate, but he stood stoically at our sides, silently offering the power of his crown in support of our union. That was the first, big step.

My mother squeezed his arm, her bottom lip trembling around a brilliant smile as she barely held back a wave of golden tears. I swallowed hard, trying to appreciate the gift I had been given in having two sets of parents when too many people never had one.

As if he could almost sense the thought, Elion cocked his head from his spot near my mother, his eyes catching mine as he offered a subtle tilt of his lips in an approving smile. Well, approving up until the moment he caught Leander standing a little too close to the Moon Court's general.

Our younger brother wore a devilish smirk as he carefully studied Celani. For her part, she appeared to be doing her best to ignore him...even if she also leaned a little closer to him.

An angry purr rippled overhead as Ahvi flew past, his eyes narrowed in mischief. For a moment, I wondered if this entire event would be over before it even began with my feraline setting fire to our guests.

Fortunately, I wasn't the only one who noticed the small predator. Just as he geared up to light an unsuspecting scribe on fire, a portal opened in the air beside him. Leander yanked him through, whispering an admonishment like he would to a child.

Ahvi sulked, and Nyx stood straighter at my side, as if to demonstrate how much better behaved she was. I bit into the inside of my cheek, trying to stifle my laughter. Unsuccessfully, if Hadeon's raised eyebrow was any indication.

He sucked in a breath to announce the beginning of the coronation but closed his lips as the room stirred with reverential murmurings. A smile tugged at my lips, even as Hadeon scowled.

Only one person could elicit that kind of response from both courts.

Sure enough, the vast crowd parted, and Abba appeared before the thrones, just as I had known she would. She had never missed an important event in my life. Hadeon must have known it, too. It was probably why he was in such a hurry to get started without her.

A tear slid down her flawless face as she took me in, her lavender gaze lingering on the crown, then the throne, and finally on my arm where it was linked with Hadeon's.

Smiling, she offered a private blessing to both of us.

Of course, he accepted it with all the grace of someone who would never forgive her for my death, even when she had brought him back from the very same.

I shook my head subtly at him before standing and throwing my arms around her. Hadeon might not be willing to move past the time we spent apart, but I would spend the rest of my life grateful for the time we had left — the time she had given us.

Once her blessing was finished, Hadeon began the ceremony. His eyes burned into mine while he asked me to repeat a set of vows about caring for his people. *Our* people.

Then he turned back to the people to formally announce me as Queen Ember. The room broke out in an uproar of approval, cheers, and even a whoop or two. My lips parted, my eyes widening in shock at the support of the Moon Elves.

Hadeon shared none of my surprise, nor did Celani and Kallius, or even the rest of my family.

"Did you think they wouldn't care about what you did for them?" Hadeon demanded, as close to outright smiling as I ever saw him.

I took a breath, the air around us heady and intoxicating with the promise of a future I never would have dreamt of before.

"I didn't think about it at all, I guess," I answered honestly.

Hadeon took a step closer, his fingers gently tracing the tattoos on my arms, the constellations woven into every inch of my skin that told the world I belonged to him.

He lowered his voice, his gaze boring into mine. "They know that they're lucky to have you as their queen and their protector. And I'm lucky to have you as mine."

"Your protector?" I teased.

He gave me a knowing look, stretching out his hand. "Just mine."

Warmth spread through me. Belonging to Hadeon was as

easy as breathing. It was right. I was his, and he was mine, written in the stars by the Goddess herself.

I took his hand, and we faced our people together. Our future.

For the first time, I let myself believe that we would spend every moment of it together.

The End.

If you're not quite done with Ember and Hadeon yet, you can find a steamy bonus epilogue by signing up for our newsletter through our website www.mahleandmadison.com

If you're curious about what happened to Adira and the mages, make sure you keep turning the page for a sneak peek from **Of Mischief and Mages** by LJ Andrews!

You can also find out what happened to Ember's friend Ivy by checking out her story in **Of Shadows and Fae** by Jen Grey.

OF ELVES AND EMBERS
PRONUNCIATION GUIDE

PHAEDRA	FAY-DRA
HADEON	HAY-DEE-ON
AELVARIA	EL-VAHR-EE-UH
CELANI	SEL-AH-NEE
KALLIUS	KAL-EYE-US
FERALINIA	FER-AH-LEEN-EE-AH
LEANDER	LEE-AN-DER
ELION	EL-EE-ON
NYX	NIX
AHVI	AH-VEE
FENGARI	FEN-GAR-EE
ZANTH	ZANTH
AEREON	AIR-EE-ON
MITERA	MIT-ER-AH
FERALINE	FER-AH-LEEN
ANAMISI	AN-AH-MEES-EE
DRYOHPS	DRY-OEPS
ELIOS	EEL-YOS

FORGOTTEN KINGDOMS
PRONUNCIATION GUIDE

ERREA
(ORLD NAME)

TER-AY-YUH

AVESTIA
ESTIVAL WHEN THE VEIL
TWEEN WORLDS OPENS)

HAV-EST-EE-UH

ELVARIA
BER
DEON

EL-VAHR-EE-UH
EM-BURR
HAY-DEE-ON

RACONIA
HIRA
KER

DRAH-CONE-EE-UH
SA-FEE-RUH
RYE-KURR

RAMAYA
ODELIA
RAN

IS-RUH-MY-UH
ROW-DEL-EE-UH
VAIR-EN

RAMORTA
RGANA
LON

IS-RUH-MOR-TUH
MOR-GAHN-UH
AV-UH-LAHN

AGIARIA
RA
GE

MAYJ-AIR-EE-UH
AH-DEER-UH
KAYJ

PEAZIA
LLA
NDT

SEH-PEE-ZEE-UH
STEL-UH
BRANT

ALAMH
NA
RAN

TAL-AHV
AH-LEEN-UH
KEER-AN

ARGR
RA
L

VAR-GUR
EH-VEER-UH
AX-EL

A Message From Us

We need your help!

Did you know that authors, in particular indie authors like us, make their living on reviews? If you enjoyed this book, please take a moment to let people know on all of the major review platforms like; Amazon, Goodreads, and/or Bookbub!

(Social Media gushing is also highly encouraged!)

Remember, reviews don't have to be long. It can be as simple as whatever star rating you feel comfortable with and an: 'I loved it!' or: 'Not my cup of tea...'

Now that that's out of the way, if you want to come shenanigate with us, rant and rave about these books and others, get access to awesome giveaways, exclusive content and some pretty ridiculous live videos, come join us on Facebook at our group, Drifters and Wanderers

You can also get exclusive access to free books and stay up to date on all our bookish news by joining our newsletter here: mahleandmadison.com/newsletter

Acknowledgments

We were so honored to be invited to be a part of a world with so many talented authors. We want to thank all of our Forgotten Kingdoms ladies first and foremost. You've been sounding boards and support systems and a source of constant laughter and memes, along with all the hard work you've given to this set.

Really, we are fortunate to have so many amazing friends in the author community, too many to name here but every one helping us shape our worlds and books and careers.

Thank you to Emily, as always, for managing our lives and hydration levels while we trudge through another grueling deadline. <3

To our alphas who read every version of every line until they lived and breathed all things Embeon, we could not do this without you. You send booze and dessert and cheerleading and sometimes very deserved chastisement, and we are so grateful for all of it.

Our beta team, thank you so much for combing through this manuscript so quickly for us so we could release it on time! Your feedback was invaluable and this book would not be the same without you!

Drifters and Wanderers, your shenanigans and gushing

and participation in our ridiculous polls help us through the worst part of every editing rush. We <3 you all so much!

All of the readers who have supported us by buying our books, reading them in KU, checking them out from the library, or left us reviews, we could not be more appreciative! You're the reason we can keep doing what we do.

Finally and most importantly, our families. We know sometimes writing means long hours and crazy amounts of rambling and brainstorming sessions and late nights. We know that sometimes we wear the same pajamas for three days in a row, even when they have coffee stains on them. But you love us anyway, and really, that's all we could ask for.

About The Authors

Elle and Robin can usually be found on road trips around the US haunting taco-festivals and taking selfies with unsuspecting Spice Girls impersonators.

They have a combined PH.D in Faery Folklore and keep a romance advice column under a British pen-name for raccoons. They have a rare blood type made up solely of red wine and can only write books while under the influence of the full moon.

Between the two of them they've created a small army of insatiable humans and when not wrangling them into their cages, they can be seen dancing jigs and sacrificing brownie batter to the pits of their stomachs.

And somewhere between their busy schedules, they still find time to create words and put them into books.

www.mahleandmadison.com

Also By Elle & Robin

The Lochlann Treaty Series:

Winter's Captive

Spring's Rising

Summer's Rebellion

Autumn's Reign

The Lochlann Feuds Series:

Scarlet Princess

Tarnished Crown

Crimson Kingdom

Obsidian Throne

The Lochlann Deception Series:

Hollow Court

Fragile Oath

Twisted Pages Series:

Of Thorns and Beauty

Of Beasts and Vengeance

Of Glass and Ashes

Of Thieves and Shadows

Of Songs and Silence

The World Apart Series By Robin D. Mahle:

The Fractured Empire

The Tempest Sea

The Forgotten World

The Ever Falls

Unfabled Series:

Promises and Pixie Dust

OF
MISCHIEF
&
MAGES

USA TODAY BESTSELLING AUTHOR
LJ ANDREWS

Of Mischief and Mages
Sneak Peek

ADIRA

Fog gathered in my skull. A fierce kind of panic took hold in my chest as I looked around, searching for an outlet. There was only one way to go—to the trees again.

Whatever nightmare this was, it was a place where I could feel, where pain was as real as the air in my lungs.

Head down, I kept a rapid pace until the wood thickened. Heavy tree limbs drooped under the weight of wide leaves. Knotted branches shielded the faint light from the storm overhead.

One hand shot into my bag, removing one of the phones. I flicked on the flashlight, using the beam to guide my steps, until I found a natural clearing. In hasty swipes, I removed a few mushrooms off the mossy bark of a fallen log and perched on the edge.

My lungs burned from the trek, my body ached from the

altercation with the cruel wizard. But alone, the world seemed to fall into a silence—peaceful and soft. I lifted the strap of my bag over my head, returned the phone to the pocket, and leaned onto my elbows over my knees.

I needed to decide, and fast—was this a dream, a delusion, or was I truly, impossibly *trapped* in some other world?

Blood pounded in my sore hand the wizard had manipulated, as though responding, as though my own body wanted me to know this was real. I blew out a rough breath, shaking my head.

"All right," I whispered. "Real, then."

At least for now. Until I found a way to escape this horrid place, I'd assume it was real. In truth, that seemed to be the only way to survive.

One by one, I checked off the next steps. Constant lists were formed in my mind with a plan of what I would do at each hour, each day. All of it was meant to help me survive, to get through the days as painlessly as possible. Whether it was tricky ways to avoid foster siblings as a kid, bullies at school, or Loyd and his goons' wandering hands, I planned out the moves to take.

I was wandering through a forest in a pencil skirt and heels.

First thing should probably be shelter. I scanned the trees. Being raised in the desert did not proffer many survival skills in a cold forest that was filled with magical bone wielders.

Water, then. Every survival show insisted the first thing to do was find fresh water. Okay, this place was clearly free of cars and any ounce of technology—I could take the risk and drink straight from a river or creek.

Second, my damn hand. Morphed fingers trembled. The bastard told me they could fuse this way, so I would need to find a way to stop that from happening. Maybe I could go find the woman I'd met first. She was eccentric but kind enough.

I glared at the battered flesh, recounting everything I knew about the man who'd done this. His face was square and built like he had armor on his bones. Thick and bulky and fierce. Dark hair, and deep set dark eyes. But he'd had curious tattoos . . . almost like mine. Some on his fingers—I'd noticed when he'd closed his damn fist to curse my hand—then a beautiful row of runes down his throat.

Obviously a prick for his little spell with my bones, but his tattoos had been fascinating.

A slow grin split over my lips, and I reached down the front of my dress. Tucked between my breasts was a slender knife. Small enough to conceal swiftly. I'd noted he kept it in a bracer on his bicep, and when I'd knocked against him, wrenched it away. I'd planned to use it before he sicced Aelfled on me.

The handle was lovely, made of a sleek jade stone rimmed in gold. And the blade was a clash of bronze and dark iron. Unique, likely custom. Good. I hoped it was sickeningly expensive and his favorite knife.

With a spin of the blade in my uninjured hand, I tucked it into my bag. Footprints littered the forest floor near the leather pouch. Large footprints, made from a heavy boot. A feverish heat flooded my cheeks. The trail of steps led deeper into the trees, and if I had to guess, the size and shape of the boot matched the same sort as a horrid wizard with lovely tattoos.

Reckless, but I was lost here. Cruel as he was, the man who'd done this to me was the only one who could likely undo it. I didn't know how long I had left to reverse it if his threat was legitimate. Nor did I know the way back to the kind old woman.

I looked to the shadows swallowing his footsteps. He couldn't be worse than Loyd. I had his blade and enough intuition to think it must've been favored if it had a custom sheath on his arm.

The knife for my hand. Seemed a fair enough trade.

Before I could dwell too long on the stupidity of my plan, I grabbed my bag, and followed the muddy steps carving through the forest.

Only once I discovered a wide dirt road did I consider the instant he had his knife returned—hand healed or not—he could kill me. If he did, I doubted I'd wake to the kindness of an old woman and her mushrooms.

Chatter filtered from up the road. Men spoke, some deep and gravelly, another a low rasp. Once or twice a pitchy voice would follow in laughter or word—a woman had to be with them. I'd known enough brutal women not to be foolish enough to trust straightaway, still it couldn't be helped to feel a bit more at ease if there were other women around.

I crouched behind a thick oak and took the knife from my bag. My heart stilled when a twig snapped underfoot. There was a stutter in the voices, but not long enough to think anyone truly thought much on the sound.

The smooth jade cooled my palm as my grip tightened. I stepped around the tree and entered the road. Empty.

My pulse thudded in my ears. No, I was certain there'd been voices—several—right here.

A small whimper drew my focus. What the hell? Down the road a few paces, a wooden cart was slumped off to the side of the road, a wheel broken off the axel. In front, seated on a stump, was a girl, no older than twelve.

She kept her head down, hugging her knees to her chest, crying into a dirty skirt. Dark ringlets draped over her face, and a few blue ribbons were tied in loose braids. On her waist was a belt with a fur-lined pouch, like an old money purse from history books.

I tightened my grip on the knife, hair lifted on my arms, but took a slow step toward the girl. A fierce shriek startled me back, knife outstretched. Perched on a tall branch was a hawk, its piercing gaze burning through me. Another cry slid from its beak before it flew away into the trees.

The girl had looked up, eyeing the bird, then realized she wasn't alone. She drew in a sharp breath and started to scuttle backward.

I held out a hand. "Wait. I'm not going to hurt you."

I made quick work of hiding the knife behind my back.

The girl looked like she'd popped out of a small feudal village, and I was still dressed in a revealing cocktail dress with a battered hand.

I gestured to her cart. "Do you need some help?"

The girl tilted her head to one side. "You'd help me, a lady like you?"

What kind of lady did she mean? I peeked down at my exposed thighs. Doubtless I was the village prostitute in her eyes.

"Believe it or not, I'm pretty handy." I smiled and reached out my hand that hadn't been attacked, tucking my bruised fingers under the fur wrap.

"A Soturi?" The girl gasped, glancing at my tattoos. "You?"

That word again. The man had called me the same. I waved it away, anxious to aid a child on her way, then be on mine.

But before I could question her odd word choice, the girl's innocent features twisted up into a crooked sneer.

When the girl spoke again, her voice was a deep baritone. It belonged to a damn man. "Pity you cannot tell the difference between illusion and reality."

I screamed when the little girl's lips bubbled with fountains of blood. Her skin peeled off her bones until they crumbled into dark, ashy mist and fluttered away. From behind the cloud of mist stepped three figures.

Two wore cowls, another a simple scarf over the mouth. The one with the scarf appeared to be a woman with her flowing crow-black hair and defined curves. Based on the size and thigh width of the other two, I took them as men.

I stumbled backward when a slice of wings sailed over my head. The hawk from the tree shrieked, the sound boiling in brain, then took up its place on the leather clad shoulder of one of the figures.

"Well done, Habrok." The same gravelly tone I'd heard

before crooned at the bird as the man handed the creature a limp mouse. "Not that it was all that difficult. I've never seen such a skittish battle mage."

"Ah, but this is the Soturi who does not deserve the title." Through the center of the group, a man stepped forward.

My insides backflipped. Built like that bastard from the star tent, he moved like a threat, heavy steps yet lithe like the ground would bow to him should he demand it. Broad shoulders, strong arms, only now his face was covered with half a skull.

A cracked forehead, empty sockets, and the upper jaw covered his lip, revealing a black cloth covering what was left of his chin.

This was no Halloween disguise—the skull mask seemed to protrude from his flesh, like it was his own facial structure surfacing from the muscle. But on the side of his neck were beautiful lines of runes tattooed along his throat.

"You." Pathetic, but it was the only word that seemed to match the frenzy of my brain and succeed in escaping my tongue.

The open skull eye sockets gave up little to the color of the gaze behind them, but when he tugged down the cloth over his mouth, his white teeth burned bright in the fading sunlight, a glistening, mocking threat.

"Me. We must stop meeting this way." Skull face tossed back the edge of a black cloak draped on his shoulders, revealing a belt laden in knives and a damn sword with boiled leather wrapped around a sturdy hilt.

I scrambled to my feet and tried to run, but an arm

wrapped around my waist, holding me tightly against his firm chest. I kicked and thrashed and scratched.

He tossed me onto the side of the road, landing me in a patch of wildflowers. I had no time to move before the man with his horrid mask, pressed his knee to my chest and leaned his hidden face close.

"By now, I'm aware you, little thief, took something of mine."

"According to you!" I grunted, desperate to shove his knee off my chest. Breath tightened the more pressure he added.

"I think it is safe to say, in present company, my word over yours will be accepted." He chuckled. "Your second foolish act is passing through Swindler's Alley unaccompanied, lady." He slipped one of his gloved fingers under the strap on my satchel. "If you'd like to keep both your eyes, we'll be needing you to pay your toll."

Made in United States
Troutdale, OR
08/11/2024

21887899R10322